# FROM LINEN TO SACKCLOTH:

## Vol. 1. A Voice Among The Four

Charles Lite

*Existence, it is such a complex, confusing and yet such a wondrous thing. So many questions without answers, so much curiosity with no explanation and so much mystery with no knowledge to tell the story. Even though the story does have an unlimited amount of ways it can be told, an unlimited number of theories that have potential and an unlimited number of questions to be asked. The majority of people don't even know where to start. Even those who are hungry for knowledge are limited to their own willingness to accept a logical explanation. Especially when their personal bias and opinions cloud their judgment so much so that they may refuse to accept it even when presented with a new logical idea. Knowledge is vast, and understanding something as complex as our existence is quite a difficult thing to achieve. That is of course only true to those who haven't been given the information or enlightenment that would enable them to decipher that which actually is the meaning of our existence. Or they were given the explanation and refused to believe it. Or maybe they just simply do not possess the mental capacity required in order to understand or comprehend that which they have been told. All these things are possibilities, depending on the person. Regardless of all that, this book was written with the intention of simply encouraging one to think. I, the author, do not wish to teach you what to think or how to think. I simply want you, the reader, to think more. However, if you do not wish to do that then I invite you to simply enjoy this fictional story that may or may not spark a new thought or two in your mind. Thank you.*

# PART: I

*"Blindly believing something in ignorance without question is the act of a fool."*

# CHAPTER: 1

**M**ARTIN heard the sound of gunfire coming from behind him as he floated in place above the thick vegetation that covered the forest floor. Taking a moment to think about how he got there and why he was floating he suddenly heard a twig snap to his right. Turning his attention to see what it was he noticed, to his surprise, that it was actually he himself running through the brush and ferns below. He was carrying a military style rifle and Martin could see that he was obviously in quite a hurry. However, even in his apparent state of superior being, looking into the physical world through some kind of supernatural vision, Martin could not remember what he had been running from or why he was being chased. He thought about it for a moment and he actually didn't remember this event at all. He could never have imagined himself to be a coward, so whomever was chasing him certainly must have been an enemy of overwhelming force.

After watching himself begin to disappear behind the trees on the ground below he decided to follow, hoping to find out a little more information about what was going on. As time progressed and the sunlight began to fade, the gunshots from behind became more faint and less frequent. Still hovering slightly above, he saw himself stumble and almost fall. Driven by curiosity he got a little closer to himself. As he did so it became obvious that his body was damaged and he appeared to be getting extremely weak.

"What the hell is this?" Martin said to himself, trying to understand what was happening. "When did this event even take place, and why am I seeing this now?"

He watched as his physical self attempted to push on, but as he took a few more steps he stumbled and almost fell once again. Still partially in the supernatural, Martin's complete 360 degree field of vision began to subside; going black around the edges as if darkness was bearing down on him. Martin then descended and moved around to directly in front of himself; matching his speed while he looked into his own eyes. As soon as he saw himself in the refection of his glazed pupils, he was suddenly sucked back into his physical body. And even though he seemed to have little control of himself at this time, he could at least feel once again.

After taking a moment to process his situation, he suddenly realized that his back felt wet and sticky. He slowed to a jog, then using his free hand he reached over his own shoulder to feel what it might be. When he brought his hand back around and held it in front of his face, he saw, to his displeasure, it was indeed blood. Slowing to a walk he dropped the rifle he had been holding, letting it fall carelessly to the ground. Then as he looked at his bloody hand once again, the scent of gunpowder residue suddenly became strong in his nostrils. The smell seemed to be coming from both his hands and his clothes, as if many shots had been fired all around him in very close proximity.

Taking a seat next to a tree he began to examine himself, trying to assess the severity of his injuries. A few moments later he had gathered that he had been shot at least twice. Once on the left shoulder, and once towards the center of his lower back to the left of his spine. Not wasting any time he quickly tore off the legs to his pants and tied one of them tightly around each wound. After sitting there for a few minutes to catch what breath he could, he decided it was time to continue on. Even though he was beginning to feel as if delusion of some sort was setting in and he was not exactly sure where he was going, he slowly stood up anyway and his vision immediately faded to complete black.

As his body fell away from his vision, allowing him to see once more, he began to understand something. Sight with the human eye is nothing in comparison to sight in the supernatural and humans in comparison to what he was now are simply weak, feeble and pathetic. As a human he could never have even imagine the power that he as a supernatural being now had. Nor could he have understood the level of knowledge that he now possessed, or see what he could currently see.

"How strange." He said to himself, looking around the forest in all directions at once. "It would appear that only mortal beings require eyes to see, and ears to hear. Yes, very strange indeed. I wish to know more."

With that simple thought, he was immediately removed from the physical plane of existence, and all at once he was in the supernatural. And before he even realized he had asked a question, he already new all of the answers, and he knew all that there was to know. He then looked around and he saw as it were, all that existed. And all of that which he saw was all happening now, and everything he was experiencing was in only one single moment.

"I can see everything." Martin thought. "I see all that exists and all that is. All of time, all at once. How is this possible? It feels more real than life did. Wait, am I dead? Am I in the next life? Or have I just gone insane?"

No sooner had Martin realized that he had finished those thoughts did he begin to fall uncontrollably through the moment. Falling back into the physical world and down towards his human body once more. As he hit the ground where his body lay, all became black and he could now see only his thoughts. He was back in the world of the living and he could no longer recall any of that which he had seen only a moment or so before. And as he lay there in thought waiting for his body to regain enough strength to awake, he tried to remember anything that could help him figure out what was happening.

"Why?" He asked himself in thought. "Why is this even happening? Was it just not yet my time to go? How did I come to be in such a state as this?.. How did I even get here?"

He pondered these questions, trying to understand, hoping that a memory of any kind would come back to him.

"Wait, I remember something!" He exclaimed in his thoughts. "Yes, I remember being part of a tactical strike team. We were fighting against the Chinese. But... if I was part of a team, then why am I alone? Where is everyone? What even were their names? Come on, Martin, think. I got it! Gabriel, James and Jacob! That's who was on my team. But then who are Brian and Scarlet? Why do I know their names and faces but have no memories of them? Out of all the things that I could have remembered, why did I remember the names of people I've never even met? This is so confusing. Send me back! Whoever is doing this to me, I wish to know and understand everything again!"

Aggravated, and still trapped within the confines of his own mind, Martin began to feel lost, abandoned, and utterly confused.

"Mr. Blank, my mysterious old friend and mentor. I remember him. He would know what it all means. He always had all the answers. But where is he now when I need him most? What happened? Why do I feel so empty and so completely alone?"

No sooner had Martin spoken did he begin to hear a voice. Soft at first, almost unintelligible, then clear and distinct.

"Rest now." Said the voice. "It is not yet come time for you to leave this place."

"If it was not my time, then why torture me with the sight of knowing the beauty of what comes next?" Martin asked.

"The answer is in your mind. If you can discover it on your own, then you are worthy of knowing."

"What must I do in order to find the answer?"

"You must do that which is asked by he whom you will serve."

"And who might that be?"

"He will be revealed when it is all over." The voice said after a short pause.

"When will it be over?" Martin asked.

"It will be over when he says, It Is Done."

"Who are you?"

There was no answer.

"Maybe I have gone insane." Martin said to himself once he realized that he was alone again. "I wouldn't be surprised. Maybe I'll ask somebody once I finally wake up. That is of course if I actually do ever wake up."

# CHAPTER: 2

*Hammett Pennsylvania. 2 Years Prior.*

**T**HERE was a cool breeze in the air as Martin Chapel stepped out onto his front porch. He was a well trimmed young man of twenty four with a casual haircut and short but neatly groomed facial hair. He was right around six feet tall and his face was quite symmetrical. He had a relatively chiseled jawline, hollow cheeks, high cheekbones, hunter eyes and a Roman shaped nose.

Currently dressed in his running clothes, about to go for an early morning jog. he stood on his front porch and looked around to take in the sight that the day beheld. It was a beautiful spring morning in mid May and the trees were just about in full bloom. He took a deep breath of the spring air as he heard a pair of small birds chirping overhead. With a smile he then turned around to lock his front door. Once he had removed the key he tested the handle to make sure that it was properly locked. Satisfied, he then turned and began his average Saturday morning jog down to his favorite spot in the park where he liked to just sit and look out at the view of his small town. With a spring in his step he made his way down the sidewalk, just carefree and excited for whatever the day might bring.

Halfway through his run he stopped to walk for a moment to catch his breath. After walking for a short time he began to whistle a joyful tune, imitating the song the birds out front of his house had sung earlier that day. He walked for a few more minutes then jogged the rest of the way till he arrived at the bench that overlooked the town. Still humming a cheerful tune he took a seat on the end of the bench and looked off into the distance where the steeple of the town church rose high above the small buildings that surrounded it. Looking over from that, he could just make out the geese bathing in the pond that was located only a few blocks from the church, with a grove of apple trees beyond it.

After soaking in the view for a short time he suddenly noticed that on the side of the bench opposite from where he sat was a man wearing a black cloak. The man was sitting with his arms crossed and his hood pulled down just far enough that it was completely shading his face from view. Martin had not seen him sitting there when he had arrived only a few minutes before, and had not heard him sit down only a few feet away. This kind of startled him for a moment but then he just assumed that he must not have been paying attention. The man then slowly raised his head as Martin glanced at him out of the corner of his eye. He was wearing a full face mask that appeared to have almond shaped lenses for eyes, and the edge going from the nose to the chin was about an inch wide down the center.

"They say that the one thing that is for certain in life is death." The man said in a low raspy voice; the sudden words catching Martin a little off guard.

"I'm sorry, what?" Martin said with a touch of surprise in his voice as he turned to look at the man.

"They say that the one thing that is for certain in life is death. So if that be the case, then why do people fear it so much?"

"Kind of a randomly creepy way to start a conversation... I'm not sure, I do believe I've actually never really thought about it."

"They fear it because there is no person on earth that can explain what death is with any proof or certainty, and people fear that which they do not understand." Said the man.

"Well of course people would be afraid of things they don't understand... it is an interesting thought though. What do you think death would actually be like?" Martin asked with a touch of curiosity in his voice.

"I could give a million completely logical and believable theories and ideas about what death is and what might happen after it. I could also end up being completely wrong, because the only way to know for sure is to go through it personally and also retain the knowledge of the experience. But even though it can not be explained, you should not fear it."

"Fear is natural though. Why shouldn't I fear death?" Asked Martn.

"Every person throughout history knew that they would die at some point. The fear of death is actually just the fear of losing what you have now and not knowing for sure what comes next. Or if what comes next will be better or worse than what came before. The part that scares people the most is the uncertainty of it all.

People are so afraid of that which they do not know or understand, and what they can not see or feel. I am not trying to tell you how to live your life, but try not to allow yourself to feel fear if you can help it. Fear is unnecessary to life... actually fear is unnecessary altogether, because no good has ever come from losing your head to the emotion of fear."

"What about when fear is an instinct that kicks in for survival?"

"If you get to the point when you must use fear in order to survive, then you probably should not be the one to survive. Relying on instinct and luck to save you, rather than simply keeping a cool head and thinking your next move through using logic is proof that you are not strong enough, and you probably do not deserve to survive. However, if luck is in your favor then I suppose you did something right at least." Said the man.

"Well, that's a pretty harsh and unhealthy way of looking at it. Are you not scared of death?"

"No, I am not."

"Everyone is at least a little afraid of dying. What makes you unafraid of it?"

"I am no longer afraid of dying because I have become completely content with life. Therefore I envy those who have died in my lifetime, but only because death is the final answer to the only questions that can never truly be answered in this life. It is also the only true way to prove to myself whether or not I was right or wrong in every question I have ever asked. There is a good chance I am completely wrong about literally everything, but at least I asked all the questions I could, and was able to find a satisfactory answer to some of the questions I did ask."

"What kind of questions?"

"You will find out for yourself soon enough, Martin, my friend." The man said as he stood up from the bench. "We do have much to discuss. But it will have to wait until a later time. Because right now, unfortunately, I must be going."

"Huh? Wait, who are you, and how do you know my name?" Martin asked in a confused tone.

The man didn't answer immediately. He simply turned his head and gave Martin a slight nod.

"Until we meet again." He said flatly as he began walking away.

"I don't even know who you are!" Martin called after him.

Without turning or slowing the man continued walking away and a few moments later he disappeared around the corner of a building and was gone.

"Well, that was super weird." Martin said to himself in a low voice. "But I guess since I'm now officially creeped all the way out, I might as well go see what the guys are up to."

Martin then stood up from his seat on the bench and began walking in the direction of his friend's house which wasn't too far from the park. After walking a few blocks Martin's eyes reflexively followed his ears up to where the birds were chirping in the trees on either side of the street. Looking ahead again, he saw a young well dressed couple joyfully walking arm in arm down the sidewalk past him. Martin smiled and thought about what he wouldn't give for something like that. For someone to love. He then looked to the sky where a few small fluffy clouds were hanging weightlessly above the buildings. The day gave him a feeling that somewhat reminded him of his younger days back home. Back when he didn't have a care in the world.

Walking up the front steps to his friends house, Martin knocked then waited. A few seconds later the door was opened by a dark haired man who was about the same height and had a similar build to Martin himself.

"What's up, Gabriel?" Martin said to the man in the doorway.

"Not a whole lot, Martin. What you got going on today?" Gabriel said as he stepped aside, inviting Martin to come in.

"I actually don't have much going on." said Martin. "Just finished up my morning run a little bit ago, then I was pretty much just relaxing a little, at least until I was interrupted."

"Interrupted?" Gabriel asked with a raised eyebrow.

"Yeah, I had a really weird interaction earlier today."

"Oh yeah? What happened?"

"There was some guy in a mask that I talked to on the park bench before coming here. He just kinda creeped me out a little is all."

"Crackheads tend to have that type of an effect on people." Gabriel said with a laugh.

"He wasn't a crackhead. At least, I don't think he was. Honestly, he was just different. I don't know how to explain it, but his presence made my blood run cold... It was almost like he was something else entirely." Martin said slowly as if he was pondering something.

"What do you mean?" Gabriel asked.

"Nothing. Don't worry about it. Do you have anything to eat? I haven't eaten since breakfast."

"Yeah, if you wanna hang out for a while, I can make a pizza or something."

"That sounds good." said Martin. "Wanna play some Xbox while we wait for it to cook?"

"Sure." said Gabriel. "You start up the system, I'll go throw one into the oven."

While they waited for the pizza to cook, Martin and Gabriel played a few matches in online Halo. As they were loading into another match there came a knock at the front door.

"There's someone at the door." Gabriel said as he stood up from the couch. "Don't kill me while I'm gone." He added as he moved to go see who it was.

"What's up, Gabriel?" Said a masculine sounding voice after Gabriel had opened the door.

"Hey, not much. What's going on, James?" Gabriel asked.

"Just came to see if you had anything going on today. That girl I've been talking to pissed me off for the last time, so I guess you could say my afternoon is more or less free now."

"Well, I'm sorry to hear that about the girl." said Gabriel. "I guess another one bites the dust. What is the tally up to now, fifty or so already this year?"

"No, It's only been a like forty-nine. Come on, man, I'm not an animal." James said with obvious, heavy sarcasm.

"Okay good. That's a relief. Come on in then. Martin and I are playing some Halo while we wait for the pizza to cook. Would you like a slice?"

"No thanks, I'm fine at the moment. Hey, what's happening, Martin?" James said as he followed Gabriel into the living room.

"Just killed Gabriel for the seventh time." Martin said with a smile.

"Dude, weak. I was answering the door, bro." Gabriel said as he picked up his controller and hurriedly sat back down on the couch.

"What? It's not my fault that you suck at this game." Said Martin.

"I bet I could kick your ass in real life though." Gabriel shot back.

"In your dreams, I have literally all the tactical equipment. I would be like a one man SWAT team all up in this bitch."

"That may be so, but I could definitely beat you in one on one hand to hand any day of the week." Gabriel said while looking at the TV.

"Bet." Martin said as he dropped his controller and immediately grabbed Gabriel in a headlock, taking him towards the ground.

"I wasn't ready!" Gabriel shouted as they both hit the floor. "This is assault! I'm calling the police!"

Martin's grip relaxed as he began laughing uncontrollably.

"You're such a bitch, dude." Martin said through his laughter as he began to stand up.

Gabriel then suddenly sprung forward, driving his shoulder into Martin's chest. He then spun around and grabbing Martin around the head with both arms he threw him over his shoulder, right through the wooden coffee table in the middle of the living room.

With eyes wide in shock, Martin looked around at the bits and pieces of wood that surrounded him. He then looked up at Gabriel's face, which was an expression of pure surprise, and then he began laughing once again. Gabriel and James both looked at each other, and a second later they joined in the laughter.

"My goodness, we are destructive." Martin said as he carefully stood up.

"It's all good." said Gabriel. "I wanted a new coffee table anyway."

"I know you guys have been out of college for almost two years now." said James. "But damn it if y'all ain't got some of that frat boy energy left."

"We can't all be 'four year retired military' like you, James." Said Martin.

"That is obvious. It is also too bad. A little bit of boot camp probably would have done you guys some good." James said with a laugh right as the timer for the oven went off.

"It's about time." Said Martin. "I'm starving."

"I know right?" Said Gabriel. "All of this 'me beating you In a fight' stuff has given me quite the appetite."

"Bitch, I know where you sleep." Said Martin.

"As do I. In my bed, with a shotgun." Said Gabriel.

"You think I don't also have a shotgun?"

"What's your point?" Gabriel asked.

"My point is that I win." said Martin.

"Hmm. Fair enough. Lets eat."

"You guys wanna have a barbecue next Saturday?" Martin asked as he finished his last bite of pizza and pushed his plate forwards.

"I'm down." Said James.

"Me too." Said Gabriel. "You gonna invite Jacob? It's been a while since I've seen the little bugger."

"Yeah, I'll invite him. I don't know why you're calling him little though." Martin laughed. "He's almost as big of a boy as we are, and he's only slightly younger."

"I know. But he's the baby of our friend group so I will treat him as such."

"Whatever you say, Gabriel. Whatever you say."

# CHAPTER: 3

**M**ARTIN opened his cupboard to fetch a coffee mug off the shelf inside. It had been almost one week now since his run in with that strange man on the bench and he had been bothered by that interaction ever since.

"How did he know my name when I never gave it to him?" Martin thought to himself, recalling when the black clad man in the mask had called him by his name then didn't answer when asked how he knew. "I'm almost certain that I didn't give it to him. I was pretty sure we never had a formal greeting... You really shouldn't talk to yourself, Martin. People are gonna think you're crazy."

Just then the coffee pot stopped percolating. Martin grabbed the pot and poured some into his mug. He then walked out to his back deck and made his way to one of the chairs beside the pool. He wanted to just sit and think for a while before he had to get ready for work. It was Friday now and that made him breathe a sigh of relief. As he sat sipping his coffee he began thinking of a memory from a time that seemed like so long ago.

"Dad, I've chosen the college I want to go and I've decided that I am going to live on campus." Said young Martin as he stood with his arms crossed in the doorway to his fathers office.

"Are you sure this is the right choice, kid? I mean, why don't you just stay here with your mother and I and go to a local college?" Said his father.

"Dad, this is what I want. The only college that is gonna teach me what I want to know is in Pennsylvania. And that would be hard to live here while going there."

"Pennsylvania?" His father said with surprise. "That's a four hundred mile trip from here. Why does it have to be so far away?"

"It's the best trade school I could get accepted into. I just think that it's time that I started acting like an adult. This is something that I feel like I need to do. I just wanna make you proud is all."

"I will always be proud of you, son. I just want to make sure you make the right choices, and that you're happy."

"I know. I love you, dad."

The memory faded and Martin was back in the present.

"Oh how I wish I could go back." He said, looking down at the watch on his right wrist that showed 6:04am.

He then downed the last swallow of coffee left in his cup, stood up from his chair and went inside to get ready for work.

Martin's morning routine never really changed much. His life was quite simple and he rather liked it that way. He never really worried about much, and unexpected things rarely happened. The talk he had with the man on the bench the Saturday before was the first time in a while something out of the ordinary had happened to him. And Martin had a strange, unsettling feeling that things were about to change, and that it wasn't the last time that he would encounter the man from the bench. It was a deep and rather dark feeling, and it made a small chill run up his spine.

"What was it about that man that made him seem so different from other people? Was it the way he was dressed?" Martin wondered to himself as he backed the car out of his driveway. "Now that I'm looking at it with hindsight It really kinda feels like he was something else. Like he had an aura about him that was more than just human."

After the short drive Martin pulled into the parking lot of the shop where he worked. He parked his car then walked into the building and clocked in. The whole day while he worked, he kept thinking about how he wished to have just a few more words with the man. There were some things he wanted to ask him.

"It's strange, it's almost like I have to talk to him again, like I'm being called by the thirst to know more." He said to himself. "Still talking to yourself... Maybe you are crazy, Martin."

The next morning Martin started off on his jog to the park as he always did. It was another fairly nice day, save for a slight overcast that seemed likely to fade as the day progressed.

"I wonder if he'll be there today." Martin thought as he made his way down the sidewalk in the direction of the same bench he usually ended up on. "It's funny, I'm only 24 and already I'm starting to live like a middle aged man. Pretty soon I'll just be working and sitting on a park bench on the weekends."

When he got to the bench he had almost hoped that the man would be there so he could ask him a couple questions, but of course, the bench was empty. Martin decided to sit down anyway. He figured a little time to think would probably be good for him.

"Hello again, Martin." Said a distinct familiar voice.

"My goodness!" Exclaimed Martin. "You really ought to announce yourself before you sneak up on people like that."

"You ought to be more aware of your surroundings." Said the cloaked man.

"Fair enough." Martin said with an exhale. "How are you?"

"I am doing well. How about yourself?"

"Well besides you almost giving me a heart attack, I can't complain."

"Good to hear." The man said with a light chuckle.
Martin quietly glared at him for a moment then lightly chuckled himself.

"Since the last time we spoke I've been wondering how it was that you knew my name without me ever telling you?" Martin said in a questioning tone.

"You did tell it to me. Do you not remember?" The man said; sounding as if he was confused. "It was right after you sat down on the bench next to me."

"I do not remember it happening that way." Said Martin.

"Sometimes it is difficult to differentiate dreams from memories. Worry not though, for it is not important at this time."

"Alright. So tell me, my completely normal acquaintance. Why is it that you are here?"

"Is it not obvious?" Said the man.

"Not even a little bit." Martin replied.

"I am here because it is where I am supposed to be."

"Okay cool, so you're insane. Why didn't you just say so?"

"I am not insane. You are just not understanding me. Allow me to explain with more simplicity. I am here to help you protect those you care about, from that which shall come to pass."

"Dude, are you okay?" asked Martin. "The way you're talking sounds kinda weird."

"I am quite fine actually. Thank you for asking."

"Whatever you say, man. So what are you talking about?"

"Our days are numbered. Time is growing short. We must prepare for what is coming, before it is too late."

"What is it that is coming?"

"You will find out when it comes to the proper time."

"I need a coffee." Martin said, rubbing his temples. "Would you like to join me for breakfast at the diner just around the corner? I'll pay, as long as you tell me whatever it is you feel like you need to tell me."

"Very well, lead the way, my friend."

# CHAPTER: 4

**T**HE diner was only a short walk from the bench where Martin and the masked man had been talking. Martin pulled the handle to open the door. And as they were walking into the entry way he noticed someone coming up behind them. He turned and held the door open as a young woman approached.

"Thank you." The woman said with a smile as she walked past him and into the diner.

"Well, she was quite a lovely woman. You should go talk to her." Said the man in a hushed teasing tone as they entered the diner after her.

"Why would I do that?"

"Why would you not?"

Martin turned to look at the man, then said.

"You're very strange. You know that right?"

"Indeed I am. What is your point?"

"What do you want me to do, just go over and randomly ask her to sit with us or something? Because that wouldn't be weird." Martin stated in a sarcastic tone.

The man cocked his head to one side while looking towards him.

"You do not even know my name, yet and you invited me here only a few moments ago."

Upon realizing this was indeed true, Martin paused for a moment to think.

"Well I can't argue with your logic." he said, finally. "You actually make a good point. hang tight, I'll be right back."

The man took a seat in a booth by the window, while Martin made his way over to talk to the young woman.

"Hi, remember me from the door a moment ago?" He said while pointing back towards the door with his thumb.

The woman looked up from the book she was reading, then she smiled pleasantly.

"Hello, yes I remember." She said.

"That's good to hear. My name is Martin by the way." He said as he presented his hand towards her.

"Ellis." She said as she took his hand and shook it gently.

"Nice to meet you. I couldn't help but notice you were sitting alone. Would you like to come join my..." Martin looked over to the man who was looking out the window with his hood still pulled down low over his masked face. "Come join my friend and I?" He finished.

"Sure why not." She said before putting the book she was reading into her purse which was sitting on the seat beside her. "I don't meet new people often enough anyway."

She then stood and followed Martin over to the booth where the man was sitting.

"No face, this is Ellis. Ellis, No face." Martin said as he pointed back and forth while he introduced them.

"I'm sorry, but who names their kid, No face?" Ellis asked with a giggle.

"It's not his real name. He just hasn't told me what it actually is yet." Martin replied.

"But aren't you guys friends?" She asked.

"Of course we are." The man Interjected. "I simply prefer my name to remain safely within the confines of my own mind for the time being. Most other knowledge and information that I possess is available upon request. My name and the face it belongs to however, shall remain mine and mine alone."

"Oh, well aren't you mysterious." Ellis Teased.

The man tilted his head a little to the side while looking towards her and gave a slight shrug of his shoulders.

"Hello, my name is Jake and I'll be taking care of you today." The waiter said as he walked up and stood in front of their booth. "Can I start you off with something to drink?"

Martin and Ellis both ordered drinks and then food, but the man clad in black sitting across from them ordered nothing.

"Is it just me or does it seem like time moves slower when you are waiting for food?" Martin asked to nobody in particular.

"Sometimes." Said Ellis. "It's almost like, when you're bored, time seems to just drag on."

"I agree. What do you have to say about this?" Martin asked, looking towards the man.

"Would you like me to explain what time is, or do you just want my opinion?" Replied the man.

"Hmm, well since you're here, would it be too much to ask for both?"

"Of course not, I would be delighted." said the man. "In the simplest of terms, I like to explain time as a series of conjoined sequential moments. It is in a sense like a slideshow. Each and every moment is an individual stationary yet conjoined slide that our consciousness goes through in sequence, one conjoined sequential slide at a time. However, there are no single stopped moments in time, time is a constant. We as humans, made of natural matter, can only go forward in time at the rate in which time was designed to allow us to go. In the natural realm where our minds and bodies are made of matter, in order for our matter to grow, we require time. Without time our cells cannot grow, change, age or learn. Because everything that we do is completely based on the amount of motion that time allows everything to experience. Mortal beings such as humans can only ever see one single instant of time at any given moment, in sequence, forced ever forwards by a series of these conjoined sequential moments and the growth of your natural bodies."

"I... I don't even know how to respond to that." Martin said with eyes wide.

"Would you like me to continue?" The man asked.

"Yes please." Said Ellis.

"Very well." He said before clearing his throat. "Time as we know and experience it is the way it is so that our natural minds are both able and regulated to learn at a set pace. This is so that we as natural beings are never able to learn or understand more than we are permitted to understand."

"So your saying time is set the way it is so that you can only ever learn so much in your natural life before you die?" Asked Martin.

"That would be one of the simpler ways of saying it. But yes, time is set the way it is in order to allow us to progress. Age and death however, are set in order to limit the progress of one single individual from learning too much."

"But why is that though? Why can't one person just know everything?" Martin asked.

"Knowledge is not just power, it is absolute power." said the man. "If you knew truly everything and understood how everything works including how to make it happen. You would be alike unto a God."

"Fair enough. So back on the subject of time. How does it work, why is time the thing that allows progress?" Martin asked curiously.

"Allow me to explain. You can not have matter without motion, you can not have motion without time, and you can not have any without all. Because without matter, time as we experience it would be irrelevant because there would be no reason to have a beginning or an end. If there was no physical matter that required time in order to age or learn, then what purpose would beginnings and ends have at all? Without time, matter could never come to exist, because there must be time in order for something to have a beginning."

"What about time itself?" asked Martin. "Wouldn't time also need a beginning?"

"What time is, and the way we experience it, are two incredibly different things, Martin. Time as the dimension does not require a beginning because time as a whole, is only one single moment."

"You lost me. That doesn't make much sense at all."

"Let me explain. There can't be life without time, because in order to have natural life, growth, or change, time is required for it to be so. Time as it is in the fourth dimension as one single moment, is greater than us in every way. However, time as it pertains to us is subject to natural matter, and natural matter is subject to the process of time. Neither on its own could sustain or be considered natural life, and would not be relevant or have purpose. Without both there would be no point to either. Time is the source that allows us to move, learn, grow and think, and it is an absolute necessity in order for matter to have motion. Without time, there can be no motion, without motion, there can be no natural life."

"So are you saying time is relative to us as natural human beings, or are you challenging the Theory of Relativity?" Ellis asked with a touch of disapproval.

"Some people have probably tried to tell you that time is relative." the man said; leaning back in his seat. "I however, am not. Because if that were actually true then each and every person throughout all of history would have to have had their own personal reality... which is not impossible, but it is highly unlikely. If time was relative to a particular individual, and everything is made up of individual atoms, then why would each atom not have a time that was relative to that atom alone? Because if time was relative, it would have to be relative to each individual atom or molecule.

And if that was the case, you would be torn apart at a molecular level by the clash of all your cells trying to keep the same pace as they move through time. While it is not entirely impossible, it is a statistical improbability that if there were a trillion different relative timelines in just your body alone that they would all share and retain the same rate of motion through time. Unless it is time that is the constant and we that are subject to time."

"Well, I suppose that makes about as much sense as I'm going to understand." Said Martin.

"You will understand soon enough." The man said, taking a second to look at both Martin and Ellis. "If the time of a particular object was to slow down, then our reality would outrun its presence, and it would be sucked from our existence. Imagine if you were holding an apple, and the time of that apple suddenly became relative to that apple alone. Then the timeline that it was in sped up or slowed down in even the slightest amount. That apple would exit our reality and disappear. You can not move an object if its time is different from your own. But if you could, and it was in a slower relative time, it would feel exponentially heavier than normal. And if it were in a faster relative time it would be much lighter than it usually would be. This however is not the case, because stuff like that never happens in this thing that we call 'real life."

"That is a pretty good point." said Martin while rubbing his chin. "But then why does it seem that time goes slower or faster sometimes?"

"Remember earlier when you said how time seemed to be dragging on when you were waiting for your food, and Ellis here agreed with you?" The man asked as he casually removed his hood to reveal the rest of his head.

They could now see that the mask he was wearing was more a tight fitting helmet than it was a mask.

"Of course I remember. That was only a few moments ago." Martin said, trying to focus on the conversation to keep himself from asking a bunch of dumb questions about the mans appearance.

"That happens because there is only one time that we all perceive, and we all share the same moments simultaneously. You were both perceiving the same emotion, and thought, of waiting for the same thing. So your perception of the rate at which time was passing was the same. The saying; time flies when you're having fun, is actually more or less incorrect. Time itself does not change. However, your perception of it does change based on the amount of thoughts you have and how focused you are on each specific moment. When you are bored or idle you tend to think a lot more, which makes you notice the passing moments more intently. But when you are busy with activities, your mind tends not to wander into thought quite as much. Which makes it feel as though time went by faster. In reality however, you just weren't noticing each and every moment as it was passing by. This is why the rate of time seems to sometimes fluctuate. It is not that time itself is changing speed. Only our perception and how much we consciously notice does it change. So in a way, time is kind of relative to each individual. But only that people sometimes see it differently based on how focused and concentrated they are at that particular moment. Time itself however, does not change."

"So you're telling me that Einstein's Theory of Relativity was wrong?" Ellis asked.

"Yes." The man responded. "If time was relative then we would be able to figure out the point in which relativity takes place and in turn we would understand and be able to control time. This however is not achievable because time is above our nature in every way besides the way we experience it."

"Oh, I see. So were you still saying anything else about how we perceive time then?"

"Ah yes, of course. Although there are a couple other ways that our brains perceive time. I noticed that the slower your brain thinks, the faster time seems to go by, but the faster you think, the slower time goes by. As I said before; physically the speed at which actual time goes by does not change. The speed in which your mind processes images and thoughts however, can vary at times. Depending on what mixture of chemicals your brain is making at that particular moment. Adrenalin can make time appear to almost go in slow motion, whereas being very calm makes time seem to take forever. Therefore, when your mind requires you to think at an accelerated rate, it makes everything appear to be slower because your mind is processing information at such a greater rate so that you may react faster. This is because you're having more thoughts per millisecond than you normally do at any other given time. Now, do not mistake what I have just laid out with the notion of how time seems to move slower when you are bored. If you are just sitting around doing something more calming, your rate of thought is slower, which allows you to acknowledge each moment of time more intently. There is a difference between time appearing to slow down, and time feeling as though it is taking longer."

"Do you think it would be possible for someone in the future to make a machine that could disrupt the space time continuum and travel through time? Or something like that maybe?" Ellis asked.

"I personally do not believe that to be possible for the same reasons that I have just explained only a few minutes ago. Also when someone says; space time, or time and space, they only say it because it is a statement that has been normalized over the years but it is actually such a broad statement that in reality it could be considered to be nonsensical. Time and space are so different that putting the two together as though they were related or even similar is idiotic. Time has absolutely nothing to do with space because space is a physical thing you can see and feel, and time is not."

"What if we could find a way to become a fourth dimensional being? Would we be able to travel through time then?" Ellis asked.

"There already is a way to become a fourth dimensional being." Replied the man.

"There is? What way would that be?" Asked Martin.

"Oh, I don't know, it is quite risky."

"Come on, just tell us." Said Ellis.

"Alright, I'll tell you, but you must never speak of this secret to anyone. Do you understand?" The man asked with a stern seriousness in his voice.

Martin and Ellis both nodded in unison.

"Okay then." The man said as he leaned in closer over the table. "If you want to become a fourth dimensional being." He looked around as if to make sure nobody was listening. Then in a whisper he continued. "The only way you can become a fourth dimensional being... is if you die." The man said with a light hearty chuckle.

"Good one." Martin said, leaning back whilst shaking his head.

Ellis just rolled her eyes with a smile then looked out the window.

"I believe you fooled us for sure with that one." Said Martin.

"That was my goal." The man said with a laugh.

"But seriously though, is there any way that we as humans could ever take control of time even a little bit?" Martin asked.

"I say again, we are three dimensional beings, Martin. Time is a fourth dimensional construct. And since that be the case, time is not relative to us; we are inferior to time. However, if time were relative to us, then we as three dimensional beings would be able to then figure out how to control the fourth dimension. If we knew when relativity occurred. But just as a two dimensional being could never have an effect on us in the third dimension or survive in it, we just the same can not affect the fourth dimension or survive in it. Because if we could figure out how to control the fourth dimension then we would in turn become fourth dimensional beings. Because it would require that we upset the natural laws of our very existence. Which would more likely than not, simply end our existence as a whole."

The man looked towards the ceiling for a moment as if pondering a thought then he continued.

"That is why I believe that it is 100% physically impossible for a human or anything else that is subject to the three dimensional realm to travel through time. Because in order to travel to a different time you must first travel out of the third dimension into the fourth dimension, then re-enter the third dimension at a different point. That is the impossible part, because in order to enter the fourth dimension you must be a fourth dimensional being otherwise you would either be torn apart at a molecular level or just simply cease to exist altogether. Although, if by some miracle while attempting to enter the fourth dimension, rather than only dying a horrible death you instead just transformed into a fourth dimensional being, it would not matter. If you were transformed into a superior being, even if you could return to being human you would neither try nor want to go back to the point in time that you came from originally. Because if you were to become a fourth dimensional being, the third dimension would be beneath you in every way. You would see no point or reason to return to your old restricted physical body. And no one in the time from which you left would ever know what had become of you."

"What about black holes, or something like that? What if we could just rip a hole in reality that we could slip through?" Martin asked.

"If you were to rip a hole in time while in our three dimensional world and the way we experience time. It would also rip a hole in every single moment of time since it began in our existence and also every moment until it ends. So if in the future someone was to attempt to rip a hole in reality in order to travel through time. It would tear a hole in time the moment they do it, this moment right now, yesterday, next week, last year, and every other moment that has ever been or will ever be. Therefore if you think about it from a logical standpoint. You will realize that time travel is not, can not, and will never be possible. Because the end of time has already been set and is currently being experienced by the people in the future. Yes, the way our time works as fourth dimensional beings see it, is both the beginning and the end of the world is being experienced by someone right now, both in the future and the past. The only difference is that we are perceiving it now, whereas they are perceiving it then. Just because something changes, does not mean that it is not all still exactly the same."

"How do you know all this stuff?" Ellis asked, looking at the masked man.

He turned towards her then after a second or two, he answered.

"I never claimed that I knew anything. I am simply just a man who thinks deeply, comes to realizations that seem mostly logical, then I form an opinion based on the theories that I come up with. Do not feel obligated to believe a word I say, for I do not expect you to."

Both Martin and Ellis were silent. The man then looked over at a table across the room and noticed a blonde haired man dressed in a suit was staring at him.

"And with that my friends, I bid thee farewell until we meet again." Said the man after looking at the watch on his right wrist.

"You really can't stay any longer? We've only just started getting into this conversation." Said Ellis.

"Unfortunately, no I cannot. There is somewhere I have to be. Hopefully we can continue this talk at another time." Said the man.

"If you're not busy tomorrow afternoon." Martin began. "You are welcome to come over to my place. I'm planning on having a few friends over, and I'm sure they would like to meet you."

The man leaned against the seat he had just gotten up from as if he was pondering the invitation.

"That sounds delightful." The man said, finally.

"Excellent. What about you, Ellis? Do you have any plans for food tomorrow evening?"

"I'm sorry but yes I do. I have to go to dinner with my parents tomorrow evening."

"Ah... well, I was gonna tell you to cancel your plans if you had any. But dinner with your parents changes everything."

Ellis laughed. "I am available Sunday. If you want to do something then? Just the two of us."

"I'll have to check my schedule." He took a brief moment to think and look at the ceiling before he continued. "It's gonna be tight but I think I can make Sunday work. Let me have your number so I can call you if something comes up unexpectedly."

"Of course." Replied Ellis.

She then wrote her number down on the napkin beside her plate and slid it over to him.

"Oh yeah, that reminds me, do you have a phone number?..." Martin paused as he looked up at the masked man. "Can I just call you, Mr. Blank, or something? It feels weird to me not having something to call you."

"If you must call me something then I suppose that, Mr. Blank, is fine with me. And yes I do, here is my card."

The newly named Mr. Blank handed him a black and gold business card with only a phone number etched into it.

"Okay great, that will make things a little bit simpler. So anyway my house, if you are able to make it, is only about a mile down the road from where we first met. On the right side of the road. People should start showing up there around 4pm. Actually, I'll just text you the address."

"Very good. I will do my best to be there. Have a good rest of your day." Mr. Blank said with a glace over at the blonde man who was still watching him.

Mr. Blank then turned and went through the doors of the restaurant disappearing out of sight a second later.

"Your friend is quite a strange character, isn't he?" Said Ellis.

"Indeed he is." Said Martin. "But the things that he said really got me thinking and questioning everything I've ever known."

"Do you believe the things he says?"

"I don't know. His points are hard for someone like me to argue. I just don't know enough to debate what he says. For all I know he's just screwing with us."

"Don't be too hard on yourself, most of what he said was very strange and I really haven't decided whether or not I think he's just a crazy person."

"Yeah, me either." Martin chuckled.

"How long have you known him for?"

"About a week."

"That's not very long at all. With the way you two carry on I figured that you've known each other for at least a week and a half."

Martin looked at her for a few seconds then they both began laughing. After he realized it wasn't really that funny, Martin finished drinking his coffee then he stood up from the table.

"Well I think I should probably get going now. It was very nice meeting and talking to you though."

"Same to you." Ellis said with a smile.

Martin gave a slight bow of his head then turned and walked out of the diner. He then made his way onto the sidewalk and began heading for his house.

Once back at home Martin began preparing a portion of meat to put on the smoker for dinner the following day. Once the meat was in the smoker, he went back inside and walked down the hall to the living room. He picked up the book off the coffee table and sat down in his recliner to relax for a while. He looked at the front cover for just a brief moment before opening the book. It was 1984 by George Orwell. He found his page, removed the bookmark, then he continued reading where he had left off.

# CHAPTER: 5

**M**ARTIN awoke the next morning sitting in his recliner as he had been the night before, with the book he had been reading still laying open across his lap. He closed the foot rest of the chair, catching the book as he did so. He then stretched his arms and rubbed his sore neck.

"I must have slept wrong or something." He said to himself, in a groan as he attempted to rub the soreness away.

He then placed his bookmark back into the crease between the pages and set the Orwellian novel back on the small table next to his chair.

"Hmm, 9:30am already." He said as he stood up while looking at the clock. "I suppose it's about time to start doing stuff then."

Later on that day, after he had prepared most of the food, he heard a knock at the front door. Wondering who it might be, Martin walked out of the kitchen and down the hall towards the door. Once he arrived in the entry way, he turned the handle and opened the door.

"Hey, Martin, my main man!" A blonde haired man in his early twenties said as Martin pulled the door open.

"Jacob, how are you, bud? Please come in." Martin said, gesturing for him to come inside.

"I'm pretty good. Am I the first one here?"

"You are. What time is it even?" Martin said aloud to himself as he looked at his mechanical watch. "Hmm, 4:00pm already. So, can I get you anything to drink?"

"Yes please. What ya got?" Jacob asked as Martin led him to the kitchen.

"I have whiskey, bourbon and more whiskey."

"Some things never change." Jacob said with a chuckle. "That sounds great."

Martin nodded then poured few ounces of bourbon into two whiskey glasses and handed one to Jacob.

"The food in the smoker should be about done." Martin said as he put the bottle back down on the counter. "But I believe the grill for the other stuff should be up to temperature by now. Mind helping me throw the hamburgers on?"

"Of course not, which one's are going on first?"

"These ones right here." Martin said as he took one of the two plates off the counter with his free hand.

Jacob walked around him and grabbed the other one, then he followed Martin outside.

Once the hamburgers were on the grill, and the timer was set, they both moved to sit in the chairs around the outdoor table in the middle of the deck. Once they had taken their seats, Jacob pulled a pack of cigarettes out of his pocket, and plucked one of them out. He then threw the pack on the table and lit the cigarette in his mouth.

"You want one?" Jacob asked, pointing to the pack after taking a long drag on the smoke.

Martin stared at the pack for a few seconds.

"Ah, what the hell." Martin said as he grabbed the pack, drew one out and lit it.

They sat and smoked for a little while, chatting about the previous week, and making small talk while they waited for the others to arrive.

Jacob was a barber like his father before him. Martin had met him about a week after he had moved to the area, because after the long, exhausting move, he was in desperate need of a haircut. They had been close friends ever since then. They even used to go to parties together back in the day, but those days were long gone now.

"Hey, remember that one night at that party that we got so drunk you didn't even remember how you had gotten there or how you got home?" Jacob asked.

"Barely, I remember you helped me get a local girl's number. You said she was a pretty chill chick... and she was but she definitely wasn't my type." Said Martin.

"Yup, that was back when we were both into that sort of thing. Work all week so we could party on the weekends."

"Remember why we stopped partying?" Martin asked.

"Not really." Jacob laughed.

"It was because of that night a few years back. The one where we had gotten so drunk on wine coolers that we almost spent the night in jail for disorderly conduct and public intoxication."

"Oh yeah. Those were the good days. Fun times. We never should have stopped"

"Aye!" Said a voice coming from Martin's right.

He turned to look just in time to see Gabriel and James rounding the corner of his house; one of them holding up a twelve pack of beer.

"Well if it isn't Gabriel and James. What the hell are you two doing here?" Jacob jabbed in a sarcastic tone.

"We're here to crash this party. How are you doing, Martin?" Gabriel asked.

"Not too bad, Gabriel. How about yourself?" Martin said, presenting his hand to shake.

"Can't complain." Gabriel said as he took Martin's hand and shook it.

"How about you, James? How are ya?" Martin asked.

"I'm good, buddy." James said as he also clasped and shook Martin's hand.

"Well now that we're all here, is the food ready to eat?" Asked Jacob.

"I might have one more person coming. He wasn't sure if he would be able to make it though." Said Martin.

Just then they heard the doorbell ring.

"Ah, perhaps he was able to make it after all." Said Martin.

"Who is it?" Jacob asked.

"He's an interesting character that's for sure. Just wait, if that's him you'll know what I mean in a second." Martin said as he went inside to answer the front door.

A few moments later he came back out onto the deck, followed by a masked man dressed in all black.

"Hey fellas, he won't tell me his real name. But this is, Mr. Blank. Mr. Blank, this is Jacob Turner, James Hudson and Gabriel Cooper."

"Hello, gentlemen. How are you all doing this afternoon?"

"Pretty good."

"Not so bad."

"Doing well." Was the answer from the three men still sitting in their chairs around the table.

"Please, have a seat. The food isn't quite ready yet, so just make yourself at home." Said Martin.

"Thank you." Said Mr. Blank.

"So, does anyone have any interesting things to talk about?" Jacob asked with a shrug.

"New guy initiation. Tell us something about yourself, Blank." Gabriel said, looking towards him.

"Unfortunately, I am not very good at telling stories or making small talk. I am more of a deep thinker."

"What's the point of deep thinking if your not good at talking?" Jacob asked.

"What's the point of thinking at all, if you never think deeply?" Blank returned.

"This is gonna get good." Martin whispered to Gabriel and James with a hand to one side of his mouth as to somehow direct the sound to only them.

"Thinking deeply hurts my head." Jacob said, jokingly. "I don't know about you, but I'd rather not have my head hurting."

"Just out of curiosity, Jacob." Mr. Blank began. "As a human, you are only given a short time in this life, correct?"

"I guess it would depend on how you look at it. But yes, I personally believe that to be the case."

"Then why would you wish for anything other than making every conversation you have, a conversation that expands your mind and knowledge a little farther every time you have one?"

Jacob put his elbow on the arm of his chair and rubbed his chin making an obvious gesture that he was thinking over a response.

"I'm a simple guy." He said, finally. "I do agree that deep philosophical conversations are good and quite interesting every now and then. but I usually prefer talking about stuff that requires less mental strain."

"So, you would rather intentionally waste time, instead of having conversations that require you to think and expand your mind and understanding?" Mr. Blank asked in a friendly tone.

"It's not that exactly. I just... common man. Why you gotta make me sound so dumb?" Jacob said, looking down, grinning with embarrassment.

"That was not my intention. But then again, I wasn't the one that made you look dumb. You do that just fine on your own, my friend."

"Burn!" Yelled Gabriel. "Oh, he got you good, buddy."

"Shut up, asshole!" Jacob yelled back at him before laughing at his own embarrassment.

Just then Martin's phone timer suddenly went off.

"Welp, looks like the food's done. Feel free to help yourselves, guys."

# CHAPTER: 6

**A**FTER dinner they all moved down to the fire pit where Martin lit the bonfire. They all sat in silence for a short while just watching the flames burn the logs, and listening to the crackle of the wood being slowly consumed.

"So where are you from, Blank?" Gabriel suddenly asked, turning to look towards him.

"I'm not sure. I was adopted when I was young. I never figured out where I was from originally." Blank said, flatly.

"Oh, I'm sorry to hear that."

"It's alright. I've managed just fine, for the most part."

"So then, where are you staying now?" Asked Martin.

"I have a place about five miles up the road."

"Really?" Said Martin. "What house? I might even know the one."

"I doubt that you would." Said Blank.

"What makes you say that?" Asked Martin.

"You all will probably call me crazy, but I say that because I do not actually live in a house. I live in an underground bunker."

"You live in a bunker?! That is cool as hell!" Said James.

"Thank you." Mr. Blank said with a nod to James.

"I would love to live in a bunker." Said Jacob. "I'd feel safe and secure at all times."

"I am almost never there." Said Blank. "I also don't much care for safety and security. I prefer freedom over being cramped up."

"I get that." Said Jacob. "But still, I bet you never have to worry about someone trying to break in while you sleep."

"A gun can give you just as much, if not more security than a bunker can during a home invasion. Of course it would be better to have both, but not everyone can just go buy a bunker. Also, bunker or not, if someone wanted to break in bad enough, they would."

"I'm a pacifist though. So I prefer stuff that isn't weapons." Said Jacob.

"What is more passive than owning the means to protect what is yours?" Blank asked. "Owning something for self defense is not because you are planning to use it, it is because you are planning for in case you have to."

Martin, James and Gabriel were just sitting there listening to Mr. Blank and Jacob having their discussion when James leaned in towards Martin and Gabriel.

"Do you guys wanna take bets on who's gonna win the argument that's about to happen?" He asked.

"I've got $20 on Blank." Said Gabriel.

"I'll take that action. I've got $20 on Blank also." Said Martin.

"Alright, I guess I've got $40 on Jacob then. We can't all bet against the little guy." James said with a hushed laugh.

"Let me ask you this, Jacob." Mr. Blank continued. "Would you rather have security from the government, or the freedom to die the way you choose?"

"Is it bad to want a life that's safe and secure?" Jacob asked.

"It depends on your level of weakness. Do you have the strength to live by your own power, or do you require someone else to keep you alive?"

"I think I'd be able to handle myself just fine if it came down to it."

"So then why would you even require that someone else gives you security in return for your freedom to live as you see fit?"

"Well I can't very well defend my whole country by myself now could I?"

"Probably not. But is your freedom worth giving up in order to receive some perceived security from your government?"

"I don't know. I'd just rather let the police protect me from the things I can't control."

"The only thing the police will do for you when you need them most, is get there just in time to draw the chalk line around your dead body."

"So you're saying I can't rely on the police?"

"That's exactly what I'm saying. The only things you own are that which you can protect by yourself. And one of the most effective ways to do that is to buy and learn how to use a gun."

"I understand that self reliance is important, but I don't see what owning a gun has to do with it."

"One day someone stronger than you will come along and demand what's yours is now theirs. Without the power to stop them, they are correct, with the power to stop them they are dead. For example, if I decided right now that everything you own is now mine, then I own all of your stuff. Because there is nothing you could do to stop me from taking it from you. And the rule of law does not apply here, because the only law that matters to me is survival of the fittest."

Jacob was silent, just looking down at the cup in his hands.

"Well, Mr. Blank. I don't agree with you on everything. But you might have begun to change my mind a little. You're alright." Jacob said as he presented his hand to Blank.

Mr. Blank took his hand in a firm grip and shook.

"I'm glad you think so. See, deep conversations are better. Both of us might have actually learned something valuable tonight." Said Blank.

With their eyes still in the direction of Blank and Jacob. Martin and Gabriel both put their hands out towards James who with a look of exaggerated dissatisfaction split the $80 in half and handed $40 to each of them.

"Well fellas, I think it's about that time that I should probably get going." Said Jacob. "It was nice meeting you, Mr. Blank, and I hope to see you again soon."

"Likewise." He returned with a bow of his covered head.

"I should probably get going too. I've got a lot of yard work to get done tomorrow." Said Gabriel. "Thank you for dinner though, Martin. This was fun."

"You're welcome guys. How about you, James? Are you staying a while, or are you heading out too?" Martin asked; looking over towards James.

"Yeah, it's getting pretty late. I might stop by tomorrow to help you clean up though."

"I would appreciate that. You all drive safely."

After Gabriel, James and Jacob had left, Martin and Mr. Blank just sat and stared at the fire for a little while.

"So, Mr. Blank." Martin began. "I would like to hear more about your theories on time. I've been thinking about what you said before and I'm still pretty confused by it all. Yesterday you said that we could continue the conversation at a later point, and now it is a later point."

"Of course. I shall continue from where we left off." Mr. Blank said, paused for a moment then continued. "So, how do you think that the past, present and future exist? And what do they all have in common?"

"I dunno. Maybe because they're all things that people go through?" Replied Martin.

"If you were outside the third dimension; looking in at it from the fourth, you would see that the past exists because it is happening now, just like the future is happening now. Life and existence are now, throughout time. Past, present and future, are all the same moment just at different times. The only thing that sets the past and future apart from the present is your current observation of a particular moment. Because both the future and the past are the present, just not presently at this moment."

"My brain honestly hurts when you talk." Martin said with a laugh while he rubbed his eyes.

"Would you like me to continue?" Chuckled Mr. Blank.

"Yes, my curiosity has gotten the better of me. Please continue."

"Alright, just let me know if you would rather talk about sports."

"Do you even know anything about sports?"

"No, I do not."

Both Martin and Mr. Blank laughed for a moment then they continued their conversation.

"Alright. Hear me out." Mr. Blank began. "The set motion of time is the undoing of all things in this life. If you hold onto the material things that you have, you're only setting yourself up for disappointment. Because one day, everything you have will be gone, everyone you know will be dead, and every moment you lived will be forgotten. The only thing that you actually have, and can call yours, is the exact moment in which you are in right now. A second that has passed, is no longer yours, a second into the future is not yours yet, but this moment that you are in now, is the only possession you actually have. Because it is the moment in which you are currently observing your existence. You only get one chance to observe each moment as it passes you by, so don't waste it. Make the most of everything you have, because the only thing you do have, is this moment and this moment only."

"Do you rehearse all the stuff you say before you talk to people, or is it just off the cuff?" Martin asked.

"I spent years just thinking, and I memorized all the things I learned about life. So I guess you could say that is a type of rehearsal."

"Fair enough. I was just wondering about that. When you speak, you seem so sure about the things you say."

"That is because I truly believe everything I say is as close to the truth as one can come. I'm not saying you have to believe what I say. I'm simply telling you what I know."

"How much do you actually know about existence?" Asked Martin.

"I know a little about a lot, and a lot about a little." Said Blank. "I could talk for hours on a few select subjects, but not even be able to respond to others. I am aware that I do not actually know anything, but just thinking about things gives my mind strength."

"Okay. Let's hear some more. I wanna know more about the things you think about."

"As you wish. What do you think would happen if the human race went extinct?"

"I don't know." Said Martin as he pondered the question. "It's hard to imagine life without self conscious, intelligent beings."

"Try to imagine not being here, not being alive, or ever existing. Try to imagine nothing existing."

"That's a hard thing to imagine." Said Martin. "How can you imagine that which you can not imagine?"

"Correct." Said Blank. "You physically can not imagine nothing. Because in this natural realm that is subject to time, everything requires a beginning. However, in order to have a beginning in time, your time also has to be started by something."

"Like what. God?" Martin asked.

Mr. Blank briefly looked at the fire then he turned back to Martin and said.

"Not necessarily. But in a sense, yes. Time would have had to be started by something or someone of greater nature than our own. Greater than time itself. Something more supernatural, if you will."

"Do you believe in God?"

"I believe nothing to be true, but anything to be possible. I believe in everything."

"Wait, so then you do believe time travel is possible."

"Do you want the short answer, or long answer?" Asked Blank.

"I want the logical answer. The best way you can answer it." Said Martin.

"Very well." Mr. Blank said, taking a deep breath. "Besides the theory's I have already told you, I have another. And that is, If we were to actually travel backwards in time, would it not also reverse the growth of our cells' natural development?"

"I don't know. What do you think?"

"The question was rhetorical, Martin." Blank said with a pause. "I believe that doing such a thing would cause the age of the cells to reduce backwards, reversing the previous experience of growth. In simpler terms, traveling backwards in time to a destination in time greater than your age, would either kill you, or it would reverse your existence back down to what you are before birth. But even if you were able to do that, time is not a fabric that can just be folded like an article of clothing so that you can just transport to a different time and place. Motion, growth, progress, and natural life, all require time as it is in its set motion, in order to exist. If time ceased to exist, then everything, all motion would stop. Because in order for a natural object to get from point A to point B, there must be something there that will allow motion to occur. Also even if you were able to find a way to physically travel back in time. You would be able to access those different times but you would also lose all previous memories of the future and therefore make the same decisions you had made previously because you lack the knowledge you lost when you traveled back in time. So you would in turn change nothing and simply repeat that which you had already done and you would not even realize it. You wouldn't even remember traveling back in time. This could be an explanation for déjà vu though."

Martin was slightly confused. However, he was doing his best to appear as though he was keeping up; nodding every so often as if he understood. Blank then suddenly paused, but after only a moment or two, he continued.

"Everything that exists, every dimension of existence requires a dimension greater than itself in order to function. The first dimension would not matter without the second to support its existence, the second would not matter without the third, and the third dimension, the one that we live in, could not exist without the fourth."

"Interesting. How many dimensions are there?" Asked Martin.

"Science says that there are eleven dimensions, but there could be as many as twenty two. I say there are more than likely an infinite number of dimensions. Which would be not at all impossible, because what is impossible to us, would not be impossible to plains of existence that are greater than our own. Although, that notion is in fact outside our ability to consider. Because the fourth dimension and above are not subject to any of the things as we are. Time, matter, physics, numbers, all these things that we use to tell us what our existence means and all the things that any human could ever think of, are irrelevant in the dimensions that are above our own."

"So do you think time travel is possible, or no?"

"Pay attention, Martin. With all that I have come to understand, I do not believe physical time travel for a human is actually possible. Two dimensional time could be bent and traveled through because it is flat like a piece of paper. However, three dimensional time is more like a solid sphere. Have you ever tried to fold a solid sphere, Martin? Me neither. Because it would be pointless. No pun intended."

"It's a lot to think about isn't it?" Martin said as he looked at the ground in front of where he sat.

"These questions have tormented my mind for many years now." Said Blank. "It is actually quite nice to talk about them with someone other than myself."

"It's my pleasure to listen." Martin said, as he looked at the flames of the fire. "I know you said it before, but in all seriousness. Do you believe it could be possible for us to exit our existence into the dimension above us?"

"For us to exit our existence into the dimension above us, would be similar to the character in a virtual reality simulation game exiting the game and coming into our reality. If the latter sounds crazy, then so should the former. Because both ideas are the same idea, just worded differently."

"What does it all mean though, what does it look like? I just want to know."

"Me too, Martin. But we are the only beings who need eyes to see, and ears to hear. Those greater than us, just are." Mr. Blank said as he shuttered in his chair. "However, If you were able to see time, you would see that one conjoined sequential moment of time is actually shaped like a bell curve or a wave. That is also because time is similar to a vibration which means time is a certain type of sound. Everything vibrates no matter what it is in our natural existence. It vibrates in some way whether it be a lot or a little. There are ways to make something vibrate faster or possibly even stop vibrating completely, but there is not and never will there be a way to make something vibrate backwards. If it vibrates, it moves forward in time. And that my friend is why and how we experience time. Time is something that  is like nothing else in existence. It's more plentiful than anything, yet it's more valuable than everything. More of it has been consumed than anything else, yet it's the one thing you cannot buy. It is in every atom and molecule in the universe, yet we don't even know what it is exactly... My only explanation is that, to us time is nature, time is motion, time is growth, time is power, and time... is life."

Both Martin and Blank sat in silence for a long time, until Martin finally broke the silence once again.

"What do you think about the way the world is today?" He asked.

"I think we only have but a short time left before peace is no longer an option." Said Blank.

"What do you mean by that?"

"I mean that war is coming, Martin. Inevitable war. And we are unbelievably unprepared for it."

"What makes you think that war is coming?"

"Name a time when America was as broken, or as weak as it is today."

Martin was silent.

"Humanity is war, Martin. Just look around you. Have you seen the state of the world recently? It is as bad if not worse than Sodom and Gomorrah was when it was destroyed. We are living in the city of Mystery Babylon, and It is only a matter of time now before it must fall. And I believe it will be sooner than most people want to believe."

"What signs will there be to warn us? How do you think it will start?" Martin asked.

"It has already started. Look at the world. Riots in the streets, the rich getting richer, the poor getting poorer. You probably have not even noticed what is happening. I hate to inform you, my friend, but we are in the midst of it. This is the beginning of war. It just has not gone hot yet."

"Maybe a war would be good for us. Maybe it would be best to just get it over with." Said Martin.

"War is chaos, Martin, and the ones who push for it the hardest will be the ones who regret it the most. Nobody in our lifetime has witnessed true violence like the violence that this next war will bring. The overall state of weakness that the civil war of today will leave the country in as a whole, is setting us up for defeat in the world war of tomorrow. The left is calling for war because they do not understand that they are weak and will be the first ones to die in almost every scenario. The right is calling for war because they have the weapons and resources, so they believe they would easily win. Both sides of this current political system of stupidity are willing to fight for their beliefs but in truth nobody realizes just how horrific and bloody war actually is. Nor do they know how cruel humanity can actually be when pushed over the line. When the civil war goes into full effect there will be no winner. Everyone loses in the end. We do not want war, Martin, nobody does, some just have not realized it yet."

"I see. So what can we do about it then?"

"Time is growing short for us in this world. The civil war will come quickly and end quicker. One day soon after that, the country will be invaded by our enemies. They will most likely do it under the guise of humanitarian aid. In reality however, it will simply be to claim what is left of the country. And we are not ready for all of that at this time."

"Now that you say it, I am actually surprised that we have not been attacked or gone to war yet. It has actually worried me for a while now. I don't know about you, but I think It would probably be wise to start preparing for whatever comes."

"Why do you think I chose a bunker instead of a house? I have actually been planning to start a defense team, just in case things go sideways."

"Before I agree to anything, I just have one question... are you a Fed?"

"No, Martin. I promise you that I am not a Fed."

"Okay then I guess I'm in, but only if it is a defense team, to help people in the event of an attack. I could probably see if Gabriel, James and Jacob would want to join too. All three of them are already physically fit, and I honestly trust them with my life."

"We will still need an initiation though" Said Blank.

"Let's make a list right now." Said Martin taking his phone out of his pocket and opening his notes. "Okay so what should the initiation be?"

"I've actually already thought about it a lot." Mr. Blank began. "To be admitted as a member into the Special Task Force Unit, you must complete a list of tasks and workouts to prove the initiative is worth our time."

"Special Task Force Unit? Is that what we're calling our team?"

"Yes it is. Write out as follows." Mr. Blank then cleared his throat and began naming off qualifications required to be admitted.

Once they had finished making the list, Martin gave it a quick glance over to make sure they had a fair basis down.

"We can polish the list up later." Mr. Blank said. "That should give us an idea though."

"I like it. I must admit that it will be difficult for me to get everything together. But I don't think the guys and I will have too much trouble passing initiation."

"I like that about you, Martin. As the team leader you could easily forgo the initiation. However, a good leader always leads from the front."

"My thinking exactly. Can't very well tell someone to do something if I can't handle myself."

"That's right. Any so-called leader who leads from a safe place is not actually a leader at all. Now I know that in some cases there are some generals who make battle plans and whatnot, but they are exceptions to the rule, and not the rule itself."

"I agree, but if I'm being honest I believe that no person should tell another person how to live, or what to do unless they themselves have skin in the game."

"And that is why you will make a great leader. You have what it takes, Martin. Even if you don't know it yet. You are going to do great things some day. I can see it."

"That's the thing though. Why have an actual leader? Couldn't we just train everyone equally and just have individual one man teams, just under the same symbol?" Martin asked.

"That actually does make sense. Like having agents. But someone would still have to be some sort of leader to keep order. And give the final say." Said Blank.

"I can do that. I just think the team would be more effective if they could act on their own judgment without having to wait for orders." Said Martin.

"I like it." Said Blank. "Individual one man teams in the same group. However if any number of the agents ever team up, there will have to be some sort of rank to circumvent bickering amongst themselves."

"Easy. Best overall number in training is the highest rank."

"That sounds reasonable."

"How are we gonna pay for all this though?" Martin asked. "Just the equipment alone will be pretty expensive. I mean, I already have enough guns for everyone but there are other things I can't really afford right now."

"Do not worry. I have enough to take care of everything." Said Blank.

"How much are you planning on spending?"

"As much as it takes." Said Blank. "I retired from my previous job with $149 million. I spent a couple million on the bunker and some other things, but I think I still have about $130 million left. Do you think it will be more than that for what we need?"

Martin's eyes went wide and his mouth hung open.

"What the hell do you do for a living?" He asked, his voice ripe with surprise.

"All I can say is that I worked for a very powerful family as a quote unquote problem solver, and funny enough actually, some of those problems were Feds."

Martin leaned over and quietly asked in a whisper.

"Are you telling me that you were, like... some kind of a hitman?"

Blank was silent for a long time before answering.

"You will not tell anyone of what I have just said...ever."

"On my life." Said Martin while raising his right hand.

"Good. Very good."

# CHAPTER: 7

**M**ARTIN woke up in his bed the next morning still wearing his jeans from the day before. He couldn't remember what time it had been when he had finally gone to bed, but he could faintly remember the last of the conversation that he had with Mr. Blank.

"You know, you don't have to walk home in the dark." Martin had said the night before as he and Blank stood up from their chairs by the bonfire. "You are welcome to sleep on the couch if you want." He added.

"I appreciate it, Martin. But I think that I am okay to walk."

"I would offer you a ride, but I'm pretty sure I've drunk far too much to drive."

"It is alright. I like walking. It helps me think."

"Alright. Well I guess walk safe then." Martin said with a chuckle.

"I shall. It is not very far. Goodnight, Martin."

Martin rubbed his face, trying to wipe the sleep away. He then rolled over, sat up and looked at the clock on his bedside table.

"8:46am, I overslept a little." Martin thought. "It is Sunday though, so I guess it doesn't matter that much."

He used to go to church on Sunday mornings, but for some reason he just stopped going one week. Maybe it was something someone said, but he couldn't remember. He shook his head trying to shake himself awake. He then looked at his home defense gun that he always kept next to his bed leaning up against the bedside table where his clock sat. He reached over and picked it up to check it over.

It was a semi automatic CZ Scorpion 9mm carbine, which had in place of the buttstock what was called a pistol brace. Because of the barrel being shorter than 16 inches it would be considered an NFA item if you were to put a normal buttstock on it, and all NFA items required a two hundred dollar tax stamp that he would rather not have to pay if he could help it. In his opinion the NFA (National Firearms Act) was stupid and made practically no sense at all. Because even if you were to ban violence itself, violence would still be committed. Because human nature is violent, and humans will always find a way to do what they please. But he saw no reason to break the law at this time, so a brace it was.

Most people would say a 12 gauge shotgun was the best home defense gun. Martin however, strongly disagreed. A shotgun, unless it was semi automatic, was slow and heavy with limited ammo capacity. It also had longer reload time, unless you were a professional shooter, and the recoil was more than he would want to feel while in a tired and groggy state. Also the myth that you don't really have to aim a shotgun, often made him chuckle. Martin had always said to the people with that opinion.

"Every shotgun round is a slug until the wad breaks apart at 25ft."

But some people's minds are harder to change than others. Some people just want to believe what they believe.

Later that morning after he finished eating, he grabbed another cup of coffee from the pot and went outside to sit in the sun for a while. Just then Martin's phone suddenly rang. He looked at the caller ID to find that it was Jacob.

"Hey Jacob, what's up?" Martin said, answering the phone.

"Hey man, how'd you sleep?" Jacob asked.

"Pretty good. You?"

"Can't complain. Hey, so you know how I always give you crap for owning so many guns?"

"How could I forget? You do that pretty much every time I see you." Martin laughed.

"Yeah yeah." Jacob said, dismissing Martins teasing. "Anyway, what your friend, Blank, was saying yesterday really got me thinking. So I was just wondering." Jacob paused.

"Yes, what were you wondering?" Martin prodded.

Jacob sighed, then he continued. "I was wondering if I could shoot one of your guns. I've never done it before, but I know you do it all the time. So I wanted you to teach me about them."

Martin laughed. "Finally coming around, I see."

"Hey man, shut up. I just wanna try it, okay." Said Jacob.

"Okay okay, calm down." Martin laughed. "Yeah man, I got you. Gabriel, James and I are probably gonna go shooting again next

Saturday if you wanna tag along."

"Sounds good man. I appreciate you. I'm actually kind of excited."

"As you should be. Guns are fun, man. They're tools, but there's just something satisfying about reaching out and touching a target from a few hundred yards away."

"I believe it, man. Thank you. I'll talk to ya later."

"Alright bud, talk to you later."

Martin hung the phone up and set it on the table in front of him. He stared at it for a moment then he picked it back up again. He scrolled through his contacts until he came across Ellis's name. He clicked on it then hovered over the 'Call Now' button. After a few seconds he hit the button and held the phone to his ear.

*Ring... ring... ring*

"Hello?" A pleasant female voice said through his phones speaker.

"Hello, this is Martin from the diner the other day. Are you gonna be ready in time for us to go out later?"

"Oh yeah. Of course I will be." She laughed with what sounded to Martin like a touch of giddiness.

"Cool, I'll pick you up around 6pm."

"That sounds great. I'll text you my address in a few minutes."

Martin could hear the smile in her voice and that made him smile too.

"Alright, see you at 6." He said.

"Okay, bye." She said, lingering on the E sound as she hung up.

She seemed like sort of both a cute and goofy girl, and Martin kinda liked it. From what little he knew about her she seemed to beam happy vibes. He was actually excited to finally be going out again. It had been a little over a year since he broke things off with his last girlfriend and decided to take a break from dating after that. It had been a bad relationship and a worse breakup. Even still to this day he worried about his car getting keyed or tires slashed. His ex was not happy when her source of money, Martin, was cut off from her. He didn't feel the need to get a restraining order or anything, but he still had a little bit of worry he kept in the back of his mind just in case.

Martin's phone suddenly chimed. It was a text from Ellis. He opened his phone and went to the message. It was the address followed by a smiley face emoji. Another message from someone else then popped up in a notification at the top of his phone screen so he clicked on it. It was James saying he was on his way. Martin responded.

"Alright cool."

He then went back to Ellis's text and responded

"Got it. See you at 6."

Still thinking about Ellis he closed his phone and set it on the table in front of him.

"This girl seems different." He said aloud to himself. "She's fresh... unique. I just hope it's not an act like the last one."

# CHAPTER: 8

**T**HERE came a sudden knock at the door as Martin put the box of trash bags he was holding onto the dining room table. He then walked down the hall to the entry way and answered the door to find the smiling face of James.

"Hey man, are you ready to clean?" James said with slightly more enthusiasm than the situation merited.

"I've already started. Come on in." Martin said with a smile.

"So what needs to be done?" James asked as he followed Martin into the kitchen.

"The kitchen, the deck, the dining room and the grills."

"That shouldn't take too long. What are you doing after this?"

"Just hanging out until around 5:30 then I've got a date with a girl I met at the diner in town."

"Is she hot?" James asked nonchalantly.

Martin laughed. "Sure bro, she's pretty hot I guess."

"Sweet. Just had to ask."

"You always do, literally every time one of us meets a girl, you ask if she's hot."

"Well you never know. And I like to protect my boys from getting themselves into something dumb."

"You know that looks ain't everything, right?"

"Maybe. But all women are crazy in one way or another, and personally I would rather take my chances with a hot one." James said with a laugh.

"You're an asshole, you know that right?" Martin laughed.

"Sure do, but I'd rather be a happy asshole Instead of a depressed nice guy."

Martin shook his head while smiling.

"Just sweep that floor you heathen."

"I'm doing it!" James yelled in a joking manner with his arms outstretched, the broom in one hand and the dust pan in the other.

Once they finished cleaning up the clutter on the outside table from the night before, they threw the garbage bags into the outside trash bin then went to sit on the deck.

"So really though, this girl you started talking to, what's she like?" James asked as he sat down.

"She's different... in a good way though." Said Martin.

"What do you mean?" Asked James.

"She's cheerful, like a ray of sunshine on a cloudy day."

"Dude, what you just said... was the lamest thing I have ever heard, from anyone, ever. Like, ever in my life." James said, then after a few seconds laughed at his own joke. "I'm just kidding, man. She sounds like a cool chick. When do the guys and I get to meet her?"

"I don't know. I pretty much just met her myself. I guess we'll see how the date goes and then go from there." Martin said with a shrug.

"Sounds good bro. I wish you all the luck."

"With how long I've been out of the game, I'm gonna need a lot more than luck."

"A little piece of advice." James began. "Just make sure that you are happy before getting into something. Because if you aren't happy alone, a relationship will only make things worse."

"I'm a generally happy person."

"Good deal. I'm just saying, if you can't make yourself happy, then you won't be able to make someone else happy either. So before you even think about getting into a relationship. Just make sure that you can at least be content with being alone."

"Isn't that kind of a cliché?" Asked Martin.

"Can clichés not be true?"

"Point made. Don't worry about me though, bud. I got this." Said Martin.

"Just looking out for ya man. You know how much I went through when it came to women." Said James.

"You mean what you put yourself through?"

"Yeah, women really are incredibly simple aren't they? You treat them well and they'll cheat on you, but if you treat them badly they'll stalk you. That's really all there is to them."

"Not all women are that way though, James."

"Of course not all of them. Ninety percent however, are exactly that way. Because of social media today women have access to any man, anywhere in the world at the tips of their fingers, with just the click of a button. So the competition against the quote unquote nice guy, is absolutely mind boggling."

"How's that?"

"Because all the women are going after the same tiny group of men." James said, tapping his finger on the table pointing downward. "Ask any semi attractive woman in America today what kind of man she wants, and if she's honest, she will tell you she likes guys who are six feet tall, with a six pack, making six figures. And that makes me laugh because there are like four single dudes in this entire country that fit that description. I would know, I'm one of them."

"I've heard some girls say they like what is called the 'dad bod' though."

"Those girls are usually just lying and virtue signaling to seem like they're not shallow or basic, when they most definitely are. However there is a possibility that they might be an exception to the rule. But as we well know, exceptions to the rule do not make the rule."

"How many women have you dated, honestly?" Martin asked flatly.

"I have dated twenty-six different women?"

"Why?"

"Well the first ten were because I was a dumb kid, but the sixteen after that were for science."

"For science?"

James took a deep breath then began.

"After being the nice guy for a few years and getting trampled on by every woman I gave everything to, I decided to do a little experiment. The eleventh girl I dated, I treated like garbage. Believe me, when I say that I was an absolute asshole to the poor girl, it's absolutely true. I was manipulative, I didn't communicate and I showed no feelings of emotion to her whatsoever. Funny thing about that though is that it caused her to not only love me unconditionally, but eventually to stalk me after I tried to break it off. I eventually did, but I'm telling you man, it wasn't pretty. The twelfth girlfriend, I treated like an absolute queen, I mean, I gave her everything she wanted. What I got from her was catching her in bed with another man. Number thirteen I treated like crap, and again she ended up stalking me just like number eleven."

"I'm gonna interrupt you real quick." Said Martin. "So how did you decide how you would treat them? Was it based on their personality or what?"

"Nope, the only thing that mattered was that I alternated between treating them good and bad. It was completely unbiased and turned out it did not matter who they were or how they acted before I dated them."

"So then what was the thesis of the experiment?"

"After dating sixteen different random women, alternating between treating one good and then one badly, the conclusion was that every one of them that I treated badly, stalked me to some extent. And every one that I treated good, cheated on me, to some extent, without fail. Seriously, there was a 100% success rate in both."

"Didn't you just break up with your girlfriend the other day?"

"Yes, that was the sixteenth. I treated her good. Can you guess what happened?"

"She cheated on you?"

"Bingo."

"Are you alright?"

"Yeah man. It hurts at first. But after the third or fourth time you get cheated on, it just becomes another thing. It's pretty much just normal for me now."

"Damn. That's rough, James."

"It's really not that bad."

"So are you gonna date anymore, or are you just gonna stay single now, or something?"

"I'm most likely gonna stay single. Both Gabriel and Jacob told me that they are probably gonna stay single too. They learned what I found out and realized that dating in a western country in today's world, is not worth it in the slightest."

"So are you saying I should treat Ellis badly if I want her to stay?"

"I'm not saying that at all. Treat her however you feel is the best way of treating her. If she's a unicorn, she will mirror your treatment back to you, regardless if you're a nice guy or not."

"And if she doesn't?"

"Then she's for the streets and she ain't worth your time anyway, brother."

"I guess I'll just try to have hope that she's a unicorn then."

"I hope that too, man. Just be careful. Keep your wits about you. You don't wanna end up dying alone like I will." James laughed.

"We all die alone, James. If we're lucky, that is."

# CHAPTER: 9

I believe that I'm here." Martin said in the text to Ellis after pulling up to the curb in front of her apartment. He then got out of the car and walked around to lean on the passenger side while he waited for her to respond.

"Okay! I'll be down in a sec!" She texted back only a minute later.

After a few more minutes he saw her step outside, and walk down the front steps. She was wearing a white sundress with yellow flowers printed all over it, white converse shoes, and she had her long blonde hair falling down over her left shoulder. Ellis gave him a smile as she approached, then she casually closed in and gave him a little sideways hug. Martin returned her smile and lightly hugged her back. He then leaned over and opened the car door for her. She stepped in, sat down on the seat and shut the door while Martin made his way back around the car and got in.

"So, how's your day going?" She asked, turning to him.

"Not bad. Not bad at all. How about you?" He said with a smolder and his most charming tone of voice that sounded more Italian than anything.

"I'm pretty good." She laughed as he pulled away from the curb and began heading down the street.

"So where are you taking me?" She asked.

"Somewhere nobody will ever find you!" He said with evil sarcasm.

"Oh no, not where nobody will ever find me! Anywhere but there!" She said in a tone of voice to imitate a damsel in distress, while putting the backside of her hand to the side of her head.

"Okay, you passed the test." Martin laughed. "I guess you're alright enough to hangout with."

"Just to hangout with." She asked with a smile.

"We'll just have to wait and see what happens." He shrugged.

"So where are we really going?"

"Well, with it being such a nice warm day, I figured we could go check out the beach at Lake Erie."

"Sounds good. It's actually been a while since I've been there."

"I try to go as much as possible throughout the summer. It's a great way to just relax."

"I agree. I can't wait to get there."

Martin and Ellis actually hit it off better than Martin had expected. He figured there would have definitely been at least a little bit of awkwardness after being out of the game for so long. To his surprise though, there was none. Only just a few minutes into the drive, they were already making jokes and teasing each other as if they were old friends who had known each other for years. Martin knew this was one of those things that was far too good to last, but he was still going to at least enjoy the moment while it did.

They arrived at the lake about twenty minutes later and Martin parked in the lot designated for beach parking. After they got out of the car Martin opened the back door and grabbed the cooler he had prepared before he left his house to pick her up. He then walked around the front of the car with the cooler in one hand, sticking out his other hand in a gesture for Ellis to take it. She looked at him questioningly, raising one eyebrow and giving a little smirk.

"There are rocks we have to cross before we can get to the beach." He said. "Take my hand, they're easier to cross if you have something steady to hold onto."

"Smooth." She said with a smile as she took his hand. "Very smooth."

They carefully walked over the rocks and once they made it to the beach he set the cooler down and they both took off their shoes.

There was a light breeze causing Ellis's dress to gently flutter around as they walked across the sand, with the waves washing up to their feet every so often. The sun had about an hour left before it would set and the colors of the coming sunset were already beginning to show. Martin put out the blanket that he had brought, then as he sat down he looked out over the lake past Ellis who was standing before him. Silhouetted against the orange sky she stood like a work of art depicting the definition of beauty. It was quite a picture perfect moment. The sky as a backdrop to her beautiful golden hair and pretty face looked like something out of a romantic film. He continued to look at her until she turned and her eyes met his. They both smiled then she shied away whilst brushing her hair behind her left ear. She then glanced back up, still smiling.

"Would you care to join me, madam? I have much wine." Martin said, imitating an accent similar to that of the french.

She walked over and sat next to him, placing one hand on the ground for support.

"What kind of wine?" She asked seductively.

"The red kind." He responded matter of factly.

"Oh, sounds delicious."

Martin poured two glasses and handed one to her.

"Cheers." He said, holding up his glass in a toast.

"What are we toasting to?" She asked.

"To the future. May it be peaceful, carefree and full of happiness."

They clinked glasses then they sat talking about what they each did for a living as they watched and waited for the sun to disappear over the horizon. They talked about where they came from and how they got to where they were now. Ellis grew up all over the country. Her dad had been in the army and they had moved around a lot when she was young. When she turned thirteen, her father retired after twenty years of service, and they finally settled down in the area not too far from where she lived now. She had moved out of her parents house when she turned eighteen and she had been on her own for just under a year. Her situation was similar to Martin's except she only moved thirty minutes from home as opposed to the over four hundred mile distance he had moved from his childhood home.

The sun was now setting on the far side of the lake in a brilliant array of yellow, red and orange.

"I've seen a thousand sunsets, in a thousand different places, but for some reason, this one is a little more beautiful than the rest." She said as she sighed happily and leaned her head on his shoulder.

They sat there just absorbing the view until the sun was gone and the dark of the night was becoming more prominent.

"We should probably get going before it gets too dark to see our way over the rocks." Martin said, as he began to stand up.

"Okay, yeah. Good idea." She said as they moved off the blanket then worked together to fold it.

"It's easy to unfold a blanket by yourself, but it's actually quite difficult to fold it up again without someone to help you." Martin said.

"Very true." said Ellis. "Especially with the big ones."

"Indeed. I would know too. I live alone." Martin said with a laugh.

Ellis smiled while rolling her eyes.

They made it back to the car just before the light from the horizon was completely gone. Ellis climbed into the passenger seat while Martin put the cooler and blanket into the back seat and shut the door. He then opened the driver door and got in. The drive back to Ellis's was just as pleasant as the way there had been. When they finally arrived back at her apartment he pulled up to the curb out front in the same spot he had parked earlier.

"Well here we are." Martin said as he turned to look at Ellis who was looking at him.

She then suddenly leaned over the center console and kissed him on the cheek by the corner of his mouth.

"This was fun. Wanna go out again sometime?" She asked.

Martin, even though he was a little stunned, still managed to contain himself enough to casually say.

"Yeah, I guess that would be alright."

"Sweet! Alright, I'll see you soon then." She said as she opened the door.

"For sure. Have a good night." Martin said as she got out and started walking away.

Halfway to her door she turned, smiled and waved. He waved back, and once she was inside, he put the car in drive and pulled away from the curb.

# PART: II

*"Every question you could ever ask has a follow up question.
You either become content with the answer you were given,
or you don't know the next question to ask."*

# CHAPTER: 10

**M**ARTIN opened up a door in his hallway and began heading down to his basement. At the bottom of the steps he turned a corner then walked up to a large vault like door. He carefully unlocked it then he opened it up and stepped inside. As soon as he hit the switch to turn on the lights, the illumination revealed a fairly large room with guns on hangers covering most of the walls, and some scattered about the room. After looking around for a moment he began taking some of the guns off the wall and putting them into hard plastic gun cases. This made transporting them much easier and safer than just throwing them in the back seat of his truck. He selected a couple AR15's, some Glock 19's, an FN Scar 17S and a Desert Eagle .50ae, just because. He figured that would be enough to keep them entertained for a while. Start off with the Glocks, then move to the AR's then to the Scar and save the Desert Eagle for last. Jacob was in for a real treat. Gabriel and James had been to the shooting range with Martin a few times already and they even owned some guns themselves. Jacob however, had never even fired a gun before. Fortunately that was about to change though.

Once he had gotten everything together in the designated cases he began taking them out to his truck to load up. Jacob, Gabriel and James all arrived at Martin's house within minutes of each other. So only a few minutes after James, the last one to arrive, pulled into the driveway, they all climbed into Martin's truck and headed out.

The shooting range was only about two miles from Martin's house. It was a one hundred acre farm down the road and around the bend. It was owned by an old man who lived in a little cabin on the property, but he had become too old and frail in recent years to use the land anymore. So he let Martin and a few other people make a shooting range and hunt there when hunting season came around.

Once at the range, Martin went over proper firearm safety with Jacob while Gabriel and James started getting a few of the guns out of their cases and setting them up on the shooting benches. The shooting benches were like large wooden classroom desks. The top wrapped around from the side where you could rest your elbow, to out in front of where you would sit. They were big enough to accommodate practically any long gun. And while they were comfortable, Martin almost never used them except for sighting in his rifles once or twice a year. He preferred shooting in positions that you would shoot from in real life, not just a controlled environment.

"Okay, so the first thing to always remember when dealing with firearms, is that a firearm is always loaded." Martin began as he held up a Glock for Jacob to see. "It is very important that you always know the status of the firearm in your hand. Accidents tend to happen most when the gun is 'unloaded' and the user is negligent. So you must also make sure you always practice good muzzle awareness."

"So pretty much don't aim the gun at anything except your target?" Jacob asked.

"Exactly. Only point a gun at something if you wish to destroy it. Also never put your finger near the trigger until your muzzle is facing your target and you are ready to shoot." said Martin.

"I've heard the term, trigger discipline before. I think it was you who said it actually. Is that what you're talking about now?"

"Indeed, you must practice trigger discipline until it is ingrained into your muscle memory and becomes an automatic reaction as soon as you pick up a gun. You must also be aware and mindful of your target and also what is beyond your target before even taking aim. After you memorize these rules and there are only a few other topics and techniques we'll have to get squared away. Then we'll load the gun and let you shoot a few rounds to see where you're at."

"Sounds good."

"Do you wanna go first, Jacob?" Gabriel asked from the shooter's table with a big smile.

"No thanks, I'll go last." Jacob said with eyes wide while shaking his head. "I'd much rather watch you all go first. If that's alright with you?"

"Of course that's alright." Said Gabriel.

"Watch closely and you just might learn something." James added.

"Ears on everybody, I'm going hot." Gabriel said as he loaded a magazine into a tactical looking AR15.

"Ears on?" Jacob asked in a questioning tone.

"Hearing protection." Martin said, handing him a set of sound canceling headphones.

Gabriel then pulled the charging handle of his AR15 then released it, and with a clank the bolt chambered a round as it slammed into battery. He then hit the forward assist, shouldered the rifle and took aim.

*Bang! Bang! Bang!*

Gabriel began emptying the magazine. Once all the rounds had been spent, the bolt locked open on the bolt catch after the last round. Gabriel confirmed the gun was clear, then turned around, raising the rifle over his head with the muzzle pointed upwards.

"What do you think of that buddy?" He said to Jacob.

"With the earmuffs, It wasn't as loud as I thought it was going to be!" Jacob yelled.

"You don't have to yell, man." Martin said with a laugh. "The earmuffs are electronic. If you turn them on you can hear everything like normal. Only sounds with high enough decibels will be canceled out."

"Oh, that makes sense. That's pretty cool." Jacob said as he felt around for the dial.

"Also, hey Gabe. Ammo is very expensive these days, remember? Don't go using it all up before the rest of us get a chance."

"I know. It's just been a while and I had an itch to scratch." Said Gabriel.

Jacob found and spun the dial to turn the earmuffs on. With a click he could now hear everything. In fact he could hear even better with them on than he could with his normal ears.

"Man, I gotta get me some of these." He said with amusement.

"You should. They're actually not even that expensive. Like 60 or 70 dollars for that pair you're wearing now." Said Gabriel.

"Sweet. Alright I think I'm ready. Is it my turn yet?" Jacob asked.

"It can be." Said James.

"Let's start him off with a Glock 19." Said Martin.

"Is that big?" Jacob asked.

"It's enormous." Said Gabriel.

"No, it's not." Said Martin. "It's just a 9mm. Their recoil is pretty mild."

"Oh, okay cool." Jacob said as Martin led him to the shooting line.

James walked up and with a sly smile he handed Martin one of the Glock 19's and a 15 round magazine. Martin examined the magazine then looked over and with an amused upward nod, smiled back at James and Gabriel. He then turned to face down range.

"Okay Jacob, pay attention. The magazine goes in this way, with the bullets facing forward like this." Martin said as he slid the magazine into the grip, demonstrating the action while Jacob observed.

"Alright, then to charge it you pull back on the slide like this and that will chamber a round."

He let go of the slide and a round slipped into the chamber.

"And now the gun is hot and ready. Side note, a Glock has no external safety lever besides this tiny little lever in the center of the trigger. That must be depressed before the trigger can be pulled. Got it?"

"Yeah. Extra muzzle discipline with that one." Jacob said with exasperation.

"Sure." Martin chuckled. "I knew you would learn fast." He added as he turned slightly away from Jacob, then dropped the mag out of the gun and racked the slide.

The round that had previously been in the chamber popped into the air and Martin caught it like he'd done it a million times. He loaded the round back into the magazine, and with the muzzle still pointed down range Martin delicately handed the gun to Jacob.

"Okay, so what you're gonna wanna do is grip it with your right hand while keeping your finger off the trigger. I like to rest mine on the side like this." He showed him the position with his pointer finger above the trigger along the bottom of the slide. "Alright and once you've got your right hand situated, take your left hand and wrap it around the other side of the grip so that your right thumb lays on top of your left thumb. Don't overlap them though."

"Why not? Jacob asked. "I actually always thought you put your other hand underneath the grip."

"That's only because of movies written by people who don't know anything about guns. In reality putting your other hand under the grip offers almost no benefit or stability. As opposed to wrapping both hands firmly around the grip, which gives you so much more control over the firearm."

"I see. I guess that does make a lot of sense."

"You can try both ways if you want to see the difference for yourself."

"I can?" Jacob asked.

"Of course. You're here to learn. Just try the correct way first. We don't want you developing any bad habits right off the bat."

"Okay cool. Let's do this."

Jacob inserted the magazine, racked the slide as Martin had shown him, then he took aim.

"Aim with both eyes open. Also squeeze the trigger, don't pull." Martin said from behind him.

He nodded, then opened his previously closed eye and squeezed the trigger slowly.

# CHAPTER: 11

**C**LICK.*

Jacob looked at the gun for a moment; puzzled.

"What happened?" He yelled to the others while still aiming down range.

Martin and the others were trying their hardest to suppress their laughter, but try as they might, their effort to contain themselves was not obvious.

"Hey, what's wrong with it?" Jacob said, looking over his shoulder.

Martin stood back up straight after being doubled over with stifled laughter.

"They put a dummy round in it." He said, still chuckling, but trying to hold a straight face.

"Common guys, I'm just trying to learn stuff!" Said Jacob.

"And teaching you is exactly what we're doing." Said Martin.

"Yup! Always check your ammo!" James yelled from the back of Martins truck.

"Just rack the slide again and you'll be good to go." Said Gabriel.

Jacob nodded then looked back to the target, racked the slide, took aim once again, and slowly squeezed the trigger.

*Click.*

"Oh common you assholes!"

This time all three of them burst out laughing. Jacob didn't even ask this time. He wasn't going to be distracted by their shenanigans. He pulled the slide back and held it open to look at the bullet in the magazine. He then looked down and compared it to the two on the ground. He was pretty sure this next one would be a real round so he released the slide, took aim and squeezed the trigger.

*Bang.*

The gun went off and to his surprise he hit the target. Not the center or even close to it, but right on the edge of the paper.

*Clap, clap, clap.*

Martin and the others had stopped laughing and were now standing up straight, slowly clapping.

"That's what I'm talking about. Never let anything distract you." Said James.

"For your first shot ever, that was actually excellent. You'll be a pro in no time." Said Martin.

"Empty the mag. Let's see how many you can get on the target." Said Gabriel.

Jacob, now with a lot more confidence in himself took shot after shot getting closer to the center with each one. He was still shaking too much from the adrenaline to get a bullseye, but with this being his first time ever shooting a gun, he was happy he could hit the target at all.

After he had spent all the rounds in the mag, he carefully set the gun down on the table next to him. James retrieved it and set an AR15 in its place.

"Alright next in line we have a standard Armalite Rifle model 15, or AR15." Martin said as he pointed out the characteristics of the firearm. "It is a semi automatic, 5.56mm, with a, standard capacity, 30 round magazine. Unlike the Glock however, this gun does in fact have an external safety. It's this little lever here on the side."

He flicked it on and off to demonstrate the function.

"After inserting the magazine." Martin continued. "In order to chamber a round you have to grab this charging handle back here that works pretty much like the pull cord on a lawn mower, and looks similar. Then you release it and the bolt flies forward, stripping a round from the magazine as it goes, loading it into the chamber. I'll reiterate that you must always make sure your safety is on, and your finger is off the trigger while you're loading the firearm."

"Understood. Safety first, trigger discipline, muzzle awareness, know your target, etc. I got this." Jacob said as he took the gun and got into his shooting stance.

"Never get cocky when it comes to guns, remember that you're only one accident away from picking carrots with a stepladder."

Jacob was much better with the AR right off the bat. The combination of the low recoil and the overall layout of the rifle made it easy enough that even himself, a novice, was making consistent hits out to 200 yards after firing only about 10 of the 30 rounds.

"Alright up next we have the Scar 17s." Said Gabriel as he stepped next to the table beside Martin and set the rifle in place of the AR15.

"Ah yes, my favorite rifle." Martin said as he picked it up. "This is what some refer to as a battle rifle. It is chambered in 7.62 NATO, or .308 to the common man. It's got a little more recoil than the 5.56 that the AR shoots, so just be aware that it is gonna kick a little harder. This here is the 20 round standard capacity magazine for it."

Martin paused for a moment to hold the magazine up so Jacob could see the rounds, then he inserted it into the receiver then he continued.

"Unlike the AR platform rifles the charging handle for the Scar is located on the side of the upper receiver."

He demonstrated how to rack the bolt and Jacob nodded in understanding. Martin nodded back then dropped the mag, cleared the chamber and handed the rifle to Jacob.

"Let's see what you got."

Jacob inserted the magazine as Martin had instructed then pulled the charging handle and aimed at the steel target 100 yards away. He then squeezed the trigger until the rifle bucked.

*Ting!* Came the response as the steel rang with the confirmation of a hit.

"Oh, I like this one a lot." Jacob said with excitement.

"Let's see you make a hit at 500 yards." Said James.

Jacob aimed at the target marked 500 and squeezed the trigger.

*Bang!*

He waited for the steel to ring, but the satisfactory sound didn't come.

"You hit low and to the left. I'm pretty sure that Martin has that gun sighted in at 100yrds, so pull one to the right and hold over one." Said Gabriel.

"I don't know what any of that means." Replied Jacob.

"The dots on the scopes reticle." Said Martin. "They each stand for one MOA. Meaning one notch at 100 yards is one inch and one notch at 500 yards is about five inches."

"Oh, I have a lot to learn, don't I?"

"Even I myself am still learning, bud. There's always something else to learn or improve on."

"That makes me feel a little better." Jacob said with a laugh.

"Good. Alright if you do what Gabriel said a minute ago you

should be rewarded with ringing steel."

"Okay... what was it again?" Jacob asked with a sense of confusion.

"Hold one dot to the right of center target and one above."

"Oh yeah, got it."

Jacob aimed and squeezed the trigger. About half a second after the gun bucked he was in fact rewarded with the ringing of the steel just as Martin and Gabriel had said.

"Nice, I'm so proud." Gabriel said as he pretended to wipe a tear from his eye.

"Yeah, they grow up so fast." James added, following Gabriel in jest.

"Alright guys, I didn't discover a cure for cancer. No need to get all emotional." Said Jacob.

"You're right. Dump the mag." Martin instructed.

Jacob smiled then commenced to shoot the rest of the rounds in the magazine.

"Here it is, the gun of the hour!" James said as he walked up carrying the Desert Eagle that Martin had brought.

"Oh no. I don't know about that one." Jacob said in reference to the large handgun while shaking his head. "That thing probably weighs as much as my arm."

"Nonsense. Everyone's gotta shoot a Desert Eagle at least once in their life." James said as he handed the gun to Jacob then walked over to stand by the shooting table.

"Common Jacob. It's not that bad." Martin said, putting his hand on Jacob's shoulder. "Just go for it. The .50ae only has a tad more recoil than the 9mm. Same rules for loading it as the Glock except the desert eagle has a manual safety switch up there on the slide under the rear sight."

Jacob nodded slowly.

"I gotcha." He said as his hands began to shake slightly. "What the hell anyway, right?"

He then took a deep breath, stepped forward to the line, inserted the magazine, aimed and fired. He was not expecting it to jump as hard as it did. The gun came back so far it nearly hit him in the face.

"Whoa!" Jacob exclaimed. "Hey, you said it was only a tad more than the 9mm!"

"I lied." Martin said, shrugging his shoulders.

"I don't wanna shoot that one again. It's cool as hell, but I'll definitely hurt myself with that thing."

"It's understandable. No problem. I'll take it." Martin said as he walked over and took the gun from Jacob.

Then with the pistol in his right hand he aimed at the steel target marked with the number 25 and proceeded to shoot the remaining 6 rounds, hitting the target with every single one.

"How did you just do that?" Jacob asked in surprise.

"Recoil control. I'm not afraid of it. I respect its power, and in return it respects my wrist." Martin said as he started walking towards the truck. "If you all have had enough fun for the day, I'm pretty hungry and grilled burgers are calling my name."


"So, guys. While we wait for dinner to finish cooking, I wanted to talk to you all about something." Martin said as he sat down at his outdoor table where the others were sitting.

"Sure man, what's up?" Gabriel asked.

"So, after you all left last weekend, Mr. Blank and I stayed up talking for a little while. And we came up with an idea. We wanna start a defense team to protect the town in the event of a crisis."

"Probably not a bad idea." Said Gabriel.

"Couldn't hurt." Added James.

"Cool, well what I wanted to talk to you guys about was to see if you all wanted to join." Said Martin.

"What exactly would we be doing?" Asked Jacob.

"Standard military training and tactics. Just think of it as working out with the added benefits of attaining knowledge."

"Sounds like a win win situation. I've been wanting to get back into working out anyway." Said Gabriel.

"Yeah, it sounds like fun." Said James.

"Alright, since everyone's doing it. I guess count me in." Said Jacob.

"Awesome. So James, with your prior military experience, would you be willing to help with training?"

"Shouldn't be a problem."

"Sweet. Would you guys wanna start next weekend? I've still got a few things to set up and get ready. But I should have everything ready to go by then."

"Works for me." Said Gabriel.

James and Jacob both nodded in agreement.

"Okay, I guess we'll start next weekend then."

# CHAPTER: 12

**I**T had been exactly one month since Martin had taken Ellis on their first date. They had been on many other dates by this point, but nothing ever compared to that time at the beach where their relationship had unofficially started. It was now a beautiful Saturday afternoon so Martin decided to take her back to that same beach where they had their first date.

As they stood in the sand, wrapped in each other's arms just listening to the waves, Martin suddenly stepped away from her.

"What's up?" Ellis asked.

"Hold on, I got you something." Martin said as he turned and picked something up off the blanket that he had put out earlier. "It's your anniversary present. It isn't much but I think you'll like it."

He handed her a wooden box with an envelope attached to the top of it. Ellis took it with a smile, then she sat down to open it. She gasped with excitement as she opened the box to find a beautiful rose made of metal inside. She carefully pulled it out of the custom cut foam, and held it up to look at it more closely.

"Where did you get this?" She asked in astonishment.

"I made it, just for you."

"It's absolutely beautiful. I love it!"

"You gotta read the card too, darling." Martin said, pointing to the card with a smile.

Ellis pulled the envelope off the top of the box and broke the seal. After withdrawing the card and opening it, she began reciting aloud the words that were written inside.

> *"One metal rose as a symbol of love. Forged in*
> *the fire and formed with the glove.*
> *This rose is not fragile but it can still fade. Rust can*
> *overcome it because from metal it's made.*
> *But if you care for it deeply, like the love that it's for,*
> *it will last a lifetime and possibly more."*

A tear rolled down her cheek as she finished reading. She set the box and card down next to where she sat, then pounced onto Martin, clasping him in a loving embrace.

"I want you to meet my parents." Ellis said, finally.

"I'd be delighted to meet them. When were you thinking?" Martin said in response.

"Mom said she's making roast beef next Saturday. She asked if you would be able to come."

"Well, tell your mom I will do my best to be there."

Ellis hugged him tighter.

"Awesome! Don't worry, it'll be fun. My dad is kinda crazy but he's nice when you get to know him. Come to think of it, my mom is pretty crazy too, but she's also super nice."

"Wait, aren't all women crazy?" Martin said with a laugh.

Ellis pulled back quickly, making a face that could only be the face of a crazy person.

"See what I mean!" Martin yelled, while pointing at her crazy face.

Ellis stood up and took his hand, pulling his arm until he got to his feet. She then led him on a jog down the beach, laughing as they went. Martin never imagined something like this could happen to him. He was happy, and it was beautiful, goofy and beautiful.

After a while they stopped running to wait for the sunset, just as they had done the first time. Still holding hands, Martin looked at her long blonde hair blowing in the breeze that was coming off the lake. Her blue eyes were like a brilliant explosion of color in the light of the setting sun and Martin was awestruck. He didn't think such beauty could exist in a world so dull, but here it was right in front of him. She smiled at him and his heart felt as though it either stopped or it beat right out of his chest. He was so completely enchanted by her that he wasn't quite sure. She moved in to stand right next to him. Her shoulder underneath his shoulder and her arms around him. He placed his hand on her back and they watched the sun set, and Martin had never been happier.

That following Saturday Martin and Ellis walked up the steps of her parents house and Ellis rang the doorbell. After a few moments, Ellis's mother opened the door and greeted them with a smile.

"There's my little girl." Her mother said as she closed in and hugged Ellis. "Oh, and you must be Martin. Ellis has told us so much about you. It's so nice to finally meet you. I'm Margaret." She said, taking Martin's hand gently.

"Yes ma'am, I am Martin. It is nice to meet you too." He said with a slight bow of his head.

"Aren't you delightful? With all the things she's told us about you, it seems that she forgot to mention that you were a gentleman."

"Mom, stop embarrassing me." Ellis said in a bashful, annoyed tone. "Where's dad?"

"He's in the den, darling. Please come in."

"Your mom is quite the... happy type, isn't she?" Martin whispered to Ellis as they took their shoes off at the door.

"Yeah, I apologize in advance for them. If you think my mom is different. Just wait till you meet my dad."

Martin followed Ellis into the den where her dad sat with a shotgun in pieces on the table in front of him. Ellis gave Martin a sidelong glance and rolled her eyes.

"Dad, this is my boyfriend, the one I've been telling you about." Said Ellis.

"Good evening sir, I'm Martin." He said as he presented his hand.

"Paul." Her father replied, taking Martin's hand and shaking it.

"It's a pleasure to meet you, sir."

"Please, the pleasure is mine."

"Mossberg 500, right? I have one almost exactly like it." Martin said, pointing at the gun on the table.

"I'm gonna go help mom with dinner." Said Ellis. "Be nice, daddy."
She kissed her father on the cheek then went into the kitchen.

"Mind if I sit with you?" Martin asked.

"Not at all, please have a seat." Said Paul. "Yes, it is a Mossberg 500. Do you know a little something about guns?"

"Just a little bit."

They heard laughter from the kitchen so they both turned for a moment to look. Ellis and her mother were going on about something that appeared to be an inside joke while they set the table.

"She's a sweetheart, isn't she?" Paul said as more of a statement than a question.

"Yes sir, she is." Martin replied in agreement.

"You're her first boyfriend. Did you know that?"

"I did not. I don't think that topic ever came up in conversation, and I'm not one to ask about ex's."

"She's never even given a guy the time of day before. She must have seen something extraordinary in you."

"It's obviously my looks." Said Martin. "I am quite the 'Chad' after all."

Paul smiled.

"I think she saw more in you than just your looks. There's been plenty of attractive guys that she's turned down. You're the first she's taken an interest in."

"I see."

"You gonna treat her well?"

"Of course I am, sir."

"Alright, then you and I shouldn't have any problems." Paul said with a crooked smirk.

"Dinner is ready." Margaret called from the dining room.

"I guess we better get in there. Wouldn't wanna get on the old ladies bad side." Paul whispered to Martin with a nudge.

Martin smiled. "Old man is kind of a character." He thought to himself as he followed Paul into the dining room.

They all sat at the table and Paul said grace. After the prayer they began eating.

"So, Martin, what do you do?" Paul asked.

"I work in a steel plant Monday through Thursday." Replied Martin.

"Interesting, and what do you do for fun?" Paul continued.

"Well sir, for fun, usually myself and my three friends, Jacob, Gabriel and James usually go to our other friend, Blank's, property to train in military tactics and maneuvers."

"Why do you do that?" Paul asked, sounding a little more interested.

"Just in case something goes down, or someone needs help. It's more of a hobby, but we are like a first response defense unit for our neighborhood, if you will."

"Huh, well at least you're doing something. That's more than most people are doing these days."

"It keeps us in shape, so we didn't see a reason not to do it."

"That's understandable. Have you told anyone else about this? Like your neighbors?"

"No, we have told no one. We figured that the less people who know about it the better. Don't want any rumors coming back to bite us."

"I know what you mean. So are you planning on having my daughter take part in your little defense unit?"

"That's up to her. But if she did end up wanting to be in the unit, she would have to pass the same physical and mental initiation as we did before she could be admitted. That's if she even wanted to though."

"Ah. True equality I see. You don't have separate standards for the different genders. Same thing for everyone. I like that. It's definitely a better idea than what our current weak ass military is doing. All this damn nonsense and inclusivity. It's pathetic."

"I've heard about that stuff. Yeah we don't do any of that. We have set rules and requirements, and if you can't make it through, then you will be turned away until you can."

"Glad to hear it. I actually wish the military would have done the same. And with that being said, honey, I'm finished eating. I'm going to sit on the back porch. Would you like to join me, Martin?" Said Paul as he stood up from the dinner table.

"Of course, sir. It would be my pleasure."

"Ellis, mind helping me clean up?" Margaret asked.

"Of course not, mother. You boys go on. We'll be out shortly."

"By the way, Martin. You can call me, Paul. There's no need for such formality in calling me 'sir."

"Yes sir... I mean, yes Paul." Said Martin.

"There ya go." Paul said with a chuckle. "So tell me more. Your team actually has an initiation, and you don't allow just anyone in?"

"No sir." Martin said as he took his seat on the deck after Paul took his. "We modeled our training after the Navy seals and other Special Forces groups. We pride ourselves on being a very hard team to get into. My friend James was in the military for a while, so he was able to build a fairly substantial training program for us off of what he learned while he was still in the service."

"Interesting. I would like to meet your team one day. I was actually  an Army Colonel myself, before I retired, so I'd be interested to see what you and your guys got."

"We can probably work something out. Maybe we'll have a bonfire next weekend at Blank's place and have you over."

"That sounds great. I like to at least have an idea of who my little girl is hanging around. If you know what I mean."

"I do, sir. I'll let you know what we plan out."

"Sounds good. Oh and, Martin. It's just, Paul."

"Yes sir... Paul."

# CHAPTER: 13

**H**OW'S the food coming, Martin?" Ellis asked as she leaned around the side of the grill. "My parent's should be here any minute."

"Don't worry, sweetheart. It will be done by the time they get here." Said Martin.

"Okay, if you say so, that should be fine." She said with a smile and a dismissing wave before turning and walking back over to the picnic table.

Martin was just shutting the grill lid after removing the food when he heard the sound of a car coming up Blank's driveway.

"That must be them." Mr. Blank said as he stood up from his seat by the picnic table.

"Where are Jacob, Gabriel and James?" Ellis asked.

"I'm sure they'll be here shortly." Martin said with a smile.

Mr. Blank walked over and stood next to Martin beside the grill.

"What should I do?" Blank asked.

"The food is done. There's not much left to do." Said Martin.

"No, I mean when her parents get here..."

"What do you mean?"

"I don't know."

"Just be normal, man. Only try not to go off on too many philosophical tirades if at all possible. Don't wanna scare them off on their first time out. Pretty much just need you to stand here and look pretty." Martin said, putting his hand on Blank's shoulder.

"No promises. I will do my best though." Blank said with what Martin could only guess might have been a smile curling in his voice when he spoke from behind his always present mask.

Martin looked at him with a smirk. They both shrugged as if to say, whatever. Then as the car was pulling in they made their way over to where Ellis was waiting.

"Hey, Martin, how are ya?" Paul said as he walked over and gave Martin a somewhat unexpected hug.

"I'm pretty good, sir. How are you?" Martin returned while giving Paul a pat on the back.

"Never better, kid."

Margaret smiled and waved as she walked around them.

"Since you boys cooked, we'll set the table. Come along, Ellis."

"Yes mother." Ellis said as she followed after her mother.

A few minutes later they all had their food and seats at the table. Blank however, sat on the end with only a clean empty plate.

"Oh, introduction." Martin said suddenly. "Paul, this is, Mr. Blank. He owns this property. Blank this is Ellis's father, Paul."

"Blank, I've heard about you." Said Paul. "You're the one who doesn't show your face for some reason."

"That is correct, sir." Said Blank. "I prefer not to be recognized if the need ever came that I were to disappear."

"You aren't disappearing here are you?" Paul said with a laugh.

"I intend no disrespect, but believe me sir, if I was you would never know about me."

"Oh, and why is that?" Paul asked curiously.

"Because no one has seen my face since I was 9 years old."

"Really?" Paul actually looked surprised at this. "Not a single person?"

"Never even once. There is not one single person alive today that knows my current face."

"Man, I can imagine it wouldn't be too bad in the colder months but in the summer it must be miserably hot in that." Said Paul.

"Nope. My whole suit, including the head and mask are both heated and air conditioned. Climate controlled, set to the perfect temperature all year round."

"Damn, I could have used one of those in the sandbox back when I was in the military. Would've made my job a lot easier."

"I'm sure it would have. Unfortunately it most likely did not exist back then."

"What makes you say that?"

"I invented, designed, and developed it myself. It is state of the art and revolutionary."

"Dang. I'm surprised you haven't gotten a military contract yet."

"I have gotten offers. Offers that I immediately refused."

"What? Why would you do that?" Paul asked in surprise.

"Because the government has enough. Also they would only try to find a way to turn it into another weapon of war."

"So I take it you are anti war then?"

"I am anti unnecessary war. However, war is inevitable. I only wish to have the means required in order to protect me and mine in the event of war."

"I agree. Self preservation is essential to survival."

"It is the way of survival." Blank corrected. "It is why Martin and I started the Special Task Force Unit."

"Oh yes, Martin told me a little bit about that last weekend. When will they all be getting here?" Paul asked.

"They are already here, Paul." Said Martin.

Paul raised one eyebrow and looked at Martin questionably, waiting for an explanation.

"I'll show you."

Martin then raised his wrist to his mouth and whispered something Paul could not hear.

Martin waited a few seconds then nodded.

"Do you scare easily, Paul?"

"Not particularly. Why?"

All at once three men appeared around the table as if they emerged out of the shadows themselves. Paul was obviously startled by their sudden appearance but tried to play it off.

"Alright. Disappear." Martin said with a wave of his hand.

The three men then slumped back into the shadows like ghosts, without a trace.

"Well that was unexpected. I'm actually Impressed. I'll admit that I underestimated you."

"That's the way we like it. We hope that all of our possible future adversaries underestimate us just as you have. It makes our job that much easier."

# CHAPTER: 14

IT was a brisk spring morning as Martin stood on his back deck sipping his coffee. He looked out into the distance at the rising sun and wondered how much longer the peaceful times would last. It had been a little over two years now since they formed the STFU and they had trained every weekend since then. They also worked out in the gym together every day, so their little team had actually become a force to be reckoned with. They had now become incredibly good at stealth and lethal in hand to hand combat. They had also become proficient with almost every weapon platform from handguns to sniper rifles. They could even provide emergency medical aid if a situation required it of them. They were ready for anything, and Martin was confident in their abilities to protect both themselves and their families.

Martin and Ellis had gotten married a little over a year prior. However, they hadn't gotten married in the normal sense. They had agreed that they didn't need any government contracts to tell them they loved each other. They had the idea to just get married in the really old fashioned way. In only the eyes of God and in the presence of their friends and family. Nine short months after that they had the blessing of a son. He was four months old now and Martin had pretty much everything he could have ever dreamed of. He only hoped that it would last forever.

From his deck where he stood he heard his doorbell ring. He turned his head to listen and it rang again. Setting his coffee mug down on the railing; he walked inside, heading for the front door. The bell rang again as Martin opened the door.

"Martin!" Jacob said, attempting to control the tone of his frantic voice. "China and Russia declared war on NATO! The others are en route now."

"Okay, slow down. Just tell me what you know, Jacob." Martin said as he led him inside and sat him down at the table.

"Last night my contacts in Taiwan informed me that the Chinese were planning to declare war. He also said that they had aircraft carriers and battleships loitering about a hundred miles off the coast of Great Britain. He said that he would keep me updated on the proceedings. Well, one hour ago his transmission signal went dark. The last transmission I received was him telling me that they have all either gone underground or disappeared."

"What about the American Military?" Martin asked.

"I have heard no information about how the military plans to react or retaliate. Our government doesn't want to let people know what's really going on."

"That's typical. What about your guy in Taiwan, he didn't give you any more information?"

"I'm pretty sure he's gone into hiding now, Martin. Taiwan is China now, remember. He'd be killed for transmitting information to us here in America." Jacob said coldly.

Just then the door opened. It was Gabriel, James and Mr. Blank who all walked in and took seats at the table.

"You guys got here fast!" Jacob exclaimed.

"We were all taking care of some stuff at Blanks place when you called, so we all just rode here together." Said Gabriel.

"So what's going on?" Asked James.

"The Chinese most likely just declared war on NATO." Said Martin. "I believe that It's only a matter of time now before they attack us. We need to prepare for the worst case scenario."

"But won't the military be able to hold them back?" James asked.

"What military?" Martin began. "Our quote unquote 'Leadership' made good on screwing that all to hell these past few years. No, at this point the American military is about as weak as a baby on the street without a pacifier."

"What's the plan then?" Blank asked.

"We need to move supplies to multiple safe locations and make more weapon caches. We need to allow ourselves more options in case of an invasion, and in the event we have to bug out multiple times."

"I'll start making a list of contingency plans, and the process that we will follow to get from safe house to safe house." Said Gabriel. "The specific events will dictate when, and where we should go."

"Excellent. James, Jacob you start putting caches together. Blank, you come with me. We have much to discuss." Martin said as he walked into his office.

Mr. Blank followed Martin into the other room and closed the door.

"Would you like a drink?" Martin asked as he pulled the cork out of the whiskey decanter on the side table in his office.

"No thanks. I am fine." Said Blank.

"Of course you are. I forgot about your mask. Please have a seat."

They both sat on the couches in the middle of the room that faced each other on opposite sides of a mahogany coffee table.

"This is the beginning of how it all starts. You know that right?" Blank asked.

Martin only nodded as he stared at the table in front of him as if he was absorbed in thought.

"Do you still feel fear, Martin?"

"Yeah. I'm scared of a lot of things actually."

"Like what. What are you afraid of?"

"Well, for starters. I'm afraid of the unknown. I'm also afraid of failing."

"What about death, do you still fear death?" Asked Blank.

"Yes, I believe that I do." said Martin. "That is a hard fear to overcome. But more than anything I think I fear the death of those whom I love. Even more so than my own death."

"If you still fear death after everything I have taught you, then you truly understand nothing about life, my friend. All those things you think you are afraid of are pointless and there is no reason for you to fear any of them. In fact, you really should fear nothing at all."

"But without fear, how can you have courage?" Asked Martin.

"Without fear, there is no need for courage." Said Blank. "Because if you are not afraid of anything, then there is nothing to stop you from doing what is required of you. You will also do it better because you will be relying on nothing but yourself. If you truly have control over your emotion of fear, and you can accept that you might die. Then when your flight or flight kicks in, you will be able to choose to feel nothing. Courage is just a lie that weak men tell themselves so they can have the illusion that they are strong. If you feel fear at all, or if you care about losing something, then someone can use it against you. And the amount of courage you previously got from that fear will be overpowered."

"Everyone has to have at least a little bit of fear in them." Martin said stubbornly.

"Incorrect. It is actually quite easy to feel no fear. Only a fool would tell you that fear is a necessary emotion. It is not. Fear is weakness. And it would be in your best interest to remove it from yourself."

"So, you're telling me that you not only aren't afraid of dying but you also don't even have a single fear?" Said Martin.

"Correct, I do not have one." Said Blank.

"Come on. Everyone has to have at least one thing that they're afraid of."

"Obviously not. Because I do not."

"How do you know?"

"Because I welcome both suffering, and death."

"What does suffering and death have to do with being afraid of stuff?"

"All fears stem from the fear of suffering, death and loss. So if you always welcome the worst that can happen to you, then everything that happens, good or bad, is exactly what you hoped for. Remember this, if you are afraid to lose anything, then you will eventually lose everything."

"How can someone get to that point though? Not everyone has the ability to think the way you do."

"Incorrect. I am only a common man. There is nothing I have done that is not achievable by anyone who wishes to have what I have or be what I have become."

"Honestly though. Some people are actually weaker both physically and mentally than the average."

"Then they are too weak to survive. Nature will do with them as nature eventually does with all weaknesses. It will root out the weak of today and they will become fertilizer for the food of the strong of tomorrow."

"That's cold, Blank. Even for you."

"The world is cold and cruel, and if it could speak, it would say the same as I do. If you die, it is only because you were too weak to live."

"But what about children, or babies? They can't survive on their own."

"If you die, it is only because you were too weak to live." Mr. Blank said again more sternly. "It is not my problem that babies are too weak and feeble to stay alive on their own, they do not have a choice in the matter. Their hypothetical parents should have done better. I survived just fine as a child until I was adopted at the age of seven. But even after that I still had to survive by my own strength. I was never given anything for free and I never asked for anything to be given. Be strong of mind, heart and body and your chances of survival go up substantially. Because strength beats weakness every single time."

"And strength comes from not feeling fear?"

"In the absence of fear, strength is all that is left. However with strength comes power, and attaining power is something with which you should be weary of and tread lightly."

"But isn't power the goal?"

"No, power almost always leads to preying on those without power. Absolute power corrupts absolutely. Although, true power is knowing you have the ability to do awesome and terrible things and choosing not to. That is something only the strongest of men can achieve. The ability to refuse the controlling of others, because they themselves do not wish to be controlled."

"How can you stop someone who possesses strength from achieving that power though?"

"Unfortunately, you can not. Because If there is power to be had, then someone will have it. You must not underestimate the power that power possesses over the minds of men. Power can change a man from good to evil in an instant and corrupt even the most pious of men. No matter how strong you become, Martin. Never forget to practice self control. And above all else, never forget who you are."

"Well we're wasting time. And you know what they say. If someone only ever kills time, time will end up killing them."

"Time is the thing that ends up killing everyone. It doesn't matter how you spend it. We will get to making battle plans in a moment. First I would like to explain something to you."

"Alright then. let's hear it."

"If something exists, everything exists. If nothing exists, then there is nothing else that can exist. There is either everything, or there is nothing. There can not be both in the same plane of existence."

"Where are you going with this?" Martin asked.

"Let me explain. Free will. The only way free will could exist is if we could see the future and choose the one that we wanted, or if we wrote our own story and chose the ending. The ability to choose one thing or another based on the choices of someone else which led to those decisions, is not free will. It is a forced decision. Because it is impossible to not make a decision. Even if you just sit in the same spot for the rest of your life, it was still you deciding to do that. Because you are required by the laws of nature to make a decision, always. If you truly had free will you wouldn't have to choose anything."

"Yes, and the Chinese decided to declare war on NATO and are probably coming for us next. So what are we going to do about it." Martin said impatiently.

"Yes, or no?" Blank asked.

"Yes or no, what?"

"When the time comes to make a decision on that, what would you choose, yes or no."

"Some decisions are more complicated than just yes or no." Said Martin.

Blank paused for a moment then took a pack of cigarettes out of his pocket.

"Yes or no?" He asked, presenting the pack to Martin.

"Sure, thanks." Martin said, taking one of the cigarettes and lighting it.

Blank set the pack on the table between them. Then drew out a deck of cards.

"Yes, or no?" He asked once again.

"What does this have to do with anything?"

"Yes or no?" He repeated while still holding up the cards.

"No... I'm confused."

Blank then took out a knife and held it up at eye level between them.

"Yes, or no?"

"No?" Martin said, with a look of confusion.

Blank set the knife on the table and drew out a pistol.

"Yes, or no?"

"Is this some kind of a game?" Martin asked, with just a touch of concern.

"No, it is not a game. I'm trying to help you understand that every decision you could ever make is because someone else did something first. Also, every desision can be boiled down to the answer of a simple yes or no question. You do not need an actual reason to say yes to a cigarette, and you don't need a reason to say no to a gun. Context is not a requirement in the event you need to make a decision. The only decision you can ever make in this life is yes or no, do or don't. And they call it free will. When we are actually nothing more than slaves to this natural prison of existence without the ability to even choose the path we want to take. We can only choose what we are permitted to. If I had the chance to choose peace instead of war, I would choose yes. However, nothing in this world is free, including our own will. The sooner you understand how little power we have the better off all of us will be. The luckiest people to live are those born after the end of the war and die before the next one starts. It would seem that you and I are the unlucky ones."

Martin looked at Blank with pleading eyes.

"What can I do? I'm still practically just a kid. I was hoping for more time before I would have to do this stuff."

"You are no younger than the great men of old were when they took on their enemies."

"That was in a different time though."

"Martin, what is the thing that separates us in this moment right now, from the Sumerians who were the first documented human civilization?"

"I don't know."

"What is it that separates the first words that you heard and understood, from the words you're hearing now, and what is the difference between the moments in which you heard them?"

"My mind is too jumbled for this philosophy crap at the moment." Martin said while rubbing his temples.

"We are in the same place, on the same planet. What is the thing that is there, that allows life and objects to move and to progress forward, but never to go backward?" Blank asked then paused for effect. "It is time through the motion, development and movement of atoms and molecules, which in turn make up the fabric of physical time. What time is to us on the natural level is a material and molecular process, that is the same throughout all the universe. No matter where you imagine, in our existence there is always something there, and that something is made up of the same physical matter as all other things. They all grow and move through time at the same pace and motion. Whether it is the unknown substance between molecules, the inside structure of an atom, or the invisible particles that make up what we call space. No matter how big or unbelievably small you might think something can be, there is always something there, and it has a set motion for it to advance through existence. And that set motion of growth is what allows progression. The smallest of atoms or particles through their requirement to move in order to learn and age. Every atomic particle is the cause for what we know as time, and they are sternly limited to the set motion of the matter in which every particle is made out of. The aging of particles is what we perceive time to be."

"What's that got to do with anything?"

"Everything. You have the means and ability to do what is required of you. So stop making excuses. There is no difference between you now, and those men of greatness then. Do you have what it takes to become who you truly need to be? Yes, or no?"

Just then Ellis entered the room cradling their little son, Mark, in her arms.

"What's going on, darling?" She asked as she sat down on the couch next to Martin.

"You remember when the civil war started a year ago and how we refused to be a part of it?" Martin asked.

"Yes. Of course I remember."

"Well a lot of people died that year because of it, and the country has never been weaker than it is now."

"Yeah, so?"

"The Chinese must have taken notice of America's weakness, because we believe that they just declared war on NATO. And the American military is just a group of weaklings now so their probably not going to be of any help to us. We predict the Chinese will try to invade the American homeland in the not so distant future."

"How long do you think till that happens?" She asked with fear in her voice.

"We're not sure yet. But don't worry, no matter what happens, you and Mark will be kept safe at all costs. We will be ready in the event of an attack. We have already begun preparations."

"What about those who haven't begun preparations?" Ellis asked.

"If you are hungry in the days of little, you should have bought food in the days of plenty." Said Blank.

"Obviously?" Ellis said with an eyebrow raised.

"When the time comes, those who did not prepare or plan ahead, will die, and they will deserve it. Nothing more, nothing less. Those people will die as savages, painfully and hungry, and it will be their own doing."

"Okay. Well we did prepare so I guess I'll go get dinner started. Is there anything in particular you would like me to make?" Ellis asked.

"Whatever you feel like making is fine, sweetheart." Said Martin.

"Should I make enough for everyone?"

"Yes, dear. We've got a lot to take care of and the sooner we get it done, the sooner our minds can be eased."

"Okay, I will holler when it's ready." She said as she left the room.

"I can help transport supplies to the undisclosed locations for a little bit, but there are some things at the bunker that we must address before the night is out." Said Blank.

"Is it that important?" Martin asked.

"Unless we want to be caught off guard, we need to plan as though an attack is coming in the morning. We can't afford to put anything off till tomorrow."

"Very well. Let's get going then."

# CHAPTER: 15

## *Quantico USMC Base, Virginia.*

**S**TAFF Sergeant, Brian Parker of the US Marines strapped himself into the seat of one of the two UH-60 black hawk helicopters. He had been ordered that morning to tag along on a training exercise to accompany a few Private's that hadn't been in a chopper before. They were all young and fresh. Some looked like they didn't even belong there but recently, since the rumors of war had began, the military seemed to take pretty much anyone who was willing to sign on the dotted line. The saying, "If you can walk, you can fight," that Brian's grandfather always told him, used to mean something different. Something much more masculine. Now it seemed like It was actually literal.

Brian would never pick on anyone who was willing to serve, he respected anyone who at least tried. However, some people really just weren't cut out for real world fighting. Because of the relaxed requirements of the PT tests and the pandering of the leadership to the weakest of people, almost nobody could fail anymore. So the military had gone from quality, to just quantity. Which only meant they had a lot of personnel, but almost no actual soldiers.

As the rotors began spinning up, Brian reached over and picked up a set of headphones and comms then put them on.

"Alright you maggots." Said a voice through the speakers in his headset. "I know they're delicious but it's time to put down the crayons, and pick up your manhood."

The voice belonged to Gunnery Sergeant Matt Vista. He was a fairly tall man from Texas that reminded Brian of a good ole fashion cowboy every time he saw him.

"For some of the Private's this is their first ride in a whirly bird, so let's show them a ride they won't soon forget!" Sergeant Vista added.

The more experienced soldiers laughed, while the Private's only chuckled nervously at the Sergeant's joke.

The chopper began to lift off the ground. Brian saw the obviously anxious private across from him lean his head back and clutch the seat. Brian kicked at his foot. The private opened his eyes and looked at him. Brian then mouthed the words. "Breath, just relax." So that the rest of the crew didn't hear him over the comms. The private nodded and began to control his breathing.

Brian looked out the side door window at the ground getting farther away. The two helicopters pitched forwards and they began to move rapidly away from the base. They flew over the trees as they made their way in a big loop. Periodically dipping down fifteen feet, then flying in a zigzag pattern, just to give the private's a good first experience.

"Are you boys having fun yet?" The Gunnery Sergeant laughed through the comms.

The Private's all shook their heads in response.

"Well, that's just fine. And just so you have something to look forward to, when we get back to base, the only way you're leaving this chopper is by fast roping out from 50 feet!"

"Don't worry, Privates. He's just messing with you." Brian said through the comms. "This time anyway."

As they came about and began to head back to base Brian saw, through the window, a flashing light zipping down from the sky.

"Sir, what is that, a meteorite?" Asked one of the Private's who saw it too.

The Sergeant leaned over to look out the window trying to see what he was talking about. Suddenly there was a brilliant, blinding flash of light.

"No kid." The Sergeant said gravely as he turned to look at the Private. "That was a bomb. And it just hit Quantico."

"A bomb?! What are you talking about?" Asked one of the other Private's.

As soon as the words had left the Private's mouth, the shock wave hit the helicopter like a solid wall. Alarms began to ring as the pilots tried to regain control of the chopper.

"I can't hold it! Call it in!" Yelled the pilot to the copilot as they spun farther out of control.

"Mayday, mayday. This is Falcon one to base. We're going down. Oh shit! Brace for impact!"

Still moving forward at speed, the helicopter hit the top of a large tree, breaking one or two of the rotor blades as it severed the wood. Still spinning they pitched to the left into another tree, hitting the trunk lower down this time, breaking off the tail and rear rotors, along with the rest of the main rotor blades. They then free fell to the ground and hit hard. The impact was the last thing Brian felt, and black was the last thing that he saw.

# CHAPTER: 16

*Virginia, 7 miles Northwest of Quantico.*

**B**RIAN awoke feeling drowsy and disoriented. He was still strapped into his seat on the Blackhawk, but was now hanging almost upside down, suspended by his still intact harness. He looked around at the mangled helicopter that surrounded him and groaned.

"Sargent!" He shouted, remembering what had happened and realizing where he was. "Is everyone okay?" He added, coughing a little as he did. "Hey, can any of you hear me?"

None of the others responded, or even seemed to be awake yet. He found and pressed the button to release his harness which resulted in him falling and hitting the other side of the chopper harder than he had anticipated. He tried to stand, then thought better of it being as his legs were quite numb and weak.

After resting for some time, the feeling in his lower body slowly came back, so he decided that he would try to stand up again. Slowly he got to his feet on the wall of the sideways chopper, carefully stepping over the heads of the Private's who were still in their seats, unmoving. He checked their pulses as he walked over them and every one he checked was unfortunately already gone.

He made his way to the cockpit to find both the pilots still in their seats, slumped to the side. One with only half his face left, the other with a large tree branch through his chest. Brian reached past them to the radio, grabbed the transmitter and depressed the talk button.

"Mayday, mayday. Blackhawk down. Multiple casualties. Requesting immediate emergency response. Over."

There was no answer. After waiting a few moments, he repeated.

"Mayday, mayday. Blackhawk down. Multiple casualties. I am requesting immediate emergency response. Can anyone hear me?

Over."

There was still no answer. Aggravated, he threw down the transmitter, then turned, carefully walked over to where he fell from his seat and picked up his M4 carbine. His old friend Sargent Matt Vista who had been sitting across from him a few seats down from the pilots, now laid with his head resting back on the wall of the chopper. Brian squatted down next to him and checked his pulse, there was nothing. He put his hand on Matt's chest and gave him a light pat before standing back up. He then checked his equipment and pouches to make sure he had all his own gear. Then he moved around the chopper collecting any useful gear he could find that was left by his now dead fellow Americans.

Once he had found all he was going to find he moved to a hole in the floor of the Blackhawk. Before exiting the crashed aircraft, he stood by the hole for a moment and looked in at his fallen brothers.

"I will try to come back for you all shortly. Gotta go figure out what the hell is going on first." He said before he turned and began heading away from the crash site.

As he walked he wondered about what might have happened to the other chopper. He didn't have to wonder long though, because as he walked through the trees he came upon it about five hundred yards away from the first. Unfortunately, unlike Falcon one, Falcon two must have exploded on impact. Being as it was in multiple pieces and burnt to a crisp. Not wanting waste any time fumbling around through the wreckage, Brian quickly ran around the crash site yelling for anyone who might have survived. After a few minutes of finding and hearing nothing, he reluctantly decided that he would continue on.

As he walked away from the Falcon two crash site he took his compass out of the pocket on the chest of his armor plate carrier and flipped it open. Once he had read it, he put it away and adjusted his heading in the direction of the Quantico.

He wasn't quite feeling 100% but he just had to figure out what was going on. He was pretty sure it couldn't be more than a five mile walk back to base. Which he was more than capable of making in one go, even with his current jelly legs.

After walking about a half mile he happened upon a farmhouse.

"I sure could use some information." He said to himself. "Might as well see if anyone is home."

He made his way up to the fence and jumped over, then walked across the yard to the front porch. Once he was up the steps he opened the storm door to the house and knocked. He waited for a few moments, but there was no answer. He knocked again harder this time, while yelling.

"This is Staff Sergeant, Brian Parker. Open up, I need to use your phone."

He looked through the window to see there was any movement inside. That's when he saw a door on the other side of the room slowly begin to open. Once the door was opened most of the way brian could see a man at the top of what seemed to be a stairway into the basement. The man looked around then crossed the room to the front door that Brian was waiting on the opposite side of. The man first unlocked, then opened the door just a crack.

"Who are you?" The man asked.

"I am Staff Sergeant, Brian Parker, of the United States Marine Corps. I need to use your phone."

The man opened the door the rest of the way.

"What is going on? Are we under attack?"

"That's why I need to use your phone. I need to call my command to find out what the hell is happening."

"The phones are down. The power is out too. Whatever that explosion was, it carried an EMP with it or something. Do you think it was nuclear?" The man asked.

"No, it didn't appear to be." Said Brian. "I was still in the air when it hit and it looked like the blast radius was much too small to even be a tactical nuke. It seemed more direct, more accurate, like whoever did it wanted as little destruction to the land around as possible. I also don't think it was an EMP. The power going out is probably just because of a blown transformer."

"Okay. Well that's good at least. That would explain why my phone still turns on. However, the internet went out just before the blast so I have no signal."

"Did you try 911?"

"Of course I did. The line was dead though."

"Of course it was."

Brian rubbed his face in frustration as he walked over and took a seat in one of the chairs on the man's porch. The man followed and also took a seat across from him.

"What happened, why are you here? Actually, why are you the only one here?" The man asked.

"My Blackhawk crashed about half a mile away from here after the blast, shockwave, or possibly something else, knocked us out of the sky. I'm the only one who survived."

"Dang, I'm sorry to hear that. Is there anything I can do?"

"Do you have a family?"

"Yes."

"Get them, collect all the supplies you can and get as far away from here as possible."

"Where is there to go?"

"Just head West. Move as far inland as possible. And tell everyone you see to do the same."

"Why?"

"Just in case. I have a bad feeling that the bomb wasn't the only surprising thing we've got coming our way."

"What about you? What are you gonna do?" The man asked.

"I've gotta go figure out what's going on. You wouldn't happen to have a spare car I can borrow, do you?"

"You can take my truck. My family and I can use my wife's car. Now that I'm pretty sure the blast wasn't a nuke I feel a little more comfortable being out in the open."

"I'm not one hundred percent sure that it wasn't a nuke, so don't quote me on that. But regardless you need to leave this area."

"Okay. I'll start packing up straight away. My name is David by the way." He said as he stood up and presented his hand.

"Brian." He said as he shook David's hand, then also stood up.

"Wait here and I'll get you my keys."

After a few moments, David came back outside carrying the keys.

"Here you go. Bring it back in one piece." He joked.

"No promises." Brian said with a grin. "Sarcasm aside, I appreciate it."

"It's no problem. We would have left it behind in any event where we had to leave anyway. The single cab won't fit my whole family."

"I understand. And again, thank you."

"Don't mention it."

"Do you need any help loading stuff up?"

"Sure, if you're offering."

"It's the least I can do."

"Alright let's get to it then."

They began loading David's wife's car with all the supplies from the house that would fit. David's wife, who Brian was introduced to as Stacy, was not thrilled about leaving her home. After a few minutes of talking though, they eventually convinced her that it was the best course of action at this time.

Once they had just about finished loading the car, Stacy walked outside carrying a cardboard box full of an assortment of foods. She walked up to Brian and held the box of food out towards him.

"I put this together for you." She said. "A little something for helping us. It isn't much, but it'll get you by for a little while at least."

"You don't have to do that." Brian informed her.

"It's the least we can give to show our thanks. Besides, we're not gonna use it."

"You know that you guys are letting me take your truck, right?" Brian said matter of factly.

"Yes, and this stuff won't fit in our car. So you'll just have to take it." Stacy retorted.

"That's very kind of you. Thank you."

"No problem. Stay safe out there."

"You do the same, ma'am."

David finished buckling his kids in the car then shut the door. He then turned and with a nod he shook Brian's hand one last time.

"I hope to see you again someday, Brian."

"Likewise, David. Drive carefully, and be safe."

Brian stood and watched as the car carrying David and his family faded into the distance. Once they were no longer in sight he turned and walked over to the truck that David had lent to him. He threw the box of food into the passenger seat, then walked around the front of the truck to the driver door, opened it and climbed in. He put the key in the ignition, turned it and the engine roared to life. He then put it in drive and made his way down the driveway to the road. Once he was out in the open he could now see multiple pillars of smoke billowing up into the sky off in the distance. He checked his compass once again, then continued in the direction of Quantico.

# CHAPTER: 17

*Martin's house, Pennsylvania.*

**M**ARTIN was getting ready to head out for his daily trip to find a store that still had any supplies they could stock up on. The whole team had agreed that each of them would spend at least one hundred dollars a week on supplies until the attack came, or until supplies were no longer available. If the attack didn't come by the time three months had passed without incident, they would ease up and bring the emergency level from high alert back down to medium and try to just ride out the economic hardship.

"Don't forget your wallet dear." Ellis said as she walked down the stairs and handed it to him.

"Thank you darling." Martin said as he took it and slipped it into his back pocket. "I'll be back in a little bit. Just gotta pick up some stuff, if I can find it that is."

"If you can't find it, then you weren't supposed to." She said, giving him a kiss before he stepped out onto the cold front porch.

Ellis wasn't wearing shoes so she had to hold onto the door frame as she leaned out to watch him go. He made his way down the walkway to the driver side of his car, waved, then opened the door. She waved back and then he got into his car and drove off.

Martin pulled up in front of the local grocery store, shut off his engine and got out. Locking his car as he walked up to the front door, he noticed out of the corner of his eye, someone pulling into the parking lot.

"It's closed." A voice came from behind him.

He turned around to see two police officers getting out of their car.

"It's 10am on a Saturday. Why is it closed so early?"

"Lack of inventory, nobody wanting to work anymore, people getting sick left and right for some reason, oh and also the curfew of course." Said the officer on the left.

"Curfew? Why, what's going on?" Martin asked.

"Look, Martin, I don't know what it is but there's something happening." Said the officer on the right.

Martin actually recognized him and was pretty sure his name was Tim.

"You should get your family and go somewhere safe." Tim added.

"You don't have any idea what it is? Who set the curfew?" Martin asked.

"The governor, but he got the orders from higher up. Like federal level high." Said Tim.

"That's strange. I'll look into it. I don't like being so uncertain of things."

"Okay, but you should really get going, Martin. We don't wanna see you get into trouble."

"Thanks, officers. If this is the beginning of what I think it is. You two should do as you instructed me. Get your families and yourselves somewhere safe."

The officers nodded to him as he unlocked his car and got in. He eyed them as he backed up and then pulled out onto the road. There was almost no traffic at all. On his way to the store he figured everyone must have just had a late morning. Now he knew something was up. He pulled out his phone, opened the group chat for his team and hit the voice chat. He wasn't a fan of texting and driving but this was too important to wait.

"Something is going down. Meet at base camp one." Was the text he spoke into the phone.

Once he finished speaking he hit send, then he put the accelerator pedal to the floor.

He whipped the car into his driveway; leaving it running as he got out and ran into the house. He yelled for Ellis to grab Mark and get in the car. Ellis didn't even question what was happening, she just did exactly as he said. She trusted his judgment and if he was this distraught about something she knew it was probably serious.

As Ellis took Mark out to the car Martin ran upstairs to grab a few of their Go-Bags. They were bags set up for seventy two hour survival and had almost everything you would need in a survival scenario. He put them by the front door then went downstairs to grab two ready to go gun cases and a backpack out of the armory.

He ran them out to the car and threw them into the trunk, then ran back and grabbed the Go-Bags he had left by the front door. Once back in the car after locking the house and throwing the bags in the back seat, he tore out of the driveway and sped in the direction of Mr. Blanks bunker.

They were the last to make it there. Jacob, Gabriel, James and Blank were all unloading some of the supplies out of vehicles and bringing them into the hidden underground storage container. The entrance to the container was camouflaged to look like a rock, and look like a rock it did. If you didn't know it was there, there was almost no chance you would ever find it.

"So what's going on, Martin. Why'd you send out the code red?" James asked as he walked over to where Martin was helping Ellis out of the car.

"Something is wrong. The town is under curfew. There were police out front of the grocery store and they told me I should get my family and go somewhere safe." Martin said as he unloaded the stuff that he had brought.

"Which officers? Did you know them?" Gabriel asked.

"I knew one of them." Said Martin. "Officer Tim Becket, if I remember correctly. He never seemed like the type to play around with such a serious matters."

"If you're all thinking the same thing that I'm thinking and if it is the Chinese or the Russians, how much time do you think we have?" Jacob asked.

"Hopefully we have at least a few more days before things potentially get bad. I don't think anything will happen tonight so I propose we all go home, gather everything that we still have at our houses and meet back here tomorrow morning. Then we can just ride out whatever this is."

"Sounds good." Said Mr. Blank. "I'll hold down the fort until you all get back. Stay safe."

"You too, Blank. We'll see you tomorrow." Said Martin before they all dispersed back to their own homes.


## Road to Quantico, Virginia.

Brian pulled the truck around to the side of a broken down car in the middle of his lane. He looked in through the driver window, but there didn't appear to be anyone inside. Deciding that it wasn't worth the time that it would take to investigate why the car was there, he continued on by it. After driving a few more miles he came upon the town that was about a mile from Quantico military base. Upon further observation he could plainly see that the town was deserted. Almost all of the windows in the houses and shops had been blown out. Most likely from the blast of the bomb that had been dropped earlier that day. He continued on at a crawl through the town, carefully traversing past downed power lines and debris scattered throughout the street. He turned left onto the road that led to Quantico and followed it for about a half mile before pulling up to the bases now mangled gatehouse. He put the truck in park, got out and walked over to the gate that was now laying on the ground. He carefully stepped over it and walked closer towards the glass parking lot where the base had once been. He looked around at the devastation for a while, trying to make sense of what had happened and why. As he looked around he heard a sudden noise come from behind him. He swung around with his rifle at the low and ready to find a thin, young, brown haired girl staring at him.

"Are you a good guy, or a bad guy?" She asked.

Brian lowered his gun.

"I'm a good guy. Do you know what happened here?"

"There was an explosion, you big dummy. What do you think happened?"

He stood up straight and relaxed a little.

"Well, for a little girl I'm glad to see you've still got heart." He said.

"Of course I still have my heart. Are you okay, mister?" She asked with one eyebrow raised.

"I'm fine, kid. Where are your parents?"

"I'm not a kid, I'm sixteen years old, thank you very much. And I don't know where they are, that's why I'm out here looking for them."

"Hmm. Are you hungry?" He asked.

Her attitude seemed to change drastically at the mention of food. She nodded slowly.

"Alright, let's have something to eat then I'll help you find your parents."

She followed him over to the truck where he reached in through the passenger side window. After a moment he drew out a bottle of water, and handed it to her. She immediately started gulping down the water as if she had spent the last week in a desert.

"Not so fast. Drink slowly. Your body needs time to catch up." He said urgently.

She nodded then slowed to just sipping the water. Brian reached back in through the window and pulled out a box of crackers that Stacy had packed for him earlier that day. He opened them and took some for himself, then handed the box to the girl, who immediately dug in.

"Don't eat too much or too fast. You'll hurt your stomach." He said.

She rolled her eyes, and resorted to only one cracker at a time deliberately making a show of each one as she did.

"So, what's your name, little girl?"

"I'm Scarlet, Scarlet Vista. What's your name, big guy?"

"Vista? Was your dad in the military?"

"Yeah, he was stationed here at Quantico." She said pointing to where the base had been. "I don't think he was there when the bomb hit though. Yesterday he said something about him spending all of today on a Blackhawk. So I'm sure he's fine. I just have to find him."

Brian didn't tell her that he knew she wouldn't find him. Because her father, Matt Vista, was still in the downed Blackhawk that he alone had climbed out of earlier that morning.

"Hello, you there? What's your name?" She asked impatiently.

"Oh, right. I'm Staff Sergeant, Brian Parker. I believe I actually know your dad. Matt Vista, right?"

"Yeah that's right!" She exclaimed. "Do you know where he's at?"

Brian hesitated for only a second before answering.

"No, but I'm confident that we can find him if we work together."

"Sweet, let's get moving then! Times a wastin." She said as she ran and climbed onto the passenger seat of the truck.

He shook his head with a sad smile. Then he looked to the cloud scattered sky.

"Don't worry, Matt. I will protect her. Until my last breath, I promise I will."

## Town North of the Quantico Blastzone.

"I don't think that anyone is here. Where should we look next?" Scarlet asked as she walked into the room where Brian was looking in the kitchen cupboards trying to find anything of use.

Scarlet cocked her head to the side while looking at him as he opened another cupboard.

"Did you hear me?" She asked, impatiently.

"Yes, I heard you. We should keep going north. Your dad might have gone to Washington DC."

Brian knew this wasn't true, but it wasn't the right time to tell her the truth yet. It might not ever be the right time. He checked the last cupboard then walked over and looked out the window at the sky. It had been only a few hours since the bombs had hit and now the air had seemed to have gone silent.

"Hey... What's that sound?" Scarlet asked, as she listened intently.

"I don't hear anything." Said Brian.

"Listen, it sounds like a swarm of large bees or something."

He listened as hard as he could. After not hearing anything for a few minutes he suddenly began to hear what she was talking about. He quickly ran to the doorway and looked to the sky off to the East. That's when he saw it, not a swarm of bees, but hundreds of war planes. It was an invasion. In that moment it all made sense to Brian why Quantico and the other places were bombed. To clear the way for the invasion.

"Scarlet, get in the truck." Brian said urgently.

"Why?" She asked.

"We have to go, right now."

"Why?" She asked again.

"Because those are war planes!"

"Well, how do you know they're enemy war planes?"

"Because they're not American."

"How do you know?"

Brian then picked her up, carried her over and placed her in the passenger seat of the trunk and shut the door.

"Hey!" She shouted.

"You ask too many questions." He said through the open window before walking around the front of the truck and climbing in.

He turned the ignition, threw it in drive, mashed the accelerator to the floor and they tore off in a cloud of dust and tire smoke. He took the first road he could find that was leading north in the direction of Washington DC. He had no idea what he was going to do once he got to DC but he just felt like he had to get there as soon as possible.

"How is this happening? Where are our defenses?!" He shouted at the windshield of the truck.

"I just want my mom." Scarlet said, beginning to sob.

Brian looked over to her. For a moment he had forgotten she was even there.

"Don't worry kid, we'll find your parents."

"Okay." She said, trying to hold back the tears.

"If those planes are landing, they would most likely have to be landing at the public airport outside of Washington DC. With the runways at the military bases being more or less destroyed, that's their only option. The Idiots must not have thought this attack through very well."

It wasn't a very long drive from Quantico to DC. With the exception of the detour he was required to take in order to steer clear of the airport, which was undoubtedly occupied by foreign invaders by that time. It was getting late into the afternoon when they finally arrived in the outskirts of the city. Brian pulled the truck into the driveway of a house that looked to be deserted, then quietly opened his door.

"Stay here while I check it out." He said as he got out of the truck.

He walked up to the front door of the house and knocked. There was no answer. Upon trying the handle he found it to be locked, so he took the butt of his gun and casually hit the corner of the window next to the door, breaking the glass. He then reached inside and unlocked the deadbolt. Then he swung the door open and waved for Scarlet to come inside.

Once she was inside, he went back out to the truck, turned the engine off and took the keys out of the ignition. Then took two trips to bring all of their supplies into the house for safekeeping.

"Are you sure it's safe to stay here?" Scarlet asked, walking into the kitchen where Brian stood preparing a dinner of canned beans and crackers.

"No, I don't think anywhere is safe anymore. I also believe that it is only going to get worse."

"Dang, man, I love the positive vibes." She said sarcastically.

"Dinner is ready. Come eat."

"So, you're like a no nonsense type of military guy, aren't ya? Just strictly business. It's okay, I get it. It's probably for the best."

"My no nonsense way of doing things is what is going to keep both of us alive."

"I get that, but seriously though, it's more or less safe here. You can loosen up a little."

"Sometimes I wonder."

"About what?"

"If it's even possible for me to loosen up."

They stared at each other until a smile formed on Brian's lips.

They both laughed lightly and then finished eating in silence.

"I know that my mom is dead." Scarlet said out of nowhere.

Brian looked up so suddenly he pinched a nerve in his neck.

"What?" He asked, then immediately grabbed at his neck.

"She was a receptionist in the lobby at Quantico. There's no way she could have survived." Scarlet said flatly as she scooped up some beans onto her fork then let them slide back into the can.

"Are you gonna be alright?" Brian asked in hopes that she might be stronger at heart than her looks made her appear.

"Yeah, there's no point in getting all worked up over it. It's not like you can bring anyone back." She said.

He could see the tears in her eyes as she spoke, but he wasn't about to point them out.

"I must admit you're stronger than you look." Said Brian. "You did good out there... for a little girl."

She looked at him and smiled. His attempt at humor was successful in lightening her mood, even though it was probably only a little bit.

"Thanks, you did pretty good yourself." Said Scarlet; wiping away the tear from her eye.

"We should try and get some sleep." Brian said after a few moments of silence. "I'm not sure what we're doing or where we should go next. All I know is that whatever we do, it at least has to be something that involves moving."

"Okay."

"You should go upstairs to one of the bedrooms." Said Brian. "I'll stay down here to keep watch and sleep on one of the couches."

"Alright." She said.

Scarlet then started heading for the stairs.

"Oh, and Brian." She said turning to face him. "Thanks for saving me. I probably wouldn't have made it out of there without you."

"Don't mention it, kid." He said.

With that she went upstairs and Brian moved into the living room. He took his rifle off and leaned it up against the coffee table then removed his plate carrier and sat on the couch.

Until he had sat down he hadn't realized how tired he was. He looked over to the front door where they had broken in, and after thinking for a moment he stood up, grabbed a chair, then walked over and wedged it underneath the door handle. He then went back to the couch to sit down. He began to nod off almost immediately, and after only a few moments, he was asleep.

# CHAPTER: 18

*Martin's house, Pennsylvania.*

**M**ARTIN and Ellis woke up just before dawn. While she made breakfast, he began gathering up the majority of their supplies and loading them into the truck. Besides a cache of a few weapons and some supplies, they had decided to leave hidden in their house, all the survival items they had were going to the bunker.

Once they had finished eating, Martin went to the living room and turned on the TV. As he stood in front of his chair, with the remote in his hand, he noticed that the screen was blue and wasn't picking up a signal. Confused, he walked to the side of the TV to check the connection. It was good, so he figured it must be the internet router. When he went into the other room to see what the problem was he quickly found that the router wasn't picking up a signal.

"What's up honey?" Ellis asked as she entered the room and walked over to see what he was doing.

"The internet is out." Said Martin.

"What do you think the problem could be?" She asked.

"I don't know." He said with a raised eyebrow while looking at the router. "Maybe they're just working on the line somewhere and had to shut it off for a while."

"Did you receive a text from the service provider?"

"I haven't checked." Martin said, as he pulled his phone out and opened the screen.

"That's strange." He said. "I don't have any signal on my phone either."

"Let's just get going. I'm sure they'll have it fixed shortly."

"Okay sweetheart. Go put the baby in the truck. I'll be there in a minute."

Ellis left the room and Martin stared at the router for a short while, wondering what the problem might actually be. Finally after much thought, he decided that he was just being paranoid. So he left the room to collect the rest of the stuff they would be taking to the bunker.

After loading everything up, they hopped into the truck and began heading to Blank's place. While driving down a back road Martin noticed a large truck round the bend a ways off and start coming up the road towards them. As it got closer he noticed there were actually three of them. Martin's eyes then suddenly went wide with surprise.

"That is Chinese writing on those trucks." Martin said in disbelief. "There's no way that could be the Chinese military this soon."

"How?" Ellis asked.

"I don't know. Keep your head down."

As the trucks approached Martin noticed they were slowing.

"I guess they want to talk." He said as he pulled up to where the soldier was standing beside the army truck.

"Hello there. What's going on?" Martin said in a conversational tone.

"There civilian lockdown. Civilian should not be out." The Chinese soldier said with a deep Asian accent.

"I'm just headed home from my parents house. They're old so my wife and I went over to check up on them."

"I don't care. We in hurry. Now move along. Get back in your house and stay there, or we put you in camp." The soldier demanded as he climbed back into the truck and shut the door.

The soldier scanned Martin's truck as they drove away. Once they were out of sight, Martin let out a long sigh of relief. He was glad he had the idea to cover up the supplies with garden tools and trash bags of grass before they left. He did it just in case some nosy person decided to have a look in the bed. He never imagined the nosy people would be the Chinese military.

"How did they get here so fast?" Martin asked, more to himself.

"I don't know." Said Ellis. "Wasn't it only a few days ago that they declared war on NATO?"

"Yeah. But for all we know, that information could have been weeks old."

"What are we gonna do now?"

Martin looked up through the windshield and saw the sky had

suddenly become heavy with air traffic.

"We're gonna have to move all of our plans up." He said. "There's no time left for procrastinating now."

They pulled down the driveway to the bunker and Martin got out of the truck. After helping Ellis out he ran inside.

"The Chinese are moving into town!" Said Martin as he entered the bunker.

"I heard." Said Blank as he stood up to greet them.

"Where's everyone else?" Martin asked.

"Not here yet."

"Okay, I pulled the truck around to the supply container. Wanna help me unload stuff?" Martin asked.

"Of course." Bank said, as they both headed outside.

While they were unloading the truck, Gabriel and James came down the driveway and pulled around as Martin had done. They then began unloading the supplies that each of them managed to sneak past the invaders. Luckily for them they also had the same idea as Martin, and enough sense to either cover or disguise their goods. James got there without issue. Gabriel however, had been stopped and yelled at by a Chinese soldier to get home. Similar to what Martin went through. It seemed that they weren't really enforcing anything yet. Probably because they weren't fully settled in, but Martin was certain they would start overreaching soon, and martial law was almost guaranteed to be enacted. Once they had everything unloaded and put away, they all headed underground to the war room to discuss the situation at hand.

"Did they even drop any bombs?" James asked. "I don't remember seeing anything about any kind of attack on the news. There was no warning."

"You don't bomb that which you wish to occupy." Said Martin.

"Yeah, China owns like 30% of America's farmland." Gabriel added. "They wouldn't want to damage those crops. Those farms supply their people too."

"How did they get into the country though?" James asked.

"My best guess. Our government let them in." Martin said, crossing his arms. "The government has always been corrupt, but these past few years they have been on a whole other level of corruption. They most likely sold the country out and just handed ownership over without even attempting to put up a fight."

"Those rat bastards are probably living lush comfortable lives on private islands by now. Without a care in the world." Said Gabriel.

"There are people in the military that wouldn't stand for that.

There would definitely be resistance." Said James.

"Those in power would undoubtedly know who those people were." Mr. Blank began. "Therefore they would simply just take care of them before they even put their plans in motion. Also do you really think the news would report an attack if the power's didn't want them to? They only tell you what they want you to believe."

"Yeah, but how would they do it?" Asked James.

"Do what?" Blank retorted.

"Take out the soldiers who didn't agree with them?"

"Simple. Government mandate." Said Blank.

"What?" James asked with a raised eyebrow.

"If you are in a position of power, and you have an agenda that you need the military on your side in order to accomplish it, all you need to do is mandate something that people with different views would oppose. Then those who do oppose it will simply leave on their own. That way they do not have to worry about who will or will not comply. They already did. Them leaving on their own was the true plan all along."

"Do you think that's the main reason why there were no bombs dropped?" James asked.

"I am willing to bet that either there were bombs dropped already and the news of it was suppressed, or some will be dropped soon." Said Blank.

"Screw it, let's go get 'em." Said James.

"Who? The corrupt people in power? How are we supposed to do that?" Asked Martin.

"There has to be someone out there who knows where they are." Said James.

"A secret is only a secret if you tell no one." Said Blank.

"That's right. And I doubt they built their hiding places by themselves. We just need to find them. We will just have to work our way up the line of potentially knowledgeable people, questioning as we go." James said as Jacob suddenly burst into the room, quickly walking over to the table that the others were standing around.

"It's about time you get here." Martin said, looking up from the area map on the table.

"They're calling for everyone to turn in their guns." Jacob began. "I just got word from the local militia that the Chinese have set up some sort of buyback type thing at the police station in the middle of town. They're saying that they will only give out rations if everyone trades in their guns. What should we do, Martin?"

Standing with the palms of his hands resting on the table Martin hung his head and sighed.

"It's all happening too fast. I really wish we had more time." Martin said seriously.

"The Chinese have already executed seven of them, and captured a few more for resisting." Said Jacob.

"What? Seven of whom?" Martin asked.

"The militia members."

"What happened? What did they do?"

"Well, as soon as the Chinese set up the gun confiscation thing, I guess some of the guys in the militia decided to attack them to try and drive them out and then just take the food. I guess a few of them were taken out in the process."

"Damn it!" Martin shouted. "Those idiots went about it all wrong. You can't just attack an entire military when you don't even have a plan." Martin stood up straight and rubbed his eyes. "If they come to your door, turn in your old hunting rifles and shotguns. We won't be using them anyway. It might throw them off our scent and buy us some time."

"Time is really the only thing we need a little more of." Said Blank. "Because they most likely do have the manpower to go door to door if they have to."

"Even if they don't. They definitely have the manpower to go to a select few houses. Like ours for instance, if they find out what it is we are doing." Said James.

"Wouldn't it be better to just not reveal ourselves at all?" Asked Gabriel. "Like instead of giving them our hunting rifles, why don't we just hide everything and play stupid?"

"Yes, that would be better in some cases." Said Martin. "However, if they were to catch us out and about they might be less likely to question us if they had previously witnessed us complying to some degree."

"I guess that makes sense." Said Gabriel.

"Now that I think about it, we should just take our old less useful guns to their bullshit gun confiscation." Martin said, rubbing his face. "We can at least get a little more food and make ourselves seem weaker than we are."

"Are you sure?" Gabriel asked.

"Not really, but it's the best idea that I've got right now."

"From what I heard the confiscation is going to be held at the police station tomorrow." Said Jacob.

"You said that already. What time?" Asked Martin.

"All day, I believe."

"Okay then, just remember to act like regular ole scared, helpless, nonthreatening civilians. We need to maintain our elements."

# CHAPTER: 19

**T**HE following day, Martin and the others all stood in line at the gun confiscation. They made sure to be spread out so as to not look like they were in a group. Martin discreetly looked around at the other people in the lines. It seemed like a majority of them all had the same idea as Martin. Almost everyone had hunting rifles. Out of everyone there, he only saw two people with AR15's and one with an AK47. This gave him hope that people might not be as foolish as he had previously thought.

"Just seem like a nobody." He said to himself. "You're just an everyday civilian."

They stood in line for what seemed like hours, until finally, it was Martin's turn. He walked up and handed the rifle to one of the Chinese soldiers. The soldier that was sitting behind the table took it then gave him a few rations and directed him to sign and print his name on a clipboard. After he signed, the soldier directed him back out to the parking lot. He made it to his truck without further interaction. He got into the driver seat, started the engine, put it in drive, then drove through the parking lot and turned out onto the street, headed in the direction of his house.

"Ellis, I'm home." Martin called as he walked in the front door.

"I'm in here." He heard her say from the kitchen.

"Where's Mark?" He asked as he entered the room.

"He's asleep upstairs. I'm making steak for dinner."

"My favorite, thank you sweetheart. It's been a weird day."

"What did you do today?"

"Just dropped the old guns off to the Chinese."

He shuttered with discomfort at the words.

"It was strange." He continued. "They were a little too friendly. It gave me a bad feeling."

"You worry too much darling. I'm sure they're just trying to make a peaceful impression."

"I worry because we've been invaded by a foreign power, and they've already killed people. Why would they be trying to make a peaceful impression now? I'm just frustrated trying to put all the pieces together."

He sat down with his elbows on the table and fists to his temples in concentration.

"Killed people, what people?" She asked with a worried expression.

"Some of the guys in the local militia. Jacob told us in the meeting yesterday. The poor guys have probably already been labeled as terrorist by the media. That way Chinese can maintain their agenda, and take over with minimal backlash. But I promise, there will still be backlash." He said, staring at the wall on the far end of the room.

"It's going to be alright." She said in a comforting tone, putting a hand on his shoulder.

"I'm not so sure. Why are they here? Why are they acting as though they belong here? They don't." He said in a harsh but level tone not directed at anyone in particular, more just to get the words out.

"Honey, no matter what happens. It will be alright. Let's just take it one day at a time. Act when it is time to act and react when it's time to react."

"Sounds like something Blank would say." Martin said as his forehead hit the table.

"It is something he said. A direct quote actually." Ellis said with a giggle.

Martin turned his head to look at her and smiled, then with a laugh he sat back up in his chair.

"Thank you sweetheart. You make life easier. But don't listen to Blank too much. He's crazy, remember? Intelligent, but crazy."

"Your advice has been duly noted." She said with a smile. "Dinner will be ready shortly. You should go get cleaned up."

"Yes dear, we should also try to get to bed early tonight. We have a lot that we need to try to get done tomorrow."

Suddenly there was a knock on the door. Martin stood up from his place at the table and walked down the hall. He opened the door, and to his surprise, he was greeted by 5 Chinese soldiers carrying sub machine guns, and one Russian soldier carrying a stack of papers.

"Is this your name here?" The Russian soldier asked while pointing to Martin's name, signed and printed on a sheet of paper.

"Sure, why not. What can I do for you?" Martin said.

"I have your ATF 4473 background check forms. I know how many guns you have, and I know how many you gave us."

"Ah, you got me. You must have searched the internet for a long time for those before you shut it down. I actually kept one bolt action hunting rifle just in case I needed it to hunt. What with the economy and all, I thought it would be fine with you."

"Show us where they are." The Russian soldier ordered.

"Alright fine, don't go getting all hostile on me now." Said Martin.

He led them to the gun cabinet in the living room and revealed a single rifle inside.

"Open the case." The Russian demanded.

Martin retrieved the key and did as instructed. As soon as the cabinet was opened, one of the soldiers grabbed the rifle.

"Good now take us to the rest." Said the Russian.

"I can't. I traded all the other ones to some old guy for canned food."

"What old guy?"

"I don't know. He was really old. He's probably dead now."

"I know you have more hidden somewhere. And I will find them." Said the Russian.

"Good luck with that, jackass. Now, if you want some Vodka I'd be happy to point you back to your homeland. The first step is for you to the hell out of my house, then you just keep walking until you get to the ocean, then just start swimming."

The Russian stared at Martin for a long time then looked at Ellis, then back at Martin.

"You have a beautiful family." He said, before he turned and led the Chinese soldiers out of the house.

Martin watched them go, and once he knew they were gone he turned to Ellis.

"We have to leave." He said with cold seriousness.

"When?" Ellis asked.

"Tomorrow morning, early. They will most likely be watching the house. So we'll probably have to wait till around 4am. That's when it is most likely that nobody will be out and about."

For the rest of the day, they tried to act as natural and inconspicuous as they could. They weren't under obvious surveillance, but Martin was almost certain they were being watched to some extent.

They got through the rest of their worry filled day without seeing any more soldiers. As Martin got into bed next to Ellis and laid his head on the pillow, he was quite troubled by everything that was happening. However, he did his best to hide it so Ellis wouldn't notice.

"Are you okay?" She asked, seeing right through his masked worry.

"I'm fine, just worried is all."

"Is everything ready to go?"

"Yeah. I got everything we'll need sorted, packed up and ready to grab as soon as we are ready to go."

"Okay good. And we're waking up at 4am?"

"Yes. Sleep now dear. I'll wake you when it's time to leave."


"Wake up, Martin!" Ellis said in a loud whisper as she shook him awake.

"What's wrong?" Martin asked in a drowsy sounding voice.

"I think there's someone down..."

*Crash!*

"There's someone downstairs." Martin said as he sprung out of bed now wide awake.

He reached over and hit a hidden button behind the headboard of his bed. With a click, a suppressed short barreled AR15 popped out on his side of the bed and the CZ Scorpion on Ellis's side. He had switched to an AR from the CZ Scorpion, because he wanted just a little bit more stopping power. Also because Ellis could use the CZ with ease if she needed to.

He had designed and installed the gun compartments in his bed, back when they first started getting serious with preparedness. He had told no one of this. Not even Ellis knew exactly what he had done to the bed. All she knew was that in an emergency she should push the hidden button.

"Get the baby, go into the bathroom and close the door." Martin whispered as he made his way over to the bedroom door.

Ellis grabbed the 9mm Scorpion from her side of the bed, checked it over, then moved to grab the baby from the crib. Martin slowly cracked the door open and leaned out. He could see the glow of multiple flashlights coming from down the stairs as he made his way down the hall. He could hear them begin to come up the stairs so he crouched down low and waited for them to get almost to the top. He watched the light as it began to make its way across the wall opposite to where he stood.

Martin flipped the selector switch on his gun to full-auto. Then in a single fluid motion he jumped out to lay across the top step, simultaneously turning on the strobe light that was attached to his rifle. As soon as the light was on he commenced to unload half the 50 round drum magazine into the team as they came up the stairs. They toppled and fell over each other as he fired. Some tried to fire back, but the dead men in front, falling onto the men below blocked most of their bullets, the rest hitting the walls and ceiling above and behind him.

Once the shooting from down the stairs had stopped. Martin stood and then unloaded the rest of the drum mag into the bodies of the trespassers. He then clicked his flashlight over to the regular 'on position' and began to examine the bodies. His eyes went wide when he saw the symbols of both the People's Liberation Army of China and the United Nations on their uniforms. Just then he heard gunfire coming from his neighbors house, then his other neighbors house.

"Ellis, it's time to go!" He yelled as he quickly reloaded his AR with the 30 round standard capacity magazine that he kept in the hall closet around the corner from the stairs.

He then heard a groan coming from the bottom of the stairs. He quickly rounded the corner with his rifle shouldered and light on. He then began putting rounds into the heads of the men as he walked over their bodies. When he got to the one at the bottom he shined the light over the face to reveal it was a Chinese woman. She put her blood soaked hand up as if she was attempting to plead for him to spare her. Unfortunately, the 5.56mm round to her forehead and the sweet release of death was the only thing that Martin had the time to give her.

"That was cold, Martin." He said to himself. "But necessary. Ellis, we have to go now!"

Ellis made her way down the stairs over the bodies carrying Mark in one arm, and the CZ Scorpion in the other.

"My god, Martin. What is going on?" She said as her voice began to tremble.

"They knew we were lying and this was how they planned to deal with us. Let's go. If we weren't before, we are definitely on their kill list now."

Martin grabbed Ellis by the arm and led her to the basement door. Once they were through he closed the door behind them and they made their way downstairs to the armory where the hidden cache of gear was. He grabbed his helmet and a set of PVS-31 night vision goggles off the shelf and put them on. They also each grabbed their spare go-bags which, just like the ones he had grabbed before, contained everything they would need to survive for up to 72 hours.

As they were just getting ready to head out they heard a commotion coming from out in front of the house.

"Sounds like vehicle's. Time to go sweetheart." Martin whispered sternly. "They must have heard the gunfire. Or they're wondering what's taking their soldiers so long."

They made their way to the back door and Martin cracked it open. He then scanned the backyard for hostiles before swinging the door open so they could make a break for it.

"Run. Make for the trees." Martin ordered.

They made it across the yard and into the trees before Martin turned and dropped the night vision over his eyes to see if they had been spotted. After about two seconds he saw a couple men round the corners of his house, scanning his back yard.

"Come back!" He heard a voice with a Russian accent yell in a friendly amused tone. "We just wanna talk to you about the mess you made in there."

"Let's go." Martin whispered softly.

They slowly crept backwards until they were well away from the tree line and then turned and picked up their pace moving deeper into the forest.

# PART: III

*"If you are afraid to lose anything, than you will lose everything."*

# CHAPTER: 20

**M**ARTIN and Ellis had been walking for a couple of hours before they came upon a clearing, giving them some relief from the thick brush they had been walking through for what seemed like far too long. Carefully moving out of the trees to the edge of the field, Martin took a knee to examine the open area, through his nightvision, before they would attempt to cross.

"Where are we?" Ellis asked in a hushed tone from behind him.

"We are almost there." Martin answered.

"Where are we going?"

"Secret entrance." Martin said as he got up and moved forward in a crouch.

They made it to the other side of the clearing where he began scanning the ground for something.

"What are you looking for?" Ellis asked.

Martin didn't answer. He took a few steps forward and began stamping the ground with his foot.

After a few moments of stamping. There was a clunk sound that came from underneath his foot.

"Found it." He quietly exclaimed.

"What is it?" Ellis asked.

"The secret opening to the bunker."

He got down to his hands and knees, putting his rifle on the ground next to him. He then began to brush away the leaves and dirt that was covering the opening. Once the leaves were cleared he removed his backpack and withdrew a key from the pouch on the front. After fiddling with the lock for a few seconds it finally popped open. He then grabbed the handle and pulled the hatch opened on new, silent hinges.

"Quickly now, get inside." He said, urgently.

Ellis nodded and began to descend down the steps into the tunnel. Martin went down a few steps after her then turned and grabbed an armful of leaves. He then threw them into the air as high as he could and quickly closed the hatch, locking it from the inside.

When he got to the bottom of the stairs, Ellis was waiting for him. She cautioned him to be quiet and pointed down the passage to alert him to the light coming from a doorway at the end of the very long passage. Martin took point and raised his rifle to his shoulder. When they drew near to the door Martin motioned for Ellis to wait. He moved forward and slowly peeked around the corner, there inside the room he saw it was just Mr. Blank, Gabriel, James and Jacob. After waiting long enough to confirm there was no threat or trap Martin lowered his rifle and knocked on the open door. All the heads of the men in the room whipped around and all eyes were on him.

"I'm glad you were all able to get out in time." Said Martin.

"I know right. What the hell is going on out there?" Jacob asked. "It sure was a hell of a way to wake up, if you get my drift."

"I was actually thinking about it on the way over." Said Martin. "It was a registry."

"What was a registry?" Asked James.

"The confiscation thing. They knew we wouldn't turn in all our guns. They just wanted to see who in the area had any. I guess they figured out that, in America, if someone has a gun, they probably have more. They also had my 4473 forms from the background checks that you get every time you buy a gun."

"So you're saying that 4473's were actually used to confiscate guns from the citizens?"

"Yeah, that's pretty much exactly what happened." Said Martin.

"Typical government. I always knew that every gun regulation was bullshit." Gabriel said from the couch.

"I agree. I also admit that I was wrong and that we should have just kept our heads down. We should have just let them come to us on their own, like they were going to anyway."

"It is alright, Martin. It is only the beginning of the end." Said Blank.

"There was something else. At my house there were NATO soldiers mixed in with the Chinese."

"Yes, what does that mean for us. Is world war 3 is here?" Asked James.

"Not exactly. Our government is a big part of NATO. I think that could mean that every country has unified against the American people alone. I think they are trying to erase the American population."

"Well then it's a good thing we killed a lot of them already. We're off to a good start." Jacob said with a smile and a shrug.

Just then Ellis came into the room.

"Ah, Ellis. Thank goodness you and the child are alright. It seems that we taught, Martin, well." Said Blank.

"I'm the one that woke him up!" Ellis laughed. "When I heard the thud sound from downstairs, he was still sleeping so heavily I had to shake him to get him up."

"I do not doubt that for a moment." Blank said with a light chuckle. "In training, Martin, always was a heavy sleeper. I am glad that you were able to get out in time though."

"We almost didn't." Said Martin. "If Ellis hadn't woken me when she did, two more minutes and we'd have been done for."

"So how did you know how to get here through the woods?" Ellis asked, turning to Martin.

"It was a last resort plan we came up with about a year and a half ago. That's why we put that hatch in. And why we put it way out there leading into the bunker. We always hoped it would never have gotten bad enough to use it, but here we are."

"Did you lock it when you came in?" Blank asked.

"Of course."

"Okay, just making sure."

"So did you guys get a similar wake up call as Ellis and I?"

"Yeah, pretty much." Said Jacob. "I got six confirmed dead, Chinese, NATO, and It pains me to say it, but there were also even some with American insignia on their uniforms. I didn't really think about it at the time, but I think your theory about everyone being against us might be correct, Martin."

"I got seven." Gabriel began. "Three possible survivors, but with lethal stab wounds. I only had time to grab my knife. I guess they didn't anticipate that the guy who's room they were standing in had two and a half years of training. I didn't care enough to see who they were, they were in my house uninvited so their shit got rocked." He shrugged.

"I got nine confirmed dead." Said James. "Six in my house, and three outside. One was Chinese, two NATO, two Russians and one American. I couldn't tell you what the three I got from the tree line were, I was too busy trying to make my escape. It was strange though."

"Strange? What do you mean?" Martin asked.

"Some of the soldiers didn't seem like they wanted to do it. They were scared. I looked into the eyes of one of them as he died. I think they're just following orders."

"Who is more guilty, the one who gives the orders or the one who carries them out?" Blank asked.

"Well the man who gave them of course." Said James.

Blank shook his head.

"A king without subjects is just an idiot with a crown."

"What does that mean, bro?" Jacob asked, injecting himself into the conversation.

"It means the only way the orders from above can be carried out is if those below do as they are told. If all of those who are just following orders said no, then those in positions of power would have none. The only time a government, or anyone for that matter, possesses power, is when they are permitted to by those whom they rule. If every person just said 'I will not serve.' There would be no people in power. Mass noncompliance is the most powerful weapon against any government, and any ruler. Unfortunately for us, mass noncompliance requires many, and we are few."

"And now we know we can't trust anyone. Especially our own military." Said Martin.

"What if they're being forced?" James asked. "I mean, what if their families are being threatened?"

"What about it?" Blank continued. "They can either choose to say yes and follow their orders, or they can say no and face whatever comes. The truth is, only cowards follow orders out of fear. If you can be controlled Into doing something because of a threat, you are a weakling. A strong man would refuse and then happily watch everything he knows and loves be taken from him. Because true strength is doing what you want without anyone being able to control you. If you are afraid to lose anything, then you will lose everything."

"We talked about this a few days ago." Said Martin.

"It is still just as true today as it was then." Said Blank.

"Some people don't have the strength required to lose some things." Martin said, glancing at Ellis who was sitting on the other side of the room, holding Mark.

"Freedom or security?" Blank asked.

"Freedom of course." Replied Martin.

"Then you better be ready to lose everything you have, everything you know, and everyone you love. Because the cost of true freedom is everything."

"Is freedom actually worth that cost though." Martin asked in little more than a whisper.

"Freedom and death, or slavery and death? Just like everything else. You can only choose one of these phrases."

"Freedom... I'd choose freedom."

"Then you better be ready to live for it, and you better be ready to die for it. If you are not both willing and able to lose everything for the sake of freedom. Then you do not deserve it, and you will never have it."

"We have to retaliate. They attacked us first. They initiated this." Said Gabriel.

"We will. But first, what allowed them to attack?"

"What do you mean?" Asked Gabriel.

"We did." Blank said, in answer to his own question. "The stupidity of our own people is what allowed this. Twenty years ago. The Chinese would not have dared to invade this country's homeland or attack its people. Because the American spirit was strong in those days. The weakness of our own society is what allowed this. That is what got us here."

"We are a nation of law's, by the people, for the people." Said James.

"There is no such thing as a nation of laws. There are only nations of people who submit and do as they are told, and nations of people who do not. The world is never different from what the people allow, it is always exactly what they ask for."

"So what are we supposed to do about it? Why not just let whatever happens, happen?" Asked Martin.

"That's up to you. It's only a matter of time though before they come for you. So would you rather fight now on your terms, or fight later on theirs? Will you fight for the freedoms we once had, or will you lay down like the weakness that allowed this to happen in the first place?"

Blank paused to look at each of them.

"Will you fight everyone who is responsible, all enemies both foreign and domestic, yes or no?"

"Yes." They each said in turn.

"What can we do against the entire Chinese, Russian and American armies and everyone else who agrees with them?" Jacob asked, staring at the table. "Because you know there will be propaganda and idiot American citizens out there who believe the lies that the Chinese are here to save us or something."

"How does a mouse overpower a lion?"

Jacob looked up at Blank with one eyebrow raised, and they all shook their heads in confusion.

"It attacks with stealth, while the lion sleeps." Said Blank. "After you gather intelligence on your target, it is just as simple as removing it. How you remove it is up to you, but it is usually all the same idea."

"Will you be going with us when we go out to gather intelligence?" Martin asked.

"No, I am retired. It is not yet the time that you need me. However when the time comes and things get to that point I will go forth into the world and torment as I once did." Said Blank, lowering his head slightly.

All but Martin looked at him with confusion, but even he was not exactly sure what Blank was talking about. They had all known him for over two years now and never even once had he revealed his face, name or past to any of them. Save the little sliver of information he allowed Martin to know that night long ago as they sat next to the fire. How they all trusted him completely with their lives was beyond him. Martin knew though that when the time came, Blank would be there, and based on the way he could just appear right next to you without making a sound, he was definitely capable of awesome and terrible things.

# CHAPTER: 21

## *Washington DC.*

**B**RIAN awoke with a start. It was still mostly dark inside the house, but out the window he could see the light beginning to swell over the neighboring houses on the other side of the street. He looked at his watch and the digital readout said it was 06:17am. He stood, put his plate carrier back on and slung his rifle over his shoulder. After taking a quick peek out the window to see if there was anything going on outside, he made his way over to the stairs and moved up the steps. Once at the top he quietly called for Scarlet.

"One second, I'm almost ready." She said from one of the bedrooms.

Satisfied with her answer, he turned and went back down the stairs. He then moved into the kitchen to gather up their supplies. By the time he had everything into two cardboard boxes, Scarlet was coming down the stairs.

"Need help with anything?" She asked as she walked into the kitchen.

"If you can carry this other box, that would be great."

"When do you wanna head out?"

"As soon as we get these and ourselves in the truck."

"Okay. Did you decide where we're going?"

"I think we should move closer to the city to see if we can get a better view of what's going on." Said Brian.

"Sounds good."

They both walked out to the truck and put the food into the bed. Then they hopped into their seats and Brian started the engine. He put the truck in reverse and then looked out the rear window before he began to back up. Once they were out on the street he noticed the front door of the house across the street from the one they stayed in, swing open. He kept an eye on the doorway as he began to pull away. That's when he saw a family of four exit the house in a hurry, all of them with suitcases and luggage bags.

"It's probably a little late to be bugging out, people." Brian said more to himself.

"Yup, and let the looting begin." Scarlet said in response.

They turned left onto a main road then took the on-ramp to the interstate headed northbound then eastbound to circle around to the other side of the city. As they drove, Brian noticed the Southbound and Westbound interstates were backed up for miles, while the North and Eastbound were more or less clear.

"Guess everyone is getting out of the city." Said Brian.

"I'm just glad we're not stuck in that traffic. Because I hate traffic." Scarlet said matter of factly.

"Me too, kid. Let's just hope we're heading in the right direction."

"Do we need a map?"

"That's not what I meant. I know exactly where we're at."

"Oh, gotcha… You lost me."

"Sometimes the path you choose to take can often lead you in the wrong direction."

"Eh, don't worry about it. I have faith in you."

Without saying anything else, Brian took the exit off the eastbound highway then turned into a parking garage that was next to a tall building. He drove up to the level right before the roof, pulled into a parking spot and put the transmission in park. He then shut off the engine and pulled the keys out of the ignition.

"Be careful not to slam your door." Brian said, quietly. "We want to keep a low profile, and the less noise we make the better."

She nodded in understanding then they both got out.

After quietly closing his door, Brian made his way across the parking garage to look out over the city. Scarlet followed him over to the edge of the platform where she leaned on the metal railing that was atop a concrete wall.

"So what's the plan?" She said in a low voice.

"Probably just gonna lay low and observe for a while. See what our new enemies will do, and if anyone will fight back."

"Then what?"

"Hopefully join the fight."

They watched the military planes land and take off all throughout the morning and into the afternoon. Brian never imagined that it would have been this way.

"Could this be world war three?" He thought to himself. "Because if it is then pretty much everyone was wrong."

It was hard to believe that America's homeland was under a full scale invasion. What baffled him even more was the fact that there had been absolutely no response, retaliation or defense efforts made yet. Where was the rest of the military? Was he maybe the only Marine left? He pondered these questions in his head, just trying to make sense of it all. It was funny to think about how if someone would have told him even an hour before the bombs dropped that they would be invaded that day, he would have called them a loonie. In fact if someone would have told him ten years ago that he would have been in the Marines he probably would have laughed at them for that too. He never was a very serious person before he joined the military. When he was younger, he always seemed to be able to turn everything into a joke in one way or another. In recent days though, he had become more than just the punk kid he used to be. He was a Marine now, and he took pride in that.

Brian had grown up around the DC area, so naturally he got into a little trouble here and there. Skateboarding on private property, and a few street fights, but nothing too serious. At least until the time he got into a fist fight with a cop that was arresting a man he knew as Mr. Pip.

Mr. Pip was actually a marijuana dealer, but Brian still considered him a friend. Therefore he was going to protect him, even if it meant that he would pay the price for it. The next thing he knew after that was he was joining the marines. The judge on his case had given him that same old offer that a lot of troubled juveniles got. Go to jail for a few years and live with a permanent record, or join the military. He of course chose the military, and he was happy that he had.

It had been nine years since that day, and he had enjoyed it up until this point. Now he was just a confused soldier on his own, without orders or a chain of command. He pushed the thoughts away and then looked at Scarlet. She was now sitting cross legged on the platform using a piece of chalk she had found to play Tic-Tac-Toe against herself on the blacktop.

"Hey, you up for a little adventure?" Brian asked.

Scarlet looked up at him.

"Where are we going?" She replied.

"I wanna try to get to the top of that building for a better view."

He said pointing to the top of the tall building that was next to the parking garage.

"Okay, I'm in. Let's go."

They made their way over to the bridge that connected the building to the garage, then walked across it. The door to the building was unlocked so they were able to simply walk right in. Once inside they walked down a hallway to the elevator and Brian hit the button marked with an 'up' arrow. He didn't really expect it to work, but then with a sudden ding, the doors opened. They both got on without comment, or complaint. Brian hit the button marked 'roof' and the doors closed.

The elevator ride to the top of the tall building took quite a while, but when the bell sounded again, the doors opened up into a stairwell. Brian looked out the door and then looked up. At the top of a set of stairs was a door marked 'roof'.

"Come on." Brian said as he started up the stairs.

Scarlet followed him and they exited onto the roof. He held the door as she passed by him then he bent over and grabbed the chunk of wood someone had left up there to be used as a doorstop. He didn't wanna take the chance of being locked out on the roof so he put the block in the opening to keep the door from closing all the way. As he walked over to the railing where Scarlet was standing, he looked off into the distance, and what he saw was worse than he had thought. From where he stood, he could see the ocean, and the shoreline. He could also see the hundreds and hundreds of battleships in the harbor and the carrier's docking at the shipyard.

"Well, this is just fan-freaking-tastic." He said in annoyance. "Not only are we hopelessly outnumbered but there's even more coming."

"It's not looking too bright now is it? Who even are they?" Scarlet asked.

Brian raised his rifle to his shoulder and flipped the magnifier scope into the upward position so he could look through it.

"We're too far away for me to say for sure, but the color of the emblem on the sides of all the vehicles is definitely red. So if I had to guess I'd say either Chinese or Russian, maybe even both." Said Brian.

"Is that bad?" Asked Scarlet.

"Yeah, kid. That's about as bad as it could get."

"Do you think we should leave? Ya know, maybe try to get farther away from the city?"

"I don't think so. Right now we are right where they'd least expect anyone to be. Everyone else is either leaving the city or has already left. They probably wouldn't expect many people to stay."

"What do you think we should do next?"

"Well, since we know we have this vantage point the only thing left to do is to see if we can find another one." Said Brian.

"Where?"

"Underground."

"Oh. Eww. Do you mean the sewers?"

"You don't have to come. You can stay in the parking garage if you want."

"I'll go." She said with a shiver. "I'd rather not be left alone. In the movies bad things always happen when the characters split up."

"This isn't a movie though."

"Nope. However we are wasting time talking about it being one."

"Right."

Once they were back at ground level, Brian led the way over to the side door of the building. Before exiting the building he checked the sky for any possible flight patrols. Then opened the door and walked out with Scarlet following behind him. He made straight for the first manhole cover he saw and pulled it open, revealing a dark hole that led to the sewers below. He clicked on his flashlight and pointed it down the hole.

"I'll go first, you follow when I give the all clear." He said.

"Okay." She replied.

He slung his rifle over his shoulder with the light pointing downward. Then he lowered himself onto the ladder and began his descent into the darkness.

It was a fairly long way down before his feet hit solid ground. As he let go of the ladder he grabbed and started raising his rifle as he turned. He stopped abruptly upon seeing the end of a rifle barrel six inches from his face. He slowly lowered his own rifle then raised his hands.

"Who are you?" Asked the voice on the other side of the gun.

Not seeing a reason to lie, Brian said.

"I am Staff Sergeant Brian Parker of the United States, Marine Corps."

"Why are you here?" Asked the voice.

"I could ask you the same thing." Said Brian.

The person holding the gun said nothing, just continued to aim at him. Realizing that he was getting nowhere, Brian continued.

"I'm trying to figure out what's going on up there. I was stationed at Quantico, but it's been wiped off the face of the earth by whoever it is that is currently moving in."

"You mean to tell me that even you don't know what's going on?"

"Correct, It all happened out of the blue and without warning. I was in a Blackhawk when the first bombs hit; I was the only survivor in my squad."

The barrel of the rifle lowered away from his face.

"Come with me." Said the voice.

"Can you promise not to hold me captive?"

"Yes. We are both Americans, therefore we are on the same side."

"Okay cool. Just hold up one second."

Brian turned and looked up the ladder where he could see Scarlet looking down at him.

"All clear, Scarlet, come on down." He called.

When he turned back around the person still stood in the dark, waiting for him.

"Who are you calling to?" They asked.

"Just a young girl that I am traveling with. I'm just trying to get her to safety."

"Very well." Said the figure.

Scarlet's feet found the ground and she walked up behind Brian. The shadow figure of the person in front of them gave her a start, and she almost screamed.

"I'm a friend." Said the figure. "Please, follow me."

They both followed the black clad figure down a passage then took a right, then a left down another passage. They had been walking for a while turning this way and that, before Brian finally saw a light source at the end of the passage. They made it to the end and entered into a large, well lit room. The light was blinding in his eyes which had adapted to the darkness, but once his eyes adjusted to the light, he made out about twenty people moving about the room.

"What is this?" Brian asked.

"We're the DC militia." Said the figure.

"Is this everyone you have?"

"Most of our member's turned out to be cowards and dipped out as soon as the invasion started."

"So why did you stay?"

"I'd rather die on my feet than live on my knees."

"You're probably the first person I've heard say that and back it up with your actions." Said Brian.

"I'll take that as a compliment."

The black clad individual then removed their hood and pulled down their mask to reveal the dirty yet pretty face of a young woman. Brian wasn't surprised, he had guessed by the tone of her voice and the stature of her body, that the person who had held him at gunpoint back at the entrance was, in fact, a female. Not that it made a difference though. A gun doesn't care who pulls the trigger, so neither did Brian.

"So, is there anything that we can do to help?" Brian asked.

"Of course there is. The more people we have the better." She said as she leaned her rifle up against a table.

"What do you need me to do?"

"You're a Marine, right?"

"Yes, that's correct."

"Well, in that case, we could use you for pretty much everything."

"Give me something more specific."

"Recon. We need to know what's going on, and I'm sure you want to know just as much as we do. So what do ya say? Are you feeling up for some recon?"

"Count me in. What about the girl though?"

"She can stick around down here for the time being. How long are you planning on staying?"

"We'll just have to wait and see. It depends on what happens." Said Brian.

"Sounds good. I'm Lynn by the way." She said sticking her hand out.

"I'm Brian. And the girl is, Scarlet." He said as he shook Lynn's hand.

"Pleased to meet you. And in case you're wondering. No, I'm not the leader of this, I'm the second in command. Our first in command, Thomas, is currently away, visiting one of his old friends in West Virginia. He went there hoping to buy weapons and he won't be back for a couple days or so."

"How long ago did he leave?"

"He left right after the bombs hit." Said Lynn, "He wanted to make sure that he could get out of the city before the traffic got too bad."

"No problem. That is sensible. But going back to what you said before. Just for the record I wouldn't have cared if you were the leader. You seem to be responsible enough."

"I appreciate that." She said with a smile. "If you wanna get some rest we have plenty of extra cots in the other room and you are welcome to one of them. I'll come wake you when its time to go to work. Everyone's gotta at least pull their own weight around here."

"I wouldn't have it any other way. And thank you. I could use some sleep. Come on, Scarlet, let's go settle in."

Brian and Scarlet walked into the room that Lynn had pointed out, each of them choosing an empty cot and stowing their gear underneath. Brian then laid his head down on the pillow and shut his eyes.

"It wasn't much of a resistance." He thought to himself. "However it was a start, and was definitely better than nothing."

He wasn't sure yet how long he would be staying with the group but at this point he was almost certain that the American government had been toppled, in one way or another. He just couldn't figure out how that could have happened so easily. After thinking about it for a while with no success in coming to a logical explanation. He decided to tuck his thoughts away for the time being and try to get some rest. He then turned onto his left side and drifted off to sleep.

# CHAPTER: 22

## *Mr. Blank's Bunker, Pennsylvania.*

**I**T had been four days now since Martin and his group were forced to flee their homes. They had spent the first three days getting themselves situated and taking inventory on their supplies. This was the first night they were going to run a scouting mission to gather intelligence in order to put together a plan of retaliation.

"We can't fight their entire force head on, but we can cause them problems. Be a wrench in their machine, if you will." Martin had said a few nights prior.

They had agreed that with them being such a small group, they would be the most efficient and effective if they acquired specific high priority targets and took them out. In theory it was a good way to disrupt the chain of command, and hopefully slow things down.

"Gather around boys. Have a seat." Martin said, gesturing to the couches on either side of the table.

After they sat, Martin continued.

"Alright so here's what we're going to do."

Pointing to the map on the coffee table he showed the spot they would be headed that night.

"See this location here, just outside of town. We received intel through Jacobs connections that this is where the Chinese have set up their base of operations. The plan is that, once we get out there, we're going to split up into two teams of two and flank the base. One team on either side to observe from the hills, but stay concealed in the trees. My plan is that for three hours after we get there, we are going to document everything we deem to be useful then head home. Taking pictures with those long distance cameras." He pointed to the cameras on the shelf in the corner.

"We will also be writing down descriptions and taking notes. We are to closely watch the attitudes of the soldiers to try and identify those in command. It's common knowledge that commanding officers don't wear anything that could signify rank while either stationed on, or visiting a field base. So we simply need to watch body language until someone is foolish, or sloppy enough to give it away."

"All it would take is for one, less than disciplined soldier to throw out a salute to someone else. Then the identification of the one saluted will be put on the list of targets of interest." Blank added.

"Just remember guys." Martin continued. "This mission is solely for recon and gathering intelligence on the enemy. No one is to shoot, or engage, unless the target in question is an obvious, once in a lifetime opportunity, and you are given permission by your spotter to do so. Understand? No getting trigger happy. We can't afford to be discovered just yet. Unless the kill was worth the cost."

"Understood." They all said more or less in unison.

"We are also going in quiet and comm silent. You guys already know pretty much everything that I do about tactics. So if we need to say something, it's hand signals only. Comms are only to be used in the event that something goes terribly wrong and we are calling off the mission."

"Sounds good to me." Said James.

The others nodded in agreement.

"Alright, good." Said Martin.

"And so begins the retaliation. Because by their actions our enemies have sewn the seeds of revolution. And come harvest time we will see to it that they will reap what they have sewn." Said Jacob.

"What?" Martin asked while looking at Jacob.

"Nothing, just trying to sound smart. Did it work?"

"Not really." Martin said. "I was beginning to think that you might just be going crazy. Anyway, boys, do your gear checks, we're moving out as soon as night sets in."

It was a clear night with a full moon rising over the trees in the east. Martin was sitting at a table by the entrance to the supply container installing new batteries into their PVS-31 night vision goggles. While the others were swapping out uniforms and putting equipment bags together. They had given up their standard Olive Drab Green uniforms for the time being. They also weren't going to be wearing their standard plate carriers or ballistic armor on the mission either. Instead they were going with more stealthy black camo, gillie hoods and the PVS-31 dual tube night vision goggles. A load out far more ideal for night ops.

They had to be incredibly cautious. Ever since Martin and the others had collectively killed around 30 of the enemy soldiers, they were undoubtedly being hunted. The Chinese had executed a few more Americans two days prior as a punishment or a warning. They must have thought it would instill fear, and deter any American citizens from fighting back or revolting. Unfortunately for the enemy, complying with tyranny just simply wasn't the American way. Revolution was the American way. The saying that Jacob had said when he was trying to sound smart, actually wasn't far off. The fate of the Invaders was sealed and their death warrant was signed, the moment they executed those innocent civilians. Those actions gave Martin and his team all the justification they needed in order to destroy those who were responsible for the death of their fellow Americans. Martin finished checking the night vision, then turned to the others, who had just finished making sure the gear, guns and ammo were all ready to go.

"Good to go." Said Gabriel as he closed the zipper on the last bag they were taking.

"Alright, everybody suit up. We need to get moving."

It took them a little under three hours to walk the five miles through the thick woods that separated the bunker from the Chinese base. As they approached the point where they were to split up, Martin gave James and Jacob both a pat on the back, then a thumbs up. They were now in enemy territory so they had switched to communicating in hand signals only. Just in case there were scouts hiding in the area. The last thing they wanted was to be compromised by verbal communication when it was unnecessary.

Martin and Gabriel watched the moon rising bright overhead, illuminating the night as James and Jacob moved ahead in opposite directions. After about fifteen seconds Martin gave Gabriel a fist bump then hefted his rifle and followed about 30 feet behind James. Gabriel did the same; following in the direction of Jacob.

As they worked their way around the base, they made sure to keep well back into the trees to avoid being spotted. Fortunately, the camp was brightly illuminated with flood lights on the inside. So for them, being outside in the trees and up the hill, the light pollution would be enough to shield them from being spotted by anyone from inside the camp. Once they made it to their spot, Martin and James moved into position. Martin scanned the area while James set up the spotter scope, the camera and his notepad. Then they switched so James could scan the area while Martin set up his suppressed AR10. By this time, Gabriel and Jacob would be doing the same.

Just like an AR15, the AR10 was semiautomatic. The .308 cartridge it was chambered in however was much more powerful and an ideal round for this occasion. The 20 inch barrel that Martin had installed in place of the standard 16 inch barrel, made the rifle deadly accurate at farther ranges. That is if the shooter had the nerve required for those distances. The rifle was also fitted with a sunshade on the scope, so as to not reveal their position to the enemy by reflecting the moonlight off the lens. Both Martin and Gabriel were the riflemen while James and Jacob were the spotters. Gabriel's rifle was similar to Martin's. Same AR10 platform with a suppressor, only Gabriel's was chambered in 6.5 Creedmoor.

"I agree that it's an excellent round." Martin had said back when he was helping Gabriel build the rifle. "I just prefer the .308 because of its commonality and that it's easy to find in any situation. Whereas the 6.5 Creedmoor is much more scarce. So once you run out of that ammo type, the rifle will only be good for use as a fancy club."

Gabriel wanted it though, so Martin only said his piece and relented to help him finish the build.

Once Martin was all set up and situated, he looked around for a moment to scan the area. Satisfied there was no immediate threat, he flipped his night vision goggles up and out of the way, then looked through the scope of his rifle. As he scanned the grounds of the base he noted there was not much military activity, but then, scanning over to the far side of the base from where they had come, he noticed something. He focused his scope to the distance and what he saw just about overwhelmed him with anger. He saw hundreds of people being held in dirty cages and pens, like mistreated farm animals.

After taking a mental note of that, he scanned over to outside the fence where it appeared they had dug a pit to act as a mass grave. It was inhuman. People were being beaten and abused in all manners and disgusting ways. That's when he realized that by this time Gabriel would have discovered the same things he just had. Martin could only pray that Gabriel would be able to stay calm. It wasn't worth it to blow their cover so soon, they needed to continue with the mission as planned. Martin held his breath waiting for the gunfire from Gabriel to start. One minute passed, then two minutes, and to his relief the shots never came. Gabriel had been able to control his anger as they had been taught in training after all. Martin knew he could count on Gabriel in almost every scenario, but this was all very new and almost made even Martin himself lose his ability to think rationally. Satisfied that no shooting was going to happen at this time he slowly let out the breath he had been holding, and went back to observing.

By the time the three hours were up they had cataloged how the guards moved, their patrols and what kind of weapons they used. They also witnessed and recorded all manner of unspeakable things that were occurring at this place. It couldn't be called a base, it was a concentration camp for abusing American citizens. There was a sudden tap on Martin's shoulder. Martin looked up from his scope, turning his head to look at James who was tapping on his wrist watch. Martin nodded and got to a knee from where he was laying. He dropped his night vision goggles back over his eyes and looked around. After a second he gave James the hand signal for all clear, then picked up his rifle. James started off and Martin waited to follow just as they had on the way there. They did this in case of a landmine or if one of them was to be spotted. The distance between them gave them a better chance of individual survival. If one of them was to get hit, or anything else, the other would be just the right distance away to either get away, or retrieve the injured man if the situation allowed.

They met up with the others where they had split up, and with tired minds and heavy hearts for the people in the camp, they began their walk back to the bunker. They could not help yet, but they would be back, very soon. Their people needed their help, and so they were going to help them.

They made it back to the bunker in the early hours of the morning. Martin walked up to the door and knocked the secret knock. He knew that Mr. Blank would be waiting to open the door, and Ellis would undoubtedly still be awake, waiting for them to return. She had always been worried even when they went on training exercises, and this was now the real deal. There was a clunk sound and then the door swung open. They all entered, shutting and locking the door behind them. As they walked down into the living area, Martin saw Ellis sitting on the couch reading a book. Upon seeing him enter, she quickly put her book down, then arose and walked over to embrace him.

"It's about time you got back. I was beginning to worry." She said.

"Beginning to worry?" Martin retorted with a smile.

Gabriel patted Martin on the back as he and the others moved past him into the other room where they began removing their gear and stowing it away on the shelves in the corner.

"I'm gonna go change out of these clothes and put my gear away. Go back to your book darling. I'll see you in a little bit."

Once they had put everything away and gotten into more comfortable clothes, they all sat around the table in the conference room.

"So what did you figure out?" Blank said as he entered from the control room where the security system and the button to open the door was.

Martin and the others then told all that they had seen. Come to find out, Gabriel had in fact discovered the same things that Martin had and he had also hoped that Martin wouldn't shoot either. Martin smiled and knew now that he had absolutely no reason to mistrust any of them ever again. They knew exactly what to do and that gave Martin a sense of relief where doubt had once been. They were ready for this. It's what they trained for, and they would only get better.

They stayed up till dawn looking over the pictures and notes and eventually came to a decision on their first course of action. They still possessed the element of surprise. So they decided that they were going to free those American citizens from that awful camp, no matter the cost.

# CHAPTER: 23

## *Mr. Blank's Bunker, Pennsylvania.*

I need to go check on my parents." Ellis said as she walked into the war room where Martin was sitting in his chair at the table.                              "They should have been here by now. I think something might be wrong."

"It's on the itinerary, Ellis. There's a lot of people that need saving. We just have a lot going on right now. We'll probably be able to go check on them tomorrow night."

"No, Martin, it's already been too long. If you and the team can't go tonight, then I will just go by myself." She said sternly.

"Easy now, sweetheart. Alright, I'll make preparations to go tonight." He said as she moved towards him.

"Okay. Thank you, darling." She said as she finished walking around the table and gave him a kiss on the cheek.

"You know your dad is gonna be pissed and want to help us fight, don't you?" Martin asked.

"So, isn't that a good thing?" She retorted.

"Your dad isn't as young as he once was. While he is very knowledgeable and a great shot with a rifle, there is no way he could ever keep up with myself and the others. And I mean that in the nicest way possible."

"Well once you bring him and my mother back here, I'll make it a point to keep him on the couch and out of trouble." Said Ellis.

"Thanks, sweetheart. I'd appreciate that. It's not that I don't adore your old man, it's just that we can't afford the liability he would be if he were to go with us."

She put her right arm around his neck and looked him in the eyes while placing her other hand on the side of his face.

"I can understand that. Okay, well if you're gonna be out all night again, you should probably get to packing." She said, patting him on the shoulder.

Martin nodded thoughtfully, before Ellis stood up straight then walked back around the table to the door. Once she was at the door she turned around.

"Would you like me to pack something special for you all to eat while you're out?" She asked.

"Yes, please. That would be great." He said.

She blew him a kiss then exited the room. Martin sat in his chair for a while longer, thinking about how they should go about getting to his in-laws, without drawing too much attention to themselves. Should they just go for it and take a vehicle, or play it safe and go by foot? After thinking about it for a few minutes longer he decided it was probably best to play it safe and go by foot. He then stood up from his chair and walked out of the room to gather the others for the unexpected pre-mission briefing. They most likely wouldn't be too happy about having to walk a few miles on a day that Martin had previously told them was going to be an off day. It didn't really matter though, unexpected things tend to happen when you're starting a war.

After the briefing, they all got into their standard OD green equipment and armed themselves with AR15's, their standard weapons of choice.

"So, why aren't we taking a vehicle?" Gabriel asked pointedly. "It would only be a one hour round trip, instead of the six hours it's gonna take us on foot."

"Gotta get used to walking someday, and there's no better day than today." Martin said in response to Gabriel's moping.

"A car will draw too much attention to us." James added. "They're definitely looking for us after what we did that first night. The time we'd save by driving isn't worth the risk of getting caught."

"Are you sure? We could just drive with NOD's on. We wouldn't even need to use the vehicle's headlights." Said Gabriel.

"He has a point." Jacob said with a shrug.

"Let's put it to a vote then." Said Martin. "All in favor of driving, raise your hand."

Gabriel and Jacob both raised their hands right away. Martin looked at James who seemed to be mauling it over. After a few moments he raised his hand with the others.

"Alright, that settles it then. We will drive under night vision." Said Martin.

With that they all piled into Gabriel's four door truck and started out in the direction of Martin's in-laws. Martin just hoped that the bad feeling that he currently had was nothing, and that his in-laws were fine. He also hoped that the noise of the truck wouldn't draw any unwanted attention.

It was only a twenty five minute drive by way of the back roads to Ellis's parents, which they made without seeing a single soul.

"I can't believe that so many people are complying with the lockdown. It seems unnatural for Americans to act so cowardly." Gabriel said as he turned the truck into Paul's driveway.

"Americans are not as they once were." Said Martin. "It only takes one generation to go from warrior to spoiled brat. The children of yesterday's strong become the parents of today's spoiled and weak."

Gabriel put the truck in park out front of the house and they all got out with their rifles at low ready. They made their way to the door in breaching formation, with Martin taking point. He tried the handle, it was unlocked. This worried him greatly, and he prepared for the worst. As he swung the door open and entered the house with his rifle shouldered, he used the pressure switch on his rifle to turn his Infra Red weapon light on. As soon as he did, his worries were confirmed. Because no sooner had the light came on, did it illuminated the body of Ellis's father, laying at the bottom of the stairs, in a pool of his own drying blood.

"Fan out. Sweep the house." Martin said in a raspy whisper.

The others broke off in all directions to clear the house. Martin moved closer and crouched down next to Paul's body. Out of sheer foolish hope, he touched Paul's neck to feel for a pulse. His body was cold as ice and Martin calmly withdrew his hand.

"Clear." He heard the others calling periodically, until one of them said.

"In here. Found another body."

Martin arose and walked into the other room to find Gabriel looking at the body of his mother in-law. Martin lowered his rifle to rest on the strap around his neck and then just stared at the bruised and beaten body.

"What do you think happened here?" Gabriel asked.

"They probably tried to fight back." Said Martin.

"How much time do we have? Should we bury them?"

"No, go help the others search the rest of the house. Take anything that we can use. Then we'll burn the house." Martin said flatly.

"Are you sure about that?"

"Yes, it may not be what they wanted. But it's more of a burial than most people will get these days."

"Okay. I'll tell the others."

After Gabriel had left the room Martin walked over and gently moved Margaret's stiff body onto the couch. Once he had her situated in a more modest position he walked out of the room and over to where Paul was laying at the bottom of the stairs. He carefully picked up his body and moved it into the room where Margaret lay. He then set Paul's body down on the other couch, then he pushed both the couches together. That way they could both rest next to each other. They had built the house, lived in it and died in it. Now they would be buried in it. Martin thought it was only right that no one else should ever live in the home that they had built. Their memory was all that mattered now. And after that night, their memories would be all that would remain.

"That's everything. We're ready to go." Jacob said from the doorway to the room.

Martin nodded in the darkness which Jacob could see through his night vision, then he followed Jacob out to help the others carry everything useful out of the house and put it into the bed of the truck. Martin followed them out onto the porch holding his zippo lighter. He looked over to the side of the house and saw Gabriel coming out of the shed, carrying a can of gas. Martin moved to the side to allow him to pass by. Gabriel then spread the gasoline all throughout the house. Once he had expelled all the gas from the can, he walked out the door throwing the can into the house behind him. They both walked down the porch steps together, then turned.

"You want me to do it?" Gabriel asked.

"No, I should do it. Thanks though."

"No problem, man."

Gabriel took a tentative step back as Martin opened and struck up a flame on the wick of the zippo. After looking at the flame for a moment, he tossed the lighter through the front door of the house, the fire igniting as soon as it landed on the floor inside. Satisfied that Paul and Margaret's house would never be used by the enemy, Martin turned, walked over to the truck, got in and shut the door.

They could see the glow of the flames for about a mile as they drove down the dark road in silence. Martin looked back just in time to see a hill block the glow of the house from view. Luckily for them any first response or military that might be coming to investigate the fire, would be coming from the opposite direction that they were heading. So the drive back was uneventful. Once they arrived safely back at the bunker, they all got out of the truck still without speaking a word. They all headed down to the armory, where they began putting their gear and weapons away. It was at this time that Gabriel finally broke the silence.

"So, taking the truck was a good idea. Am I right?" He said, trying to ease the tension.

"Yeah, it was the right way to do it this time, but probably won't have that much good luck if we do it again." Said Martin.

There was a long pause before anyone spoke.

"How are you gonna tell her, Martin?" James asked.

Martin looked at the floor without answering the question.

"I heard you all come in." Ellis said as she entered the armory. "Where are my parents, are they okay?"

Martin paused in the middle of putting his rifle on the rack. After a moment's hesitation he finished placing it, then he turned to face her.

"We couldn't find them." Jacob said, cutting into the conversation.

"What do you mean?" She asked, turning towards Jacob.

"They weren't at their house. They either bugged out, or got captured. We will find them soon though."

Martin turned and looked at Jacob who gave an almost unnoticeable small shrug.

Martin looked at Ellis and she looked back at him.

"You will find them, right?" She asked.

"Yes. Don't worry dear. They're out there somewhere."

She gave him a hug, then with a sad smile she walked into the other room. Martin waited till she was gone before turning to Jacob with a disapproving look.

"What?" Jacob said, playing innocent.

"You know what. Why would you lie to my wife?" He asked incredulously.

"Because." Jacob whispered, leaning over to make sure Ellis was out of ear shot. "Because, there are some things that some people are better off not knowing. See, I'm not like our good friend, Mr. Blank. I don't think everyone should know everything. Telling her now will only make her life harder than it has to be. Which will in turn make everything worse."

Martin didn't respond for some time. Rubbing his chin

thoughtfully he finally said.

"Just don't do that again, please. I'm the one that has to deal with it if she finds out on her own."

"I know." Jacob said with a touch of cheeriness in his voice. "That's the best part, bro. For me anyway."

"What about all the rest of our parents?" Gabriel asked. "Should we try to get to them?"

"If they are farther away than a half hour drive, then we must consider them to already be dead." Said Martin. "There is no sense in trying to make it across the country to save someone that might need saving, when there are plenty of people here that we know need saving."

"Fair point. Kinda cold hearted, but I can't really argue with your logic."

The next morning after breakfast Martin grabbed a rifle off the rack. He checked the mag-well and chamber to make sure it was clear and unloaded, then held it up to examine the exterior. It was the AR10 he had used a few nights before. He was debating on taking it out again, once they left for the mission to free the camp later that night, but he wasn't sure yet. He looked up from the rifle in his hands and scanned over the rack of rifles on the wall. His eyes stopped when they fell on his FN Scar 17s. It seemed like it had been forever since he had used it, even though he trained with it quite often. For some reason, at that moment the beautiful golden brown and FDE color was calling to him like an old friend begging for attention.

He hadn't had time to make another one yet so he twisted the suppressor off the AR10 and put the rifle back on the wall. He then grabbed the Scar and twisted the suppressor onto the barrel. It was a .308 suppressor and both the AR10 and the Scar had the same thread pitch on the end of the barrel so the same suppressor worked well for both guns. He selected four magazines for the rifle, inserted one into the mag well and the other three into the pouches across the front of his armor plate carrier. They would be going in full kit this time. Being as it was more of an assault mission, as opposed to the stealth mission a few nights before. There was a much greater chance of being shot. So having armor was a precaution worth the extra weight. Just then Martin noticed someone standing next to him in his peripheral vision. He turned to see Mr. Blank standing there in his usual black clothes and mask, with his hood on.

"I am going to scout the opposite side of town tonight." Said Blank. "I overheard some chatter as I was walking past a bread line earlier today. They said there's something going on over there. I figured if I am not going with you to fight, the least I can do is scout out the team's next target."

"I really would like it better if you came with us. We could use your expertise and abilities." Said Martin.

"It is not yet the proper time. It would not be fair for me to interfere so soon."

"Fair to whom?" Martin asked.

"Anyone." Said Blank.

"Very well. I won't argue with you. It's not my place to tell you what to do anyway."

"I know it was never made official that you were the leader, but if anyone was to be the leader, it would be you, Martin."

"I appreciate your confidence in me, but I do not want power over anyone. I know the guys listen to me, but that's only because they trust in my plans. Nothing I tell them to do are orders. I only request them to follow my plans. They do so by their own choice."

"They respect you, Martin. You are just humble and cannot see what a great leader you could be, if you allowed yourself to become one."

Martin nodded in understanding.

"So when are you heading out?" Martin asked.

"In a few minutes. I will most likely be back by the morning."

"Okay. Just be careful."

"I am always careful, Martin. Please try and do the same."

In one silent graceful movement, Blank was gone. Martin knew he didn't have to worry about anything when it came to the well-being of that man. There was almost no chance he could ever be discovered unless he wanted to be. He was pretty much the closest thing to a phantom that a person could be, in Martin's eyes. Which explained how Blank had made so much money back when he was still working. He just wondered what made him retire. Maybe one day Blank would tell him his story, but until then he could only wonder.

# CHAPTER: 24

**M**ARTIN met Ellis at the door to the bunker before heading out on the mission to free the people being held in the concentration camp. Gabriel, James and Jacob were doing a final weapons check outside as they waited for him to say goodbye to his wife.

"Do you really have to go back there? Why can't someone else do it? We don't even know them." Said Ellis in a sad tone of voice.

"We have to go, Ellis. I don't think there is anyone else who's willing to do it."

"Then why should you? If they won't, then why not just let them be?"

"Your parents might be there though." Jacob said as he walked past them.

Martin glared at him for a second then turned back to Ellis.

"We must do everything as if we are alone and there's nobody else that will fight alongside us." Martin said, looking into her eyes. "Those are our people out there, and they need our help. This country will only become truly lost, if we don't fight to keep it. That is the whole reason why we formed the Special Task Force Unit. To defend the people and to fight for our home."

"I know how good you guys have become, and you probably will survive this time, but for how long? You may survive tonight, but what if you go out again tomorrow and you don't make it back? If you keep going out there every night for the sake of others, It's only a matter of time before something happens." She said, holding back tears.

"No matter what happens. We will always find a way to make it back. It'll be just like the past few nights."

"The past few times you went out were different than tonight. Those times you weren't going out with the intention of conflict, this time you are. I just can't lose you. I'm scared by where this will all lead. Mark and I need you now more than ever."

"Do not fear, sweetheart. Fear is unnecessary. Death is the answer to the question that is life. Survival was never part of the plan, darling. I will fight to the bitter end. Because If we are going to stay alive, then I want us to live, not simply survive. Regardless, I will see you soon either way. I love you."

He leaned in, and as he kissed her on the forehead, she closed her eyes to savor his touch. After a moment he pulled away. When she opened her eyes a moment later Martin and the others were gone. She looked around and then in a whisper, she said.

"I love you too. Please stay safe."

Martin caught up to the others and crouched next to Gabriel who was sitting opposite from Jacob and James.

"Took you long enough." Jacob said with a smile Martin could just barely see through the darkness.

"I was only like seven seconds behind you." Said Martin with confusion in his voice.

"Yes, and those few seconds could mean life or death one day. You shouldn't allow yourself to become so easily distracted." Said Jacob.

"Yes, dad. I'll keep that in mind next time I'm saying goodbye to my wife." Martin said sarcastically.

"You make your daddy proud boy." Jacob said, imitating the voice of a gruff old man.

Martin looked at him for a long time before saying.

"That's just weird, bro. Why are you the way you are?"

"Never allow your sense of humor to abandon you. One day you may rely on it to survive."

"Duly noted. Let's go." Said Martin as he put his mask on and dropped his night vision into place over his eyes. The others followed suit and then with a thumbs up, they were off in the direction of the Chinese camp.

They moved silent, swift and effortlessly through the woods until they came upon a path about an eighth mile out from the enemy camp. As they waited to make sure it was safe to cross they suddenly heard voices coming up the path towards them. Martin gave the hand signal that they should wait to see who it was. After about five minutes, two men in Chinese uniform, casually walked by where they were hiding just off the path. Once the soldiers had passed, Martin tapped Gabriel on the shoulder. Gabriel looked over, and Martin made the gesture of a knife sliding across his throat.

Gabriel nodded, then drew the knife out of the sheath attached to the shoulder strap of his plate carrier. Martin did the same while signaling the others to wait. They moved up behind the soldiers, quickly and quietly with carefully placed steps. Martin going for the left, Gabriel for the right.

Once they were close enough to strike, they both sprung into action. Cupping a hand over the mouth of each soldier, they simultaneously jammed their knives to the hilts into the side of each man's neck. As soon as the blade had been fully inserted they immediately pushed forward, forcing their razor sharp blades to slice through the soldier's esophagus on its way out. They then gently lowered the limp bodies to the ground as Jacob and James quietly moved over and grabbed their feet. They then carried them off the path and began to cover the bodies in the bushes. It was almost like they were one single person in four different bodies. Thinking the same, acting the same, and doing the same. All without even saying a word. It was like art, and Martin bet that they would be beautiful to watch, if they were ever to record their operations that is.

Once the bodies had been hidden under the brush off the path, they continued on. Moving like the shadows themselves, they stalked ever closer to their prey. Prey who had no idea they were even being hunted, or that they would only be alive for a short time longer. They stopped right at the edge of the trees to take stock of what they had waiting for them. Martin looked around for a few seconds, then he pointed to Jacob and James, then pointed at the two guards standing on either side of the front gate. He then pointed at his Scar 17, then to the guard up in the watchtower. All of them gave a quick nod of understanding, then James and Jacob both faded into the shadows as Gabriel turned to check their six.

Martin took aim at the man in the tower as he waited for the others to take out the guards by the gate. He didn't have to wait long. He saw the shadows moving, then in a blur of movement both guards had hands over their mouths, and knives in their necks. As the two gate guards were violently pulled into the darkness, Martin fired. The suppressor on his rifle masked the muzzle blast, but it couldn't cover up the sound of the bullet breaking the sound barrier. With a crack of sound the man in the guard tower collapsed, and with a sense of urgency that he knew the others felt too, Martin whispered.

"Move your ass."

# CHAPTER: 25

**L**IGHT was just beginning to appear on the horizon as Martin stood in the center of the concentration camp; the dead scattered on the ground all around him. It had only taken them mere minutes after entering the base to locate and dispatch the life of every soldier in the camp. No alarms were sounded, the enemies were all dead before they had the chance. There were only ten outside on patrol, being that it was 4am most were still in the barracks sleeping. After more or less silently eliminating all the soldiers outside, they moved inside. Drawing the short swords they kept on the backs of their plate carriers, they commenced to go from bed to bed, quietly ending the lives of every person sleeping in the barracks. Fifty six Chinese, NATO and American soldiers in all, died that night. If they were in that camp helping it run, they were all equally guilty, and therefore, were all killed without remorse.

This actually wasn't the first time any of them had deliberately, or intentionally taken a life. They had actually been doing it in training for the past year. With the help of Mr. Blank, they had hunted down pedophiles, rapists who escaped justice, corrupt police who were abusing both their power and the people, and they even assassinated a drug lord once. Blank would find them through registers and investigation, Martin and the others took care of the rest. They did not kill just anyone at the drop of a hat though. Every person they took out was always thoroughly researched beforehand to make sure they were actually bad enough to eliminate, without anyone innocent being harmed as a result. If the target had a family who they were good to, or if they were actually trying to better themselves, then some of the things that one did could be overlooked. However, every target that was found guilty was taken out quickly and quietly, and they were gone without a trace. They knew it wasn't their place and that they had no right to take these things into their own hands, but the justice system in America was broken. Those with money or the correct political leanings were judged lightly, and given lenience. While the poor and undesirable were judged with the harshest of punishments. In Martin and his team's eyes, a double standard of law means there is no law. All men were created equal, so all people must be judged equally. If not, there is chaos. Now that the Chinese had occupied the country though, none of that really even mattered anymore.

Martin looked down at the dead American soldier laying on the ground before him. He crouched down next to him and looked into his open staring eyes.

"Why did you have to betray us?" He said with a touch of sadness pulling at his voice. "If you had kept your oath to the people, you would still be alive."

This wasn't his first time killing someone, it was however, the first time he felt remorse for killing someone. This man had been a traitor, and deserved to die, but there was a chance he was probably just following orders like all idiots do, and didn't even know any better. Martin reached down and closed the man's eyes. Then he stood; looking over to check on how the rescue was going. Jacob was opening cages, Gabriel was passing out food and water he took from the dead soldiers and James was helping wrap blankets around women and children. Just then Martin noticed a young man slowly walking towards him. It was one of the ones that Jacob had just released.

"I just wanted to come over and say thank you." He said in a trembling voice.

Martin nodded but did not say anything in response.

"Please, will you take us with you." He pleaded with his hands folded together.

"We have nothing to offer you but the freedom you now have. Go back to your homes, and prepare for the revolution." Martin said in a flat tone that was slightly muffled by his cloth mask.

"The revolution?" The man said questioningly.

"Freeing you was a favor. We gave you your freedom back. It is your responsibility now to keep it." Martin said sternly.

"Oh, I see. I'm Brad by the way. What's your name?" He said as he stuck his hand out.

"Martin." He said as he shook Brad's hand.

"I will not forget this, Martin. Nobody will. When the war comes, we will fight."

"Brad, my friend. You need to understand something. The

war began the minute these bastards invaded. This is only the beginning of the war, and you need to get your shit together. The time to fight is now, and my team and I are going to fight, even if we have to go alone."

Martin and his team silently moved through the trees next to the road that led back to the bunker. They had waited at the camp until all the people had gotten out and were all on their way back to their homes. Some of the people that the team had freed took in others who lived too far away, or no longer had a house to go back to. It was only a matter of time before the enemy would discover what had happened, and they were worried about how they might retaliate. So with that on their minds they all agreed that they needed to be ready for anything.

It was a long tiresome trip back to the bunker, but they pushed through it and even jogged most of the way. As they drew nearer, Martin got an uneasy feeling again that something wasn't right, and as they rounded the last bend before the entrance, they all stopped dead in their tracks. To their horror and disbelief, the large door to the entrance of the bunker... had been smashed in. On the verge of complete panic, Martin rushed to the opening where the door had been. Shouldering his Scar 17 he entered the bunker, with his team on his tail scanning in all directions. Once they made it down the stairs they found the place had been completely ransacked and torn apart. With the muzzle of his rifle following everywhere his eyes went, he continued to scan and clear the rooms of the bunker.

"Ellis! Where are you?" Martin said. in an elevated yet demanding voice, just in case someone was still hiding down there.

"Clear!" One of them called from around the corner.

"There's nobody here, Martin." Gabriel said as he came walking into the room.

Martin lowered his rifle to rest on the sling attached to his shoulder. With his right hand still on the pistol grip, he used his left to rub his eyes with his thumb and first finger.

"Do you know why that's a problem, Gabe?" Jacob asked.

"Well yeah. Ellis and the kid are gone." Gabriel paused for a moment, pondering the word he had just said. "Ellis and the kid are gone... shit. My apologies, Martin. I was in battle mode and forgot that they were family and not just any ordinary civilians."

"It's okay, Gabriel. We'll find them." Martin said as he lowered his hand from his eyes and looked up. "What's the damage? Is there anything left that we can use?"

"The secret armory is untouched." Said James as he walked into the room. "They must have forgotten to check under the floorboards."

"Good, at least we'll be able to replenish our ammo and supplies before we go after them." Said Martin.

"I also found this."

James then handed Martin the metal rose that he had given to Ellis on their two month anniversary. Martin took it from him with an approving nod then put it into the side pocket of his backpack.

"How the hell did they find us so fast? We're in the middle of nowhere!" Gabriel said, kicking an empty crate.

"Someone must have followed us, and then waited for us to leave again so they could strike, and rob us." Said Jacob.

"I don't know, man. That door looks like it was hit with a battering ram, and only one group around here has that kind of portable machinery." Said James.

"Indeed, the Chinese and NATO." Gabriel said in answer to James.

"Why would it have to be portable? What if they were farmers and just used a piece of heavy machinery?" Jacob asked.

"Because there were no tracks. No, whoever did it, was on foot." Said James.

"Do you think that they might have tracked us via satellite or something when we took Gabriel's truck to Martin's in-laws house?"

"It's possible, but if they knew we were here, why would they allow us to leave and go attack their base?" Gabriel asked.

"Maybe they didn't see us leave." Said Jacob.

"Or they're laying a trap." Said James.

"That sounds pretty cliche, if you ask me." Said Gabriel.

"Sometimes the simplest answer is the correct one. And that's what it seems like to me." Said James.

"Enough, all of you." Martin said over them. "It doesn't matter. They have my wife and son. So I don't really care who it was, or where they are. We're going to track them down and we are going to kill them. Do you understand?"

They all went quiet and looked at the ground.

"You're right, Martin. How long until you want to head out?"

"Replenish supplies and ammo. Then run a full weapons and equipment check, and grab anything else you think we'll need. I wanna be out of here in ten minutes."

"Yes sir."

A second later they all dispersed to take care of the preparations. Martin never wanted to be the one in charge, but for some reason it always appeared that he just was, and the others didn't question it. He leaned up against one of the kitchen counters then looked at the overturned table where he had eaten dinner with his wife and son the night before. After staring at it for a while he knelt down to examine the clutter on the floor. He brushed around with his gloved hand for a few minutes, moving torn paper, broken glass dishes and other debris until his hand found something underneath some splintered wood from a broken cabinet. It was his wife's locket, simular to the one that he himself wore at all times. He picked it up and clenched it tightly in his hand as he put it to his forehead. After a few seconds of silent cursing, he put the locket into the right side pocket of his pants. As he did so he looked to his right, and underneath the cabinet he saw the blink of a little red light. He reached over and grabbed at the source of the light, a second later he withdrew a little square box, and instantly knew what it was.

"Ellis, you smart girl."

It was a tracking device receiver and he could plainly see on the digital screen, once he had clicked it on, that it was activated and receiving a location signal. Martin got up and walked down the hall towards where the others were. He entered the room holding up the small screen of the receiver so they could see.

"Boys, on the double. We have somewhere to be, and we need to get there now."

Martin looked at the tracking device receiver periodically as they moved through the thick woods. All of them were just about completely drained of energy by that point, and they were moving much slower than Martin would have liked. After a while he looked at the tracking device screen again. It showed that they were only about 100 feet out from the transmitter. Martin signaled the others to disperse in a flanking formation just in case something was waiting for them. Martin approached the transmitter alone. He moved the tall vegetation away to reveal something laying on the ground. He bent over to pick it up, and darkness suddenly overtook his eyes.

# CHAPTER: 26

*Washington DC, local militia sewer base.*

**B**RIAN... Hey Brian, wake up."
"What, what's going on?" Brian said as
he pulled his mind out of his sleep.
"Lynn, told me to come wake you. Apparently their leader,
Thomas, is finally back from his trip and wants to talk to you."

Brian sat up rubbing his eyes.

"Oh, hey Scarlet. You're up early." He said.

"Yeah. I wasn't very tired. Are you good?"

"Yeah, I'm fine. Tell them I'll be there in a minute."

Scarlet left the room and he just sat on the bed for a short while longer. Once he had woken up enough to stand, he arose from the bed and grabbed his pistol from underneath the pillow. He inserted it into its holster, then strapped it onto his hip.

As he walked into the large room to meet the others he saw Lynn and Scarlet both standing next to a man he hadn't met or seen in the time since they had arrived there.

"You must be, Brian. It's a pleasure to meet you." Said the man as Brian approached them.

"That's right. I'm guessing you must be, Thomas."

"That's correct." Thomas confirmed.

"I heard you wanted to see me?" Brian said as he stopped in front of them.

"Yes. Lynn, told me that you were willing to help us. So I thought we might go over some plans that we came up with using the information I gathered while I was away."

"What kind of information were you able to get?" Brian asked.

"Some of the information I got was actionable intel, some of it was just useful intelligence. I figured we should focus on the actionable intel first and move onto the other stuff if we have time."

"Sounds good. So what's the plan?"

Thomas set a brick of C4 explosive down on the table in front of them and locked eyes with Brian.

"Just hear me out." He said, pointing at the C4. "I don't know how you're gonna feel about this, but I think we should just like, blow up some of their shit or something."

"I'm listening." Brian said, crossing his arms.

"Okay, so I was able to get my hands on a whole crate of this stuff from an arms dealer I know in West Virginia. I was thinking if we could place it strategically on different things all around the enemies armaments, then we could inflict maximum damage without too much risk on our part."

"Who is the enemy anyway?" Brian asked. "I couldn't tell from where I was when I was observing them from the top of the building the other day."

"Mostly Chinese and some Russians, from what I've gathered., but I really don't care who they are. If you know what I mean."

"Yeah, that is as I suspected. It was kind of obvious actually. They really are the only nations who possess the strength required to invade America's homeland. Unfortunately."

"I don't disagree. They are very formidable foes for us. Especially since our tiny group has been the only thing that has shown any kind of push back since they landed on our shores." Said Thomas.

"Yeah. So back to the plan."

"Ah yes. I think we should place the explosives at the airport, here, here and around here." Thomas said pointing to spots on the map that was laying on the table. "I think that will cause the most destruction and confusion, which will hopefully give us enough time to get far enough away to evade being tracked down and captured."

"Sounds good to me. When do we head out?" Asked Brian.

"How soon can you be ready?"

"About five minutes. I've been down here for too long."

"Sounds good, I guess we'll head out in five minutes then." Thomas said before turning to the others. "Mission is a go, we're leaving in five."

Brian took his leave and walked back to the sleeping quarters to retrieve his M4 carbine and the rest of his gear. After completing his pre-mission equipment checks he walked back out into the main room to await departure.

"Are you ready to go?" Lynn asked as she walked past him, turning slightly as she went.

"Yeah. So, how many are going?" Brian asked as he began walking beside her in the direction of the tunnel's exit.

"We have twenty bricks of C4, so ten of us will be going, carrying two bricks each." She said, "That way we can spread it out better and faster."

"You all seem to have this pretty well thought out."

"Yeah, we had contingency plans for this already, but we did minor tweaking earlier to make everything specific to the situation."

"If only more Americans still thought like you guys, we probably wouldn't even be in this mess." Said Brian.

"Probably not, but we are in it, so the only thing we can do now is react. I just hope it's not all for nothing."

"Don't we all?"

When they made it to the ladder, Brian gestured for Lynn to go up first. As she started up the ladder Brian saw the other eight militia members in their company approaching down the passage in his direction. Once they all arrived they stopped and waited for their turns to climb up to the surface.

Brian made it street-side only a few moments after Lynn. Through the darkness he could see her waving at him to come take cover in the building she currently occupied. One by one the rest of their group followed. Once all of them had made it into the building, Thomas rehashed the plan one more time. He then split everyone into teams of two at random.

"Alright, you're with him, you're with her, you and you." Thomas said, as he pointed to each member of the team.

Brian was teamed up with a young man by the name of Tyler, who seemed eager, yet skilled enough in his own right. Judging from the information Brian gathered from some of the others, the boy was an orphan who had said that he joined the group simply because he wanted something to fight for.

"Snipers take either the windows or the building tops once we get there." Thomas said, looking towards the two men holding bolt action rifles. "If you choose to shoot from a window, just be careful not to make too much noise when you break the glass beforehand."

Both men only nodded their understanding. This made Brian realize that as far as he could tell, none of the members of this militia required any formal way of addressing Thomas, or each other. Which was fascinating to him, they seemed to just listen to his orders, and if they were reasonable then they followed them through.

Once the plan had been relayed and understood, they all dispersed in different directions to seek out their designated targets. It was very dark by this time so they used the cover of night to their advantage, sticking to the shadows as best they could. Brian and Tyler made their way to the fence that surrounded the airport, where the enemy was landing a portion of the many planes. Most were flying past the airport, heading farther inland, causing Brian to wonder how the rest of the country was faring, or if the rest of the world even knew what was going on. Not that it really mattered at this point. It was pretty much already too late. If what was happening now was any indication for the future, most Americans would be getting very hungry by now. And when normal spoiled Americans get hungry, they will all but beg to go to a concentration camp, if it means they get food or some false sense of security. Brian personally thought those types of people were absolutely pathetic, weak, a disgrace to the American way, and a detriment to the human race. True Americans would die before submitting to anything or anyone. Proud and stubborn, like the people currently in his company. They at least believed in something with enough conviction to risk their lives for it. Brian respected their bravery, he also respected their stupidity for going against such overwhelming odds without a second thought.

After locating a point of entry in the fence around the airport, Brian and Tyler made their way through the rows of parked Boeing 727's. They checked for guards as they went, then quietly snuck up beside of one of the large hangars. As soon as they were relatively hidden behind some cases, a guard suddenly walked into view about twenty feet away. He stopped and stood in front of the building for a second just looking around. After a few more intense minutes, he flicked his cigarette out then turned around and disappeared from view. They waited another minute or two, just to make sure he wasn't coming right back out, before quietly getting back up to resume their mission. Once they were both up, Brian pointed to a large fuel tank that was towards the back corner of the hanger.

They carefully moved over next to it, and Brian took off his backpack, retrieving one of the bricks of C4. He armed it, setting it to the time that they had all been instructed, then placed it on the fuel tank. They then moved onto the next hanger doing the same thing. Once they had placed Brian's charges they moved on to Tyler's designated target, which was the main air traffic control tower. Trying to get to it would be difficult, luckily for them however, Tyler was small, fast and agile. Brian figured that he probably wouldn't have too much trouble getting to the tower, setting the charges, and getting back safely.

They both crouched by the corner of the hangar and peeked around the edge to scan the area for guards. Fortunately, there were only a few of them out on the runway, so far as Brian could tell.

"They must not have the personnel required to guard the entire airport yet." Tyler said in a whisper. "Or maybe they're just not guarding as much at night."

"Doesn't really matter. We're gonna blow them to hell regardless." Brian responded as he placed his hand on Tyler's shoulder.

Tyler looked at Brian who held up three fingers then began putting them down one at a time. Tyler understood and prepared himself to run. On the count of zero, Brian took his restraining hand off and Tyler bolted for the control tower. He reached the base of the tower, taking off his backpack as he came to a sliding stop where he would plant the first of the explosives. He armed them both and after laying one of them down, he ran around to the other side and placed the second.

"Hey you, what are you doing!" Someone shouted in a deep Asian accent.

Tyler didn't wait around or even pause for a second, instead he took off at a full sprint in Brian's direction. Brian shouldered his M4 and took aim past Tyler. As soon as Tyler was out of the way he fired, hitting a man directly in the head. He then looked towards the tower and saw a man start reaching for one of the explosives. They just couldn't have that, so without hesitation Brian aimed and squeezed the trigger, a half second later the man was on the ground, writhing in pain. With both the potential pursuers now incapacitated, Brian turned and chased after Tyler. There was no way the entire airport didn't hear those gunshots and he was sure that there would be more coming. They would most likely be forced to blow the C4 remotely now, and earlier than they had planned. He just hoped they were all far enough away by the time of the detonation.

When he drew near to the spot in the fence where they had entered through, he wasted no time in slowing his pace. Instead he ran full speed and then broke into a slide barreling right underneath the fencing, tearing his pants and one of his sleeves in the process. Scratched and bloodied he carried on, catching up with Tyler a moment later.

"You good?" Brian asked.

Tyler, being well out of breath, only nodded.

"What's going on?" Said Thomas as he and a few of the others came running up to meet them.

"Blow the C4, now. We were seen." Brian said as he flipped up his Eotech X33 magnifier, then turned and aimed back towards the enemy. "They will undoubtedly figure out within the next ten seconds exactly what is going on, if you don't blow it right now.

"Where's everybody else?" Thomas asked.

"Hopefully well out of the blast radius because we are out of time. Hit the button now, Thomas!"

Thomas held out the remote trigger for the C4 and looked at it for a moment. He then looked to the sky, closed his eyes and clicked the button.

# CHAPTER: 27

## *Outside the Washington DC, Airport.*

**B**OOM!* The sound from the multiple explosions resonated through the still night air. The C4 had definitely done its job even better than they expected. They all looked at the burning airport. Planes were crumpled and broken, hangars were collapsed and on fire, and the control tower was now laying across the runway making it no longer usable. Brian turned to Thomas who was looking at the destruction they had wrought, his mouth hanging open in disbelief. Brian patted him on the shoulder and gave him a nod as to say well done. Then he turned and started heading for the city, to again take refuge underground.

"Are we heading back now?" Tyler asked.

"Yes, common everyone. Our work here is done." Said Brian.

As soon as he had finished saying the words, Lynn suddenly burst through the bushes coming towards them at a full run, showing no signs of slowing down.

"Run!" She said as she passed right by them.

They all looked at her in confusion as she went, then all at once they started after her. Being one of the most physically fit in their group, Brian caught up to her first.

"What's going on?" He asked as they ran.

"They're coming!" She said, trying to control the fear in her voice.

"Who is coming?"

"Who do you think?!" She shouted.

That's when they heard the sound of vehicles coming up the road behind them.

"Pick up the pace!" Brian yelled so everyone in their group could hear.

They continued running down the main street for a few blocks, then took a right onto a side street between two buildings.

"We should all split up, it will make it harder for them to catch all of us." Thomas said as he ran up next to Brian.

"Agreed." He responded. "Everyone split up, buddy system, pick a person and a direction and go!"

All at once, those who followed, broke off in pairs with whomever was closest to them. Disappearing to the left and right, down alleyways and side streets, or into buildings. Brian and Lynn continued running straight for a few more blocks before taking another side street. They then zigzagged randomly through the alleys, trying to throw off their scent as best they could.

Brian and Lynn ducked behind a dumpster and waited for the troop carrier to pass by. They had been running and hiding for hours but they finally made it back to the street right before the entrance to the underground. Since their pursuers had caught up with them and now had patrols frequenting the streets, they had been forced to move much slower. Brian looked down then bent over and picked up a small piece of rebar. Once the truck had passed and turned around the bend they made a break for the manhole cover. Brian sprinted then broke into a slide, skidding over and slightly past the lid. He shoved the piece of rebar into the small hole and lifted the lid. As soon as the lid was up, Lynn quickly slid into the hole and grabbed a hold of the ladder, immediately beginning to descend. As soon as she was out of the way, Brian spun around and saw the light from a vehicle's headlights shining on the building at the end of the street from around the corner. As quickly as he could while holding the lid with one hand, he stepped onto the ladder and took a few steps down so only his head was above ground. He held the lid for a few seconds as the headlights began to round the corner. He then carefully lowered the lid and waited for the truck to pass by before he continued to the bottom of the ladder. Once he arrived at the bottom, he found Lynn standing there waiting for him.

"It took you long enough." She said, still trying to catch her breath.

"There was a truck coming, I wanted to wait to see if it stopped."

"Sure you did, slowpoke." She teased.

"Probably." He said in an attempt to confuse her.

She didn't respond to it, so Brian figured it must have worked. She smiled sarcastically as he walked past her, then she followed him down the tunnel towards the underground camp.

## Somewhere in Pennsylvania.

Martin awoke to the sound of approaching voices. He was laying on the floor of a jail cell, his head throbbing with pain. He looked up and through his blurred vision, he saw Ellis holding Mark in the cell across from his own.

"Ellis! Are you alright?" He asked in a loud excited whisper.

She looked up with tears in her eyes.

"Martin! When they brought you in, I thought you were dead." She sobbed.

"I'm alright. Did they hurt you, how's Mark?" He asked urgently.

"We're both fine. What is going on?"

"They're smarter than we thought. We knew it was a trap so we counter acted for it but they still managed to capture me. I'm not sure what happened to the others, but I'm certain they are either around, or out there somewhere."

"How are we gonna get out of here?" She asked.

Just then the door flung open and three men walked in and came over to stand in front of Martin's cell. He slowly stood, staring with defiance into the eyes of the one in the center.

"You have been causing a lot of trouble for us in recent days. What are we going to do with you?" Said the Chinese man in the center.

"I'm a big fan of freedom. You could just let us go. Don't worry though, you're guilty so I will only kill you slowly and painfully."

"That's some big talk for a man in a cage." Said the Chinese man.

"This is only temporary. Soon I will get out, and I will stick a knife right in your stupid face."

"How ever did you come about such a foolish way of thinking?" The man asked with a chuckle.

"You underestimate the proud stubbornness that is the red, white and blue American blood."

"Well, in that case I guess we'll just have to deal with you before you have time to escape then."

The man stared at him with a smile curling the corners of his mouth, then he turned and started heading for the door.

"What do you want us to do with him, Commander?" One of the other two men asked.

"Let's teach him a lesson he'll never forget, for as long as he lives.

Even though that will only be a short time. Grab them all, and bring them outside."

"Yes sir." Said one of the Chinese soldiers.

"All of you turn around and face the wall." Said the other soldier as he pointed to Martin and then to his family.

"All of you? My son is only a few months old. He can't stand up yet. I think you meant to say, 'both' of you." Martin corrected.

The cell doors to both of their cells slid open with a loud clang. One of the soldiers walked up and roughly cuffed Martin's hands behind his back.

"Let's go, joker boy." Said the soldier.

"Come on, move it." Said the other as he pushed Ellis forward.

As they were all led outside, Martin looked around to get an idea of his surroundings. The place appeared to be set up similar to the base they had overtaken the morning before. There were cages of people and a razor wire fence around the whole camp. They were led through the gate on the far side of the camp, to the outside of the fence. Martin looked over his shoulder at the faces that watched as they were most likely being led to their deaths. Once they were about thirty feet away from the gate, they stopped and turned Martin around to face Ellis.

"kneel, both of you." Said the soldier next to Martin.

"I prefer standing." Martin responded.

He immediately felt a kick to the back of his knee that forced him to fall to the ground. Ellis glared at the soldier then with an expression of defiance, she stood taller. The soldier pointed his gun at Martin's head.

"I said, kneel."

Then in a loud enough voice for all to hear, she said.

"We are not afraid, and we kneel to no one!"

With an angry expression the soldier walked over to her and smacked her to the ground. Martin started to get up but the soldier noticed and pointed his gun at Ellis as she got to her knees.

"This is true power." The one in charge said with a smile.

"No it isn't." Martin laughed. "Power attained by using fear or inflicting pain is not power at all. It is a weakness underneath the illusion of strength. Power through pain is weakness, power through knowledge is strength. Using overwhelming numbers to beat up on the helpless, does not make you strong or powerful. The only ones who are strong and have power, are those who cannot be controlled, and also do not require subjects in order for them do what they wish. Power is dying when you wish to, freedom is dying without submission to another."

Tears began to form in Ellis's eyes as the soldier cocked back the hammer of the double action Beretta aimed at her head.

"Keep your eyes on me sweetheart. It's gonna be alright." Martin said with urgency.

With a smile the soldier snickered in amusement.

"Remember when you told me that survival was never part of the plan?" Ellis asked with a teary eyed smile.

"Yes. Life or death, I will see you soon either way. I love you. Are you ready?" Martin said while staring into the eyes of his beloved wife, kneeling in the mud across from him.

With tears now falling down her cheeks Ellis nodded, closed her eyes for a moment and mouthed the words.

"I love you."

Still smiling and aiming the pistol at Ellis's head, the soldier next to her looked at Martin.

"This is what happens when you go against the will of The Order! I am Commander Wong, let this be a lesson to all of you!" He yelled out for all to hear.

He then aimed the pistol at their son's head and pulled the trigger.

Martin, so full of anguish, did not even hear the sound of the gunshot as his infant son died. He watched with no expression as the muzzle of the gun then turned back to the head of his lovely wife. Again his ears did not even register the sound of the gunshot. His vision was far too focused on memorizing her features before she also died. As her body hit the ground, the lifeless body of his son rolled from her arms, head split from the bullet that passed through his soft fragile skull. While examining her face, Martin noticed her eyes were still looking all about, as if she was trying to find a way, or maybe just trying not to believe what had just happened. It's strange how even a shot to the head doesn't always kill immediately, it sometimes takes a few minutes for the moving to stop. She spasmed one last time and then she was gone.

Martin wondered as to why it was that he suddenly felt nothing. He was pretty sure he should have been feeling at least some sort of way about what he had just witnessed, but he didn't. It was as if his ability to feel had died with his wife and son. Commander Wong then turned to look at Martin.

"Your family is dead now. How does that make you feel?"

Martin stared directly into the eyes of the man who had just killed his family, and to the surprise of the three men around him, Martin smiled.

"Now, I am empty." Martin said as he began to laugh.

With a look of confusion the commander just scoffed then stalked over, pointed the pistol at Martin's head, and pulled the trigger.

*Click.*

The gun was jammed.

"Aww, that's too bad." Martin said in a mocking tone. "Don't worry, it happens to everyone."

With a scowl, Wong racked the slide, clearing the misfired round and took aim at Martin's head once again.

"Good luck." Said Martin.

The Commander squeezed the trigger.

*Bang.*

The gun went off at the same time that Martin twitched his head to the side; the round smacking the ground harmlessly behind him. The sound of the muzzle blast however, rang in his ears to the point of deafness. Before the commander or his two guards could process the speed in which he moved, Martin jumped up and kicked the Commander in the face. The force of the kick was so great that the pistol flung out of Wong's hand as he flew backwards through the air. In a flash Martin turned around to face the two men who had only just started raising their rifles to bear on him. In what seemed like slow motion Martin ran and leaped forward, kicking into the first with both feet, while simultaneously placing his hands on either side of the barrel of the second soldier's rifle. With the handcuff chain crossing the muzzle, the startled soldier pulled the trigger.

*Bang.*

As the bullet left the barrel, the chain was severed, freeing Martin's hands of the chain that bound him. Still horizontal to the ground with both feet still kicking into the first soldier, Martin's hands caught purchase on the second soldier's rifle. Martin then began to spin, pulling the rifle into his grip. He quickly found the trigger and pulled it. The round miraculously found its way into and through the shoulder of the Commander who was still laying on the ground. Martin continued to spin until the muzzle of his newly acquired rifle found its way around to the head of the soldier that his feet were still kicking into. He squeezed the trigger sending a round through the man's forehead. Still spinning, he moved his aim towards the head of the other soldier and pulled the trigger again. The round went up through the corner of the man's jaw and out the top of his head. It had only been ten seconds now since the Commander had fired the round that was meant for his own head. To Martin however, it had felt like ten minutes from the moment the gun fired, to the moment that he finally hit the ground. He quickly got to his feet and began observing his handiwork.

"All of that had happened in only a few seconds." He said as he looked down at his family. "A few seconds too late."

He thought maybe he was just in too much shock to grieve for them at this time, but he knew that one day, he would avenge them.

"Run!" A shout came from the cage of people inside the fence.

He then heard the alarm sound and a clatter of troops coming his way. The guard in the lookout tower was yelling frantically in Chinese, trying to bring his rifle up to aim at Martin.

"Run!" A few people in the cage shouted again.

"I'll come back for you!" Martin yelled as he turned and began running for the trees.

With rounds smacking the ground at his heels and whizzing past his head, he somehow managed to make it to the tree line. He didn't stop running till the noise and the clatter of troops and bullets, faded into the distance behind him. He ran as hard as he could, trying to put distance between himself and his pursuers. As time went on and the gunshots became more faint and less frequent, he began to grow very tired. He ran for a short time longer until he suddenly began to feel extremely weak. His adrenaline rush lasted for what seemed like hours, but now that it was beginning to wear off, he began to feel a little light headed.

"What the hell is going on with me?" He said, trying his best to shake off whatever was happening to him.

He attempted to push on, but as he took a few more steps, he began to feel faint and his vision was starting to go black around the edges. After taking a moment to mentally process his situation, he suddenly realized that his back felt wet and sticky. Slowing to a jog, he used his free hand to reach over his own shoulder to feel what it might be. When he brought his hand to in front of his face, he saw, to his displeasure, it was indeed blood. Slowing to a walk, he dropped the rifle that he had been holding, letting it fall carelessly to the ground. Then as he looked at his bloody hand once again, the scent of gunpowder residue suddenly became strong in his nostrils.

Taking a seat next to a tree he began to examine himself, trying to assess the severity of injuries. A few moments later he had gathered that he had been shot at least twice. Once on the left shoulder, and once towards the center of his lower back, to the left of his spine. Not wasting any time he quickly tore off the legs to his pants and tied one of them tightly around each wound. After sitting there for a few minutes to catch what breath he could, he decided it was time to continue on. He slowly stood up, and his vision immediately faded to complete blackness.

# CHAPTER: 28

**M**ARTIN awoke to the sunlight shining across his face. Confused, he wiggled his fingers, then moved his arms to see if he was restrained. To his relief, he was not. His vision was blurry but he could just make out that he was in a somewhat large room, lying in a soft bed that was pushed next to the wall on his left. He was covered up to his neck in a white blanket, which was actually quite warm and comfortable. He blinked rapidly trying to clear his vision to get a better idea of where he was. Once his vision was clear, he looked around to find that he was in a log cabin. The sun was shining through a small window above the bed where he lay, and he could hear birds chirping outside. After lying there a moment longer he decided he would try to get up and see where he was and how he got there.

He pulled the covers off his body and noticed his clothes had been changed. He was now wearing jeans and a tee shirt, which he had no idea how they got on him or to whom they belonged. He sat up slowly and instantly began to feel the pain from his bullet wounds shock through his body. He powered through the pain, then swung his bare feet out of the bed and onto the floor. That's when he noticed the IV drip that was attached to his right arm by a tube. He pulled the needle out, then attempted to stand up. He was a lot more sore than he had originally thought he was when he first woke up., but after his second attempt, he was on his feet and standing straight. He was wobbly, but he didn't think he would fall over or anything like that. Regardless, he moved slowly so as to not tear any of the bandages that he could now feel were on his back. Once he finally made it down the hall and to the door he paused for a moment to listen if there was any noise coming from outside. Hearing none, he turned the handle and opened the door just a crack to peek out. Satisfied there was no imminent danger he swung the door open and slowly moved outside.

"Well look who's up." Said a familiar voice.

Martin was stunned for just a moment before he looked over; his eyes falling on none other than Mr. Blank.

"Martin, this is Parker. He's the one who owns this cabin. He bugged out here soon after the bombs hit, when he saw the Chinese coming."

"What bombs?" Martin asked.

"You don't know?" Parker said, questioningly. "The Chinese dropped bombs on all or most of our military bases before making landfall."

"That's not surprising. How did I get here?" Martin asked.

"Well." Blank said as he leaned forward slightly. "When I got back to the bunker the morning after I went scouting, I found it was ransacked, with nobody to be found, so I began tracking you. After a few hours of walking, following your trail through the woods, I began to hear gunfire a ways off in the distance. Thinking it was probably you and the team, I decided to head towards it. After I walked for a while, I heard rustling coming towards me, so I took cover. I waited a few minutes for something to pass by. When nothing did, I peaked my head around the tree where I was hiding only to see you collapse onto your face. I then rushed over to see what happened and I noticed you had been shot twice. So I picked you up onto my shoulders and carried you till I ran into this fine gentleman who offered to help us. After he made sure we were Americans first, of course."

"I see. I guess I owe you both a debt of gratitude then." Said Martin.

"If you're killing the invaders. Your debt has already been paid, my friend." Said Parker.

"Thank you." Replied Martin.

"Oh, Martin, by the way, I have something for you." Blank said as he pulled out and presented Ellis's locket, the one that Martin had found on the floor of the bunker the morning that they were taken. "It was in the pocket of your old pants. I figured you would want it back."

Martin carefully took the locket from Blank with a nod of thanks.

"So what happened, Martin? Where is everyone?" Blank asked.

It all came rushing back to him. And Martin collapsed into the empty chair on the deck next to Mr. Blank.

"My wife and my son are both dead." Martin said flatly, without emotion while staring at the deck.

Parker looked up from his pipe and scowled.

"Those damn bastards." He said, shaking his head in anger.

Mr. Blank was silent for a long time just looking downward. He knew Martin's pain was much greater than he portrayed it to be, but he didn't press the matter.

"And the others?" Blank asked, finally.

"I'm not sure where the guys are. I imagine they probably got captured like I did. I didn't see them in the camp though, so they must've either been kept in a different area or I just didn't see them. Wait, how long was I out?"

"A little over a day. I found you the night before last."

"Then there is no time to lose. If they are captured we need to break them out before they're executed for being in league with me. I killed a few of them when I made my escape. I also promised the people there that I'd be back for them."

"You are in no condition for a rescue mission, young man." Parker said sternly. "Your wounds should have killed you. I'm honestly very much in disbelief that you're alive at all. But still, you're nowhere near healed up enough yet. You can barely even walk. I really don't know how you even got out of bed."

"I'll be fine by the end of the day." Said Martin.

"Like hell you will. Nobody heals that fast." Said Parker.

"He's right, Martin. You have to rest." Said Mr. Blank.

"I'll rest once I know for sure the guys are safe. I've lost enough, I can't lose them too. I'm leaving tonight to find them and you can't stop me. All I need is a rifle."

Parker and Mr. Blank looked at each other. Then after a second of hesitation, Blank spoke.

"Martin, you must look at this from a logical standpoint. If they are prisoners, there is no way you will be able to successfully get them out, while in your current condition. You will only get yourself killed along with everyone else there. Jacob, Gabriel and James are strong and smart. They can take care of themselves while you heal, and if they were here, you know that they would agree with me."

Martin looked at the ground and took a deep breath.

"You're right. In my current state, I'd only make things worse. I guess maybe you can stop me."

"I've got some special ointment my wife made that will help you to heal faster." Parker said. "I've been saving it in the event that I need it but I think now is as good a time as any to use it."

"You don't have to do that for me. You've already given me more than I could ask for." Said Martin.

"The way I see it is that you and your friends are the resistance to the communists. I am too old to fight, so I will gladly give everything I have in order to help rid our land of those pests."

"How long do you think it will take for your medicine to heal him?" Mr. Blank asked.

"I don't know, maybe a week or two if he's lucky and a fast healer, but I can't be certain until I see his progress over the next day or so."

"Well we're wasting time then." Said Martin.

"I'll get the ointment. Hold your horses." Parker said with a chuckle as he stood up.

Martin sat at the table in Parker's dining room just thinking about how to go about rescuing the others. He had spent the past week just resting and applying Parker's medicines to his wounds. By the fourth day he had been healed enough to walk around normally. By the seventh day he was back up to about 90% of his normal ability. The wounds still caused him discomfort and even pain at times, but he was now feeling well enough to at least find his team.

"Since strength in numbers is not on your side, I think it's probably best to have the element of surprise." Parker said as he entered the dining room carrying a black case.

"What's in the case?" Martin asked.

"Something I think you will like."

Parker lifted the case onto the table and flung it open. Inside was a black compound bow and a quiver of arrows.

"I do also have the tools to set the peep hole, poundage and draw length to your specifications."

"You are incredible, Parker. I will be forever in your debt."

"Don't mention it." Parker said with a chuckle. "It belonged to my son, he's no longer around and I am too old to use it anyway."

Martin paused then asked.

"You have a son? If you don't mind me asking. What happened to him?"

"He was a marine. I stopped hearing from him after the day of the attack."

"I'm sorry. I know how it feels to lose someone you love." Said Martin.

"Meeting someone who has also lost someone close to them seems all too common these days."

"What was his name?" Martin asked.

Parker looked up from the coffee cup he now held in both hands.

"Oh, his name was, Brian, Brian Parker."

"So it's your last name that is Parker?"

"That's correct. My first name is Elijah."

"Would you like to talk about him? Your son, Brian."

"Oh, no. I'll be fine. I'd rather not think about it all. What about you? Would you like to talk about your family?" Parker asked with a touch of sadness pulling at his voice.

Martin stared at the table for a long time without speaking.

"My wife will forever be the most important woman I've ever known." Martin said flatly. "Losing her was definitely a great misfortune, and a detriment to my life. I new her well, and I loved her greatly. However, the loss of my son stings in a different way, because I will never even get the chance to know him. Or to see the kind of man he would become."

"Five years ago, after I lost my wife to cancer, my son was all I had left. Then when they bombed Quantico, the base my son was stationed at, I realized that he was now dead too. I was so paralyzed by grief that for a long time I could barely move about. You are definitely stronger than I am, Martin. But just so you know, it is okay to let it out in situations like this."

"To show emotion is to show weakness." Martin said, even though he could feel a sense of sadness starting to well up inside him.

He lowered his head in thought. The memories that were once so happy, near and dear to his heart, now held nothing but emptiness. He remembered the day of his wedding, when Ellis, so breathtakingly beautiful, walked down that aisle in his backyard with her father. The day in the hospital when he held his son for the first time. All the happy memories of back when he had everything he ever wanted, now only brought anger and disgust. To the point that he found no relief, and no happiness in their remembrance.

Blank was sitting cross legged in the corner of the living room and upon hearing Martin's words, he looked up.

"One day, everything you have will be gone." Said Blank from where he sat on the floor.

After a few seconds of silence Martin raised his head.

"Everyone we know will be dead."

"And every moment that we have lived will be forgotten." Blank finished.

There was a pause before anyone spoke again.

"Emotions are human, Martin. You can find strength in them, but by having them you can never become more than human."

Martin turned to face Blank, then he said.

"I will never allow myself to revel in sorrow. I will become better. I will become more."

Once Martin finished speaking, Blank gave him a nod of approval then stood up and without another word, walked outside to the porch.

# CHAPTER: 29

**T**HERE, that should do it." Parker said, putting the final torque onto the compound bows upper cam; finishing with the adjustments. "Here, give it a try, I wanna see how well it fits you." He said handing the bow and an arrow to Martin.

"Thank you, Parker." Martin said; taking the bow in his hand. "You have done so much for me, and yet you've asked for nothing. What is there that I can do to pay you back?"

There was a pause and Martin's words hung in the air for an almost uncomfortable amount of time.

"If you ever come across my son, dead or alive." Parker said finally. "I would like to know. In this situation, any news is better than no news. So, if it's not too much trouble, please find out what actually became of him."

Martin nodded his acceptance to the mission, then he turned towards the door.

"If it's alright with you, I'm gonna go sit with Blank for a while." Said Martin.

"Of course. You go on, I'll clean up here and take care of the tools."

"Thank you, Parker."

Martin then walked out onto the porch where Mr. Blank was sitting.

"I'm going to get my team back tonight." Martin said as he sat down next to Mr. Blank. "For such a short amount of time, I feel better than I thought possible. So I figure I better get on with it."

"Indeed, you've healed quickly, my friend. I think you're well enough now to do what you must do."

"Are you not coming with me?" Martin asked.

Mr. Blank looked off into the distance.

"The time has now come for me to be on my way, Martin."

"What? Where are you going?"

"It is time for me to stop fighting it and do what my father put in place for me."

"Your father? What are you talking about?"

"I was trained for many years to be a killer, that however was not what I was meant to do. I have killed many... many people in my life, Martin. More than I can remember. So to repent for some of those things which I have done, I tried to live my life differently. I tried to find people like you to train to become more than just human. To become better. That way, once that which has been prophesied has come to pass, people will be able to look to you, and find hope. I have come to realize that I am not good enough at heart to do this. There is far too much evil inside me, that I can no longer ignore the duty that I was sent to do."

Martin stared at Mr. Blank with a confused look.

"I must leave soon." Blank continued. "So I will ask you this now. As my friend and most dedicated student, are you willing to take this burden upon yourself? Are you willing to do as I have done and to complete what I attempted? Are you also willing to never show your face to anyone ever again, for as long as you live?"

"What? Never show my face to anyone at all?" Martin asked.

"You may choose one living person to reveal your face to. Choose wisely though, for if you change your mind, then that person must die."

"Seems reasonable enough. Very well, if it is what you wish for me. So be it. I have nothing left anyway."

Blank paused for a moment, then he said.

"My words have always been spoken in truth, Martin. If you are afraid to lose anything, then you will lose everything. There is another part to this saying though. It goes as follows, 'Those who have lost everything, have the potential to achieve anything'. You were afraid to lose them, Martin. Therefore you did. You had every right to feel everything you felt, they were your family, but now that there is nothing that can be used against you, there is nothing that can control you. Every negative has an equal positive. If you allow yourself to see the positive and use the negative to give structure to your strength, then there is no force great enough to stand in your way."

With his eyes staring downward, Martin put his hand on Blank's shoulder and shook him gently. Blank nodded then he reached up, removed his hood and un-clipped his mask so that it fell away from his face. He then removed the helmet, revealing the rest of his head. With his mask finally removed for the first time ever in front of Martin, he saw a face with young handsome features, a shaved head, and pale white skin. So pale in fact was his skin that it looked as though it had never been touched by the sun ever before. Martin looked on in total surprise at the face of a man whom he had always assumed would be much older, but was actually no older than Martin himself.

"How old are you?" Martin asked in a somewhat stunned tone.

"In human years, I am twenty six." Said Blank.

"You are younger than I am, how can this be? And how old were you when you started your training to become a killer?"

"I was seven years old when I was adopted into that life."

"That's so young. How old were you before you started killing?"

"Do you remember how old I said I was when I first covered my face?"

Martin looked at him with a questioning expression for a few moments, then his eyes went wide.

"You were nine the first time you killed someone?!" He said in surprise.

"I did not actually ask for my life to be this way. My story was written long ago. I am simply playing the part. For today I am human, tomorrow I am not. As for my age. My body may still appear to be young, my mind however is as old as time."

"What do you mean?"

"Life is strange, Martin, but death is stranger. I have seen the beginning and the end, and all eternity in one moment. The experience was so overwhelming that my human mind did not have the capacity to contain the information. So in order to return to this life with all the knowledge I acquired, it was necessary that I become more than human."

"What do you mean, more than human, I am very confused?"

"The supernatural has a way of doing things. And when things in the natural world aren't going in the direction that they desire, they send people to manipulate the way things are going in order to get them back on the proper track.

"This is too much all at once." Said Martin. "Life is becoming too complicated."

"You will remember it yourself soon enough. In only a short time, you will understand exactly what it is that I am talking about. Because you yourself have witnessed it."

"What's the point though? I tell ya, sometimes I think it would be better to just put a gun to my head and hit the delete button so I don't have to worry about this shit anymore."

"No, Martin You must live." Blank said sternly.

"But what if I've had enough, and I don't want to do what I must anymore." Said Martin.

"If that was the case, I would tell you to stop being a weakling. You need to understand something, Martin. There is nothing in this life more deserving of punishment in the next, than self-inflicted death. The level of absolute weakness someone must possess in order to do something like that, astounds me. I have no respect or sympathy for those of such pathetic weakness that they do not even have the strength to live, or the patience to die at their set time. I have died once and I remember it very well. Your troubles do not leave you with the death of your body. Instead they increase in clarity and all of them at once, instead of simply one or two at a time. The difference is that in this life you can overcome them, whereas in the next life you have to live for eternity with the remembrance of everything you did not overcome. You do not have to believe me, be patient and you will see for yourself soon enough when you remember. This temporary existence in which we currently live is either a prison, or a paradise. It can not be both, it can not be neither. You must make a choice. What mindset will you have, Martin? Are you in paradise, or prison?"

"It's all in how you look at it." Martin said rhetorically.

"Correct. I will forgive it this time, but you will never again speak of ending your own life. You will die when it is your time, and not a moment sooner."

"Okay." Martin said, looking at the ground.

They sat in silence for a while, then Martin asked.

"Why did you wait till now to reveal your face?"

"This was always my plan. I had to make sure that you were worthy enough to wear it as I wear it. I now know that with your face also behind it, this mask will become the symbol of true freedom that I always envisioned it would be. The freedom to die at the exact moment you are meant to. This is why I did not reveal my face, and why you must not either. People like us must not allow others to see what we look like. Because if they know my face they will know my works. And if they know my works they will know my charity. And if they know my charity, my works and my face will become my pride. And my pride will in turn become my destruction. For pride and destruction have always walked hand in hand. That is why we must never show our faces. I did it all these years to set an example for you. To prove that people can trust you and be your friend even without ever seeing your face. You must now take up the mask and wear it until the end. And just as I have, you must find more people like yourself to carry on this burden. As I have done so also will you do. This is the only way it can be stopped."

"The only way what can be stopped?" Martin asked looking over at Blank.

"You must find that out on your own when the time is right. I will however tell you this. When the time comes do not hold back, do not give in, fight until the very end, no matter what or who is in the seat of your enemy." Said Blank as he presented Martin with a box.

Martin took the box and opened it. Sitting on top was a new set of PVS-31 night vision goggles.

"I noticed you must have lost your old set when you got captured." Blank said. "Just try not to lose them again. Night vision is extremely hard to come by these days."

Martin set the night vision down beside him, then he reached in and withdrew a mask that was very similar to the one that he knew all too well. He held it up, looking into the eyes of the face he had always known as Mr. Blank.

"Ramiel." Said Blank as he leaned back in his chair while putting his mask back on; covering his face and head.

"I'm sorry, what was that?" Martin asked.

"That's my real name. Ramiel Asmodeus."

There was a click sound that came from his mask and then Ramiel stood up from his seat. Before Martin could ask anything else Ramiel walked across the deck, down the steps, across the yard, and disappeared into the trees without looking back. Martin watched him as he went. It was actually quite a curious thing. Even though he didn't even know who Ramiel even he was still the closest friend Martin ever had, and he would always love him like a brother. The brother he hadn't even gotten the chance to know, or the time to understand.

Martin sat alone on Parker's deck for some time, thinking and wondering how he could possibly fill the shoes, or more accurately the mask that he now had to wear. As he sat there, he suddenly noticed the sun reflecting off of something on the other side of the chair where Blank, Ramiel, had been sitting. Martin reached over and grabbed it. It was a case that was a little bigger than a briefcase, with Martin's name engraved on the tag. He set the case across his knees, then pulled the latches and opened it. Inside was a tactical looking black suit made of cloth and leather. It actually seemed to be extremely well made as far as he could tell. He pulled the suit out of the case to get a better look at it. Holding it up with arms outstretched, he could see that it was most likely made for stealth, but could also be for combat, being as it appeared to have built in ballistic armor plates, and a full climate control system running through it. He examined it for a few moments then looked back into the case, there sitting at the bottom, was a book with a black cover. He put the suit down on the chair next to him then pulled the book from the foam cushioning of the case. The single word inscribed in gold on the cover read "Existence." His curiosity was now quite peaked, so he moved the case off his lap and placed it onto the deck in front of him. He then carefully opened the book to the first page and began reading.

Later that day, Martin stepped out onto the front porch dressed from head to toe in the all black suit that Ramiel had left for him. He had entered the house as Martin, and emerged as the new Mr. Blank. He threw his hood up, looked over to Parker who now sat where Ramiel had been sitting a few hours before. They nodded to each other, then Martin hefted his new bow, tightened the straps to his backpack and quiver of arrows, then walked down the steps and away from the cabin.

# PART: IV

*"Believe nothing to be true, but anything to be possible."*

# CHAPTER: 30

## *Washington DC, Militia Sewer Base.*

**C**OME on, Brian. I'm done being cooped up down here." Scarlet said in a typical teenage style groan. "Let me go help scavenge with the others."

"Since when did teenagers start asking to do chores?" Brian asked, looking up from the table with a confused expression.

"Since they were kept in a sewer for days at a time." She said, "I just wanna breathe some fresh air and feel the sun on my face."

"Who will be going with you?"

"All the other kids and teens."

"Do all the kids do the scavenging?"

"Uhh, yeah. Where have you been this whole time?"

"Apparently not paying attention to what the children are doing."

"So, can I go."

"Yeah, sure. Just be careful."

"Sweet! Thanks, Brian!" She said with a big smile as she ran off.

"I'm not your dad, kid. Why do you keep acting as though I am?" He said just loud enough for himself to hear, but not loud enough for anyone else to.

It had been almost two weeks now since the invasion, and he still hadn't been able to go back to the crash site to collect the bodies of his fallen brothers in arms. However, he did have every intention of doing so as soon as the time allowed. But if fate decided otherwise, at least they were on American soil, and inside an American aircraft. He figured that was at least better than nothing anyway. Pulling himself out of his thoughts, he walked over to the other table that acted as the planning station of their war room and sat down in one of the chairs. Thomas and Lynn were standing on the other side of the table leaning over one of the maps of the city.

"It won't work." Thomas said while pointing at the map. "I'm telling you right now that it's a bad idea."

"It will work, we'll just have to have everyone go at different times so that we aren't identified as a group." Said Lynn.

"What are you two going on about?" Brian asked.

They both turned and looked at him sitting in the chair across from them.

"We're discussing our plan of escape." Said Thomas. "It's getting to the point that it is no longer safe here."

"Yeah, but this big dummy thinks it's a good idea to try to drive out." Said Lynn.

"Yeah, that might have been a good idea a week ago. But now that we've actually declared war on the invaders, there will be no driving unless your plan is to get captured." Said Brian.

"That's what I've been trying to tell him."

"I'm sorry, Thomas, but for whatever my opinion is worth, I'm gonna have to side with Lynn on this one."

"Yeah yeah, I know. I'm just worried about the youngsters making the trip on foot."

"We should only have to walk until we're out of the city. Then we can get a vehicle that can carry everyone to wherever it is we decide to go. We should actually send some runners to the outskirts of the city to find and position vehicles for us before we leave." Said Brian.

"That actually makes a lot of sense." Thomas said. "This is why a counsel of people is always better when you're making a plan. You sometimes miss things when you have just one or two people."

It was nearly dark by the time Scarlet and the other kids got back from scavenging. They had managed to scrounge up an entire wheel barrow worth of non perishable foods from surrounding apartments and other buildings.

"This should be enough for at least a couple of days. Good job, all of you." Thomas said as he looked at the kids' success.

"Does this mean you'll let us go out farther next time?" Scarlet asked with excitement.

"Don't push it." Brian said as he walked up to greet them. "It's still dangerous out there and the farther out you go the more likely you are to get caught and questioned."

"But there's other people with kids still in the city. We could just say we were playing."

"They have passports, and even those people are still under curfew."

"Brian, is right." Said Thomas. "It's better to play it safe and stay within the area that we know the enemy doesn't patrol as often. Going out a little farther is not worth getting captured over. Let's just stick to the current perimeter for the time being."

"Don't worry about it though, kid." Said Brian. "We're heading out of the city sometime in the next couple of days. So hopefully wherever we end up, it will be safe enough that you can go as far out as you please."

"Oh, alright. I just wish you'd lighten up a little bit, and stop treating us like a bunch of children."

"You are a bunch of children."

Without arguing farther, Scarlet crossed her arms and let out an aggravated huff.

"You can be as angry about it as you want." Said Brian. "But one day you will learn, one way or another, that being young and following orders is a hell of a lot easier than being old and giving the orders."

"That's easy for you to say because you are old, and speaking from a position of power." Said Scarlet.

"When you become an adult, you will see that things are not as easy as you might think. The biggest difference between the young and the old in situations like this is that when you make a mistake, you die, whereas when we adults make a mistake, everyone dies. That's the difference. Which one would you prefer?"

Scarlet didn't know how to respond to that. She actually wasn't even entirely sure what he meant exactly. So she just looked at the ground and hoped they would all leave her be.

"Oh leave her alone you two." Lynn said as she came over to see what they were talking about. "She's just adventurous and wants to explore new parts of the city."

"That may be so, but is it worth compromising our whole group over? I didn't think so. There will be time to go exploring once we get to somewhere with less, or preferably no hostile forces. That sound good? Great. Good talk." Brian said with a smile as he dismissed himself.

## Somewhere in the forest, Pennsylvania.

Martin slowly crawled up and peaked over the top of the hill that overlooked the base where his family had been killed only a week prior. Seeing the place again now, with the memories still so vivid in his mind, under normal times he probably would have become emotional. This time however, he did not. He was just as empty now as he had been right after it happened. It was a curious thing, feeling nothing. It was actually quite odd to Martin how pain born of such extreme and overwhelming sorrow broke his ability to feel. It was as Ramiel had said long ago.

"Emotions are a weakness that allow you to feel fear. Without emotions there is no fear, and in the absence of fear there can only be strength."

As he looked around scanning the area, his eyes suddenly and unexpectedly fell upon the back of a masked head. Surprised that he only just now spotted him, Martin reflexively ducked down a little and took out his knife. After taking a moment to size him up, Martin began to stalk closer. As he made his way up behind the man, something on the man's shoulder caught his eye. He carefully leaned over to get a better look, and right there like a shot of pure relief he saw the familiar patch of the STFU. The same patch that he himself was currently wearing on his own shoulder, was also on the shoulder of this man in front of him. He slowly and silently put his knife back into its sheath, then bent over and picked up a small rock. After looking at the man for a few seconds he realized that he was actually asleep. Martin shook his head in disapproval, then he released the rock. It flew through the air and hit the man right on the side of the head. His hand came up in a flash to nurse the sudden pain, and he quickly realized that he had fallen asleep. Seeing Martin out of the corner of his eye he quickly drew his handgun and aimed at Martin who put his hands up as if to surrender. The man quickly registered who he was aiming at and lowered his gun.

"Mr. Blank, what are you doing here?" He said in a hushed impatient tone.

"It's a long story, Jacob. I'll explain later."

Jacob raised one eyebrow and cocked his head to one side in puzzlement.

"Wait, why do you have Martin's voice?"

"Because, I am Martin. I'll explain later. Where are the others?" Martin said as he moved past him.

Jacob turned towards Martin with his hands out to his sides in a questioning shrug.

"Why are you wearing his clothes? Bro, wait up." He said in a loud whisper as he chased after Martin.

Martin took a knee at the edge of a ridge that overlooked the enemy's base. Jacob caught up with him a few seconds later and crouched down beside him.

"Where are the others? Gabriel and James?" Martin asked, turning to Jacob.

"James got captured about an hour after you did. He went to scout out a way to get you out, but they were waiting for him. After that, Gabriel and I had to retreat to try and come up with a plan to get you both out. We knew we couldn't take the base with just the two of us. So after about a day of thinking, Gabriel came up with the idea to get himself purposefully captured as a citizen and try to get you out that way. He dumped all his gear so that he looked like a normal citizen, then he went to the camp saying he was seeking shelter. They must've bought it because they took him in gently. Wait... How did you get out? We never saw you leave."

"You were about a day too late. I was only there for abaot a half hour or so, I think."

"Did you get Ellis and Mark to safety?" Jacob asked with excitement.

Martin paused for a moment before answering.

"They are safe."

"That's great! Where are they? Do we have a forward operating base set up?"

"They didn't leave the camp with me. There's no forward operating base." Martin said without looking his way.

Shocked, and slightly confused by this new information, Jacob wasn't exactly sure what to say.

"So any idea how we're gonna get the guys out?" He asked, deciding to just change the subject.

"Wait for nightfall, go in, kill everyone who isn't an American citizen, grab the guys, get out."

"Do you really think that just you and I can pull it off?"

"If you want to stay here, I will not hold it against you."

"No, I'm going. I was just curious if you're thinking clearly." Jacob said with a sideways glance.

"My mind has never been more clear, Jacob."

"Well, alright then. I guess we're doing rescue mission stuff tonight. This should be fun."

The shadows lengthened as the afternoon drew the night.Martin sat with his back against a tree, holding both of the very simular lockets that he and his wife had shared. With one in each hand he stared into the gap between them, where even though the distance was small, the longer he looked at it the larger it appeared to grow. As he stared he began to remember the day he had given her the other matching locket. He closed his eyes and allowed himself to be absorbed into the memory.

"You really didn't have to bring me to such a fancy place, you know." Ellis said, sitting across from him on the other side of the table. "I would have been fine with anything really."

"Alright then, fast food it is." He said as he took the napkin off his lap and stood up, holding out his hand to help her out of her chair.

"Oh sit down, you big goof." She said, gently slapping his hand away. "I'm not saying I don't actually really wanna eat here. I do. All I'm saying is that you don't have to spend money on me. I'm fine with even just going for walks in the park."

"If I'm being completely honest, I came here because I wanted to. You just always seem to tag along with me for some reason." He said with a shrug.

She put her hand to her chest, and her mouth dropped open in surprise and shock.

"Heavens! How dare you." She said in astonishment. "I'm just kidding, I know it's because it's our 6 month anniversary."

"Correct. I'm actually impressed that you remembered." Said Martin.

Ellis scoffed.

"It's supposed to be the guy that forgets important things. It's not my fault that you have such a stupidly good memory."

"Nope, your compliments and female trickery no longer work on me, sweetheart." He said in jest.

"We'll see." She said while flicking her hair over her shoulder.

They stared into each other's eyes for a short time. Until Martin broke their eye contact by dangling a necklace between them. She looked at it, smiled and rolled her eyes.

"Didn't we just finish discussing how you don't need to spend money on me?" Ellis said with a smile.

Martin got up and moved around to stand behind her, holding the necklace in front of her with both hands.

"I didn't spend money on it. I made it. It is close to an exact copy of the one I wear."

She looked up at him then held her hair out of the way so he could put it around her neck. She let her hair fall back to her shoulders, then got up and hugged him tightly.

"You're the best, Martin. How is it that you're so good to me?"

"Because, I love you." He said.

She hugged him tighter. To the point he thought she might be trying to break him. Then she responded.

"I love you too."

"Hey, are you asleep?" A hushed voice came from a few feet to his left.

Martin lifted his head from where it had been leaning back, resting against the tree. He then shook his head without expression. Not that Jacob would be able to see through the mask anyway.

"It's about time to go." Jacob whispered. "It should be completely dark within the next few minutes."

Martin looked off to the horizon where the last glimmer of light was fading into darkness.

"Good. Let's get this over with."

Martin grabbed his bow and they began heading in the direction of the camp. The place where their enemies would soon be laying their heads down to sleep, for the last time.

# CHAPTER: 31

**M**ARTIN and Jacob silently moved through the trees that surrounded the Chinese concentration camp. They worked their way around until they came to the spot with the least amount of open ground between the tree line and the fence surrounding the camp. Martin then knocked an arrow to his bow string and he exited the cover of the trees. With Jacob right behind him, Martin followed the shadows as they made their way to the recently installed outer fence. He looked around for the best source of entry, then looked down to where the fence met the ground.

"Lazy bastards. They didn't even bury the bottom portion here." He thought to himself as he grabbed a hold of the fencing and lifted it so they could duck underneath.

Once on the inside, Martin hand signaled Jacob to go in the direction of the captives. Martin knew that he would know what to do. So as Jacob disappeared into the darkness Martin decided that he would head for the barracks. On his way there, he spotted two men sitting on the porch of a house trailer that was located towards the center of the camp. He made his way around the crates and vehicles that were sitting off to the side, then he quietly stalked forward to get a closer look. The men were both sitting across from each other, chatting as if they didn't have a care in the world. Martin moved to a better position then raised his bow. He had practiced with it a little after it was given to him, but even in that short time he had become extremely proficient with it. The muscles in his back stung slightly from his injuries as he drew the bow back to full lock, but the pain was manageable. He then took aim at the head of the soldier closer to him, and squeezed the release. His aim was true, and the location he chose to shoot from was perfect. The arrow soared through the air, through the first man's head, and into the throat of the man sitting beyond him; pining him to the wall while the first fell out of his chair onto the ground. Neither of them even had the chance to scream.

As soon as Martin had loosed his arrow he was on the move. The clock was ticking now, and he had no time to waste. He silently swept through the camp in the direction of the barracks, killing three more soldiers on the way there. One had been sitting with his legs propped up on a table drinking coffee and playing on his phone. Martin's knife had slid into the side, then out the front of his fleshy neck with ease. The other two were standing next to each other off to the side of the main building. One got an arrow through the side of his head, as Martin silently ran, and the other got decapitated by a swing of his sword as he passed between them. Martin then rounded the corner and headed for the entrance to the barracks. That's when he saw another soldier standing on the porch.

With his short sword still in his hand he leaped into the air, kicked off the wall and hacked his blade halfway through the of the man's head. He then kicked him away; forcing him to fall off the porch onto the soft grass below. After the dead man had landed softly on the ground, Martin turned and opened the door slowly. He then slipped inside without a sound.

"You think they would have learned by now." He thought to himself as he set his bow down next to the door and readied his already blood soaked sword.

He approached the first cot holding his sword with the hilt next to his face, in a pose ready to strike. Gripping the tip of the blade with his other hand, he gently directed the point to his first victim's throat. With one quick, silent, fluid motion, the blade was plunged into the soldier's throat; down through the space between his fourth and fifth vertebrae, severing at least most of the eight pairs of nerves in his cervical spinal cord. Leaving the soldier in almost complete paralysis to mitigate the risk of him making any noise as he died. When Martin removed his blade it left an inch and a half wide sideways hole through the man's throat. If the move was executed well enough, the victim would normally drown in their own blood before they would have the chance to make a sound. Skipping over an empty bed he moved on to the next sleeping, soon to be dead soldier in line, who was unfortunately sleeping on his side.

"Too difficult to aim." Martin thought before leaning down and gently whispering into the man's ear. "lay on your back."

To Martin's surprise, the man obeyed, and with a groan, he turned to lay on his back. Martin swiftly ended him just as he had the first, then he moved on to the next, then the next, then the next.

Fifteen nearly perfect kills later Martin heard a door open then close. He quickly stabbed the man he was currently standing over, missing his spine by about an inch. The man coughed a little as Martin withdrew his blade, so he lined back up and tried again. His aim was better this time and it quickly ended the man's life as he had done the rest. After mentally noting the count to be sixteen, he quickly moved to the darkest corner of the room. As soon as he was hidden, a man walked into the room in shorts and a white T-shirt, tiredly moving towards the empty bed. Martin waited patiently for the man to lay down. Counting this newcomer there were only seven left for Martin to eliminate. He silently wondered if the bastard who killed his family was in there somewhere.

"Not likely." He thought. "With the amount of smugness that asshole had, he was definitely an officer and probably had his own personal room."

The tired man sat down on his bed rubbing his face and Martin began to move his sword out from behind his back. He then suddenly stopped at the sound of a loud bang that originated from the far side of the camp. The man's head whipped around in the direction of the sound as he stood up from his bed. Probably with the intention of investigating the source of the bang. Unfortunately for him, it was time to go.

On silent feet Martin rushed across the room and slashed. The man's hands shot to his throat, his eyes wide in surprise as crimson blood gurgled from his mouth and between his fingers. He stared at Martin in shock as he fell back to sit on his bed. Martin turned away from him, and walked back over to continue dispatching the rest of the sleeping soldiers. Leaving him to helplessly sit there watching as he himself slowly died.

Martin looked towards the man who was looking at him, then he stabbed the last sleeping man without looking away. The man still sat on his bed holding his throat trying to breathe through the blood as Martin moved over next to him. Putting a hand on his shoulder and patting twice he leaned in next to the man's ear and whispered.

"This was all completely personal."

He then raised his sword, and with an expertly precise movement, he inserted the blade into the space between where the man's shoulder met his neck; plunging the cold steel down through his heart. The soldier's hands then fell away from his neck and Martin withdrew his blood soaked sword. As the man began to fall to the side, Martin turned and started for the door. He heard the thud of the man's head hitting the metal bar of the bed frame, but his work was done, so without looking back he walked out of the room and left the building.

Once he was outside in the night air again, he heard another explosion from the other side of the camp. He took off at a full sprint in the direction of the blast. And as he rounded the corner of the building, a green Hummer appeared out of nowhere, nearly running him over.

"Get in, jackass, we gotta go!" James said from the passenger seat as the back door flung open.

Without hesitation, Martin jumped into the open door, shutting it as soon as he was in the seat.

"Where's, Martin?!" Gabriel shouted as he slammed his foot down on the accelerator.

"This is, Martin!" Jacob yelled. "He said he'll explain later!"

"Why is he wearing Blank's clothes?" Gabriel asked.

"It's a long story. I'll tell you once we are somewhere safer." Said Martin.

"Okay, sounds good to me. I'm done with this shithole!"

He turned hard to dodge a parked Jeep then tore through the grass and blew through the gates without even slowing down.

"Did you get the rest of the civilians out?!" Martin yelled over the sound of the roaring engine and rushing wind.

"Most of them! But I don't think the rest will have any problems escaping. What with pretty much all the guards being dead." Gabriel laughed loudly.

"If they're all dead, then why are you driving like we're being chased?" Martin asked.

"For cinematic effect! And because after being in prison for the past few days, I wanna go fast!" Gabriel said, leaning back to look at Martin for a few seconds.

Returning his eyes towards the road, he then stuck his head out the window and yelled.

"The boys are back together again, baby!"

"Don't forget your stuff, Gabriel." Jacob said from the back seat.

"You're right!" Gabriel said with a snap of his fingers before pulling a U-turn a little too quickly, side swiping a street sign with the rear fender.

"Oops. Good thing it's a rental." He said, earning a laugh from the others.

They drove about a mile down the road back past the concentration camp then they took a left. After following that for about half a mile, Gabriel stopped the Hummer.

"Go turn the vehicle around, I'll get your stuff. I know where it's at." Jacob said before jumping from the Hummer and running into the woods.

Gabriel drove down the road until he found a place level enough to turn around. The ditches on either side of the road were much too deep and they didn't want to take the risk of getting stuck. By the time they got back to the spot they had let him out at, Jacob was standing just outside the tree line. He was less than patiently waiting for them, holding Gabriel's plate carrier, rifle, and backpack. Jacob threw everything into the back storage area of the Hummer with the rest of their stuff, then climbed back into his seat.

"Took you guys long enough. I was waiting there for a whole thirty seconds." He said after shutting the door.

"Why are you complaining about thirty seconds?" James asked.

"A lot of things can happen in thirty seconds." Said Jacob.

"You were fine. You're just paranoid." Said Gabriel.

"Probably, but still you need to work on your recovery time and punctuality."

"Yeah yeah, whatever you say, dad."

"So where are we heading?" James asked as he turned to look at the rest of them.

Before anyone else could answer, Martin said.

"Go south. There's nothing left for us in this town."

Gabriel looked to Jacob who was sitting in the seat behind James and mouthed the words.

"Where's Ellis?"

Jacob just shook his head then gave Martin a sidelong glance. Gabriel faced back to the road. He knew what that meant, and he could not even imagine how much pain Martin must have been going through. But there would be plenty of time to help comfort him, once they were somewhere safer than the open road.

# CHAPTER: 32

## *Valley Grove, West Virginia.*

**M**ARTIN and the team had been driving for a few hours before they came upon a motel located smack dab in the middle of nowhere. Gabriel drove past the motel then turned onto the street right after it. They slowly drove down the lane as everyone, except Gabriel, quietly got out of the Hummer one at a time. Once they were all out and off to investigate, Gabriel drove around the block then pulled into the parking lot behind the motel.

Martin quietly crept around the side of the building to the back door. He tried the handle and to his surprise and satisfaction, it was unlocked. He cracked the door open and peaked inside. From where he was he could see a light coming from a room down the hall. He carefully pushed the door the rest of the way open and stepped inside. Once he arrived at the door where the light was coming from, he slowly made his way around to see the source of the light. Inside the room behind a desk, sat a woman with piles of paper stacked all around her. As Martin examined her, he could clearly see that she was distraught over something.

"Maybe she's just stressed." He thought to himself. "Might as well go in and ask for a room. Ain't getting much done from out here in the hallway."

He stepped into the room, which was probably her personal office, then he moved to the center and stood in front of her desk.

"Don't scream." He said softly.

She slowly looked up. And when her eyes fell upon his masked face, she started shaking uncontrollably and was without a doubt going to scream.

"Heavens me. Since when did cutting throats become easier than speaking through them?" He thought.

"Don't scream." He said again, a little louder this time.

She put both of her hands over her mouth and gave a muffled cry that was loud but not as bad as it could have been had she just let it out.

"Calm down ma'am. I Just need a room. Off the record would be preferable." He said.

She just stared at him, hands still covering her mouth.

"Look, I have gold." He said as he held out a small bar of gold that he had found in the pocket of the suit that Ramiel had given him. "I will pay you ten times what the room is worth for the night if you keep it quiet. And for god's sake, please calm down."

He stepped forward to place the bar on her desk. Seeing his arm in the light he suddenly realized why she was so scared. It turned out that during all the chaos, he had forgotten that he was actually still covered in splatters of deep crimson colored blood.

"Yeah, I guess I can understand her reaction to seeing me. Actually pretty rational." He laughed to himself.

He set the gold down on her desk then took a step back, with the woman's wide eyes still staring at him. She slowly lowered her hands from her mouth and then looked down at the gold laying before her with just a smidge of blood seared across it. She knew full well that it would have been worth enough to buy a car a few months ago, but that was back when there was actually still an economy. Martin then pointed at the gold and said.

"I need a room... please."

"Who are you, and why are you covered in blood?" She blurted out.

"I am... you can call me, Mr. Blank. And as for the blood, my best explanation for that is, shit happens."

"I'll say. And speaking of shit, I think you definitely might have scared a little out of me." She said, now sounding more angry than scared.

"My apologies, ma'am. I assure you that I had no intention of scaring you. I would just like a room for the night. That is all. I can select a key myself if it's all the same to you." He said as he turned to go.

Still breathing heavily but seeming like she was on the way to calming down, she asked.

"Why are you wearing such a frightening mask?"

"I wear it because I must. It was given to me by a good friend who said; that in order to wear it at all, I must wear it forever and never again show my face."

"Why?" She asked.

"Because if a symbol has a face, then that symbol dies with the host. But if a symbol has no face, it can be passed from host to host. Therefore that symbol can never die. It also restrains one from feeling personal pride or vanity. Except for the pride that is of the symbol."

"Symbol for what exactly?"

"Revolution, ma'am. The symbol for revolution. My men and I have already destroyed two Chinese camps and freed a few hundred American citizens. That's actually where we're coming from now."

"You're fighting back against the Chinese?"

"Yes ma'am."

She suddenly became visibly more calm.

"Then you can have the room for free. Those damned bastards stayed here for a few nights when they first got here. It took me literally days to clean up the rooms after those disrespectful pigs."

"Keep the payment. You need it, I don't. And I like to pay people what they are owed."

Martin left the room and went to the front entrance. He threw the lock and opened the door to see Jacob waiting right outside. Martin led Jacob inside to see the woman was now standing in the hallway outside her office door, facing them.

"How many of you are there?" She asked.

"There are four of us, ma'am." Said Martin. "Can you accommodate that many?"

"I think I might have an apartment that would fit you all more comfortably than just one of the little rooms."

"An apartment will do just fine."

"So, where is everyone?" Jacob asked, looking around. "I haven't seen any citizens who weren't in a camp in like a week."

"Most of the people around these parts are either dead, bugged out west or they were taken to the camps. You're actually the first people I've seen come through here in a while now."

"If there's no people then how is your power still on?"

"The Chinese have taken over and are now maintaining all the power plants. I guess as it turns out, they rely on electricity as much as we do."

"So why are you still here when nobody else is?"

"Because I gave them what they wanted when they asked. As much as I hate to admit it, I didn't have the courage or the strength to fight back. When they arrived, I just folded."

"Not everyone was born to be a warrior. You did what you had to do to survive." Said Martin.

"I know, I just wish I could have been more brave. But I always end up being afraid of everything."

"Boo." A voice whispered in her ear.

She screamed loudly this time, frantically throwing her arms in the air.

This gave Martin and the others all a good laugh.

"Wow, you all are a bunch of assholes aren't you." She said, shaking her head. "I understand now how you stand up to those Chinese rats."

"Hmm, yeah I'd say that's probably accurate." Gabriel said, rubbing his chin as he walked past her. "Life is easier when you're an asshole."

"Yeah, I'm sure. Anyway, here's the key. It's room number 17."

She held out the key toward Martin and he took it.

"Thank you, ma'am. We'll stop by to check out in the morning."

With that they all turned and walked out the front door, heading in the direction of their room.

Once they were settled in, with their gear stowed away in the corner, they all sat around the breakfast table off to the side of the room. They talked for quite a while, taking turns sharing their stories of what had happened in the past week while they were separated. Apart from some light torture by the Chinese, James and Gabriel's week has been mostly just boring, waiting for the moment they could strike. Jacob had spent the whole time alone, observing the camp trying to figure out what to do. When it was Martin's turn, he told them the whole story of what had happened. He told them of Ellis and his son, meeting Elijah Parker, and how Mr. Blank's real name was Ramiel. He also told them the fact that surprised them all. Ramiel was only twenty six, which was around the same age as the rest of them. Martin then told them of how he had been given the mask he now wore, and how Ramiel had appointed him with the task of becoming a symbol of hope and revolution.

"Do you know where he was going?" Gabriel asked in reference to Ramiel.

"He didn't say. As soon as he had given me this stuff he just got up and left without another word."

"I wonder if we'll ever see him again." Said Jacob.

"He does have a knack of just showing up out of nowhere. I

wouldn't be surprised if we crossed paths with him in the future." Said Martin.

"Not trying to change the subject." Jacob began. "But I find it pretty disturbing how a little over a week ago I was stuck in a traffic jam, and now its as if everyone on earth has disappeared. Do any of you feel the same or is it just me?"

"It actually only takes about three weeks for two thirds of the American population to die after a societal collapse." Said Martin.

"Really? Why such a short time?"

"Well one of the reasons is, famine and lack of all resources. Another reason is that humanity had became addicted to pharmaceuticals. So the only people who really survived after the invasion, were those who never went to the hospital or got subscribed any synthetic drugs."

"Why is that though?" Jacob asked.

"Well, when you keep the weak alive by artificial means, as soon as those means are halted, those people die. Because after being altered by drugs, they become reliant on then to the point that they they are no longer strong enough to survive on their own."

"I don't know about all of that. It sounds a little conspiratorial, if you ask me." Said Jacob.

"Anyone who believes that synthetic health is actual health, will always be unhealthy. Questioning the legitimacy of the pharmaceutical companies is not a conspiracy, the companies themselves are the conspiracy."

"Are you guys hungry yet? James asked out of the blue. "I mean, we have a full kitchen for the first time in a while, so I was thinking that we should probably use it."

They all agreed then got right to work preparing the thing that was now far too uncommon. Something that they had taken for granted their entire lives up until that point. A warm meal.

# CHAPTER: 33

**G**ABRIEL sat down on the couch in the apartment, grabbed the remote and turned on the TV. He then flipped through the static channels until he eventually ended up on a news channel.

" You know, I'm actually not surprised that the news is still up." He said as he continued on flipping through the channels. "I mean, every mainstream media organization has been working for either the Chinese or the Russians for the past few decades. So why wouldn't they keep it up? Gotta brainwash the remaining people somehow."

He changed from one news channel to the next then back again, just looking for something more interesting to watch.

"Wait, stop!" Martin suddenly said with a sense of urgency. "Go back."

Gabriel clicked back to the channel before the one that it had been on.

"There, that's him. That's the piece of shit that killed them."

The man on the screen that Martin pointed out to the others, walked up onto the stage. He then went over to the podium where a few microphones had been attached. His right arm was still in a sling from when Martin had shot him, and in that moment, he just wished that the bullet would have hit just a few inches to the left.

"It brings me much sadness to inform the public that the terrorists attacked again a few night ago." The Chinese man said from the podium. "This recent bombing unfortunately left twenty of our brave soldiers, dead."

He paused for a few seconds, then continued.

"We don't know who they are, or why they are attacking us. We are, however, working with our American counterparts to find out who is responsible for these attacks. So that we may bring them to justice. I regret to inform you that until we find them we are putting the entire DC area under complete lock-down and martial law. Anyone with any information on this matter is urged to come forward. We are here for you, the people. We will get through these trying times as long as we all work together. Should you need anything please do not hesitate to come forward. Thank you."

Once he had finished speaking, Gabriel turned off the TV.

"Well then. So I guess we're terrorists now." He said, throwing the remote onto the seat next to him.

"He said there was a bombing. I think that there might be others who are fighting back." Said Martin.

"What makes you say that?" Gabriel asked.

"We haven't bombed anything yet."

"Do you think that they know about us attacking their camps?"

"No, I don't think that they even knew that it was us that attacked the first one."

"How could they not have put that together?" Asked Jacob.

"It's possible that they're just not as smart as we give them credit for." Said James.

"Or we just don't appear that impressive at face value. Maybe when they found the bunker they thought we were just random people trying to hide, and weren't capable of doing what we do. I imagine that the militia was more than likely the first people that they would think did it."

"Hold up. So what you're saying is that they just came across the bunker, and then after they took... um." Gabriel paused, searching for the proper words.

"You can say it." Said Martin. "It doesn't bother me, man. Please continue."

Gabriel hesitated for another second then continued.

"After they took Ellis and Mark, maybe they thought we were just a few crazy preppers coming after our people?"

"That's actually kinda what we are though." Said Jacob.

"Yeah, I guess you're right." Gabriel huffed out a laugh.

"Why are they saying we're terrorists though?" Said James. "What we are doing isn't for political reasons. And I'm sure anyone else who is fighting back is doing it for the same reasons as we are. We're defending our land. 'Terrorist' really isn't the proper description."

"Don't worry about it." Martin said from behind the couch, standing with his arms crossed. "They're probably just running damage control for the stories that are already being spread by the people we freed from their inhumane treatment. They will do whatever it takes to paint anyone who stands against them as the bad guys, even when they are clearly the ones who are mistreating our people."

"Don't let them get to you, Martin. They'll get what's coming to them all in good time." Said Gabriel.

"I would say I hope you're right. But unfortunately, hope is for fools. I know that it's nice to believe the lie that good always prevails in the end. But it does not. Evil wins almost every single time in this messed up world. And it doesn't matter how hard you try to win by being good, evil still wins because it doesn't even have to try."

"Damn. Way to be a downer, bro." Said Jacob.

"What are you saying? Are you giving up?" James asked.

"No, in fact just the opposite. I will fight to my last heartbeat if I have to. I have accepted that I will die one day soon, and it makes no difference to me when I die, but rather how I die."

"What do you mean?"

"There are no winners in a war. There are no good guys or bad guys, because when both sides believe they are good, that is only proof that neither sides are good. To be good is to be charitable, and in war there is little to none. I freely admit that I am not charitable towards my enemies, but they have not been charitable to me either. The only difference between us and them is that we fight for others without regard for our own well-being. They fight to oppress and prey on the weak, for their own benefit. We may not be good, but I know for a fact that we are better than them. And because of that, we will die. I have accepted that. No matter what I do to escape or outrun it, it will happen. I will die, and it will be soon. So I am just going to make sure that I die in a better state than those who kill me."

"How long will we do this for, how long can we?" Jacob said, looking at the floor while shaking his head.

"Until either it is over, or my life is. You all can stop at any point and I will not hold it against you. But I have chosen to live by the sword, therefore I must die by the sword."

"We have killed about a hundred of them already. I don't wanna be a dick but don't you think vengeance has been achieved?" Asked Jacob.

"They kill one of ours, we kill all of theirs. That rat bastard killed my family, Jacob. Right in front of me. Now I want them dead. All of them. And they shall be. I will go by myself if I have to, but I would prefer your company, if you are willing to follow me."

"Alright, fair enough. So how are we gonna do it?" Jacob asked.

"Do what?"

"Kill the asshole that killed Ellis and Mark?"

"Rifle. There's no way any of us will be able to get close enough to him to use anything else."

"What caliber are you thinking?"

"A .50BMG would be nice, but that's obviously out of the question, so I'll make due with anything bigger than a 7.62x51."

"Maybe not out of the question." Jacob said thoughtfully. "Do we still have a map of the area?"

"Yeah it's in my bag, I'll grab it." Said Gabriel, reaching over to his backpack.

He handed the map to Jacob who placed it out on the table.

"Okay, so I believe that we past through Valley Grove, a few miles before we stopped, so we should be somewhere around here right now." He said, pointing to a spot on the map. "And according to the map it looks to be about an hour drive."

"What does?" Martin asked.

"I have an… acquaintance who may or may not own and want to sell a Barrett M82a1."

"For how much though?"

"His prices are usually pretty reasonable actually."

"Okay. I guess we'll head there first thing in the morning then. No sense wasting time."

"That's right. We've got places to be, and people to kill. You know, the things normal everyday people do on a Sunday afternoon." Said Gabriel.

"Let's just get some sleep. It's been a long day." Martin said with a sigh.

"Who gets the bed?" Jacob asked.

"Don't care. You all fight over it if you want." Said Martin as he laid down on the floor in between the couch and coffee table.

"Why are you laying on the floor, Martin?" James asked with his mouth full as he walked by, carrying an open bag of potato chips that he found in one of the cupboards.

"Because I'm tired."

"Fair enough." James said before turning to the others. "So who's taking the first watch?"

"I'll do it." Said Jacob, raising his hand.

"I'll take it next." Gabriel said. "Wake me up in two hours. James, you can take the bed until your shift on watch."

"I guess I'll take the last watch then." Martin said from the floor on the other side of the couch. "Wake me up when it's my turn."

"Alright, let's get some rest. We've got a big day tomorrow. I think."

# CHAPTER: 34

**M**ARTIN sat at the table looking out the window at the sun beginning to rise over the hills in the distance. It was around 7:30am now and he had been on watch for the past hour and a half. Even though it had been an uneventful night and so far a peaceful morning, he hadn't slept a wink. Looking around the room, he figured that he would wake the others to begin preparing to head out after another half hour or so. As he looked back to the rising sun, he sat deep in thought, and for some reason, his mind began to wander back to the first official assignment that he and his team had been sent on.

"Hey, I found a job for you and the team." Mr. Blank had said to him a few years back. "He is a problem that needs to be solved. We have been asked to take care of it."

"Asked by whom?" Martin said curiously.

"That is not important. What is important is that we have our first job. Make it happen. The address and all relevant information is in this mission folder."

"Okay, I'll tell the others." Martin said, taking the folder. "We will prepare to leave as soon as possible."

Once they arrived at the address they had been given, they began staking out the house, taking turns in shifts two at a time. They had parked on the other side of the street from the target's house in order to observe his activities without being too obvious. After about two days of observing, at around 7:00pm, they saw a little boy about the age of twelve, carrying a backpack and coming up the street. They watched with unexpressed concern as the boy walked up the target's driveway, then up to the front door to ring the bell. The target answered, then invited the boy in and shut the door.

"Oh, hell no." Gabriel said from the passenger seat, beginning to open his door.

"Wait, wake the others." Martin said in a whisper as he got out of the car. "Tell one of them to stay and be ready to drive in case we need to make a quick getaway."

"Okay, sounds good."

The sun had just gone behind the hills in the distance as Martin made his way across the street. He couldn't afford to wait any longer for the others to be up and ready. It was just about dark enough now, so he was mostly concealed as he casually walked up the driveway to the house. He entered the backyard through the gate and stepped onto the patio behind the house. Carefully moving over to the back door, he tried the handle.

"Of course it's locked." Martin mumbled to himself before getting down to eye level with the lock.

He then took out his lock pick set and went to work. After a few seconds the lock was open and the handle turned. Just as he had begun to open the door he heard a noise behind him. He turned to find Gabriel and James standing there. He waved them in after him, and they entered into the entryway where a washer and dryer sat up against the wall to their right. Down the hall they could see light coming from what appeared to be the kitchen. Martin gestured for them to take different directions through the house as he made his way forward, towards what he thought might be the living room.

"You said apple juice right?"

Martin froze. The voice had come from the kitchen. Martin slowly peaked around the corner to see the boy sitting on the sofa eating a snack as though he didn't have a care in the world. Martin ducked into the dark room around the corner. That's when he heard the man enter the living room from the kitchen, then the squeak of the sofa as he undoubtedly sat next to the little boy.

"What kind of a disgusting human being could take advantage of a child like this." Martin thought to himself. "This has already gone too far."

Martin started to stand up when he heard movement coming from the living room once again.

"I'm gonna go freshen up for our extra curricular activities, you can go wait in the bedroom and I'll be there in a moment."

Upon hearing this, Martin could barely contain his anger. He heard footsteps leave the room in the opposite direction and the sound of a door shutting. Then he heard smaller footsteps coming down the hall in his direction. The boy walked right by the room that he was hiding in, so Martin crept out of the room and up behind him. Cupping a hand over his mouth, Martin whispered.

"Don't scream. We're here to save you."

The boy, surprised but not quite startled, looked up at Martin and he saw that tears had already been forming in his eyes. Gabriel appeared out of the other room and took the boy by the hand.

"Let's go." He whispered. "Keep very quiet."

Martin removed his hand from the boy's mouth and Gabriel led him out through the laundry room where they had entered. Once the boy was safely outside, Martin turned and stalked back towards the living room. He heard the toilet flush and then the bathroom door open. He looked to his left and saw James enter the living room from the other direction. They moved closer to where the man would be coming from and both stood on either side of the doorway. The man entered the room still drying his hands on a towel. He threw the towel onto a chair then looked up, right into the eyes of Martin's ski mask. The expression on the mans face was complete and utter shock as he looked at Martin. He then turned and looked at James, then back at Martin, then back at the wall where James had been standing. He frantically looked around then turned to check behind him, letting out a yelp as he did. James was there. They had him surrounded.

"Who are you?" He said trembling with fear as tears started to run down his cheeks.

Martin tilted his head slightly to the side and stared at him.

"S.T.F.U." Was the last thing the man ever heard.

Because as soon as the words entered the man's ears, so too did Martin's knives enter into both sides of his neck. Martin stared into his eyes as he slowly died, then placed his foot on the man's chest and kicked. The blades tore through everything on their way out, leaving a gruesome V shaped wound that would give any detective a rather interesting day.

"First kill. How do you feel?" James asked flatly.

"He may not have deserved to die, but the world is a better place now that he is no longer in it."

"Yeah, I hear ya. By the way, what do you call that move?"

"I'll probably call it, the Chapel V neck, or something."

"Interesting, I like it."

"Jobs done. Let's get out of here."

The man that Martin had unceremoniously executed was actually a school board member. Blank had discovered him to be having multiple affairs with children aged six all the way to fourteen years old. He had been caught red handed, was tried and convicted on multiple separate occasions. Charges like sexual assault, child molestation, pedophilia, child abuse and providing explicit content to minors. However, before conviction, the prosecutor allowed him to plea down the charges and he was released with only a slap on the wrist. This was most likely because he was considered a minority by society. And apparently some people thought it was okay to abuse children as long as your skin was the right color and your political views lined up with the favored side. To Martin and the team however, justice must always be applied equally, or there is no justice at all. Therefor, being as it was not always upheld by the state, from time to time it would have to be upheld by the people.

When Martin came back to the real world from his thoughts, he was still staring out the window at the tree line where the sun had been hidden a moment before. He looked down at his mechanical watch. It read 8:03am. He stood from his chair next to the table and walked over to Jacob and gently shook his shoulder to wake him.

"It's time to move out. Wake the others and load everything up. I want to be out of here in fifteen minutes."

Jacob sat up and rubbed his face.

"Alright. Are you going to go check out of the room while we are loading up?"

"Yes, I'll take care of it." He said before walking over to his bag to double check its contents.

Jacob moved across the room and began shaking James awake.

"Time to get up, buddy. We're heading out in a few minutes."

With his eyes still closed James nodded, stretched then stood up. Once he was up he began grabbing bags and weapons to carry out to the Hummer. Jacob made his way into the bedroom to wake Gabriel. Martin slung the strap of his backpack and quiver over one shoulder, and his bow over the other. Then he walked out the door and headed in the direction of the lobby. It was a clear morning with a blue sky peppered with small fluffy white clouds. He made his way down the walkway then entered through a door into the hallway that led to the main lobby. As he entered the lobby he saw the woman from the night before, sitting behind the front desk. He walked up in front of her and stood there until she noticed him. She looked up and gave him a friendly smile. He couldn't return the gesture on account of him wearing his mask. So as a substitute he used his pointer finger to draw an imaginary smile across the face of his mask where his mouth would have been.

"Good morning, ma'am." He said. "I'm just here to let you know that we'll be checking out now."

"But, normally the checkout isn't until noon." She said in a questioning tone.

"Indeed. Nevertheless, we must be going now. We appreciate the accommodations."

As he finished speaking he placed the key on the front desk and began to walk away.

"Okay... My pleasure. Good luck with everything." She said, sounding somewhat confused.

Martin stopped then turned and looked at her.

"Remember, tell no one that you helped us. No matter what. Lie if you have to. Believe me, when I say that it is for your own self preservation, it most definitely is."

"Okay. Well then, I hope to see you all again someday." She said as he opened the door to leave.

He looked over his shoulder while holding the door open.

"Hope is for fools. It is very unlikely that you will ever see us again. And that is for the best."

With that he stepped outside letting the door swing shut behind him.

He walked around the motel to the parking lot in the back and saw the others standing by the back door of the Hummer. They were all standing around just discussing how to load a couple rifle cases.

"Shotgun." Martin said as he walked up behind them.

"Cool, here ya go." Jacob said as he threw Martin a Benelli M4 shotgun, then climbed into the passenger seat.

Gabriel let out a single loud laugh, and James raised an eyebrow. Martin stood there for a second holding the shotgun, then shook his head in disbelief.

"Bro, what?"

Jacob put his hands out to the sides in a questioning manner.

"What. You said shotgun, and that is a shotgun. A good one too if you ask me."

"I was calling shotgun seat, you retard, not shotgun... gun." Martin said with a laugh.

"Ah, well you should be more specific next time." Jacob said as he got out of the passenger seat.

Martin was going to say some words but instead he just said them with his middle finger.

"How's that for specific?" He asked.

"Overused, but I'll accept your offering." Said Jacob with a smile curling the corners of his mouth.

"Alright kids, quit playing around. We've gotta get moving." Said Gabriel.

"You're the driver. Lead the way." Said James.

"I drove last night. Why can't you drive?"

"Because you're the best at it."

"You're right, I am pretty great. But seriously, can you take the first shift?"

"Sure thing man, I don't mind driving."

"Quit fighting mom and dad. You're traumatizing me!" Jacob said in a mocking tone.

"Let's go! We got places to be." Martin yelled from the passenger seat.

"Boss says it's time to go. Everybody in." James said with a shrug.

They all climbed in. James in the driver seat, Gabriel in the seat behind him, and Jacob behind Martin.

"So, what kind of weapons do we still have to work with?" Martin asked as they turned onto the street, heading south.

"Well since all the hostiles were dead, we were able to raid the armory before we left the concentration camp." Gabriel said from the back seat. "So first off we got your backpack, scar 17 and Desert Eagle back. We also grabbed a couple Steyr AUG's, M4 carbines, seven Glock 19's, and the Benelli M4 that Jacob threw at you. Oh, and your compound bow, of course. Also my AR10 that we got back from where we hid it with the rest of my stuff."

"Yup, but it's not enough." Jacob said as he put a magazine into one of the AUG's. "So let's go get us some of the bigger guns, boys. And by the way, I call one of the AUG's."

"When you found my backpack. Was the metal rose still in the side pocket?"Asked Martin.

"Yes. I actually checked that specifically." said James. "I figured that it must be really important to you if you would be willing to carry it at all."

"It is. Thank you."

"No problem, man."

James looked at the map then took a left turn at the next street that came up.

"Well, we're only gonna get more guns if your guy is still even where you say he is." Martin said in response to Jacob. "If he's anything like we were, then he's probably either dead or about to be."

"Who, Franklin? I doubt it. If he was like us then he'd be out here kicking ass and taking names. He's actually more like a drug lord though. Only more dangerous and with way more guns."

"Great. I always thought it would be the Chinese who killed me. Not some crazy arms dealer that Jacob brought me to see." Gabriel said with a sigh.

"We'll be fine. Don't worry. He's cool, if we don't give him any shit then he won't give us any either."

"So how do you even know this guy?" Asked James.

"I met him at a gun store about three months after you all took me shooting for the first time. It was when I decided to buy my first AR15. I guess he saw me struggling to pick one out, so he came up and asked if I wanted his opinion or advice. So I told him, sure. Then we talked for about an hour, and we became friends, more or less."

"Fair enough."

"Okay, well it's about an hour to our destination. If you all wanna take a nap, Jacob just needs to show me on the map how to get there and then I'll wake you up once we're close."

None of them opposed this idea so Martin laid his head back on the headrest and immediately fell into a strange type of sleep.

# CHAPTER: 35

## *Washington DC.*

THE sun was setting fast as Scarlet and the other kids slowly made their way back towards the underground base. It was now their third trip out in two days and they were quickly realizing that their looting options were dwindling.

"We need to go out a little farther." Scarlet said from atop a concrete wall.

"Scarlet, no." Tyler said in a serious tone. "Thomas and Brian said not to go past the perimeter that's been set for us. We need to follow their orders."

"Tyler is right." Said one of the other kids in the group. "We should just head back. We found everything we're gonna find."

"And that's alright. We're leaving the city soon anyway. So let's just head back." Tyler added.

"You all are a bunch of sissies. Common, let's just check that one last building over there, then we'll head back."

Tyler looked at the others, some of them shrugged but none seemed to have much disagreement.

"Okay then, we'll check that one last building." He said, turning back to Scarlet. "But then we're done for today."

"Good, at least I don't have to go alone." Scarlet said lightly as she began moving towards the edge of the perimeter.

The others looked around then reluctantly started to follow.

As they quietly crept up to the front doors of the building, a hand lightly grabbed Scarlet by the shoulder. She turned to see Tyler with a finger over his lips in a shushing gesture.

"What is it?" She whispered.

"Something doesn't feel right." He whispered back. "It's probably nothing but I'm gonna go around to the back just in case."

With that he removed his hand from her shoulder then quickly moved down the front of the building and disappeared around the corner. After Scarlet had watched him go she turned, grabbed the handle of the door and pushed it open. Once they were all inside, Scarlet turned to the others.

"Ground floor first." She said in a loud whisper. "Check everything, then we'll move upstairs."

"We need to hurry up, Scarlet. It's gonna be dark soon." Whispered one of the others.

Scarlet moved forward without further addressing their concerns. She knew it was about to be dark, but she had a feeling that there was something in there that she needed to find.

After about five minutes of searching, she moved out of the last room on the ground floor. Finding nothing of real value by that point, she began to think this was a waste of time. She made her way upstairs followed by the rest of the group, all except Tyler who had not yet met back up with them.

"Hey, where's Tyler?" Someone asked from behind Scarlet.

This was the exact question that was also on Scarlet's mind, but she did not feel the need to address it just yet. She was sure that he would show up any minute, he probably just got caught up looking at something.

They finished up on the second floor and then moved on to the third. By that time it had been fifteen minutes since Tyler left, and Scarlet's wondering was now quickly turning to worry. Tyler still wasn't back and she was beginning to regret making them all come here.

"Scarlet, there's really nothing here of value." Said one of the girls as they approached. "We should just cut our losses and go. The sun is already down, but if we leave right now we might not have to walk the whole way back in complete darkness."

"Okay." Said Scarlet. "Gather the others. We'll leave as soon as we find Tyler."

Scarlet looked out the front door into the quickly fading daylight. There was no movement outside so they quietly exited the building. With the others close behind, Scarlet began moving to the corner where she had last seen Tyler. Peeking around the side of the building she saw nothing, so she moved around to the side and continued to the back corner. She slowly peeked around to look behind the building, and immediately she saw a figure standing right out in the open. Horrified that it might be one of their enemies, she quickly ducked back around the corner, her heart now racing.

After taking a second or two to calm down she slowly peeked around the corner again, just hoping it was only her imagination. Her eyes found the figure again, and upon seeing it more clearly this time, to her relief, she realized that it was only Tyler. He was standing about twenty feet away from the building, facing away from her.

"Tyler." Scarlet said in a loud whisper. "Tyler, let's go."

Hearing her he turned around with a look of disappointment on his face.

"What are you waiting for? Let's go." She said a little louder.

"It's a trap." He said in a normal speaking voice, not even trying to be quiet.

Upon hearing him say those words, Scarlet's heart stopped for a moment and she suddenly found it hard to breathe.

"It's a what?" She said, trying to control the trembling in her voice.

"A trap."

Just then she saw someone else step out from behind a wall. Then another in her peripheral vision. A few seconds later, they were completely surrounded, and it was obvious that there was no escape. With tears beginning to well up in her eyes, Scarlet looked at the others and did the only thing she could do. She mouthed the words.

"I'm sorry."


## Road to Franklin's House, West Virginia.

"Alright guys. Wake up, we should be there in a few minutes." Said James, rousing them from their sleep as he drove.

Jacob sat up in his seat, rubbing the sleep away from his eyes. He looked around at the buildings and houses for a moment to analyze where they were, then he said.

"Yup, this is the right area. I remember these buildings. Franklin's place should be just up the hill and around the bend."

"So why have you never told us about this guy?" James asked.

"I guess I just never thought it was important." Jacob said with a shrug. "I've only ever been down here once, and that was back when I knew little to nothing about guns. Maybe I just forgot to mention it because we never needed any guns that we couldn't just get from somewhere more local."

"Seems like something you would do." Gabriel said with a chuckle.

Jacob just gave an exaggerated shrug, without elaborating further on the story.

At the top of the hill Jacob pointed out the driveway. James turned in and pulled up to a large rod iron gate. Jacob then got out and walked up to the panel and hit the button labeled 'talk'. He waited for a moment, but after nothing happened, he hit the button again and waited. A few more minutes of silence passed.

"Maybe he's not here." Gabriel called from the back seat."

"Come on, Franklin." Jacob said in a whisper to himself. "We didn't come this way for..."

"What do you want?" A voice said through the speaker, cutting off Jacob's whispers to himself.

"Franklin, this is Jacob Turner." He said holding the talk button. "We want to look at your inventory. If you have anything left to sell."

There was a long pause and Jacob began to wonder if he had dipped out on them.

"Yeah, we have a couple things left. Come on in." The voice finally said through the speaker.

"Thank you." Jacob said as he began to turn to head back to the Hummer.

"Also, I hope you'll understand." The voice said suddenly. "For security reasons, my guards are equipped with live ammunition and will be trained on your vehicle until it is deemed safe."

"Understood."

Jacob jogged back to the Hummer and hopped in. By the time he was in the seat, the gate had split down the center and began to swing open. They drove up the long driveway until they came to a stop in front of what could only be described as a mansion. The driveway had gone in a big circle around to the front steps and there was a flower garden with a fountain in the center. The house had a large set of steps that led from the driveway to the base of the marble coulombs that were polished and clean. Giving the mansion a similar look to the front of the White House. There were also guards out front, lined up and standing on every fifth step. Guards were also spread all throughout the perfectly maintained grounds of the property.

The guard closest to the vehicle waved for them to get out. Jacob stepped out of the vehicle, Martin and the others followed a few seconds later. The guard then gestured for them to walk up the steps. Once they were about halfway up, a man in a suit stepped out the double front doors and stood on the landing at the top. They crested the top of the steps where he spread his arms in a welcoming fashion. He walked forward to meet them and in a friendly manner he embraced Jacob.

"Welcome my friend. How have you been?" He said, now holding Jacob at arms length.

"I've been better. If you haven't noticed, the world has kind of gone to shit."

"Indeed it has. It is unfortunate that your visit could not have been under better circumstances, in more peaceful times."

"It is what it is. So anyway, Franklin, these are the other members of the STFU. The ones that I told you about a while back. This is Martin Chapel, Gabriel Cooper, and James Hudson. Guys this is, Franklin Diaboli."

Martin and the others nodded in greeting as Jacob introduced them.

"I'm honored to meet you all." Said Franklin. "I've heard much about you. I am here to help with whatever you need. Please come inside."

"Thank you. We appreciate it." Said Jacob.

"It is my pleasure. Can I offer you anything, a drink perhaps?" Franklin asked as they walked through the front doors of the house.

They moved through the entryway and into a massive open ball room that was completely lined with marble. The tile was so expertly placed that the room appeared as though it had been cut out of one enormous solid block of marble.

"What kind of drinks do you have?" Gabriel asked.

"Name what you want." Franklin said with a smile.

"I could go for a glass of whiskey." Gabriel said as they were led over to the seating area on the left side of the large room.

"I think we could all use one of those." James added.

"Very good. I will forward the order to my butler. Make yourselves at home. I'll be back in just a moment." Franklin said before exiting the ball room through a large set of doors that opened so smoothly they looked as though they were weightless.

After Franklin had left the room, the four of them sat down in the chairs that were all placed around a large coffee table in front of a fireplace.

"This room is almost big enough to fit my entire house." James said, looking around, marveling at the staggering amount of wealth. "How are you friends with this guy?"

"I dunno." Jacob said with a shrug.

"It's likely that since we are a somewhat highly trained team, he wanted to keep contact with us in case he ever needed us." Martin said matter of factly. "Not saying he did it with any malicious intent. But that is my best guess."

"That would make sense." Said Jacob. "But regardless, he's still a pretty nice dude."

"Agreed. But I will be skeptical and suspicious of him until he gives me reason not to be."

Just then the door to the room that Franklin had left through a moment before, suddenly opened. A tall man in a suit carrying a tray of drinks entered with Franklin following behind him.

"My apologies for being gone so long. I had a security breach on the far side of my property that I had to address."

"Do you need us to do anything?" Asked Martin.

"No, no, please. It was only a harmless beggar and his family scavenging for food. I had one of my men bring them a bag of supplies and send them away in the opposite direction of my house."

"Good. As long as it wasn't the Chinese or the Russians." Said Gabriel.

"Yes, they were quite troublesome when they first invaded, wouldn't you agree?" Said Franklin.

"Yeah. How did you get them to leave you alone?" Asked Gabriel.

"I'm an international arms dealer, Gabriel. Making deals with powerful people is what I do. And now that the laws of this nation no longer apply, there is no reason to hide that fact any longer."

"Not that it makes a difference, but just out of curiosity. Did you sell them any weapons?" Asked Martin.

"Just some typical semiautomatic AK47's and ammunition. Nothing that they wouldn't get from someone else anyway."

"Okay just wondering what kind of weapons they'll be using in this area when we head back out there."

"It's understandable. No need to explain yourself." Said Franklin with a shake of his head. "Anyway not to change the subject but I couldn't help but notice that Ramiel, or Mr. Blank as I'm told you call him, did not come with you."

"He left about a week ago. That's why I have this mask. He gave it to me before he took off." Said Martin.

"Ah yes, when Jacob introduced you as Martin, I figured that is what must have happened."

"Wait, how did you know his name was, Ramiel?" Martin asked.

"Oh Martin, my dear friend." Franklin said. "Ramiel is my younger brother."

# CHAPTER: 36

**H**E'S your brother?!" Jacob shouted in complete surprise. "Younger brother, yes." Said Franklin. "We are four years apart in age. I helped my father with the business, while Ramiel was the family problem solver, and there has never been anyone better."

"What do you mean by 'problem solver'?" Jacob asked.

"Professional killer." Martin said in answer to Jacob's question.

"That is correct, Martin. If we had a problem, we would send him to solve it. And he never failed even once. He was like death itself in the form of a human. He always made us proud."

"What happened?" Gabriel asked. "He never really told us anything about his past. Actually, he never told us anything about himself at all for that matter."

"He was always a very mysterious young man. I'm not exactly sure what his plan was. One day he just went to our father and told him he wanted out. My father had asked him why the sudden change of heart, but he simply said that he just wanted out and that he would give the family half of everything he had in order to be excused from all of the family's dealings. Our father was of course reluctant at first but finally decided his offer was more than reasonable. So Ramiel gave my father the key to his bank vault, shook my fathers hand then walked out."

"How much?" Asked Gabriel.

"I'm sorry?"

"Just curious how much was in the vault."

"Ah, yes of course. There was two hundred and fourteen million dollars inside. Which was actually a little more than half his net worth."

Gabriel whistled. "That is a hell of a big chunk of change."

"Yes." Franklin said with a sad sigh. "But we have never found someone who was his equal, or anyone that could do what he did with such excellence. However, with him being as good as he is, we thought it best to let him do what he wished. We could only hope that someday he would return to rejoin the family business."

"Were you worried he might turn against you?" Jacob asked.

"Not exactly. My father realized that Ramiel had dedicated his entire life, heart and soul to this family without ever asking one favor in return. So when the time came that he finally did ask for something, it was only fair that Father decided to let him. As I said before, we hoped that he would return someday, but I can see now he just might have moved on from this life entirely. Since you, Martin, now wear his signature mask, that can only mean that you are his equal. For he would not allow any other man to wear one of those, if he was not worthy."

"Ramiel, told us he was adopted. Is that true?" Asked Martin.

"Yes. My father found him when he was seven years old and when he discovered that he was exceptional at almost everything he did, my father asked him if he wanted to be trained in martial arts. He accepted. So at the age of seven he began his training."

They all listened intently to Franklin's story about the life of their friend. Martin knew some of it from his talks with Ramiel, but not with all the extra details.

"Now, on my father's behalf." Franklin continued. "I will say that he did not intend for Ramiel to become an assassin. In the beginning he actually would have preferred that he one day became a bodyguard, or something similar. However, at the age of nine he went to my father and made a request to go with our hit team on a mission. Naturally my father refused, but Ramiel persisted until my father finally decided to allow him to go with the team, but only to observe their tactics on the mission. He ended up taking out the target before the team could."

"How?" Gabriel asked.

"By expertly playing the 'innocent child asking questions' card. After learning the target and the plan of attack, he managed to get ahead of the team somehow. And he finished the job before the rest of them even got there."

"Damn! Are you telling us that Blank was a badass, even at nine years old?" Asked James.

"More or less, yes. I guess you could say that. However, once the team returned and was debriefed, they revealed the whole thing to my father. Naturally, Ramiel was punished, but after that, my father knew that he was born to do that kind of work. And his realization was reinforced when Ramiel had a mask custom made. That was the last time any of us saw his face."

"Was it this mask?" Jacob asked, pointing at Martin's head.

"No, he had new ones made as he grew up. He also had multiples just in case."

"Oh, good. Cause I was gonna say, that mask on a nine year old would be like a bobble head."

They all got a chuckle from this. Then Martin asked.

"When he gave this mask to me, He told me that I could never show my face again. Because if a symbol has a face then the symbol dies with the host. But a symbol with no face can change hosts yet remain the same. So the symbol will last forever."

"My father always told him that legacy was important. But he said to me once that he would never have children. That he would make his legacy live on through only the strongest, most lethal people the world could offer."

"Do you think that's why he started wearing the mask, even at that young age?" Jacob asked.

"He might have had some other ideas at the time he had the first mask made, but I think he still knew what he wanted very early on. He was always intelligent beyond his years."

"Did he ever talk to you about his theories and the way he thought?" Martin asked.

"He and I had a fairly deep conversation once. But I had heard from some of the other Problem Solvers that he was in fact quite brilliant."

"When I first met him, I thought he was crazy with how much he talked and all the wild things he thought about." Said Martin.

"What sort of things?" Asked Franklin.

Martin paused for a moment staring at the table.

"Everything. He told me that he wanted to understand all of existence. And I'm beginning to believe that he might have actually either done it, or at least come close. He left me a strange book that I'm still reading. But it has all sorts of weird, mind blowing thoughts and ideas in it. I think he wanted out so that he could spread what is in the book to others, in order to perhaps make more people like him."

"I would like to read this book someday, once we move into more peaceful times. If you don't mind, that is." Said Franklin.

"Of course. Someday when we have more time. It's too bad he couldn't be here so he could explain all of it himself."

"I really would enjoy his company again. We weren't incredibly close, but he is still my brother. I had visited him a couple times over the past few years to see how he was doing, but I was never able to stay long."

"Whether it's by blood or by oath we will always consider him our brother." Said Martin.

"And that makes all of you my brothers also. That is why I stayed in contact with Jacob. Just in case you ever needed my help. And now help you I shall."

"Speaking of help. May we discuss the reason we came here?" Martin asked as he stood up from his chair.

"Oh yeah. We need guns." Said Jacob.

"I have many. Anything in particular you are looking for?" Asked Franklin.

"I'm looking for a Barrett M82a1 or a M107a1. Do you have anything like that?"

"Probably, I often move quite a bit of different brands and products so we'll just have to go down and see what I've got."

"Sounds good. Please, lead the way." Said Martin as he stepped aside and held his hand out gesturing for Franklin to go ahead of them.

They walked through the double doors that Franklin had left through earlier, he then led them down a hallway with sunlight shining through the windows to their right. About halfway down the hall they stopped in front of the doors to an elevator. Franklin hit the button on the wall with the downward facing arrow on it. The doors opened and they all climbed inside. Once they were all in, Franklin turned and typed in a code on the keypad located to the left of the door. The doors closed and they began to descend. Once the elevator came to a stop, the doors opened, and Franklin led them down a short, well lit hallway to a steel vault door. He typed in a code on another keypad and with a clank the door slid open.

"Why don't you use key-cards instead of codes you have to type in every time?" Martin asked from behind him.

"Key-cards can be copied or stolen, my memory can not. Why do you ask?"

Martin shrugged.

"I was just curious. I actually preferred fingerprint locks, myself. But that was back when I still lived in my own house."

"Ah yes, it is most unfortunate that the Chinese had to run people away from their own homes. But do not worry about it too much. We will get them back for it soon enough."

"If nothing else. At the very least, we will try."

"Indeed. After you." Franklin said, gesturing for him to go through the door.

When Martin entered the room, it was like walking into an American man's dreamworld supermarket. There were rows upon rows of shelves, with every kind of weapon you could imagine. The others followed in behind Martin and they all stood for a moment just staring at the vast array of modern weaponry.

"Beautiful isn't it?" Franklin asked rhetorically.

"Can I just live here?" Jacob said as he walked over and began gently petting an M249 SAW that was leaning up against one of the shelves.

"This way to the high power rifle section." Said Franklin. "I just got a shipment of rifles yesterday, that's where the Barrett's will be if I have any."

Martin nodded and followed him around to the far side of the large underground room. As they rounded the corner of a set of shelves Martin spotted one. It was sitting on top of a table, set up on its bipod, in all its glory.

"Ah excellent. It appears that I do in fact still have a few of them." Said Franklin.

Besides the one on the table, an M107 which was Titanium Gray in color, and had a 29" barrel, there were three others. There was a black M82 with a 20" barrel, a Flat Dark Earth colored M107 with a 20" barrel, and another black one with a 29" barrel.

"What's your asking price for this one, including the scope?" Martin asked, laying his hand on the gray one.

"A Barret M107 with that specific 5-25x56 Nightforce scope, .50cal supressor and ammo would have sold for around $22,000 back when there was still an economy. But I will accept, and would actually prefer payment in other ways.".

"Like what?" Martin asked.

"Precious metals, food, water, medicine, different types of guns and ammo. Pretty much anything that has survival capabilities or actual value.

"We don't currently have much. Besides a couple guns we took from the Chinese and maybe our Hummer."

"I couldn't take your transportation. How about this. I would be willing to give it to you in exchange for a job I need taken care of. If you're interested."

"Depends on the job." Said Martin.

"Don't worry, it's nothing out of your ordinary line of expertise."

"You want us to solve a problem for you?"

"Indeed. And in return, if you complete the job, I will give you the Barrett with the scope. I will also give you three more guns of your choosing, along with ammunition for all of them."

"This must be a pretty high priority target if you're willing to give us that much for doing it."

"Have you ever heard of The Order, Martin?"

Martin had heard of it once. The Chinese Commander had said it before he shot Ellis. Even if he wasn't exactly sure that's what the commander had said, it didn't really matter.

"Yes, once." He finally said.

"Do you know what it is?" Franklin asked.

"No, I can't say that I do."

"The Order is the organization that originated under the name; The New World Order. But then they secretly changed it to just 'The Order' so that they could continue to say that they were just a conspiracy theory. They did this in hopes their actions at that time would go unnoticed."

"And you believe it?"

"Of course I believe it, Martin. I'm the one that sold them most of their weapons. However, that was back when they were just another customer. Back before I knew who they really were, or what their plans were."

"You wouldn't have sold to them if you had known what they were planning?"

"Of course not. I may be an illegal arms dealer but I still have morals. I do my best to only sell to the good guys. Or at least the lesser of two evils."

"So you've chosen a side?"

"Yes, I refuse to put money or profits above the well-being of my people anymore. I am an American citizen after all, therefore, I am on the side of all those who identify the same."

"You are on the side of the American citizens then?"

"Indeed, I am." Franklin said with conviction.

"I suppose that means we are on the same side." Said Martin.

"Good, then you should have no problem with killing a member of The Order."

"Nope, sounds like a good time to me."

"Don't get complacent. The one I want you to take out isn't a super high priority target, but he's still incredibly protected. I guess you could say that he's pretty much the mayor over this area now. And naturally I don't like being told what to do, so he has begun to piss me off."

"Not that I really care, but is that really worth killing him over?"

"He's also a power hungry prick, and he's on the counsel so he has a say in everything that's happened so far within a 250 mile radius."

Martin paused for a moment. "So he has jurisdiction from here, all the way to around where we lived in Hammett?"

"I believe so. Why?"

"So how well guarded is this guy?"

"About as well as me."

"And you'll be paying with guns and supplies?"

"If that is the agreement on how you wish to be paid, then yes."

"Good. Do we have to find him, or do you have any intel we can use?"

"I have his home address, if that works?"

"That's a little too easy, but I'll accept that. It will save time."

"When can you do it?" Franklin asked.

"I'll go ask the others. One moment."

Martin walked over to where the others were all looking at the different kinds of weapons.

"Hey guys, listen up." Martin said in a commanding voice.

They all looked at him then moved in a little closer.

"Franklin, has offered us a job. In exchange he will give us each the gun of our choosing with ammo. It will probably be the most dangerous job we've ever taken. According to Franklin, the target is somewhat high priority. And is as heavily guarded as this place. If you are interested in going to eliminate him tonight, raise your hand."

All their hands went up.

"The more danger, the more fun." Jacob said with a smile.

"Wait, you mean we're actually getting paid for once?" Gabriel said in a disbelieving tone.

Martin smiled behind his mask, then turned back to face Franklin.

"I guess we're in. We'll be back for our payment in the morning."

"Excellent."

# CHAPTER: 37

**T**HE sun was just beginning to set as Jacob pulled the Hummer into a parking lot off the main road. They had played Rock-Paper-Scissors before they left to see who had to drive this time. Jacob had lost the game, but he won the keys for the day. After pulling around behind an abandoned gas station, Jacob put the Hummer in park and pulled out the map to double check their location.

"According to this map we're about a mile away from the address that Franklin gave you in the briefing. It's just on the other side of this forest." Jacob said, pointing to the trees. "I figured we could walk from here and sneak up on the target. Then wait until dark to set in completely before we attack."

"Okay, cool. What weapon systems are we using this time?" Gabriel asked as they all got out of the Hummer and walked around to the back.

"Stealth. Put suppressors on any of the guns you're bringing." Said Martin.

"Plate carriers?" James asked as he opened the door to the rear storage area.

"Bring them. Better to have them and not need them, than need them and not have them."

"Sounds good to me. I always feel more comfortable wearing one anyway. Even with the added weight." Said James.

Since Martin was already wearing armor he just grabbed his bow and quiver of arrows. He thought for a second about bringing his Scar 17, but then decided against it. He figured the Glock 19 he kept in the holster on his leg, along with the bow he was holding should be enough for this specific job. Besides, Gabriel was bringing his AR10, James had an M4 carbine, and Jacob had the Benelli M4 shotgun and an AUG slung on his back. All of them also had sidearms. Martin figured that would be enough firepower to get the job done.

"Alright. Let's go kill some bad guys."

They could see the mayor's mansion in the distance as they waited for the darkness to set in. It was practically just a large compound at this point. With barbed wire fences all the way around it, and more guards than there should ever be for just one house. As Martin scanned the objective he could see that the only ways in were either through the main gate, or from the sky. And since they didn't currently have any way to do a HALO jump, that left them with only one option. The main gate, which was guarded by two men, one on either side. Both of them holding sub machine guns in the low and ready position. Once he had gathered all the information that he could from their current vantage point, Martin turned and looked at the others.

"Okay so here's the plan."

Martin slowly made his way through the bushes in the area between the tree line and the fence surrounding the targets house. He had to move slowly on account of the whole area being lit up like a Christmas tree, with spotlights casting light all around the compound. It was a difficult crawl but he finally made it to the corner of the four foot stone wall that sat beneath the barbed wire fence. As he peaked around the corner, Martin could see the guards were facing each other. He then slowly crept towards the guard while keeping to the shadows cast by the wall. He looked past them and caught a glimpse of Gabriel coming up behind the one on the opposite side. He then looked at his watch and he could just make out the time revealing he still had one minute left before the time they had designated that they were going to spring into action.

As Martin waited, he figured that he might as well listen to the conversation the guards were having, just to pass the time.

"Man, I hate gate duty." The first guard said to the second who was facing him.

"I hate this job." Said the second.

"It wouldn't be so bad if it wasn't for that spoiled dick of a mayor that we have for a boss."

"I know right. I mean, he wasn't even elected. He was installed. If I could quit, I'd be so out of here. But you know how it is. You can never really leave this job, you only ever get let go."

"Yeah, and the only way to get let go, is when it's off the edge of a building."

Martin thought about what the guards had been saying as he stalked his way up behind the back of the one closer to him.

"Do they deserve to die?" Martin asked himself. "They don't want to do this... but they are, so that means they are weak. And this world has no room for weak men just following orders. But..." Martin's thought trailed off as he made his decision.

He looked at his watch showing three seconds left. He rushed forward and grabbed the guard. Cupping a hand over his mouth and pulling his head to the side to reveal his neck Martin placed the point of his knife against the guard's carotid artery. Gabriel grabbed the other at the same time and followed Martin in doing the same.

"So here's what is going to happen." Martin said just loud enough that both guards could hear him. "You two are either going to open that gate and walk away, or you're going to open the gate and die. The final outcome will rely solely on your decisions within the next 10 seconds. Do you understand?"

Both men nodded.

"Excellent, open the gate."

The guard removed his glove, and with a shaking hand he reached over and placed his palm on the scanner. The gate unlocked and began to swing open.

"Hand-print scanners. Nice." Said Martin looking at the device attached to the wall.

The guard began to pull his hand off the scanner, then suddenly shot back to it and punched a red button. The alarm began to sound at the same time as Martin and Gabriel both stabbed.

"Stupid jackasses. Was it really worth your lives?" Martin asked rhetorically.

He knew they could both still hear, they just couldn't answer on account of having severed jugulars.

"They'll bleed out in about a minute. So they can use that time to think about the consequences of their decision." Gabriel said as he stepped over the dying man and moved to the gate.

"Welp, we've come this far. No sense in quitting now." Martin said as he pushed through the gate past him. "Let's get this over with."

Gabriel shrugged then followed him onto the grounds with James and Jacob moving inside moments later.

The alarm was still blasting, but there was no sense in trying to turn it off now when they could use it to their advantage. It was disorienting, but as long as they could tune it out better than the rest of the guards, then they still had the upper hand. They made their way through the bushes and around the side of the mansion as all the guards scrambled and ran all about the grounds.

"This alarm is damned annoying." Jacob said as he moved in closer behind Martin.

"Yeah. I'm man enough to admit that's my bad." Martin explained. "Should've just killed the guard as soon as the gate was opened, but my sympathy got the better of me. It won't next time though."

"Shit happens. Things aren't always easy, and they definitely can't go right every time. It's no biggie, our luck is just running out is all."

Martin nodded then waved them onward towards a ground level window. There were guards everywhere around the mansion, so moving about without being detected was quite difficult. Luckily for Martin and the team most of the guards were outside waiting for an attack that wouldn't be coming.

Under the cover of the shadows by the side of the mansion, Martin mentally timed the sounding of the alarm. As soon as it went off he stood up and prepared to smack the window with the hilt of his knife. It sounded again and at the same time he broke the window using the alarm to mask the sound of the shattering glass. He then reached in, unlocked the window and slid it open. Once they were all inside Jacob closed the window behind them so as to not draw any extra unwanted attention. Since they were already inside, it was better to have all the guards believing that the attack would be coming from outside the wall.

Martin looked around the edge of the door-frame from the room they were in and spotted a man standing down the hallway looking out a window. He put his knife back into the sheath on his lapel, while dropping his bow off his left shoulder and catching it. At the same time that he caught the bow, he simultaneously pulled an arrow from the quiver on his back. Still behind the cover of the wall he quickly knocked the arrow and drew the bow back. He took aim at the wall then breathed in, then exhaled half out and held. He leaned to the side, instantly finding the target he had anticipated, and squeezed the trigger on his bow release. The arrow flew through the air and found its mark in and through the side of the guard's head, embedding into the wall beyond him. His hand went up to the spot where it had hit, then he collapsed to the floor as his fingers felt at the hole that was now through his brain.

"Just like deer hunting." Martin whispered. "Let's move."

He reloaded his bow while the others moved down the hall in a crouch. Just then a door at the end of the hall opened. They all froze their advance as another guard entered the hallway looking down at the cups he was holding and trying not to spill.

"Hey Clint, I brought you a coffee. I don't know what's going on out there, but..." His words were cut short by the arrow now embedded in his forehead.

The cups hit the floor as his body was pushed into a backwards fall by the force of the arrows impact into the much thicker front and back portions of the skull. They began moving again, Martin retrieving and wiping the blood from his arrows as he passed by each of the two dead men.

"We have to hurry." Martin whispered to the others. "It's only a matter of time before the guards outside figure out what's going on."

Carefully moving through the door that the guard with the coffee had just come through, they made their way down another hall and entered a break room. It was empty so they moved through the room, exiting the door on the other side.

"What are we looking for exactly?" James quietly asked from behind Martin.

"The door down to the bunker below." He responded.

After sneaking around for a few more minutes Martin cracked open a door to have a peak. On the other side of the door was a large room with two curved staircases off to the right and left of the room. It was the main entrance of the mansion. Also to Martin's surprise, the mayor himself was there in the center of the room, nervously pacing as if he was waiting for something. The front door suddenly opened and Martin ducked back a little more as about twenty men entered the house from outside .

"I don't know where those lazy assholes went or why they would trip the alarms before they ditched their posts." Said the guard in front. "But I assure you, Mr. Mayor, that they will be punished severely for this false alarm."

The alarm abruptly stopped. Martin slowly and silently closed and locked the door, then turned to the others.

"How did they not find the bodies?" He asked in a breathy whisper.

"The one's outside the gate?" Jacob returned.

Martin nodded.

"We threw them in the ditch on the other side of the road. We figured it was a good idea." Said James.

"It was. Good thinking."

"They will most likely find the ones we killed in that hallway though. There wasn't anything we could do to hide those bodies."

"We'll just have to make sure we finish the job and disappear before they do."

"Captain! Sir, Clint and Tom are dead!" A man yelled as he barged through the door into the main entrance.

"Well, that was quick." Jacob said turning to unlock and open the door a crack.

"What!" Said the Captain in a harsh angry tone. "What do you mean they're dead? How and where?"

"They were found at their posts in the hallway of the East wing, sir!"

"Damn it! There's someone in the house!" He said as he pointed at one of the body guards. "Get that fat idiot Mayor back downsta..." The back of the Mayor's head suddenly splattered across the wall behind where he stood, cutting the Captain's words off in the middle of giving his orders.

"Kill confirmed." Gabriel said after taking the shot.

The 6.5 Creedmoor from his AR10 at such a short distance was definitely overkill, but he figured that it was better to be sure.

"You think so? I'm surprised you could tell. At such an incredible distance, I was wondering how we would ever know if he was dead or not." Said Jacob, his words dripping with sarcasm.

All the guards save the Captain were frozen with shock. The Captain fell into a chair and began to rub his eyes.

"This is going to be a lot to explain to The Order's counsel." He said in a groan.

"Sir, orders." Said one of the guards looking up from the dead Mayor.

"Whoever did this is better than us, and is without a doubt long gone by now. They've probably been planning this for weeks and every single thing that happened tonight was all part of their plan."

"You could just blame Kyle and Jeff for abandoning their posts. Let them deal with the repercussions of this. They got it coming anyway."

The Captain just rubbed his face. Still hidden in the other room Martin leaned over close to Gabriel.

"We should probably go now." He said In an almost inaudible whisper.

Gabriel nodded and they began to backtrack in the direction of the window they had entered the house from. They made their way through the house until they got to the break room that they had passed through earlier. There were now three men sitting at the table. Martin and the others silently snuck up behind them. The guards didn't stand a chance and definitely didn't see it coming. Their eyes were a tell tale sign to their surprise as the blades of Martin, Gabriel and James's knives stabbed into their necks.

Once they were done in the break room, they quickly made their way down the hall, through the door and past the bodies to the window. Jacob slowly began to open it, but when the window was about halfway open, the alarm sounded again. Gabriel knocked his head against the wall in aggravation, while the others jumped out one by one and ran for the gate. Once the others were out and moving, Gabriel leaped out and followed after them. They could hear a commotion coming from the front of the house, so they made an effort to run faster.

"There they are!" Shouted a guard from the front steps.

"Don't let them escape you idiots!" Shouted another. "And I want them alive!"

Martin and the team sprinted for the gate. Sacrificing stealth for speed they charged towards the five men standing in their way of escape. With expert precision they put down all five without pause. Jacob then kicked in the door to the gatehouse that sat about fifteen feet away from the gate and quickly smacked down on the big button labeled 'open'. With a clang the gate began to swing open. Jacob then ran back outside and looked towards the mansion, and the two dozen men chasing after them.

"Nope." He said as he turned and started sprinting for the now open gate.

The others were already halfway across the road, while the horde of angry guards barreled down the hill after them as they ran.

"Welp, this is probably as good a time as any." Jacob said as he pulled a fragmentation grenade out of a small pouch on his plate carrier. He then pulled the pin and threw it over his shoulder as he ran through the open gate and onto the street. After running about fifty more feet, he risked a look behind him. The guards must not have noticed what he had thrown, because they did not even slow their chase at all. As soon as the second row of them passed where he had dropped the grenade, it exploded with a deafening sound and blinding flash.

Jacob made it to the trees catching up with the others a moment later. He could hear the screaming of the dying men, and the cursing of the men stepping over the bodies as they attempted to continue their pursuit.

"Where did you get a grenade?" Martin asked as they ran.

"Where do you think I got a grenade? I stole it from Franklin." He shrugged.

"You shouldn't steal things, Jacob."

"I know, but it saved our lives so you're just gonna have to live with it."

"Just shut up and run you crazy bastard." Martin said, shaking his head and smiling behind his mask.

# CHAPTER: 38

**M**ARTIN and the team had run the entire mile back to the Hummer without slowing. It had been a difficult run that they made in about ten minutes, but besides being quite out of breath they did finish the job and escape without too much issue, all things considered. They all then jumped into their seats and shut the doors. Jacob turned the ignition and the engine came to life. He then threw it in gear and hit the accelerator, tearing out from behind the store. Turning out of the parking lot and onto the street Jacob took the road heading back in the direction of Franklin's.

"Mission accomplished boys. Good job." Gabriel said from the back seat, still panting from the run.

"Wait to celebrate till we get to safety. There's no way that we're not being followed." Said Martin from the passenger seat.

"Right, good thinking. Wouldn't wanna jinx us."

"I don't know about you guys, but I'm going to sleep. Wake me up when we're back at Franklin's." Said James.

"Sure thing. Are you two sleeping also?" Jacob asked.

"I am." Said Gabriel. "I'm beat. Wake us up if we get attacked."

"I'll stay up with you." Said Martin. "I'm not that tired."

"Cool." Said Jacob. "What do you wanna talk about?"

"Is there anything to talk about?"

"Sure there is. Remember that time when we beat the hell out of that guy in the back alley of that bar for harassing that one girl?"

"Yeah, he cried like the little bitch that he was." Martin said, laughing lightly.

"Yeah." Jacob said with a smile that soon faded. "I miss those days. Everything was so simple back then."

"It is what it is."

"Do you miss those days?"

"No, I don't. I'm glad they happened, but I do not miss them."

"Why not? I miss them."

"A moment in the past is no longer yours. A moment in the future is not yours yet. This moment now, is all that matters. Because it's the only moment you actually have, and the only thing you can truly call yours."

"Okay, Mr. Blank. Whatever you say." Jacob said sarcastically.

They were silent for a little while until Jacob began humming a tune. Then quietly singing the words to a song.

"I don't yet remember tomorrow, I haven't yet planned for yesterday, if there was time that I could borrow, I'd take out a loan each and every day."

"What is that?" Martin asked.

"Oh, it's just a song by this unknown band that I heard before things went to hell. What you said reminded me of it. I don't remember their name. They're probably dead now anyway."

"What does it mean?"

"I think it's about a guy that ends up losing everything, and so he spends his life wishing for the days of his past back, instead of allowing himself a future. That's what I got from the music video anyway."

"Sounds interesting. It's too bad that I didn't get the chance to see it. Probably never will either, since there's no internet anymore."

"Yeah, I remember at the very end of the video it had a quote that read 'Appreciate everything you have while you have it. Because everything has a timer, and it is set to go off when you least expect it.' I don't know how I remember that, I guess it just stuck with me for some reason."

"It is good advice. I think it's for the best that you continue to remember it. And also try to follow it."

"Alright, I will."

They were silent for a short while before Jacob spoke up again.

"Man, I know shit has gotten bad, but seriously where is everyone? I feel like it's been forever since I've seen another regular person."

"Not counting all the people that died before the invasion. Anyone less prepared than we were is either dead from starvation, was killed during the invasion or is still in a concentration camp somewhere." Said Martin.

"You really think that many people have died from starvation?"

"America worked on a just in time delivery system, remember? Also most Americans were overweight. As soon as the supply chain stopped, the people who relied on it were starving within a week, tops."

"Damn, I can barely believe that our system and society was really that fragile."

"It was all by design. This was all part of the plan. Control the food, control the people. Control the information, control the minds. It's all very simple if you understand how things operate, and how both the corrupt and the weak minds work."

"Makes sense. But how do the corrupt people actually win if there's nobody left to do their bidding?"

"Slavery. It's always been how they get anything done."

"Slavery? But wasn't that made illegal a long time ago?"

"Of course. It was definitely and rightfully made illegal… for you and me that is. But for the elite, of course not. Nothing is illegal if you have enough money and power."

"That's messed up if that's true."

"Of course it's true. Laws don't mean, or do anything. Laws only ever exist for the plebes like us. They don't apply to criminals or to those with power and influence, but I repeat myself."

"Is that why you want to kill them all?"

"More or less. Their greed and selfishness is actually the only reason we are even in this mess or doing any of this in the first place."

"But how are we supposed to kill them all?"

"One at a time."

"How are we supposed to find them so we can do that?"

"Simple, stop the supplies to wherever they are, and they will either come out of hiding, or they starve to death. Either way is fine with me.

# CHAPTER: 39

**T**HE light from the sun had just begun to appear on the horizon as the team drew near to Franklin's. They had ended up having to take a detour to evade the pursuit from the Mayor's men, which added a few extra hours onto their trip. And they had made it with barely fumes of gas to spare.

The gate at the end of Franklin's driveway opened as they pulled up to it. Jacob then drove through and headed up the drive. He pulled up and parked out front of the house. As they all exited the Hummer, Franklin stood up from his chair next to the table that was off to the right of the front doors. He then walked over to the top step and waved for them to come up. Once they were all at the top of the steps he shook their hands in greeting.

"So, how did it go?" Franklin asked.

"The mission was a success." Martin answered.

"Excellent. Would you like your payment now, or after breakfast?"

"After breakfast would be preferred. We are all quite hungry."

"I believe it. How long has it been since your last actual meal?"

"About a day and a half."

"Heavens! I'll have something prepared right away."

Franklin snapped his fingers and the butler moved to his side.

"Have a four course breakfast made and set out for our guests, as soon as possible." He said.

The butler gave a slight bow, then turned and walked into the house.

"I believe it shouldn't take but thirty minutes for the food to be done. Now please come in. I want to hear of all that happened on your mission."

They all made their way inside and sat in the living area off to the left of the ball room where they had sat the day before. They then proceeded to tell Franklin all they had gone through since they left for the mission.

"My goodness. So you probably wouldn't have made it back if it wasn't for that grenade?" Franklin asked.

"There is a good chance we would not have outrun them otherwise." Said Martin.

"Well I'm glad you took it then. As long as it helped you with the mission then I will consider it as a down payment. In addition to the full payment of course. You can pick everything out after we eat."

"We appreciate your understanding." Said Martin.

"For sure. However, please just ask next time, Jacob. I try to keep a fairly strict inventory on all the products I have."

"Absolutely." Said Jacob. "To be honest I just wasn't thinking. I hadn't even realized that I was holding it until we came back upstairs. But by that time I decided to just hold onto it."

"I can see that happening." Said Franklin. "Again, no worries. I'm glad that it helped you escape."

Just then the butler appeared in the doorway.

"Breakfast is served." He said with his hand out gesturing them into the next room.

"Great, let's eat." Franklin said, standing up from his chair.

They all moved into the dining room and grabbed plates from the stack sitting on a small rolling cart.

"Remember to eat slowly guys. It's been a while and we don't want anyone getting sick." Martin said as they began to fill their plates.

"We know, Martin." Said Gabriel with a smile and a roll of his eyes.

"Just making sure that you remember."

After they all had their plates, Martin sat down at the far end of the table away from everyone else. He then unclipped the bottom latches on his mask and pushed the plate that covered his mouth, upwards on the hinge that was hidden by the nose guard. The purpose of the mask opening in this way allowed him to eat while still shielding his face from the others. None of them took notice of this though. Or if they did, none of them let it on. As Martin put a piece of chicken into his mouth he immediately noticed that it had absolutely no flavor, or texture. Spitting it back out onto his plate he decided to try a carrot. It was the same as the chicken. After quietly spitting it back out also, he looked around at the others to see if they were having the same problem. They did not appear to be having any distastefulness for the food whatsoever. Confused, Martin looked at his plate, wondering what could possibly be going wrong with him. After staring for a while with no appetite, he just closed his mask and then slid his plate forward. When the rest of them finished eating, Franklin stood and the rest of them followed suit.

"Well then, shall we get to the selection of your payment?"

"Sure. Lead the way." Said Gabriel.

Franklin clasped his hands together, then turned and began heading for the elevator. With the same process as before they made their way down to the armory. Once inside the armory they began looking at different kinds of weapons to decide the ones they wanted. Martin already selected his weapon before the mission. The Barrett M107a1. It was still sitting on the table where he had left it, so he walked over to it. Franklin followed him for a moment then went to sit behind a large wooden desk. Martin picked up the rifle, dropped the magazine, then grabbed the charging handle and racked the bolt. The Barrett M107a1 was a semi automatic anti material rifle. Chambered in .50bmg and with the 29" barrel, it was capable of delivering a killing blow at up to 2000 yards, if the person behind the trigger was good enough. Martin was confident in his ability, and with the addition of the Nightforce scope, he knew he could take out any target from wherever was required factoring in of course that being a 2 MOA gun it wasn't the most accurate but it made up for that by being semi-auto.

"How many rounds are you willing to throw in with it?" Martin asked.

"I can probably do a one hundred round can." Said Franklin.

"How much for an additional can?"

"As I said before, I'll take anything of value that I can either use myself, or resell."

Martin thought for a moment.

"Would you be willing to trade the rounds for a Steyr AUG?"

"Absolutely I would. Taking an offer like that is kind of a no brainer."

"Yeah. Before shit went to shit, people probably would've called me an idiot for making that offer, but I'll most likely need the ammo before I need a weapon system I haven't trained with enough to be familiar with."

"I can understand that. I'd be interested in taking a look at anything else you've got that you'd be willing to trade. I am a businessman after all, and a lot of my inventory is stuff that I took in on trade."

"Sounds good. We can go have a look once we've finished up down here, if that works." Said Martin.

"Sounds good to me. I'll call some of my men down to help you carry stuff, once we are all finished up."

"I appreciate it."

Martin turned and walked over to where the others were checking over the guns they were interested in.

"Find anything you like?" Martin asked.

"I've narrowed it down to the M249 and this golden Desert Eagle." James said, holding the large pistol up for Martin to see.

"I'd say go for the M249. It would be much more useful to us."

"You're right, but I've always wanted one of these."

"Is it more important to have what you need, or to have what you want?"

"I see what you're saying. Alright then, I'll take the M249."

"Maybe we can trade Franklin my black Desert Eagle and something else for the gold one. If we do, you can have it."

"Hell yeah, that would be awesome. Thanks."

"No problem. What did you pick Gabriel?"

"Russian Dragunov." He said holding it up with excitement.

"A classic, nice. What about you, Jacob?"

Jacob, who was standing next to Gabriel holding a green wooden box, looked up at Martin and grinned.

"I'm fine with my new AUG, so I decided that I'll follow my gut. Except I'm gonna take it to the next level this time and get us the entire box of grenades."

"That's probably a little more than the price of a single gun. But we can probably even out the difference by trading Franklin some of the other stuff we got."

"Sweet, let's get it done." Said Jacob. "Now that I've eaten and the food has settled, I'm getting pretty tired. I think if I don't get some sleep soon, I'll probably just pass out anyway."

"You and me both." Gabriel said in agreement.

"Well then if you're all finished picking shit out, let's get on with it, I would also like to rest for a little while before we leave."

The items they had picked out were approved, and then agreements were made to cover the cost of the differences. Once they were finished, they all went back upstairs and then out to the Hummer to give Franklin the items they had agreed on trading. Then they took a quick look through their stuff to see if they had anything else they could trade for things they needed more. When all was said and done, they had decided on trading all but one of the AUG's and all but three of the M4 carbines, for ammo, food and med-kits.

The day was drawing to a close by the time they were done finalizing all of their dealings. Once they were done, Franklin's men had brought everything up so they could load it into the Hummer.

"Pleasure doing business with you." Said Franklin, putting his hand out for Martin to shake.

"Likewise." Martin returned, taking his hand and firmly shaking it.

"So, when do you wanna get going?" Gabriel asked.

"You are all welcome to spend the night." Franklin offered. "I have plenty of guest rooms, and I'm sure you'd prefer actual beds over however you sleep out there on the road."

"We don't want to be a burden. You've done enough for us." Said Martin.

"Nonsense, I insist."

Martin looked at the others. Jacob nodded and shrugged.

"One night shouldn't hurt." Martin said finally.

"We are grateful. We will get out of your hair first thing in the morning." Gabriel added.

"Very good. My butler, Winston, will Show you to your rooms."

"I can't thank you enough for your hospitality." Said Martin.

"Please, it's my pleasure. I hope to work, or do business with you in the future."

"Count on it. It might be a while before we make it back around to this area though. Are you planning on remaining in this area for a while?" Martin asked.

"I'm not sure yet. Maybe I'll go forth to try my hand at bringing peace back to the world."

"Good luck with that."

"Indeed. Well, In case I don't see you in the morning before you leave. Good luck and stay safe."

Martin gave a slight bow of his head then turned and they all followed Winston to their rooms.

The next morning they were all up and ready to go before sunrise. As they all made their way into the main ballroom, Winston stood by the front door waiting to see them off.

"Tell Franklin thanks for everything, and that we'll be back to see him again one of these days." Martin said, setting his backpack on the ground at the top of the steps. "Also thank you for taking care of us during our stay."

Winston gave a slight bow.

"It was my pleasure sir. I look forward to your return."

They all shook Winston's hand then walked out the door and down the steps to their Hummer that was waiting for them out front. It had been taken down to Franklin's private gas station by one of the guards the night before to be fueled up then brought back around. That way it would be ready for them no matter where they were heading.

They all climbed in and shut the doors. It was Martin's turn to drive this time, so Gabriel took the shotgun seat with the Benelli M4, which was of course the proper gun for the position. James was in the seat behind Martin with his new M249 and golden Desert Eagle. Jacob sat behind Gabriel with his Steyr AUG. Martin started the Hummer, put it in gear then pulled away. As he drove down the driveway, for some reason Martin had a feeling they wouldn't be coming back there. At least not for a long while anyway. He looked in the rear view mirror and saw Winston still standing at the top of the steps, waving goodbye as they drove off.

"Everything is about to change." Martin said aloud.

"What makes you say that?" Gabriel asked.

"I just have a strange feeling in my gut."

"It's probably just the food we had last night. It was delicious but I think it's messing with my stomach." Said Jacob.

"Not that kind of feeling, jackwagon." Said Martin. "I feel like something is gonna go wrong."

"We've had good luck so far. I wouldn't worry about it." Said Jacob brushing it off.

"That's the thing about luck though. It always runs out. Because all good things must come to an end sooner or later."

"We'll worry about that when it's time to worry." Said James. "Where are we going now anyway?"

"Well we have the proper weaponry now, so we're gonna go take out the asshole that took my family from me.

"Sounds good. How are we gonna do that though?" Asked Gabriel.

"Very carefully. And from the back of a car."

"This Hummer is a little high profile for that though, don't you think."

"We're not going to use the Hummer. We're going to steal a new car once we get close to where we're going."

"Just lead the way man. We'll follow wherever you take us.".

Martin looked back to the road and thought about those words. "Lead the way. She said that once." It was the day a new part of his life began. A day that felt like ages ago.

"Is it safe?" Ellis asked him.

"Of course it is safe. I wouldn't have brought you up here if it wasn't." He replied.

"Okay then. I suppose that I trust you." She said with a smile.

He smiled back then took her hand and led her up the stairs to the walkway, then up another set of stairs to the platform. They both walked over to the railing and Martin leaned against it.

"It's beautiful from up here isn't it?" He said as he looked out to the edge of the world where the sun was beginning to set.

"It is." She said as she moved in close and he put his arm around her.

"I'm glad you brought me up here. It's perfect."

"I have something for you. Close your eyes."

He pulled away from her embrace and held her at arm's length.

"I told you that you don't have to do that." She said, shaking her head and smiling.

"Just close your eyes. It's different."

She looked at him for a second with a raised eyebrow and a half smile then closed her eyes.

"This better not be some kind of prank where when I open my eyes you're hiding to scare me or something."

"Don't worry, it's nothing like that... you can open your eyes now."

When she did, she saw Martin down on one knee, holding a ring in his fingertips. Her hands went to her mouth in surprise.

"Ellis, will you marry me?" He asked.

Tears began to run down her cheeks as she touched his hand with hers.

"Yes, of course I will." She said in a happy sob.

Martin stood up, then he moved in and kissed her gently.

"Why do I keep allowing myself to have these flashbacks?" Martin asked himself in thought, as he watched the road before him. "Am I just subconsciously trying to see if I can still feel anything? How was I once that guy? That kind man who could treat a woman with such kindness? How have I now become so different? Could I ever be that way again? No, I can't, and I don't want to. People only ever change for the worse, never for the better. It is what it is. There's nothing I can do to change it now."

Once he was finished scolding himself for trying to feel, he looked over to Gabriel who was sitting in the passenger seat, cleaning his Russian Dragunov that he got from Franklin.

"How's it going?" Martin asked.

"This thing was filthy." Gabriel said, looking up from his work. "I don't think it has ever been cleaned before."

"I bet it still would've run without a failure though."

"You're probably right, but I'd rather not take my chances with a dirty gun. Even if it is an AK platform rifle."

"Fair enough."

"So, where are we going?"

"Washington DC. Commander Wong is there. And that's where I'm gonna kill him."

"How do you know that he's gonna be there?"

"Franklin told me."

"Do you think he's right though?"

"Even if he's not. I'm sure that whatever we find there will be something worth disrupting."

# CHAPTER: 40

## *Washington DC, underground base.*

**W**HERE are they?" Brian said as he paced the floor, visibly stressed. "It's about to be dark. Why aren't they back yet?"

"I'm sure they won't be long now." Said Lynn. "They're probably just playing in the street."

Brian stopped pacing and turned to look at her.

"That might have been funny under normal circumstances. But in all honesty I am starting to get a really unsettled feeling about them being gone so long."

Suddenly, the door flew open and Tyler rushed in tripping over a stool and falling to the ground in a heap. He got up as quickly as he had fallen then moved towards them with urgency in his face.

"Brian!" He said in a panic. "Brian, they took them!"

Brian's heart jumped into his throat.

"What are you talking about? Who took who?" He asked.

"I tried to stop them but Scarlet insisted that we go outside the perimeter. Then the Chinese took all of them!"

"Then what the hell are you doing here?" Brian asked through clenched teeth.

"They let me go. They wanted me to bring you a message. Don't worry though I am positive that I wasn't followed." Tyler quickly added.

"Let me guess." Brian began. "They told you to come tell us that we should mount a rescue mission so that they can spring the trap on us as soon as we try anything. They've probably been watching you scavenging for days."

"Seems like the most logical explanation." Said Tyler.

"You think so? To figure that out all on your own you must be a genius for the books."

"Enough arguing." Said Lynn. "We're wasting time that we could be using to go after them."

"We? No, I will go alone." Said Brian. "They will be expecting a larger group. I'll have more of an advantage by myself."

"You sure about that?" Asked Lynn.

"The only thing I'm sure of right now is that I'm pissed."

"You don't have to go alone." Said Lynn. "We can send a few of the scouts with you."

"It's more important that they stay, we need as many people as possible to protect the base. Really, I'll be fine on my own."

"If those damn kids would have just listened and stayed inside the perimeter, then none of this would be happening." Lynn said in frustration.

"Is there anything I can do?" Tyler asked.

"You can show me the last place you saw Scarlet and the others and the direction they were taken. Then you will come back here and you will do nothing until you are ordered otherwise." Said Brian. "Now, I'm going to get my gear and then you will lead me there."

A short time later Tyler accompanied Brian to the spot where the others had been captured. Once they got there Tyler explained exactly what had happened.

"They were taken that way." Tyler said, pointing off towards the west.

"Are you sure?" Brian asked.

"Yes. I looked back as I was running away. Just to double check that I knew the direction."

"Okay. You can head back to base now. If I'm successful then I'll be back in a couple days. If not, well, it was nice knowing ya kid."

"Likewise sir. But don't worry, I have hope. I'm sure you'll find them and be back without a problem."

"I tend not to rely so much on hope."

"Well, that's no way to live."

"Yes, but it is the way that I live. Run along now. You're wasting valuable time just standing here."

With an informal salute Tyler turned and headed back towards their base following the way they had come. Brian watched him go for a moment then turned to look off into the west where the moon was chasing the sun to the horizon and the last glow of light was quickly fading into darkness.

"Why can't life ever just be easy?" Brian said to himself.

Then with a shrug and a grunt, he pulled the straps of his armor plate carrier and backpack a little tighter then he began walking.

"So this is my next journey into the unknown. I wonder if I'll make it back this time around."

He walked until the sun began to rise at his back and continued walking through into the afternoon until he came upon a small house that looked cozy enough to stay in for the night. As good as he was at walking, he really didn't wanna wear himself out on the first day of what was sure to be many on this new journey. He figured that he had made pretty good progress for the first leg of the trip, so he decided to call it an early day. As he walked up to the front door of the house he looked in all directions around his location, scanning for any potential threats. When he reached the door he knocked lightly.

"Hello, is anyone home?" He asked in a little more than a whisper.

There was no answer, so after waiting a few more seconds, he entered the house then closed and locked the door behind him. Once he had cleared all the rooms in the house and made sure that it was safe he sat down at the kitchen table and made himself dinner. It wasn't much, just some jerky and a can of mixed vegetables that Lynn had packed for him before he set out. Once he finished eating he went upstairs and while still fully clothed he crawled into the small bed. In the days before, the room the bed was in had probably been considered the master headroom by whomever it was that owned the house. But to Brian it was good enough. As he lay there thinking about where exactly the kids might have been taken, his fatigue finally caught up with him. A few moments later he drifted off into a somewhat deep sleep.

Brian awoke the next day feeling stiff and groggy, but still more or less well rested. He got up slowly, hanging his legs off the bed to sit for a moment while he finished waking up.

"Scarlet." He said, suddenly looking up as he remembered what he was supposed to be doing.

He quickly stood up from the bed, grabbed his M4 carbine then raced down the stairs and out the door. Once outside in the daylight he saw a convoy of vehicles traveling west down a road about a mile away from where he currently stood. He looked through his flip up magnifier scope to get a better look at the vehicles but the only real thing he could make out was that they were all military green with red dots on the sides. He thought about it for only a few seconds before deciding to follow their path. Worst case scenario, they would lead him to nothing. Best case scenario, they would lead him to where they were keeping Scarlet and the others. It was a long shot, but it was the best shot he currently had.

It was closing in on late afternoon of the second day by the time Brian finally tracked down and caught up with the trucks. He could see from the bushes where he was hiding that the trucks had been parked in the lot outside of a high school for some time now. He figured it was probably a good idea to sit and watch them for a little while before he made any rash decisions. He wasn't actually even sure yet if Scarlet was in there or not. And if she was then he didn't want to take any chances of putting her in more danger than she probably already was.

"Psst."

Brian froze at the sudden hushed sound.

"Psst. Hey Larry, turn your comms back on."

Brian slowly turned to look behind him and saw nothing but trees and bushes. Then to his surprise one of the bushes removed its hood to reveal the face of man who upon seeing Brian clearly now dawned a confused expression.

"Wait, who are you?" The bush man asked as the muzzle of a rifle trained onto him from the mid section of the bush.

"I'm an American." Brian replied gruffly.

"Oh... Okay cool." Said the man, his expression becoming instantly more relaxed. "So, are you gonna help us get rid of some commies?"

"Sure, I'll do what I can."

"Good enough. My name's Wade, by the way."

"I'm Brian. So what's your plan?"

"Hit the invaders hard and fast, leave none of them alive."

"Sounds reasonable. When are we going?" Brian asked.

Wade looked down at his watch, then back at Brian.

"From right now, like 90 seconds."

"Sounds like you've thought this plan through thoroughly enough."

"Yeah, hopefully... possibly... probably... yes, absolutely we have." Wade said finally and with much confidence.

"Well, that escalated quickly." Brian mumbled under his breath before saying. "Fantastic."

Brian turned away from Wade to face towards the school and readied up.

"Feels kinda weird that we're about to charge a school while being fully armed, wouldn't you agree?" Brian asked as he pulled his pistol from the holster and press checked the slide to make sure a round was chambered.

"Not really. We're going in there to save innocent people, not hurt them. It doesn't feel weird at all."

"I mean like, the whole taking guns into the school thing, ya know."

"You talking about school shootings?" Wade laughed. "Because you do know that If they would've allowed us to protect our children the way they protected their corrupt politicians there never would have been such a thing as a school shooting, right? Those types of things only ever happened in gun free zones, where guns already weren't allowed. The only reason the term 'Capitol Shooting' never existed is because they had armed guards. The fact that we weren't allowed to protect ourselves is proof enough that school shootings were encouraged by the very poeple who swore to protect us, all so they could push an agenda."

"Yeah, you're probably right. I'm probably just overthinking it."

"You're damn right I'm right. Because everyone knows criminals always follow all of the laws." Wade said sarcastically.

"Laws are made for the innocent who will continue to follow them. The guilty have already broken them and will continue to do so." Said Brian.

"Yeah, pretty much. You ready, my friend?" Wade asked.

Brian nodded then pulled the charging handle of his M4 back slightly to check on the round in the chamber. Seeing the gun was ready he released the charging handle then hit the forward assist twice to make sure the bolt went back into battery properly. By this time Wade was moving past him in the direction of the school. Brian followed close behind him for about one hundred feet until Wade suddenly stood up and began sprinting for the school. Brian stood in surprise wondering why Wade would give away their location so irresponsibly. That's when he noticed something in his peripheral vision, he turned to see what it was and running towards the school was another person dressed similar to Wade. Then he noticed another, and another. After taking about a second to process what was happening he guessed there were at least two dozen fighters charging the school building.

As he watched them all close in on the invaders location he suddenly understood what it was that was going on. It was actually a full scale organized attack, and he was just standing there in a field. All at once he started sprinting after Wade, who was already making his way across the parking lot to the front door. That's when the first shots were fired. Wade shot through the glass at the head of the soldier who was standing just inside the door. The bullet dropped him instantly as it scrambled his brains on its way through his skull. Wade then breached the doors and pushed inside. Brian heard more shots from the far side of the building, then more from another side. With renewed effort Brian ran harder to the aid of the men he barely even knew.

He burst through the door and immediately broke into a slide, just barely dodging underneath the hail of bullets from their enemies guns. He quickly jumped to the side of the door behind a concrete wall, just in time for a spray of bullets to hit where he had been only a split second before. Wade was on the other side of the doorway from where Brian was currently crouched. Brian made an effort to get his attention then he held up three fingers and began to lower them one at a time. Once he put down the last finger, he clenched his fist and gave the signal for GO.

They both stood up at the same time and immediately began laying down fire towards the enemy, alternating when they reloaded so as not to allow the enemy even a chance to return fire. After Brian emptied his first magazine he quickly ducked down, reloaded in a flash then was back up and shooting a moment later.

*BOOM!*

Brian and Wade both hit the deck as fragments and debris flew over the walls where they were taking cover.

"What the hell was that!" Brian yelled to Wade.

"That was part of the plan!" He yelled back.

"Maybe a little heads up next time?"

"I never said it was a good plan!"

After listening to the ringing of his ears for a moment, Brian lowered his head into the dust on the floor and began lightly laughing at the stupidity of this whole ordeal.

"Common man, it wasn't that funny. Let's go see who they've got locked up in this place. They always have some kind of prisoners." Wade said as he stood up and brushed himself off.

"I'll check in the basement." Brian said after collecting himself. "If they're holding people, I'd imagine they'd probably keep them down there."

"Get on it. I'll send some of the others down once we finish off the rest of them up here."

Brian nodded once then stood up and ran for the stairwell at the same time that Wade stood up to cover him. As he bounded down the stairs taking them multiple steps at a time he heard gunshots coming from back where he had left Wade. He only hoped that the gunshots he was hearing were pointed at the enemy and not the other way around.

Once he arrived in the basement he immediately began clearing the rooms, searching for anyone in need of rescue. Six rooms in he hadn't found anything useful. As he approached the next room he cleared one of the blind corners then he quickly crossed the doorway to clear the other one, sweeping the room as he went. He leaned in tight to the wall as he shined his light as far into the corner of the room as he could. Satisfied it was likely empty, he entered and then swept the rest of the room before opening the closet. While he was looking through the closet he suddenly heard a small coo sound through the wall coming from the room next to the one he was currently in. His adrenaline spiked and he rushed back to the door then walked around to the neighboring door and slowly pushed it open from the side.

He quickly cleared the first corner and as he was crossing to clear the fourth he saw and identified that there was a young girl tied to a desk. He quickly cleared the corner then moved through the doorway sweeping the rest of the room as he approached the girl. Once he reached her he knelt down in front of her to assess the damage. She was dirty and her hair was covering her face. Brian then carefully began to brush her hair away and breathed a sigh of relief. It was her, it was Scarlet. As soon as her hair was moved completely away from her open eyes she snapped at his hand. Brian jumped back and shined his flashlight at the ceiling to illuminate the room.

"It's me, it's me!" He said, putting his hand out to fend her off.

Upon realizing it was Brian her attitude immediately switched from wrath to tears of joy. She tried to approach him but the desk she was cuffed to was too heavy for her to move.

"How did you find me?" She said through the tears that had begun to stream through the dirt on her face.

"Luck I guess. There's really no other way to put it. It was pure luck."

"That makes sense." She snickered then sniffled. "Is it just you?"

"From our group, yes." Brian said. "I met some people outside though, and they are currently upstairs taking care of business."

"Okay. Do you have anything that can get me out of these handcuffs?" She asked.

Brian was already scanning the room for something to use but at that point he hadn't yet found anything. After a few seconds he realized that he was only wasting time. He walked back over to Scarlet and drew his pistol.

"Umm, what are you doing?" She asked incredulously.

"Never try this at home, kids." He said as he put the muzzle of the gun onto the chain where two of the links met. He then squeezed the trigger. The bullet did as intended, severing the chain with only minor spalling of the metals while the bullet fragments hit the far side of the room with damage being done only to the drywall.

"We'll finish getting the cuffs off later. Where are the others?" Brian asked, looking around.

Scarlet wiped the tears away from her face with her newly freed hands and said.

"They're gone."

"What do you mean they're gone? Gone where?" Brain asked.

"Sold to the highest bidder." Scarlet said. "I heard some men and a woman talking about it. Apparently they were saving me for the son of one of thier Commanders or something."

Before that moment Brian didn't know that it was possible to be so angry, but there wasn't time for that now so he quickly brushed his anger asside.

"Wait, how did you understand them?" Asked Brian. "The Chinese don't usually speak to each other in English."

"They weren't Chinese. I think I remember one of them saying the name, Dante Greenskin, or something like that."

"What? Never mind, you can tell me about it later. Are you hurt at all? Or are you good enough to walk on your own?"

"I think okay. I'm a little hungry but I think I can manage for a little bit."

"Okay, just let me know if you're feeling weak and need to be carried."

"I will. Thank you for saving me, Brian."

"Thank me when we're actually back to safety."

"Does safety actually even still exist in this world?"

Brian looked at her for a second, trying to figure out the answer to that question himself.

"Let's go find out." He said finally.

"Brian, where ya at, man?!" A shout came from down the hall.

Brian took Scarlet's hand then moved to the door and peaked out with his pistol at the ready. He saw Wade frantically running down the hall, looking into the rooms as he did. Brian stepped out to meet him.

"I'm here. What's going on?" He asked.

"We've gotta go, man. They must've called in reinforcements. We've gotta go now. Grab anyone you can find and let's get out of here."

"She's the only one here." Brian said before thinking to himself. "What are the odds that the one I was looking for the most was the only one left? Really, what were the odds that i'd actually ever have found her at all."

Wade looked at Scarlet then at Brian without saying anything. He rubbed his face then turned and started walking towards the stairs. Brian and Scarlet followed.

"Where are all of your people?" Brian asked as they began to move up the stairs.

"They already retreated." Said Wade.

"Alright. How long do you think we have?"

"Like two minutes, tops."

"Cutting it a little close don't you think?"

"You can't prepare for something that you don't know or foresee."

"Whatever you say, man." Said Brian.

They made it out of the school building then made their way across the back lawn. As they ran they could now hear the sounds of engines coming up the road. Brian turned to look and he saw there was a convoy of trucks moving in their direction, and they were moving fast.

"Pick up the pace." He said as he scooped up Scarlet and started running full tilt for the tree line.

She didn't protest but she did grab hold of his plate carrier to steady herself from bouncing so much as they ran. They made it to the trees at the same time that the trucks were pulling into the school parking lot. Brian turned to look over his shoulder but he couldn't make out much from that distance so they just continued running.

"Do you think they saw us?" Wade asked.

"I don't know. Let's just run till we can't anymore, just to be safe." Said Brian.

"Sounds good."

They ran for a long time before exhaustion set in and they finally had to stop.

"Let's camp there." Brian said, pointing at a flat spot on the ground in a small clearing.

A few hours later after they had all made beds out of moss and grass they just sat around in silence thinking about the events that had transpired that day.

"So, what's your story, Wade? How'd you come to be a part of a militia?" Brian asked, breaking the silence.

"We organized back when the civil war was brewing during the start of the food riots a few years ago." Said Wade. "I guess It was a good thing too. Seeing that we were able to save quite a few people over the past couple weeks after the invasion."

"Was it worth it?" Brian asked.

"I like to think so." Said Wade. "Sad part about it though is that the last of my friends and my group died today. And I'm not sure I understand how I feel about that yet. I mean, we all knew that one day we would all die fighting for what we believed in, but I don't know. I might just be in shock still."

"I thought that they retreated." Brian said, sounding confused.

"I just said that because I didn't want to believe they were actually gone yet."

"I'm sorry. I know how you feel. I lost my whole squad on the first day of the invasion."

"Yeah, well whatcha gonna do. Shit happens, I guess."

"We have a few friends back East in DC. You're welcome to come back with us if you want." Said Brian.

"That would be nice." Said Wade. "Maybe being around new people will help me cope with the loss of the old ones."

"That's the spirit. We'll leave first thing in the morning."

"You think we should try to find a car?"

"If we can find one with gas, then yes."

# PART: V

*"One man who says the right things, at the right time, in the right order, can change the world. Be it for better or worse."*

# CHAPTER: 41

**D**AWN was drawing near as Martin and Jacob sat next to the Hummer waiting for Gabriel and James to return so they could debrief. They were currently in the forest on the outskirts of Washington DC, which was now under the complete control of the communists. Luckily they met a pair of scouts on their second night there, who led them to a friendly group of people hiding out in the sewers. They had been willing to share a few different pathways with Martin and the others, that allowed them passage in and out of the city. However, even with that information they still had to be careful. They could not afford to be captured just yet.

"They're late." Jacob said quietly, looking over at Martin. "What do you think could be keeping them?"

"I'm sure they will be back shortly. They probably just had to take a different way or something." Said Martin in the same low voice.

Just then they heard a twig snap to their left. Martin drew his pistol and Jacob followed suit. Suddenly Gabriel stepped into the small clearing with James behind him.

"That twig snap was sloppy." Martin said gravely.

"My bad. I almost lost my balance back there." Said James leaning out from behind Gabriel.

"What did you find out?" Martin asked.

"The Commander is going to be doing a live press conference tomorrow around noon out front of the Capitol building." Said Gabriel.

"Where did you hear that?" Asked Jacob.

"A couple of the locals heard about it through the grapevine."

"Are you absolutely sure about this?" Martin asked.

"I'm pretty sure. I pressed them about it just to confirm and they did confirm. They said he apparently has a big announcement or something along those lines."

"How well guarded is the capitol? What kind of distance am I looking at?" Asked Martin.

"Extremely. You'll most likely have to take the shot from a few blocks away at least." Said Gabriel.

"How close were you able to get to it?"

"Me? I didn't wanna risk it. But one of the local boys told me that he was able to get within two blocks before he was asked for his papers, then told to get back inside his house. Also they were in the process of putting up more barriers so I'm not sure what it will look like by tomorrow."

"Damn it. That makes things more complicated." Said Martin.

"Are you sure you wanna do this here and now, Martin?" James asked.

"Yes I am sure. We're here, he's here and I at least want to try. And If I miss the shot, it is what it is."

"Okay so what's your plan?" Asked Gabriel.

"We need a throwaway car." Said Martin.

"A getaway car?" Gabriel corrected.

"No, a throwaway car. A car that we can dump wherever and not care."

"Gotcha. Why not just use the Hummer though?"

"Because the Hummer has all our stuff in it. It's also way too high profile. We need a vehicle we can just dump anywhere and forget."

"Okay, I'll go see if I can get one from the local group."

"See if one of them with a passport would be willing to drive too. " Said Martin. "Remember, we don't have passports of our own."

"Good point. I'm sure one of them will."

"Get going then. There's a lot to do, and I wanna be ready before tomorrow morning."

"On it."

The next day, Martin was laying in the trunk of the car with his Barrett M107 in his lap. He had the barrel facing towards the rear of the car, lining up with a hole he cut in the trunk lid. It had only been about a thirty minute drive, but it had felt like hours as they passed through the security checkpoints far too often. He had stayed up all night while the others slept, so he could outfit the car in time for the mission. He had made it so the back seat of the car could fold down to allow him more room to lay back. He had cut an oval hole in the trunk lid just big enough for the barrel and the scope to function from his shooting position back inside the trunk. Even with a suppressor, the semi automatic .50cal is still very loud. So having the entire gun inside the car would also help to suppress the sound that comes from the rifle when firing. He was pretty sure he would still be caught, even with all the precautions and the unconventional way of using a car as a sniper nest. Unfortunately, there was no way to suppress the sound of a large caliber bullet traveling through the air at over 2500 fps. The crack of the round breaking the sound barrier would be a likely giveaway on his location.

When they got to the spot that Martin had requested, the driver swung around and parked the car with the front facing away from the Capitol. The driver then got out and walked into the building trying to act as casual as possible.

"11:46am, almost time." He said looking at his watch before he took aim.

They had all decided and agreed that it was safest if Martin went in alone this time. There was much less chance of them all getting caught this way. So if he did get caught then at least it would only be one of them. The plan was that the driver would stay inside until 12:00pm exactly. Immediately after Martin had made the shot, they would drive away casually.

Still looking through his scope, Martin mapped out the stage where his target would be standing. He also noticed there was a row of chairs at the back of the stage. Most likely for the other leaders to sit. Martin decided he would be emptying the mag. Take as many as he could. Anyone that would be on that stage was without a doubt either a member of The Order, or at least partially responsible for the position the world was currently in.

Ranging the target, he noted down that he was approximately 1500 yards away. He then found a flag next to the stage and noted wind direction then estimated the speed. He gave his best guess on the temperature and humidity, then wrote down his ballpark figure. He then determined that he was facing due East, so he factored in the spin of the earth correlated with the direction he was shooting. Looking at the windage and elevation dials on the scope, he then turned them to the proper settings for the distance and windage, based on all of the factors in his notes.

"This is literally a long shot." Martin said to himself.

He quietly chuckled at the stupid pun, remembering the time that Jacob said.

"Never lose your sense of humor. You may depend on it to survive one day."

Once he had finished dialing in the rifle, he looked through the scope again. There were people beginning to walk up onto the stage and go to their seats. He checked his watch again, it read 11:58am.

"Hope this guy is the type to be on time." He thought. "At least the weather outside isn't too hot."

11:59am hit and Martin saw Commander Wong walk up on the stage. His heart skipped a beat in either excitement or anticipation. He wasn't quite sure why it did anything at all. He wasn't supposed to feel anything anymore.

"Control yourself." He said to himself under his breath.

His watch clicked over to 12:00pm. He immediately took aim, then squeezed the trigger. The first round was a direct hit on the Commander's head. Or at least would have been, if not for the ballistic glass wall in front of the stage.

"Of course there's ballistic glass." Martin said in annoyance.

After the impact of the first round the occupants of the stage all hit the deck. The nine rounds that followed on the same square foot first cracked then broke through the glass causing a panic. One of the rounds managed to hit an old woman wearing a purple dress in the back as she ran away from the stage. All the rest had been a waste.

Martin cursed loudly as the driver got into the car.

"What happened?" The driver asked.

"Mission failure. Get us out of here." Martin said as he climbed out of the trunk to sit in the passenger seat.

The driver pulled away from the curb and drove down the road away from the chaos Martin had just set in motion. They drove right through the barricade and passed four dead soldiers that had once guarded it. The night before, when Martin and the team had met up with the local group to get the car. Some of them had volunteered to clear the path and make sure that Martin and the driver had a better chance to make a clean getaway. It was apparent now that they did their part well.

"Now if only I had done my part, it would have been worth it." Martin thought.

Once they were safely back at the camp outside the city, Martin informed the others of what had happened.

"We're gonna have to move out immediately and then lay low for a little while." Martin said.

"Do you think we'll get another chance at him?" Gabriel asked.

"Probably not. Now that he knows he's being targeted, he will most likely go underground."

"Which direction are we heading once we're ready to go?"

"West, we need to get as far away from the city as possible before they start dropping bombs in random locations to snuff us out."

"We could hide out in the Appalachian mountains. It would be a good vantage point for us."

"Okay, we'll try that. In any event, we'd have to cross over them anyway, so we'll see what happens."

As they were talking, Martin noticed two people off to his right walking over to them.

"I apologize if I'm interrupting anything, but I have something to ask you, sir." The man said as they approached.

"You don't need to call me, sir. Martin is fine." He said.

"And I'm Gabriel. Who are you?"

"Oh, I'm Thomas. We met before. And this is, Lynn. She was the one that led the team in clearing the path for you to safely get out of the city."

"I am in your debt." Martin said with a nod to Lynn. Then turning back to Thomas, he asked. "What was it you wanted to ask?".

"Ah, yes. We have come to realize that the city is a lost cause and it's not safe here anymore. So most of us want to leave and possibly regroup with more forces later on. We actually have someone out on a rescue mission right now." Said Thomas.

"What Thomas is trying to say is. We were going to leave on our own, but we would prefer to travel with you. So we were wondering if you would be okay with that?"

"We normally try to avoid traveling in big groups." Said Martin.

"It will only be for a little while until we find a better location to set up a base of operations." Said Thomas.

Martin looked at Gabriel who after a short pause gave a slight nod.

"Okay you can travel with us for a while, if you can keep up. Just make sure you keep a low profile so as not to give away our location."

"We understand, that's no problem."

"Okay. Get ready to move out. We're leaving in fifteen minutes with or without you." Said Martin.

"Roger that." Said Thomas.

With that Thomas dismissed himself, but Lynn remained where she stood.

"Was there something else you wanted to say?" Martin asked.

"Yes, there was a member of our group that left right before you all got here. His name is Brian and his reason for leaving was because a few other young members of our group including his little girl, Scarlet, were captured. So he left to rescue them but we haven't heard any news about them since he left."

"What would you have us do about it?" Gabriel asked.

"I was hoping you would help us to eventually find them." Said Lynn.

"We'll see what we can do, but finding lost people these days is getting increasingly difficult."

"I know, if it comes down to it, I will go after them myself. I just don't know where to start. Brian didn't say where he was going, he just left as soon as he got word that Scarlet was taken."

"You care for this Brian a lot, don't you?" Martin asked.

She nodded. "You could say that. He's a good and honorable man. A true marine."

"A marine named, Brian." Martin said, pondering the words for a moment. "What is his last name?"

"Parker, why?" Lynn asked.

Martin turned and reached into the Hummer, pulled out his bow, then he held it out to her.

"Because his father gave me this." He said as she took it from him. "It's Brian's actually, but his father, Elijah, believed that he was dead so he gave it to me for safekeeping and to use."

She turned the bow to reveal the name 'Brian Parker' engraved into the side of the bow's frame.

"Wow, it really is a small world. So how long have you known Brian for?" She asked.

"Me? I've never met him. I only know his dad because I got shot twice and he helped to patch me up."

"Oh, I see. So will you help me go find him then?"

"We are heading in a specific direction but we will help you look. And if we end up finding his location we will help with the extraction if it is required."

"Thank you." She said taking Martin's hand in both of hers.

"It's my pleasure, ma'am." He said as he took his hand back and crossed his arms.

"You and your team are doing great things. I'm glad that our paths crossed." Said Lynn.

"Don't let appearances fool you. We are not as good as you would think." Said Martin.

"Oh, I'm sure that isn't true. You're just being humble."

Even though he was actually completely serious about what he had said, she didn't appear to have realized it. She then just smiled and excused herself, walking over to where the others had gathered in the center of their camp.

"What do you think, Martin?" Gabriel asked.

"I think this country is going to hell, taking the people with it and there's nothing left that we can do about it."

"A wise man once said. When everything around you is in chaos, move, do something, do anything. Because if you choose to do nothing, then that is all you will ever do."

"Who said that?"

Gabriel stared off into the distance then in a serious tone, he said.

"I don't know."

Martin leaned against the Hummer and put his hand to the side of his masked head.

"Why am I friends with you?"

"Because I'm awesome, probably." Said Gabriel.

"Keep telling yourself that, and maybe someday it will come true." Martin laughed. "Let's get out of here before we all die."

# CHAPTER: 42

THE sun had just begun to rise as Martin and his team, along with the group from DC, approached the Appalachian mountains. It had taken them almost two days to make the trip on account of the enemy air patrols becoming far too regular for them to travel at even a normal pace. They had driven most of the way during the night hours using their nightvision goggles instead of the vehicles headlights so as to not shine any beacons out to give away their location.

The morning light was growing brighter as they entered the foothills of the mountains so they decided that it was a good idea to stop and rest for the day. They would attempt to traverse the winding roads that lead up and over the mountains once the sun had set. As they made their way through the foothills, they all began scanning for a good place to make their camp. They turned off the main road onto a two track then drove down it for about a mile.

"That looks like a good spot." Jacob said, pointing to a somewhat flat area off to their right.

James pulled the Hummer off the road a little ways and parked. The two pickup trucks following them did the same. Once everyone was out of the vehicles, they camouflaged them with brush and tree branches to hide them in the event of a flyover. After the vehicles were well hidden they all walked about twenty more yards into the trees to get well away from the road.

The weather had turned out to be warm and clear that day so there was no need to waste time setting up tents or hammocks. The shade that the trees provided was more than enough to keep them cool while they rested throughout the day.

"Sleep in the vehicles if you prefer it over sleeping on the ground." Martin said as he walked over to the others. "We're moving to the top of the mountains come nightfall. So make sure you rest up."

"Do you think it's okay to build a fire?" Thomas asked.

"Of course. But only If you think a bomb getting dropped on top of us is okay." Said Martin.

"That means no." Said Gabriel

"But why?" Thomas asked.

"In the daylight fire makes smoke, in the nighttime fire makes light. Both are dead giveaways to our position. And in turn would make us dead too."

By that time the whole group had gathered around where they stood, so Martin turned to address them.

"There's enough of us now to have two man watch teams." He said in a voice just loud enough for everyone to hear. "I'll take the first shift. Is there a volunteer that would like to join me?"

A young man about the age of 17 raised his hand. Martin remembered him introducing himself as Tyler, before they had left the DC area.

"I'll take the first watch with you, sir. I'm not tired anyway."

Martin nodded to him then turned back to the rest of the people.

"Alright, the next shift for the watch will be chosen at random. So everyone should try to get as much sleep as possible. It might be you that is selected next." He said before leaning over to his team and whispering. "I don't fully trust these people yet. Standard watch shifts, just wake one of them to join you when it's your turn."

Martin sat on a rock towards the edge of their camp. All was calm and quiet, so he pulled the book Ramiel had left him out of his backpack and opened it to the page he had left off on. The sun had begun to rise higher through the trees so there was just the right amount of daylight for him to read a little. He looked down at the page and began reading the words that had most likely been written long ago.

*Entry: 117*

*"Chaos and disorder is a result of stupidity. Peace and order is a result of wisdom."* - Ben David.

*Entry: 118*

*"You can never truly believe in anything, unless you first allow yourself*

*to believe in everything." - Ben David.*

*Entry: 119*

*"With great knowledge comes great power, and with great power comes incredible corruption. With absolute knowledge comes absolute power and with absolute power comes absolute corruption." - Ben David.*

*Entry: 120*

*One of humanity's biggest flaws is that we always want to believe that we are in control. And so the most ignorant of us, base our beliefs and opinions on the things in which we think we have the most control and understanding of. Science for example explains much about our universe, solar system, nature, genetics, etc. but there is far more that it cannot explain, rather than what it can. Gravity, time, the human mind, the cause of life and consciousness, science itself, the list goes on. It is also constantly changing drastically, so believing that something as unreliable, inconsistent and unstable as science has all or even any of the factual answers for that matter, is quite foolish. Everything can be dis-proven, if you know the right questions to ask. If you only think scientifically, you are limited to that alone, and you will never even know the proper questions to ask, let alone understand the answer if it was put right in front of you.*

*Entry: 121*

*Humans have always assumed that they were superior beings, that's just typical human arrogance, vanity and pride. But the truth is, humans are in fact, quite inferior and insignificant, on the large scale of things. The entire human race barely has a lasting effect on the planet earth, let alone the universe. Humanity is tiny, pathetic, and the best thing that could happen to the human race, is extinction.*

*Entry: 122*

*Humans aren't actually even that intelligent, they are survivors,* animals. But what would happen if the human race were to go extinct? It's hard to imagine life without self conscious, somewhat intelligent beings. Like just try to imagine, not being here, not being alive, or ever existing. You can not, because you physically can not imagine "nothing". The way in which we experience time everything requires a beginning. But in order to have a beginning in time, you are also required to have an end. Your time also has to be started by something of greater existence than your own insignificant self.

I mostly understand how the supernatural exists, but I'm still trying to figure out why it needs to, or If anything actually needs to exist at all for that matter. But if the supernatural exists, then I don't see a reason why there couldn't be a supernatural to the supernatural. Because no matter what you do, it doesn't matter unless there is someone or something of greater being to acknowledge that you did it. In our existence, no matter how big something is there is always something bigger, also no matter how small something is there is always something smaller. If there is not something between everything including itself, then everything would be absorbed by the space between. There can not be physical existence unless there is something physical everywhere.

Scientists have spent years trying to split an atom thinking that it will change something, it will not. An atom is just a very small piece of physical matter and splitting one will have no different result than if you split a watermelon. The true answers they seek do not lie with the splitting of an atom. The answers lie within something so much smaller. The solid mass of energy that makes up the foundation that atoms rest upon, and also that which makes up the atoms themselves. The energy of existence that connects all things and bonds them together. That which is all of existence.

Martin looked up from his reading with a look of confusion behind his mask. Even after reading quite a lot of it, he still wasn't exactly sure what to make of the book. Whether it be just theory, or if it was possibly true, or was it just the ravings of a madman. After taking a quick moment to look around, he continued.

Entry: 123

There is no physical place or point where we as natural three dimensional beings can exit our natural universe. Besides the severing of our supernatural consciousness from our natural bodies. There could however, potentially be a way for us to go to a different natural universe on the same plain of existence in the third dimension. But we can never go physically or mentally outside the natural realm, without first going through the death of our natural body. Time travel would require the subject to die before being able to traverse the time dimension. At that point however, there is no point to even trying to do it at all.

*Entry: 124*

If there is something that can be learned, then a human mind can both learn and understand it. Everything in our universe that is physically and naturally in our realm of existence can be, or has the potential to be understood by any person who truly wants to know it. Everything outside our realm of existence can be acknowledged as real, but can never be observed or experienced by us as long as we remain three dimensional beings.

*Entry: 125*

However, it would be ignorant to assume that it is not possible that there could potentially be multiple infinities. Because when we are talking about the supernatural realm, we're talking about something that we, as mortal beings, do not possess the mental capacity to even be able to imagine or fathom. We could never even paint a mental image of what it could be like, because there is nothing in this universe that resembles it.

*Entry:126*

We as physical beings are completely unable to even imagine what it would be like if there was only nothing. If all things, both natural, supernatural and anything else, just suddenly ceased to exist. What would be there to acknowledge its disappearance? If there was no existence at all, with nothing to observe it then is there even a reason for it to exist, and would it actually matter if it didn't?

Existence in its entirety is without reason. If absolutely everything ceased to exist, what would it really matter? The only time something matters at all, is when there is something of a superior nature to acknowledge its existence. Some will probably ask "but if a tree falls in the forest when nobody is around, does it still make a sound?" So my answer to that question is, yes it does. However, without someone there to acknowledge the sound, then the sound that the tree made when it fell, does not matter. And the effect would not change had it fallen without any sound at all.

*Everything in this life, including that which we would concider to be nothing is still something, because if it wasn't then we would not know about it because we wouldn't have a word, or idea to explain what it was. If you can imagine it, then it can not qualify as nothing. When you try to think of nothing, your mind normally chooses to imagine either total white, or total black. But that is not nothing, that is just you thinking about the color white, or the color black. Your mind does not possess the physical capability required in order to imagine what nothing would actually even look like. Same goes for when you try to imagine what the supernatural would look like. Your mind is limited to thinking of at least one thing at all times and that something is always within the realm of the first three dimensions.*

Entry: 127

*Quantum entanglement tells us that pairs of quantum particles can be linked and affect one another no matter the distance between them. This is because every atom, molecule and particle in the universe is connected to each other, through each other. So a signal could be sent from one end of existence to the other, in an instant, by relaying a message through the particles. However, that is only after we learn the language required to do that. Every single particle is connected by the space between them. And everything is constantly sending messages. What is the difference between the space between two single particles right next to each other and the space between two particles miles apart? Simply a different amount of negetive energy space.*

*It's a curious thing to consider how there are no two atoms, molecules or particles that actually touch each other. So what is it that connects particles together, what is the physical makeup of the space between two atoms, and what would be the difference between one square inch of it and a million square miles of it? It's strings. Everything in existence is connected through a super-net of string-like energy that makes up and holds all of existence together. But that leads to another question. What is in the space between the strings?*

*In the natural third dimensional realm there is no such thing as nothing, so no matter how small something is, there must be something smaller joining it together on the ultra microscopic level. Even outer space must be a solid form of energy like mass, that connects all things together. Because if it did not, then no motion could occur. There must always be something because "nothing" does not exist, especially in the physical world. Every atom is touching every other atom through a solid connection of strings, that they themselves are connected by that which is connecting the strings like a solid yet invisible energy that binds all things together. I call this theory, "The Theory of Complete Connection."*

Martin looked up from the book once again. This time with skepticism at what he had just read. For a moment he thought about just putting the book down, but eventually decided to give it another chance.

*Entry: 128*

*Of the few people who do research on the subjects that interest them, the majority will only research so far as until they find the explanation that they wish to hear. Although in reality, if the result is what you wanted to hear and what you wanted the truth to be. It is more likely than not that whatever it is that you want to be the truth, has a higher chance of not being true at all. Or in the very least not the whole truth.*

*Entry: 129*

*Life almost never turns out the way you hoped or wanted. You can lie to yourself and create an illusion to base your life on in an attempt to hide the truth you'd rather not know. But no matter how good an illusion you make for yourself, reality will always be in the background. Just waiting for the day when the illusion subsides and you have to accept the harsh repercussions of the truth that you buried for so long. Or you can take the much simpler way of life, and believe nothing to be true, but anything to be possible.*

*Make the most of everything, and every moment you are given. Stop worrying about everything and just let life come as it will. Don't trouble yourself with the problems of tomorrow when you haven't even figured out the problems of today. Take life one single thing at a time and you'll find that stress, anxiety, and depression will all start to become less and less, until they eventually become manageable. Unfortunately there is no magic potion that just instantly cures all these common human problems, but I have found this method of living to be quite beneficial. Clear your mind, think of the one thing that is most important in this very moment, and do that. Either until it's done, or until something else becomes of greater importance in that moment, and requires immediate attention. And once you are satisfied with the completion of that task, only then should you be concerned with the next task. Don't allow yourself to become overwhelmed with so many things that you drive yourself into a deep depression and resentment. There is a time* and a place for every activity. Make sure all your other tasks are in their place before you jump the gun to add more than you can already handle.

Entry: 130

Almost everyone believes that the meaning of life and existence Is supposed to be extremely complicated and almost impossible to understand. But the meaning of life is actually so ridiculously simple, that it is one of the hardest things for a person to understand. The meaning of life is, live in the moment you have now, experience everything you can, while you can and to have the patients required to do it. Don't waste your time worrying yourself with the things that are out of your immediate control. This moment right now, is yours, and it is the only thing in your life that actually matters. Enjoy it, experience it, and appreciate it, even if you are not happy. That is the beauty of life. Happiness comes and goes, but if you truly understand all that I'm saying, then you can be content, even in the worst of times and misfortune. And contentment is more important than happiness, because happiness is fleeting and temporary. Whereas contentment can last a lifetime.

There is positivity that can come out of even the most catastrophically negative scenarios. If you know where to look you will quickly notice that even the worst, most unfortunate things that happen to you, only happen so that you can know what it feels like to suffer. It is what will make you strong, so long as you look intently to find the good in the things that upset you the most. Every experience you have, whether it's good or bad, is an important stepping stone in your life. And nothing, not even pain and sorrow lasts forever. That is why it's important to appreciate everything in the moment. Because once a moment is gone, it's gone for good, and no matter what you do, or how hard you try, you can never change them or get them back. And along with not only the time itself, all the emotions you were feeling at that time, are now the property of the past. So make sure you at least make the most of the moments you'll never get back. This moment right now, is yours, choose wisely what you do with it.

Entry: 131

"A man who only sits back and prays and refuses to do good works, is worthless. And he shall perish with the rest of the weak, worthless men." - Ben David.

Hearing a noise, Martin looked up from the book to see Tyler walking towards him. Martin set the book down beside him as the young man sat down about five feet away just staring at him as though he was in a trance.

# CHAPTER: 43

**W**HAT can I do for you, kid?" Martin asked as Tyler just sat there staring at him. Tyler paused for a few more seconds, then he asked. "Is it actually you that I've been hearing all the stories about? And if it is, I was just wondering if they were true."

"That all depends on what you have heard." Said Martin.

"Just people saying that an immortal in a black mask has been going around killing hundreds of the communists."

"No one is an immortal kid. Immortality is far too cruel a punishment for anyone in this life."

"I'm sorry if I'm asking too many questions. But what does that mean, sir?"

"Lesson number one. Never apologize for anything, ever. Always say what you mean, and ask what you want... That being said, to answer your question. Immortality is the only thing in this life that could be considered a true curse."

"Why is that?" Tyler asked.

"To live through all of history, outliving everyone you grow to care about. To see the world be built up only to come crumbling down. Watch empires rise and fall, be forced to witness every genocide, disease, and mass extinction over and over again. But more than anything never get to see the truth that exists only in the plain you enter after you die. There is nothing that could be more of a hell than being forced to live on this earth forever."

"I see. So you wouldn't want that?"

"No, I wish to die young so that I may see through my real eyes again, and see as I did when I left this place for a time."

"What? I don't understand." Tyler said in a confused tone.

"Life is strange, kid." said Martin. "But death is even stranger. There are some questions you can ask in this life that can only be answered after death."

"Death is scary though. I wonder if there's anyone out there who would want to live forever."

"The people running the world think they want that."

"Why?"

"Selfishness and greed."

"Those things make people want to live forever?" Tyler said in a questioning tone.

"Yes. However, selfishness and greed, breed stupidity and are therefore the downfall and death of man. Only those who care not, and want for nothing, will be cursed with everlasting life."

"Do you care about anything?"

Martin thought for a moment then answered.

"No, I do not. There was a time that i did, but i'm afraid that time is now the property of the past."

"What about your team? You'd have to care about them at least a little bit."

"They know and understand what they are a part of. The worst thing that can happen to any of us is death, but we all hope for the worst, because this life is more exciting that way." Said Martin.

"What about me and my people?" Tyler asked.

"I didn't ask you all to come with us. I allowed it. There is a big difference. If any of you die, it is because you were too weak to live."

"I prefer to be strong, but I'm just a kid. Also don't let some of the others hear you say that about them. Especially the women."

"I say what I want. I don't care who takes offense to it. Because if anyone does, good. Maybe it will toughen them up a little. Because in case you haven't noticed, life ain't all sunshine and rainbows, buttercup. It is cold, cruel, gruesome, messy, harsh and unforgiving. I don't give a sideways shit about anyone's feelings, or their opinion. If you can't take the heat, then you'll burn with the rest of them."

"Buttercup?" Said Tyler with a confused look.

Martin slowly began to chuckle, which evolved into a light laugh. Tyler smiled and then began to laugh himself.

"You're alright kid." Martin said, moving past the good natured name calling. "Lesson number two, kid. Always keep your sense of humor, you may depend on it to survive someday."

"I will try. Wait, but if you don't care about anything or anyone, wouldn't you be someone who could be cursed with everlasting life?"

"There are some questions that I am not at liberty to discuss. Sometimes the things you want most are taken from you, while the things you never wanted, are forced upon you."

When nightfall came they began their trek up the mountain. The trip up the winding road to the top was long and stressful, but they managed to make it only a few hours after the darkness had set in.

Once they found a decent spot and parked the Hummer, Gabriel got out and walked over to the cliff that was the edge of their new camp.

"Nice. That's some view." Gabriel said as he looked off into the dark cloudy sky.

"It's dark as hell, bro. What view?" Jacob said as he stepped over next to him.

"I'm just rehearsing for what I'll say in the morning."

"This isn't a movie, bro. You don't have to rehearse lines."

"Who knows. Maybe it will be someday." Said Gabriel.

"I doubt it man. I don't think anyone will even be alive to tell our story by the time this is all over." Said Jacob.

"Don't be such a downer. Have a little faith." Gabriel said while patting Jacob on the shoulder before walking back to join the others, who were now all sitting in a circle in the middle of their new camp.

Jacob looked out into the dark sky for a moment longer then he turned and followed after Gabriel. He then sat down between Gabriel and Martin and listened to the people taking turns telling stories. An older gentleman was telling a story about the time when he had gone deep sea fishing back before the war started. Once he had finished, everyone sat in silence for a moment.

"Does anyone know any songs?" Thomas asked, looking around at the people in the group.

"I heard, Martin, sing once." Said Jacob.

"Really? Could you please sing something for us, Martin?" Asked a girl across from where he sat.

"It was a long time ago, I don't sing anymore. Singing is for happy times of peace." Martin said, not wanting to relive the days of old back when his life was easy.

"Oh come on. Please." She persisted.

Martin was silent for a little while, then he nodded. The girl lightly clapped her hands together in excitement.

"This isn't a song, exactly. It's more like a ballad."

"Who's it by?" Asked the girl."

"I wrote it." Martin said before he briefly lowered his head in mental preparation.

After a few more moments, he began.

> *"It's cold in bed when I lay down my head*
> *but I know someday that I'll be dead.*
> *I remember the words of all the things I could have said,*
> *If my mouth wasn't frozen up, my heart so full of dread.*
> *The things I knew, there's things that I must do.*
> *I know my mind, I know my thoughts are true.*
> *I think I blink, I hope my heart won't sink.*
> *My thirst in this broken world's so choken I can't drink.*
> *It's cold in bed, when I lay down my head.*
> *I know someday my friends will all be dead.*
> *My true love is watching me from somewhere up above.*
> *Flying above the clouds, a pretty white winged dove*
> *I'll live for now and I will never bow*
> *Until the day I make my way up to stay.*
> *Sometimes I wish that I could see your face again.*
> *But the life that I'm living now is different from back then.*
> *It's cold in bed, when I lay down my head.*
> *Without you next to me reminds me that you're dead.*
> *I chamber a round into my rifle and breathe in.*
> *There's nothing left to do but to kill and deal with sin.*
> *I breathe out half to hold and take my aim.*
> *Nobody will remember me or even know my name.*
> *I squeeze the trigger and the bullet finds its mark*
> *In the head of my enemy, I fade into the dark.*
> *It's cold in bed, when I lay down my head.*
> *But I know someday everyone will be dead.*
> *I don't know, the place next I will go.*
> *But I hope he's there so that pain to him I'll show.*
> *There's nothing else I want to do, there's nothing from before.*
> *Two bullets from his firearm have shut and locked that door.*
> *One day I'll find the man I want to kill.*
> *If it's the last thing I do, I know for sure I will.*
> *It's warm in bed when I lay down my head.*
> *The blood from my enemy has warmed my heart once dead."*

Martin finished the song and they all sat in silence for a while.

"It's about your family isn't it?" Gabriel asked in a low voice. "The song I mean. Is it about Ellis and Mark?"

"It's about everyone that all of us have lost, and also about what we are going to do about it." Replied Martin.

CCXCVIII

"It's your anthem." Said Thomas.

"It's the anthem for our team, the STFU." Said Jacob.

"Even if none of us are remembered. Maybe the song will be." Said James.

"Maybe." Martin sighed, looking towards the sky in the East. "Daylight will be here before you know it. You should all get camp set up then get some sleep. I'll take the first watch."

"When are we planning on heading out?" Gabriel asked.

"Soon." Said Martin.

"What's our plan, once we leave?"

"We're gonna go hunting."

Martin looked up from the strange book once again. He had been reading for the entire first hour of his watch shift. Sitting with his back against a rock he looked out through the trees at the plume of smoke rising from the burning town far off in the distance. He wasn't sure why it was burning, he wasn't really sure of anything anymore. Looking back down at the words of the book his old friend had given him, Martin wondered if things would ever return to the way they used to be back only a year ago. Back before they were attacked, when life was so joyful, quiet and carefree, in comparison to life now. He really didn't possess any hope for that anymore. The world was just too far gone at this point. He now thought it was probably best to just let the world burn and simply not worry about it anymore.

It was around midday now and the others were all still asleep. After glancing around for another moment Martin returned to his reading. A little while later he again looked up. It was still boring and quiet, so he checked the time on his mechanical wrist watch.

"Hmm, 1:30pm already." Martin thought to himself.

He put the book back into its designated pocket in his backpack. Then he stood and walked over to where Jacob was sleeping.

"Time for your shift, Jacob." Martin said, gently shaking him awake.

Jacob's eyes opened suddenly and scanned the area behind Martin. Then he carefully sat up and put the pistol he kept in his hand while he slept, back into the holster on his hip.

"Good afternoon, Martin. I take it that it is my shift to watch?" Jacob asked in a hushed tone.

"Indeed it is. Wake Gabriel up in two hours for his shift. Also tell him to pass the word on to James that we're moving out at dusk."

"You got it." Said Jacob.

With a nod, Martin then walked over to a spot that looked comfortable enough and laid down. After only a few minutes, Martin passed into that same strange form of sleep that had been happening more and more often as time progressed.

# CHAPTER: 44

## *East of Charlottesville, Virginia.*

I**T was late morning and the sun was shining bright through the few clouds in the sky overhead. Brian, Scarlet and Wade all walked in single file down the blacktop road in silence listening for any signs of the enemy closing in on them. They only hoped they had enough of a head start to make it to safety before the enemy could catch up to them. They had actually found a car earlier that morning with a quarter tank of gas in it so they had hot wired it and used it up until they ran out about a mile back down the road.

As they walked Brian observed the countryside and the Appalachian mountains off in the distance to the West. Their attempts to avoid the enemy had forced them to stray a long way off course in the completely wrong direction. Brian wasn't even sure exactly where they were at anymore. All he knew was that there was an overpass up ahead and a small deserted looking town beyond that.

"I think we're probably safe now." Wade said as he moved up to walk next to Brian.

"I usually tend not to get my hopes up so easily. I suggest that you do the same." Brian responded flatly.

"We've been on the move for almost a whole day now. Do you think they would actually follow our trail for this long?" Wade asked.

"It's very likely that they would."

"How do you know?"

"Because if I was tracking someone, I would follow the trail till I found them. I actually wouldn't be here if I hadn't already done just that."

"While you do have a point, I say we take a quick breather to rest our feet for a minute, then continue on after we're..."

His words were cut off by a loud crack. Brian's head whipped to the side to see what it was. All he saw though was Wade's body falling towards the ground. His head was mutilated and his blood sprayed all over the road in front of where they were walking. Without taking even a second to think it over, Brian acted instead. He grabbed Scarlet's shoulder and pushed her in front of him as they ran full tilt in search of cover. Bullets whizzed by around them, one hitting Brian square on the armor plate in the rear of his vest. The impact partially knocked the wind out of him and caused him to stumble a little but he managed to keep his balance. Still under fire they both jumped and slid down the hill, taking cover under the overpass.

"Are you hit?!" Brian asked through clenched teeth on account of the pain from the definite bruising left by the bullet in his ceramic armor plate.

"No, I'm fine. How about you?" She asked.

"I got one in the back but I'm pretty sure my armor caught it."

He reached back to feel if there was any blood and to his relief, there wasn't. That's when they began to hear vehicles approaching fast.

"We have to move now. Are you good?" Brian asked.

"Yeah, I'm alright." Scaret responded.

Staying low they moved as quickly as they could down the lower street to a small building. Brian kicked the door in and no sooner were they inside did the Chinese stop on the overpass. They watched from the small building as some of the soldiers piled out of the trucks and began searching for them around where they had been only moments before.

"Let's go." Brian whispered. "We need to get to the town up ahead. We gotta try to find somewhere to hide."

They both moved through the dark room to the back window and Brian slowly opened it. After helping Scarlet out he carefully crawled out the window himself and they made their way down the street. Using the small building to block them from the sight of the enemy, they made their way down the road until they came upon a culvert pipe that led underneath the road. They quickly jumped into the ditch and entered the pipe to head in the direction of the town. Once they approached the end of the pipe on the other side, they paused for about ten minutes to make sure they gave the enemy plenty of time to move on before they would make a break for the buildings.

There was about one hundred yards of open grass to cross between them and the nearest buildings. They would have to time it just right and hope they could make it without being spotted. Brian closed his eyes and listened intently for a few more moments then opened them and readied himself to run for it.

"On three." He said looking at Scarlet who followed his example and readied up. "One, two, three."

They both darted from the pipe and sprinted across the grass as fast as their legs could carry them. They made it to the buildings and ran into one of the alleys between them. Once in the alley they hid behind a dumpster for a moment to catch their breath. Brian then stood up and walked over to a red door on the side of the building across from the dumpster. After a second of hesitation he knocked. There was no answer at first then the door suddenly opened a crack.

"Who are you?" A short gray haired man asked.

"If you're American then I'm a friend." Was Brian's answer.

The door opened the rest of the way and the short man waved them inside.

"Quickly now. It's about to get messy out there." said the old man.

"What do you mean?" Brian asked.

"It's been reported that the Chinese are moving into town. So our fighters are going to send them away."

"Are you sure you want to inject yourselves into this fight?" Brian asked.

The man leaned closer towards them and in a whisper he began.

"We've been hearing rumors of a man they call The Blank. Word is that he's been killing the invaders at such an astronomical rate that they are starting to get scared and wonder if he's even human. They say that the way he moves about like a phantom is starting to make them believe he's actually something else entirely."

"Something else? Like what? How does he move?" Brian asked with an air of urgency.

"They think he's an immortal. I hear he moves with complete silence and can simply appear right in front of you within the time it takes to blink an eye."

"That sounds like a tall tale to me."

"It probably is, but regardless, it has given people hope and made them willing to fight to get their homes back. So tall tale or not, it is having a positive effect on the people of this town at least."

As soon as the man had finished speaking, Brian heard gunshots in the distance. He walked over to the window on the side of the room where the sound seemed to be coming from and looked out. As soon as he did he could see the back end of the truck that had been pursuing them hauling tail away from the town.

"Well that's not good." Brian said in disappointment.

"What's not good?" The man asked.

"They let one of them escape."

"So? It's just one."

"One man carrying a brand new, shiny message. Everyone has to leave now!"

"Why? Do you think they'll send reinforcements?"

"I know they will. Get your things. But only what you'll need to survive. Move quickly and get out of town."

"Where is there to go?" The man asked.

"Anywhere but here." Said Brian.

"What about you? Where are you going?"

"I'm trying to get back to Washington."

"Isn't Washington occupied by the invaders?"

"Indeed."

"I see. Well in that case I wish you luck my friend. And Godspeed."

"Likewise. Come on, Scarlet."

Brian grabbed Scarlet and they stepped back outside into the alley. Brian led the way out into the street heading deeper into the town.

"Are we really gonna try to make it all the way back to Washington?" Scarlet asked.

"Yup. That is of course unless you've got a better idea."

Just then they heard a sound coming from behind them far off. They turned and Brian's heart sank. For what he saw was something he never really imagined or expected the invaders would do with such little provocation. Rising up into the sky in pillars of smoke were twelve short range ground to ground missiles.

"So that's how they're gonna play it then. Just bomb shit." Brian said, his anger obvious in his voice.

"I think we should run. Right?" Scarlet said, sounding scared and unsure.

"I guess it's worth a shot."

Brian turned to look back as they ran and saw the smoke trails from the missiles arching over the buildings and heading straight for them.

"Pick up the pace, Scarlet!" He said as they ran down the streets through the town. The buildings to either side of them were torn from neglect on behalf of the invasion. As they sprinted away from the imminent danger that was growing ever closer to them Brian noticed an old gun safe lying in a pile of rubble. It was laying next to a wall up ahead with its door partially open. It appeared to have been thrown from one of the building windows overhead.

"Quickly, climb into that safe!" Brian ordered.

Scarlet ran up to the opening and pulled up on it. Brian arrived a second after her and helped flip the door to the side on its hinges so they could climb in. The door hit the wall with a slam. Scarlet then hopped into the safe as Brian ran around the side to lift the door so it could be shut. He held the door above his head for a moment as he looked off into the distance. Above and behind him the incoming missiles were now beginning their descent.

"Wait!" Scarlet yelled. "There's not enough room for both of us, we have to find a different hiding place!"

With a tear in his eye Brian turned back to face her. She looked into his glazed eyes as he held up the door to the safe.

"What are you doing?!" Scarlet asked with anxiety in her voice.

"There's no more time." Brian replied calmly. "It appears that my journey has come to its end. But you can still survive."

"Wait, what are you talking about? I don't know where to go. And I can't do this without you." Scarlet said frantically, beginning to cry.

"You can do this, and you will. I will always be with you. I made a promise. This is just how it has to be this time."

Without letting her answer he closed the safe and then quickly piled rocks and dirt over the door. Just enough to help stop the blast but not so much that she wouldn't be able to get out after it was over. He then walked over and sat on the ground next to a crumbling brick wall. There was no use in even trying to find cover. There was no more time or places left that could save him now. He made the mistake that got him there, now he would reap the seeds he had sewn.

As he watched the sky he took the pack of cigarettes out of his pocket which contained his lucky and last cigarette. He put the cigarette in his mouth, pulled out his fathers old zippo lighter, lit the smoke and inhaled deeply. It seemed like everything was moving in slow motion as he watched one of the bombs explode about 100 feet away. As he felt the heat grow on his face he waited for the sound and shock-wave to hit. He exhaled the smoke from his cigarette as he casually threw up a middle finger to the explosion.

"You did good, Brian, you did good." He said to himself in a low voice. "Dad, wherever you are. I just hope that you would be proud."

The fire from the explosion hit and it felt different than he had expected. He figured it would have felt hot but it was in fact just the opposite. Like a thousand ice cold hands pressing unbelievably hard on his bare face and all over his body. It didn't hurt, he knew that his life was worth giving so that a young soul like Scarlet might live on a little longer. And the thought of that gave him the strength to endure whatever pain he might have felt. In his mind at least, it was worth it.

As he lay there, charred and on his way out of this life, he recalled a saying that a wise man with no name had told him before he became a marine.

"There is no man more honorable or selfless than a man who gives his life for the innocent. And does so for no reason other than simply to give all he can while asking for nothing in return, not even the recognition that he did so. This is true charity worthy of a supernatural  reward. Some people are meant to live an extraordinary life, some people are meant to live a simple life. But sometimes there are those who live in such a way that their simple life is also extraordinary. Some people are extraordinarily simple, and some people are simply extraordinary. Your actions dictate which one you will become."

With that Brian felt content enough to let go of this clutch on life, and as his consciousness began fading to black. He smiled with what face he had left, for he was proud of the way he lived, and now he was proud of the way he died.

# CHAPTER: 45

**W**AKE up, Martin." Said a hushed voice.
He could feel there was a hand on his arm shaking him awake, but he was in a mental state that he would have preferred to stay in.

"Martin, wake up. There was an explosion in the town off towards the southeast."

Martin slowly came out of his strange state of rest and looked up to see James standing in front of him. He sat up cautiously and stretched the arm he had been laying on. Then he picked up and holstered the Glock 19 that he had placed on the ground next to where he was resting.

"What is it?" Martin asked in a whisper.

"I don't know. But a bunch of missiles just hit the town over there." James said, pointing off towards what he was describing.

"The Chinese are bombing shit. What else is new?" Martin said with a shrug.

"Should we check it out?"

"If they're bombing the town over there then it means they don't know that we're over here. We'll wait for nightfall. No sense in drawing any unwanted attention."

"Okay. Sounds good."

"What time is it?" Martin asked.

"Just after 7:00pm."

"Was the message relayed to you that we're to set off at dusk?"

"Yes sir, I was going to wake everyone up in about 40 minutes."

"Well I'm awake now, so if you want to get a quick power nap in I can take a watch till it's time to go."

"Are you sure?"

"Yes, get some sleep, James."

"Cool. Thank you, Martin."

Martin turned and walked over to the rock he had been sitting on earlier that day during his first shift on watch. He then climbed up to sit atop it once more. From where he was now sitting he could see the smoke from the explosions that James had told him about. Martin wasn't really worried about it but it had most definitely shook James. As time passed, Martin became more and more curious about how much damage was done. He eventually grew to be kind of interested in going down to investigate, but it could at least wait till the night set in. It was unfortunate that whatever remained of the town probably wouldn't be anything more than a pile of smoldering ashes and rubble by then. But that wasn't really his problem.

As the last flicker of sunlight disappeared under the horizon, Martin stood then jumped down off the rock and walked over to where the others were sleeping. Leaning over, he lightly kicked James's boot to wake him.

"It's time to head out." He said as James's eyes began to open slowly.

"Why must sleep be so hard to come by these days?" James asked no one in particular.

"You'll get plenty of sleep when you're dead." Said Gabriel, sitting up from his makeshift bed of leaves.

"Can't wait. It's gonna be a good time." James said with a chuckle that the rest of them joined in on.

Three minutes later they were all kitted up in their night vision gear with all the supporting equipment required to run it properly.

"You guys heading out?" Lynn said as she approached them.

"Yeah. We're going to check out what those explosions from earlier were." Said Martin. "We might be back in the morning, but don't worry about it if we're not. There's no guarantee that we won't just head out somewhere. Unfortunately there's still a lot of assholes that need to be put down."

"No problem. You do you. But if I don't see ya. For what it's worth, thanks for what you've done and what you're still doing. And I hope that our paths cross again someday."

"We appreciate it but hoping for anything these days is asking just a little bit too much." Said Martin.

"It's always better to shoot high and hope for the best." Said Lynn.

"When you shoot high, you usually miss. I tend to prepare for the worst and hope for the worst, that way I always get what I want."

"That's a little messed up, but okay. I wish you good luck then."

Lynn stood there looking at them for a moment then with a smile, she turned and walked back over to her spot by her group.

After their final pre-mission checks they all piled into the Hummer and drove down the winding road to the bottom of the mountains. They took the first right they came to and headed in the direction of the town to investigate where the bombs had hit earlier that evening. After the short drive, they arrived at one of the blast sights. Gabriel pulled the Hummer off to the side of the road and parked, then they all exited the vehicle and moved off in different directions to look around. Out of curiosity, Martin chose to head straight down the street to ground zero of the blast zone to check out the level of the damage dealt by the bomb. On his way there he came upon a mound of dirt with an old gun safe half buried in rubble. He leaned over to look inside it and wasn't surprised to find it empty. He continued on a few more steps when through his night vision he saw a body with its back leaning up against a concrete wall. As he got closer he noticed that the body had been burnt and left unrecognizable by the fire from the bombs.

"Almost looks like the aftermath of napalm." Martin thought to himself.

He approached then knelt down to one knee next to the charred body in the street. He reached for the chain around the neck and lightly pulled to reveal a set of bloody dog tags. He wiped one of the tags off with his thumb then focused one of the objective lenses on his night vision tubes. Once the image was more clear he leaned in closer to read the name on the tag.

"Parker Brian." He said as he looked into the eyes of the man's burnt face.

"Find anything?" Gabriel called from the other side of the gun safe that was laying in the rubble.

"Nothing." Martin called back. "Let's get out of here. Head back to the Hummer, I'll be there in a minute."

Martin clenched the tags in his fist and broke the chain that held them. As he stood he carefully placed them in one of his breast pockets. Staring down on the body he wondered if he should bother going back to tell Lynn and the others. Or if he should just let them believe that Brian was still alive. He quickly decided that it was better to not tell them yet. This world was already messed up enough and more bad news was unnecessary and would only make things worse. Also Martin thought that the ignorance of people was sometimes entertaining to watch.

# CHAPTER: 46

**I**T was early morning the day after Martin and the team had left the Appalachian mountains. The sun had not yet begun to rise but they could see the light beginning to show where the sky met the hills in the distance. They had been traveling all night in search of their next potential target with few meeting even the lowest level they liked to deal with. A few small road blocks and camps which they had put down without so much as breaking a sweat, but as easy as those had been Martin had a feeling that they would come across a larger camp within the next few hours.

"Hey Martin, I'm getting pretty tired. You think we should stop soon before it gets too bright out?" Gabriel asked as they drove down the cluttered highway heading southbound.

"Yeah, let's just make it to the other side of the next town and I suppose we can stop for the day."

"Okay. Hey Martin?"

"Yeah?"

"I've had something that I've been wanting to ask you for a while that's been bothering me."

"Sure, what is it?"

Gabriel took a deep breath then after taking a moment to gather his thoughts, he spoke.

"Why are we still going around like cowardice thieves in the night instead of taking our enemies head on? Ya know, with honor or whatever."

"Where did this come from? Have you always felt this way?" Martin asked with a touch of surprise.

"Not always, just somewhat recently."

"There is no honor in dying like a fool, Gabriel. Can a mouse kill a lion in a head on fight? No it cannot. But give the mouse poison and the element of surprise and the lion who was once a predator becomes prey. I ask you this, is it better to be an effective thief or a dead hero?"

Gabriel was silent so Martin continued.

"I also ask you. How could you consider our tactics cowardly when it is only four of us taking on multiple armies? We know we have little hope of survival and even smaller hope of victory. Yet we continue. And since when are any of us worried about honor? The things we have done would be frowned upon by almost anyone who actually knew. But that's not even half of it. There is a very good chance that nobody will ever even know our names let alone remember us. My dear friend, why is it that we are doing what we are doing?"

"To avenge our families and our country."

"No, we are doing this because it is our duty as men. And we are doing it without seeking anything in return. Be it for honor, glory, fame or anything of the sort. One day we will die in a ditch somewhere and without ever receiving a damn thing for it. And if you wish anything other than this fate you may leave and I will hold nothing but love and friendship towards you."

"If we're just going to die anyway, then why do we continue?" Gabriel asked.

"Why do we do anything? Why live life at all? I don't know what your reasons are, but I continue because I'm good at it and because the only thing I have left in this world is to die. So why not die a glorious death. Why not continue, and make the most of whatever time I have left?"

"I never wanted to admit it, but I think the reason I do it is, firstly, because I hate them. Secondly, because they took my home and my life away from me. And lastly, probably the main reason I do this is because I like it and because actually I want to do it."

"So you are with me in this fight till the bitter end then?"

"I suppose that as long as I am considered honorable in the eyes of my friends, that is enough for me to be satisfied with life. And if I die fighting with you guys, I could never hope for a more glorious death." Said Gabriel.

Martin smiled behind his mask and gave gabriel an approving nod. The driver side window then suddenly burst inward sending an explosion of small glass fragments into the Hummer. Martin reflexively turned his head to see what happened. And as the blood and glass spattered his mask he saw the exit wound in the side of Gabriel's head. His body slumped in his seat and the Hummer began drifting to the right side shoulder of the road. Martin reached over and pulled the emergency brake causing the Hummer to come to a hard screeching halt.

"Everybody out!" Martin shouted as he grabbed and tore off Gabriel's dog tags. "Shots fired from the left flank!"

James racked the bolt on his M249, and Jacob readied his AUG, while Martin grabbed his bow. Then they flung only the passenger side doors open and all jumped out as bullets began to rain down on their location.

There was no time to worry about the dead man in the driver seat. The only thing Martin and the others could do for Gabriel now was remember him. Once they were on the street Martin waved for them to follow him to the nearest building to take cover. James glanced inside the passenger side window of the Hummer to have one last look at their fallen brother.

"Rest easy, my friend." James said, putting his hand to the glass for a moment before moving off to follow Martin in the 30 foot spacing as per their standard formation.

Jacob watched as James crept away, ducking behind the broken down cars as he went. He then turned to look through the window at Gabriel.

"We are born for death." He whispered. "It's not about when you die, but how you die. And you died well. You had a glorious death, brother. Goodbye, Gabriel, I'll see you when all this is over."

With that he reached into the back seat of the hummer and pulled the pin on one of the grenades in the crate he got from Franklin. He then turned and followed after the others. It wasn't much of a eulogy but Gabriel would have understood. It was a hard thing to believe that after all they had survived together it was a lucky shot from a sniper that ended Gabriel's life so suddenly. He was the first of their team to die but feeling what he was feeling now, after listening to him and Martin talking mere minutes before. Jacob only wished it would have been himself that died so he wouldn't have to endure the loss of his friend.

Jacob was about halfway to the building when the Hummer finally exploded with everything inside being destroyed. Immediately after the explosion, bullets from a machine gun suddenly cracked just over Jacobs head and buried into the ground and the wall of the building as he ran towards the door. He dodged to the left behind the engine bay of a truck as a hail of bullets peppered both the truck and the ground around it. He waited hoping that the gunfire would stop just long enough for him to reach cover. When the gun finally stopped, James swung out of the doorway with his M249 and began laying down suppressive fire. Jacob waited for what felt like a one minute long second then broke cover and ran. He leaped through the front doors and was immediately grabbed from the side by both Martin and James, who aggressively pulled him out of the line of fire. Bullets immediately tore through the doorway and impacted on the floor inside the entryway. The machine gun kept firing for only a few more seconds then stopped for no apparent reason.

"You can't run forever!" Said an Asian accented voice through what sounded like a loudspeaker. "Even if we have to pick you off one by one! It's only a matter of time before we kill all of you demons!"

"They'll be upon us before we know it." Said Martin. "We have to keep moving."

The others nodded in silent agreement and they all carefully moved to the opposite side of the building then exited out the back door to the street beyond. They could hear the enemy closing in so they quickly moved across the street and into the next closest building. Careful not to let the door slam as they entered, Martin caught then gently pushed it shut as he took one last peek outside to see the enemy enter the building they had just left.

# CHAPTER: 47

**Y**A know, I was actually beginning to believe that we really were immortal." Jacob said, looking down at the unopened food rations he held in his hands. "I was really starting to believe that nobody could ever kill us."

The sun was just about gone for the day and even though they were tired they were preparing to move out once again. It had taken them almost all day to give their Chinese pursuers the slip and to get to the relative safety of a farmhouse a few miles away from where Gabriel had been killed. In the light of only one candle the middle of the small room James said in response to Jacob.

"Yeah, that was more of a reality check than I would have liked."

"It feels weird without him, doesn't it?" Jacob asked. "I mean like something is missing."

"Something is missing. Gabriel... Gabriel, is what's missing." Said James.

"I know. What are we going to do?" Jacob asked.

"First you are going to eat. Then we are going hunting again." Said Martin.

"Did you get something to eat, Martin?" James asked.

"Actually now that you mention it, I can't even remember the last time I saw Martin eat anything at all." Jacob said, first looking at James then looking at Martin who said nothing.

"Yeah are you feeling alright, man? You should probably eat something if you wanna keep your strength up." Said James.

"I'm fine. I do not require food to sustain me anymore." Said Martin.

"What?" Jacob asked with a laugh. "What do you mean you don't require food anymore?"

"It's fine if you don't wanna tell us. But we are your friends so just know that you can if you want to."

"I'm not really sure what it is yet." Martin said with a sigh. "But there is something strange happening to me. A change of some kind."

"What kind of change?" James asked.

"It's hard to explain. I haven't felt hungry for a while and I'm beginning to no longer feel tired or the need for sleep either."

"Shit, that must be nice." Said Jacob.

"Not when you don't fully understand why it's happening."

"Well how do you feel? Do you feel like you're catching something?"

"No, I feel perfectly fine. It's almost like my body has just stopped needing anything. I tried to eat something a few days ago but my stomach feels full and hydrated at all times now. Like I've been put in a bubble where the required time for my cells progression has stopped."

"When did this all start?"

"After I got shot when I was running away from the Chinese camp where my family died. It started a few days after I woke up."

"Why? What could getting shot have done to trigger such a reaction as making you no longer require food or sleep?"

"It wasn't the bullets that caused it directly. I believe they only did their part to kill me. I believe that it was me dying and coming back that made me no longer require natural sustenance."

"Wait, you died?"

"Yes. I died. But I came back somehow."

"How? I mean, what was it like? Did you see a light?"

"No, there was no light. Light is a natural thing and in the supernatural it is not required in order to see."

"What did you see then?"

"I saw everything. All of natural time, every moment of existence from beginning to end. I saw all of existence and everything that exists in every plane of existence. I saw everything, from every angle and all at once."

"Damn. How long did that take?"

"It was only one single moment. Everything I saw, was now."

"How is that possible?"

"Without time, I guess a process is not required. I saw everything all at once... and I understood it. The craziest part is that I remember it now. I remember what the supernatural was like. The images currently in my mind should have undone my existence. Yet here I am. The only explanation is that I am no longer a human and that I am slowly becoming more."

"That's super crazy, bro. If you're screwing with us I'm gonna be pissed." James with a chuckle.

"I am not screwing with you. I died, and what I returned as, my very existence as I am now is not fair to the rest of the world."

"Because you've seen the supernatural and don't have to eat? That's really not that much of an advantage."

"That is not even half of it."

Jacob only blinked his eyes and Martin was gone.

"Dude! What the fuuuu?!" Jacob and James shouted as they stood up, looking around.

"As I said." A voice came from behind them. "It is not fair to the world that I exist."

"Yo, how did you do that?" Jacob asked, pointing at Martin in surprise.

"I can only do it if nobody is looking."

"But we were both looking directly at you just now."

"You blinked." Martin said matter of factly.

"Why didn't you do something to save Gabriel?!" Jacob shouted, after suddenly realizing what Martin could do.

"It is not so simple. I cannot do it unless no living person will see. And I have not yet figured out how to make people blink when I want them to."

"Why is that?" James asked.

"There are natural laws, then there are supernatural laws. The only reason I'm telling you anything at all is because I'm your friend. I'm literally tiptoeing the line by saying what I already have."

"What would happen if you just straight up told us something you're not supposed to?"

"They will take away my existence and leave no memories in the times where I have been."

"Who's they?"

Martin tilted his head to the side slightly.

"That would be the line, Jacob." He said.

"Gotcha, never mind then. What else can you tell us?"

"What I have already told you was pushing the limits as it is."

"Can you see the future?"

"I've seen the future, but what I saw is one of the things that I cannot recall clearly. Foresight is not a privilege granted to spiritual beings. I currently experience the process of time as you do."

"So why just you? Why couldn't Gabriel be like you and come back?"

"I do not have the answer to that, I only know what I myself am permitted to remember."

"Like a whole new level of classified information." Said James.

"More or less." Said Martin.

"You know what?" Jacob began. "I bet that Ramiel is like how you are now. It would explain how he would always appear out of nowhere. He did it to me a couple times now that I think about it. I caught him out of my peripheral vision once or twice."

"So, when was the first time you found out you could move like that, Martin?" James asked.

"About a week ago. It's quite strange, and it's almost impossible to put it into natural sounds in the form of words. The best way to explain it, I think, is to say." Martin paused for a moment, then he continued. "I know that I know things, but I haven't figured out how to know what I know that I know."

"Say that five times fast." Jacob laughed.

Martin and James also both laughed briefly.

"I hope you guys don't see me any differently. I am still, Martin. I am still the same guy you have always known. I am just... more now."

"Don't sweat it, man. It's cool." Said James.

"Yeah, I'm sure once you figure out your new skills you'll be able to run those invading bastards out of our land for good." Jacob added.

"That isn't exactly why I was allowed to come back. But in a sense, sure."

"Good enough for me." Said Jacob.

"We should probably get going now. We've been here for too long already." Said Martin, walking towards the back door of the farmhouse.

It was fairly dark now so Martin pulled his night vision goggles out of his backpack and attached them to the forehead of his mask. He then flipped them down over his eyes and looked out the window. Seeing that the coast was clear he quietly opened the door and stepped out. Leaving the candle burning in the small room, the others followed after Martin and they all silently ran across the back yard of the house and disappeared into the field of withering corn stalks.

# CHAPTER: 48

**S**HOTS rang out from the left as a bullet impacted the tree right next to Martin's head.

"Time to go, boys." He said, as he calmly stood then moved behind a tree for cover.

The others followed suit, taking cover behind the trees closest to them as more bullets struck the ground and trees around them.

"How did they find us so fast?" Jacob asked from behind his tree.

"It's the Chinese military. Now that they know who they're looking for, I would be surprised if they weren't using some kind of thermal imaging to find us." Said James.

"It doesn't matter how they found us. What matters is that they did. Let's get moving." Martin said as he broke cover and ran, heading northward.

James and Jacob followed him, trying their best to keep trees between themselves and the incoming bullets as they ran. James quickened his pace to catch up with and run beside Martin.

"Is there anything you can do about the assholes shooting at us? I'm getting tired of all this running." He said hoping for a positive answer.

"Unfortunately, I am still mostly restricted by the part of me that is my human body." Martin said as they ran. "There is nothing I could do about this that you yourself could not also do."

"So we just continue running then?" Asked James.

"I am open to any suggestions."

James looked around through the darkness until he fixed his gaze on a source of light emitting from something a ways off in the distance.

"There!" He said, pointing in the direction of the light. "That might be a town where we can hide out for a little while and potentially catch our breath."

"Or it's a town that is already occupied by the enemy." Jacob said from behind them.

"Likely, but it's at least worth a shot." Said Martin.

"Yeah, pretty much. Lead the way I guess."

They approached the first house at the edge of the town. Martin knocked an arrow into the string of his bow and readied to fire, just in case. They circled the house through the tall grass and came around to the front.

"Yup, definitely occupied by the enemy." Martin whispered as he pulled his bow string back to the cheek plate of his mask aiming directly at the soldier sitting on the porch.

A fraction of a second later the man's head was nailed to the outside wall of the house by Martin's arrow. Immediately after the arrow hit, all three of them were out from their cover and sprinting for the small house. James flung the door open and Jacob followed him inside. Martin grabbed his arrow from the soldier's face as he passed by, then stepped inside after the others. As he shut the door he saw James and Jacob holding a Chinese soldier at gunpoint.

"What do you wanna do with this one, Martin?" James asked.

Martin drew out his sword then slowly walked up in front of the kneeling man. The man looked up with tears welling up in his eyes, causing Martin to cock his head curiously to the side. After they had stared at each other for some time, Martin suddenly stepped forward and stabbed downward. Driving his blade into the man's shoulder and down through his heart.

"Damn, why'd you do that?" Jacob asked, turning to look at Martin.

"I didn't like the way he looked at me."

"Harsh." Said James.

"We'll stay here for the remaining hours of the night." Martin said, changing the subject and turning to look around the room. "Maybe the enemy will pass by us without searching too hard."

While it was well furnished, It was a somewhat small home. However, it was still a step up from what they had become accustomed to. After settling in they set up the shifts for the order in which they would be on lookout. Now that they had one teammate less they would have to take slightly longer than their usual two hour shifts now.

Martin had been correct in his hopes that the enemy would pass them by. Because one hour into the first watch the enemy trucks drove down the road about a mile off and kept going north ignoring the town and their location altogether, for the time being.

The next morning Martin came out of his meditation still sitting on the floor where he had been all night. It wasn't that he needed to meditate, but now that he didn't need to sleep he just felt like he had to do something to help pass the time. At least until he could become used to just staying awake and active for extended periods. After waking the others up they took a moment to check for hostiles. Once they confirmed all clear they stowed their night vision in their bags then they exited the small house. And just out of curiosity they began walking towards the town.

"I wonder if they have a shop or something." Jacob said to the others as they walked. "Since we lost the Hummer we are already running low on supplies."

"This town looks to be very run down and poor. I wouldn't be surprised if we currently have more than they do as a whole." Said Martin.

They entered into the town square and Martin had been more or less correct. The townspeople were not doing well at all.

"A little slice of paradise, if you ask me." Said Jacob, in reference to the state of the town not even trying to hide his sarcasm.

"It's a thing of beauty, no matter what way you look at it." James added.

"In all seriousness though. Why do you think they stay in this actual hell hole?" Jacob asked, now in a more serious tone.

"These people are NPC's." Martin said without emotion.

"NPC's?" James asked.

"None Playable Characters. They're the same people as the everyday normal people from the days before. Remember the ones that only watched the mainstream media and never thought for themselves? This is what those people become when the times get tough."

"Really? I actually used to know a few people like that. Do you think it's like this everywhere?"

"No, this place is fairly calm. I would imagine that some places are far worse." Said Martin.

"Why is that? Is it simply because of stupid NPC's as you call them?"

"Indeed. Come and observe, I'll show you what I'm talking about."

Martin walked over to an old man sitting on the ground and stood in front of him.

"Hey there, old man. Do you wish for freedom?" Martin asked. "We can take you someplace with better accommodations if you so desire."

The dead eyed man just gazed off into the distance; after a moment he looked up in Martin's general direction and responded.

"We are safer here. Food, water, shelter. They take good care of us here."

James raised an eyebrow at the old man's response as Jacob moved around them.

"You are obviously malnourished and you are sitting in a mud puddle... you know that right?" Jacob said, crouching down in front of the old man.

"Don't waste your time. This is what I was talking about. He's been brainwashed. The same as everyone else in this god forsaken place."

Jacob stood up and with a smile turned to say something that was probably going to be a good natured joke when his facial expression suddenly went grim.

"Welp, I guess the party's over. It appears they might have found us." He said pointing down the road.

Martin and James turned to have a look and sure enough the enemy trucks were coming up the road heading in their direction, about two miles out.

"What's the plan?" James asked as they began walking out of the town square, moving down a side street that led behind the buildings.

"We have to end this. I'm tired of them pestering us when all we're trying to do is pester them." Jacob said as they began walking down the street.

"Agreed. I think we currently have more or less the element of surprise. So we should definitely try to exploit that advantage to its fullest potential." Martin said as they took a right down the first alley they came across.

"So what are we gonna do?" Asked James.

Martin suddenly stopped, then grabbed an old black blanket off a clothesline. After throwing the blanket on the ground he pulled out his combat knife and began fashioning it into something else.

"Whatcha doing there, Martin?" Jacob asked.

"Making a cloak."

"Why?"

"So I can act like one of the town people in order to get close, then execute."

"Should we do the same?" James asked as he reached for another blanket.

"No, you guys should go to the upper floors of the buildings on either side of the square to pick off any that try to get away. The last thing we need is one of them going for reinforcements."

"Sounds good. You think you can handle them on the ground by yourself?"

"Yes, I'm positive."

"Fair enough. Let's go, Jacob. I'll circle around to the building on the far side of the square. You head up this one right here." James said, while patting the brick wall of the building they were currently behind.

He then gave a slight nod and ran off in the direction of the building on the far side of the fountain.

"You ready, Martin?" Jacob asked as he looked over at him.

"Whether it was before my death or after, I have never been more ready in my life, and I have never felt so alive." He said staring off into nothingness before throwing the cloak over himself.

The rough fashioned hood covering his masked face almost completely, for some reason unknown to Jacob, the sight of Martin now in his newly acquired cloak sent a cold chill down his spine, and caused his blood to run cold.

"I'm just gonna head up there now." Jacob said before turning and running up the steps to the back door of the building and going inside.

"I wonder what that was about." Martin thought as he began walking past the building to head towards the square.

As soon as he rounded the corner, the enemy was pulling into town. The trucks came to a stop next to the dry fountain and soldiers began filing out of the covered troop carriers and lining up to receive orders. Martin began slowly limping his way in their direction trying his best to go unnoticed, or at least seem nonthreatening.

"I know they are in this area." Said the one who appeared to be an officer standing before the rest. "Spread out and find them. The masters would prefer if they were taken alive, but if that proves to be problematic and they push back or resist, then you have permission to shoot them."

"Yes sir!" The soldiers chorused all together.

"Alright everyone get move..."

The officer's words were cut off along with his head as Martin's sword severed it from the neck in one clean stroke.

"Well hello, my alien acquaintances." Martin said. "I would say welcome to America, but you are simply not welcome here at all."

He darted quickly to the side as they brought their guns to bear on him. Then in a blur he moved towards the soldiers who were visibly shocked by his staggering level of speed and agility. Seeing the opportunity granted to him by the surprise of the men at the front of the line. He dashed forward, lobbing the head off the first soldier he came across. He then spun around and ran his blade through the heart of the second, who was standing across from the first. As he was moving on to the third, chaos erupted. Upon realizing what was happening, all at once the soldiers around Martin converged on him in an attempt to use their sheer numbers to overpower his speed. They began striking at him as he stabbed another one of them. Then he swung and chopped the hand off another. Quickly growing tired of the odds being against him, Martin began shoving the soldiers back one by one. After he had pushed five or six backwards into the men behind them, he waited a second or two then he turned and jumped over the wall into the fountain, laying flat. No sooner had he hit the ground did the group of soldiers begin to explode one after the other.

"Wow, just like a magic show." He said as he sat up, covered in dirt from the multiple explosions.

His hastily made plan had actually worked more or less perfectly. It turned out he wasn't only pushing them back, he was also pulling the pins on their grenades. It was a risky thing to try, but it had actually played out better than he thought it would.

The few soldiers who weren't injured by the explosions or the shrapnel saw the destruction and immediately decided to flee in hopes they would not meet the same fate. They sprinted down the road leading out of the town when shots began to ring out, dropping the fleeing soldiers one by one.

Martin stood up then climbed out of the dry fountain as James and Jacob came running up to meet him.

"Well, that went better than expected." Said Jacob.

"You think so?" Martin asked as he brushed the dust and dirt off his entire body.

"Well sure, from the window up there you looked like an artist."

"Yeah yeah, we should search these trucks for supplies before reinforcements come to see what happened to these sorry bastards."

"What are you doing! They were here to save us!" A female voice screamed as she ran across the square to where Martin and the others were standing.

Without even a second of hesitation Martin pulled out his sidearm, turned around and shot the woman right between the eyes at point blank range.

"This world has no room left for such pathetic stupidity." Martin said, returning his pistol to its holster as her body collapsed to the ground.

"Damn dude... that was a little cold, don't you think." Said Jacob.

Martin stood looking down at the dead women. And with a coldness that the others hadn't seen from him before, he said.

"I didn't come back from the dead to have sympathy for the weak."

James looked down at the dead women, then at the pieces of dead soldiers.

"Well in any case I guess what is left of the gene pool is a little bit stronger now." He joked.

"Still man, for the record I don't like how you just did that without hesitation or remorse." Said Jacob.

"Duly noted, Jacob. Let's get going."

Jacob walked over and climbed up into the covered area of one of the trucks and began searching it. After a few seconds he returned to the opening at the back with a box in his hands.

"It's MRE's." He said, tossing the box to Martin.

"Is that all there is?" James asked.

"No, there's a couple more cases up front."

"Leave them in there." Martin said, throwing the box back up to Jacob. "James, go check the other truck. We'll load everything into this truck and take it."

"Do you want to leave anything behind for the townspeople?" Jacob asked as he set the box on the bench seat to his left and climbed down out of the truck.

"No, we can't help them. These people died a long time ago, Death just hasn't gotten around to them yet." Said Martin.

"So leave them nothing?"

"Anything we leave them will only prolong their suffering. If they aren't strong enough to keep themselves alive on their own, then they will die anyway."

"Damn. Alright. If you say so." Said Jacob.

"Hey I found something." James called out from inside the other truck.

Martin and Jacob walked over to the back of the truck where James already had a pile of boxes ready for them to grab.

"What did you find, James?" Martin asked.

James set a large case onto the tailgate and opened it.

"It's a bolt action 20mm anti material rifle." He said pointing at the gun inside the case.

"Load it up with the rest of the stuff. It might come in handy later on since we lost the Barrett."

Halfway through transferring all the supplies to the truck they would be taking, Martin noticed they had begun to draw the attention of some of the locals.

"Pick up the pace. It's about to get exciting again." He said.

"That's the last of it." James said as he jumped down off the tailgate.

By that time the townspeople were quickly forming into a small mob. Jacob ran to the driver door and climbed into the cab. The truck roared to life as Martin and James climbed into the back.

"Go!" Martin yelled.

The truck lurched forward causing James to grab a hold of the canvas to keep himself from losing his balance and falling out. The mob instantly turned into a riot as the truck began to head in the direction of the open road out of town. All the people descended on the truck as Jacob slammed his foot down on the accelerator.

"If any get in the way, that is their problem. Don't stop, don't even slow down." Martin said as he walked up to the opening between them and the driver seat.

Jacob glanced back, then gave a nod before turning his eyes back to the road. As soon as he did his eyes fell on a man stepping into the road about thirty feet in front of them. He was probably thinking that they would see him and slam on the breaks. Unfortunately, reality hit him like a truck as Jacob accelerated over top of the man without even attempting to slow down in the slightest. Once they were back out on the open road, they continued west for a while then turned down a back road, passing a sign that read "Now Leaving Locust NC".

"I know where we're at now." Martin said, leaning over towards Jacob. "We somehow made it all the way to North Carolina. We're on 24 now, follow it until 485 then take 85 north. We want to try to avoid Charlotte at all costs"

"Why, what's in Charlotte?"

"I don't know. And I'd rather not find out."

"Okay so after we head north. Then what?"

"Just head north towards not Charlotte but Charlottesville,

Virginia. I think 85 will lead up to 29, which leads right up through Charlottesville."

"Are we going back home?" Jacob asked.

"Not exactly, just heading in that general direction."

"I'll take what I can get. It would be nice to just see our old area again though if at all possible."

"We'll see what happens." Said Martin. "We managed to come out on top again, more or less, but we probably just got lucky. We need to start being more careful."

"Just a little bit." Jacob said, looking in the rear view mirror at the road as it faded into the dust left by the truck.

"Why does it have to be like this?" James asked standing next to Martin.

"It doesn't have to be, it just is." Said Martin as he took a seat on the bench. "Things tend to happen the way they are supposed to in order to serve a purpose."

"What purpose could all this possibly be happening for?" James asked.

"I do not know. Any knowledge I had of the future was erased from my memory when I re-entered my body."

James exhaled loudly, then took a seat on the bench across from Martin on the other side of the truck.

"Man, why did you come back?" James asked.

"What do you mean?" Martin returned.

"Why didn't you choose to just stay in the other place and be free from the hardships of this world?"

"Firstly because at that time I knew you guys needed my help. Secondly because something told me there was still something I had to do. I just can't remember what it was."

"Is it wrong that I want to know what it's like? To see what you have seen?"

"No, it's not wrong. All will be revealed to you on the day that you have been designated to be shown. If you wish to see what it's like, you need only have patience. It will come soon enough, because it must. Everything that begins, also ends. The real and only question is, when will it."

# CHAPTER: 49

JACOB turned the truck into the parking lot of a Walmart and pulled to a stop in one of the parking spots. They had been driving for a little more than a day now on gas they had siphoned from a few abandoned cars on the side of the road. However, those with fuel still in them were few and far between and they had actually only been able to make it as far as they did because of pure luck. They came dangerously close to running out of fuel on more than one occasion so after their last attempt to find fuel they had decided to stop and scope out the area a little before attempting to continue on in their journey into and through Charlottesville. Because if there was still anyone alive by this time they would undoubtedly be hostile, or worse.

"So what do you think we should do, Martin?" Jacob asked as he looked back into the covered part of the truck where James and Martin were sitting.

"Probably should just try to stay alive." Martin said before standing up from his seat.

"Sounds like a plan to me. Stay alive." James agreed before following Martin to the back of the truck.

"Seriously though, what are we gonna do?" Jacob asked again as he opened the door to get out of the truck. "Should we try to go around the city, or should we just send it right down the middle?"

"I say we go down the middle and then just plan as we go. It's a waste of time planning for the unknown when we can just improvise." James said as they walked around to the driver side door where Jacob had just jumped to the ground.

"Makes no difference to me. As long as we get to wherever we're going then I don't really care." Said Martin.

"Where exactly are we going?" Jacob asked.

"I'm not sure yet. I just have this feeling telling me to go back north." Said Martin.

"Alright cool. So no real plan, no actual destination. And we're just gonna wing it. Awesome." Said Jacob.

"More or less. Maybe we'll get lucky and everyone in the city has already starved to death." Said Martin.

"Maybe we'll get lucky. That's funny because we already push our luck past it's limits." Said James. "Also I wouldn't really consider everyone being dead as being lucky."

"It would be lucky for us in our current situation though."

"Actually, being lucky would be us sitting at home in a free and protected nation. Not the bullshit we're stuck with now."

"I'll take what I can get, and accept what I am given." Said Martin.

After locking the truck up as best that the old vehicle would allow, they all spread out for different ways to enter the Walmart. Martin took the main center entrance going through the already broken glass of the automatic sliding doors that were of course no longer functional. Jacob jumped over the fence of the garden center, then through a broken window into the toy section. James simply opened and walked through the surprisingly unbroken door to the grocery section as if he was a normal shopper from the days of plenty. Back when great spoils were so common and so taken for granted. The simple act of opening an unbroken door actually brought back happy memories to his mind. Memories of the days before, causing him to smile briefly as he walked past the broken metal detectors and into the desolate, ransacked store.

Martin continued down the bare center aisle, stepping over broken plastic and empty cardboard boxes. He kicked a box of Triscuits over as he walked by, only to confirm that it was empty just as he expected it would be. He took a right at the end of the isle and made his way to the hunting section. That's where he found James crouched down, looking through a pile of what appeared to be just junk.

"Hey Martin, fancy meeting you here." James said as though it was a coincidence.

"Find anything?" Martin asked, looking to his left down another aisle.

"I found a shaving kit down that aisle over there." He said, pointing back towards where he had entered the store. "But that's pretty much it. To be honest I don't think there's anything left."

"I would be more surprised if there was. This is normal for the scenario we are currently in. If the store had items left, then it would mean there not only aren't people in the area, but that there weren't people in the area. And that would be slightly more puzzling."

"Makes sense. So what should we do now?" James asked as he stood from his mission of searching through the garage pile.

"Go find Jacob and check out the rest of the camping section. I'm gonna go check out the loading docks. If you don't find anything of importance, meet me back there."

"On it."

James jogged off in the direction of the garden center, while Martin went in the opposite direction towards the back of the store. Upon going through the double swinging doors he noticed immediately by the sun shining through the skylights that the docks were in the same situation as the rest of the store, ransacked and trashed.

"Damn savages." Martin said under his breath. "It's no wonder the human race keeps almost going extinct. They can't control themselves, or their emotional response to hard times."

He looked around for a moment before his eyes came to rest on a small body laying on the dock. He made his way over and knelt down to one knee next to it so he could get a better look. It was the body of a boy that looked to be about ten years old, laying face down on the concrete. Martin removed his glove to check for a pulse and upon touching the boy's neck he knew immediately that the boy was dead. Probably had been for at least a few days now.

"Martin? Where are you at?" Jacob's voice called from the doorway.

"Over here." Martin said just loud enough for the others to hear him.

They walked over to where Martin was kneeling over the boy and stopped.

"He probably came here looking for something to eat, only to find out there's nothing left." Martin said without emotion.

"This is probably one of the worst parts about what's going on in the world today. The kids without parents and without a clue as to what's going on." Said Jacob.

"Yeah. Do either of you have a shovel?" Martin asked.

"A shovel? You actually want to bury him?" James asked in amused surprise.

"Yes. I do not remember what it feels like to have a heart, mine has gone cold."

"So? The kid is dead along with millions of others that aren't buried. Why should we waste our time on this one?"

"I never got to bury my own family. I never even found out what happened to their bodies. Their only crime was choosing to be a part of me, and a part of my life. And they died for it. They died for what I had chosen to do. Gabriel died for similar reasons and we had to just leave his body to burn in that Hummer. This kid laying here did absolutely nothing to deserve this fate. He never had a chance or a choice. A proper funeral is the least that he deserves."

"Didn't you shoot a lady in the face and leave her in the street the other day? Was she deserving of that fate?"

"Yes, she was. She chose to sympathize for and side with the very people who put her in that unfortunate position. She was a fool, and there was no positive effect that she could have had in any way had she been left alive. There are some people in this world who deserve to die in order to make the world better. There are some people who are weak, worthless objects that are unworthy of mercy, and I shall give them none. For I have no sympathy for the foolish, I am all out of empathy for the weak and I no longer possess the ability to give a damn about the worthless."

"Alright then, point taken. Common, Jacob. Let's go find some shovels." James said as turned and began walking towards the doors that led back into the store.

Jacob remained for a moment looking at the ground. He then looked at the boy's body then turned his gaze to Martin.

"I'm glad that I never found love." Jacob said before looking back down at the boy. "Staying single and never marrying was the right choice. Losing Gabriel was one thing. But I don't think I would have survived this long had I gone through the same level of loss that you went through, Martin."

Martin knelt unmoving and silent, looking off towards the wall to Jacob's right.

"I really don't know how you stay sane, or even calm for that matter. But for what it's worth, I'm here if you ever wanna talk about it."

Martin turned and looked at him then stood up.

"It's alright. What's done is done and those gone are gone. It's not about the things that happen, it's about what you do and how you choose to act after the fact that matters. I appreciate you being there for me though."

Jacob nodded once then after a short time standing in silence he turned and walked off in the direction James had gone a few minutes before, leaving Martin standing alone on the loading dock.

# CHAPTER: 50

**T**HE young boy's body was cold and stiff as Martin carefully lowered him into the hole they had dug for him. It was hard work but It had only taken them about half an hour to dig the hole deep enough that it would be unlikely the body would be bothered by any animals before it could have time to decompose.

Once the body was laid into the six foot deep hole they all stood around the grave looking down in silence until Martin spoke up.

"We may not know your name, or the kind of child you were, or the man you might have become. We all lose things as time goes on. Some lose more, some lose less, some lose everything and some lose everything sooner than others. Loved ones, family, friends... enemies. So many lives have been lost unnecessarily, many of them by our very own hands. I hope this small act of kindness and charity towards you will help us to see the world through less cynical eyes that we might become better than those we fight. Rest In Peace now little one and may we meet at a better time in the place where both time and natural life are beneath us. Rest now... and we shall see you in a moment."

They gave a few seconds of silence then James and Jacob began shoveling the pile of dirt back into the hole, covering the body and burying any memory of the boy. The boy who just like so many others would never be considered anything more than a statistic. That is if any history books ever got the chance to be written after these days had passed on into better times. Once they had finished covering the grave and packing down the dirt they began walking back in the direction of the truck. As they rounded the side of the building into the parking lot, it was Jacob's turn to break the silence.

"I'm not exactly sure why but somehow burying that kid feels like we also buried some of the others that we lost. Do you guys feel similar, or is it just me?"

"It isn't just you." Said Martin. "I do feel somewhat different. It's as if I've had a small amount of closure. Unfortunately there are some wounds that no amount of charity could ever heal."

After arriving back at the truck a few moments later. They unlocked the doors, climbed inside and took their respective seats. Martin in the passenger seat, Jacob in the back and James, who had taken the driver seat, started the engine, then put the truck Into gear.

"This whole stop was kind of a waste of time. Wasn't it?" James said, pondering the thought for a second before pulling out of the parking spot and heading for the main road.

"If nothing else. We at least got a good workout out of it." Jacob said from the bench in the back of the truck.

"I mean, we've been consistently exercising for years now, but I suppose a little more didn't exactly hurt us."

"Do good when you can, do evil when you must. It doesn't really matter what you're doing, as long as you're doing something. It's not that complicated." Said Martin.

"Sounds about right. That is if I understand you correctly anyway." Said James.

"It doesn't matter if you understood it or not. Everyone eventually understands everything. However, some just understand after it's too late. I recommend that you try to understand sooner rather than later. But I won't force you to believe that which you physically cannot."

"Are you talking to me?" James asked.

"It's possible. Were you listening?"

"Yeah, but you seemed like you were talking to someone else. Like your words were directed elsewhere."

"Almost everything I say is directed to anyone who is willing to listen. Even those who would disagree."

"I get that. I was just curious what you were getting at."

"Exactly what I said." Martin stated. "Everyone will eventually understand everything. Some will figure out a portion in this life and in turn they will be okay with what comes next. Some will refuse understanding in this life because of personal bias and in the next they will realize that they were sorely mistaken. But at that point it will have been too late."

"I'll have to think about all that when I get a spare moment." James said as he adjusted his seat to a more comfortable position.

"Not to butt in and change the subject." Jacob said, popping his head between James and Martin. "But we're coming up on Charlottesville. We should probably come up with a plan, or at least something we can use as an excuse."

"Turn there." Martin said, pointing to a side road up ahead on their left.

They approached the turnoff that Martin pointed out. James did as he was instructed and turned down the narrow road. After following it for some time they mae a right turn onto an overgrown dirt road that appeared to lead deeper into the trees. They drove on until Martin noticed they were coming up on the other side of the woods.

"Go a little farther down, then park before exiting the trees. We'll leave the truck there then we'll go scope out the city on foot." Said Martin.

"What do you guys think we'll find in the city?" Jacob asked as they parked.

"Hopefully unicorns and fairy dust. We're running low. And I could go for some right about now." Said James before shutting off the engine and getting out of the truck.

"What? Are you high, bro?" Jacob asked walking around the side of the truck looking slightly confused.

"He's screwing with you." Martin said as he walked between them and around to the back of the truck.

"I know. And It's not like him. So the only explanation is that he's high, right?"

"I'm not high. Not yet anyway." James smiled.

"Good luck finding anything to get high on. I'm sure that all the good stuff was used up a long time ago." Said Jacob.

"Damn, way to just crush all my dreams." James huffed.

"You don't even like drugs."

"You're right... how did we even get on this topic?"

"Because, you're both retarded." Martin said through the canopy from inside the truck. "Now come help me with our kit."

"I don't know, Martin." Jacob said in a less than serious tone as he walked around to the back of the truck. "That sounds pretty difficult. Are you sure you want us to help? I mean, what if we break something?"

"Well, you'll only be handling your own stuff. So I don't really care If you do."

"Ah, well that just takes all the fun out of it." Said Jacob.

"Does it?" Martin asked impatiently.

"Prossibly." Jacob said thoughtfully.

"Prossibly?" Martin asked after a pause.

"Indeed."

"That's not a word, Jacob."

"You may be correct, but there is a prossibility that it could be."

"What does it even mean?"

"It's a cross between probably and possibly."

"That's actually super dumb, bro." Said Martin.

"That's prossible." Said Jacob.

"We're wasting time. Are you guys gonna get your stuff together, so we can head out?" Martin asked.

"Yeah, we're on it." James said as he climbed into the back of the truck.

Jacob followed a second later, gathering the supplies and gear they would need for scouting in urban environments.

"How long do you think we'll be out for, Martin?" Jacob asked.

"Just long enough to see what kind of a situation the cities have devolved into." Said Martin.

"So like a day's worth of supplies?" James asked.

"Yeah, I think that will work."

"What about if something goes wrong?" Asked Jacob.

"Standard contingency plan. The truck will be our base camp. If anything goes wrong and we have to split up just try to get back here and hold down the fort until we can figure out whatever it is that needs to be addressed."

"Alright, sounds good. Let's get on with it then."

A short time later they were all geared up and ready to move out. Martin still wore the same style of clothes he had worn since Ramiel had assigned him his new role, given him the mask and made him swear to wear it. James and Jacob both wore their same old green uniforms of the STFU that seemed to be pretty much their everyday attire now.

From the spot where they had parked the truck at the edge of the woods they could see the edge of the city about a mile away. There were some houses they would have to clear or avoid before they could get to Charlottesville, but they didn't think those would pose much of a threat. Being as, almost everyone in this part of the world had died either from exposure, starvation, or disease. Or they were murdered by other people or complications from the mandated medical operations from the prior years. They could only hope that this was the case, because less people in this situation meant less potential trouble.

They made their way to the edge of the woods and looked out through the fading light across a small field. On the other side of the field there was another line of trees with a house beyond them. It was a small farmhouse with a little barn sitting off to the right side of it. It also had what appeared to be a chicken pen attached to it.

"Should we check it out?" Jacob whispered.

"Yeah. That property seems almost unaffected by what has been happening. And that makes me quite curious." Said Martin.

They slowly and silently crept towards the house, listening and watching it carefully as they went. There was no movement inside or outside, apart from the chickens, which were just busy doing whatever chickens do. They made their way up the front steps and onto the deck. Jacob and James moved to look through the windows on either side while Martin went up to the front door. He first looked at James who gave him a nod, then he looked at Jacob who did the same. Martin then knocked on the door and moved to the side just in case. No sooner had he moved out of the way, did the center of the door explode outward in a hail of splintered wood and metal.

"Friendly!" Martin yelled as he crouched down against the wall.

"Who the hell are ya?" The person inside the house asked, in a southern accent. "And what do ya want?"

"Just travelers passing through." Said Martin.
"We were only looking for information on the area and if there was anything we needed to be wary of."

"Come out where I can see you. Nice and slow and with your hands up."

Martin bumped the remains of the door to open it up the rest of the way. It opened easily since the rounds had removed the entire area of the door where the handle had been only seconds before. He then put his hands up as instructed and slowly stepped into the opening.

"How many of ya are there?" The southern man asked.

"There's myself and two more out here on your deck."

"Tell them to stay where they are. You can come closer."

Martin nodded to the others to stand down then stepped forward into the dim light. The resident inside the house stood up from behind the couch and aimed his shotgun with aggression as he did so. Martin could now see that it was a man in his mid to late 40's, with graying hair and a somewhat short beard.

"You need not fear us. We mean you no harm." Martin said as he moved fully into the room with his hands still raised.

Surprisingly the man slowly lowered his shotgun.

"What's yer name?" He asked as he slowly continued to point the muzzle towards the ground.

"My name is, Martin. But you can call me, Mr. Blank, if you'd prefer." He replied while slowly lowering his hands.

"I'm Aron. You ain't from around here, are ya?"

"No, we are not. We came down here from the Hammett Pennsylvania area when everything went sideways."

"Interesting. A while ago someone told me what I thought at the time to be a tall tail about a man in a black mask they called The Blank. They say that he's been traveling the land, fighting for the people. Your appearances fit the description of that man, but the question is, are you actually him?"

"Unfortunately, I do not actually fit that description." Said Martin. "For I do not fight for the people because there are no people left to fight for. There are individuals, but we are no longer a people."

"What type of person would someone have to be for you to fight for them?" Aron asked curiously.

"Honest, innocent, honorable and deserving."

"That's quite a tall order for anyone in this day and age, don't you think?"

"At this point, I'm now of the opinion that the less good people there are, the less I have to worry about helping."

"Well then, if you won't fight for those who remain, would you fight for payment instead?" Aron asked.

"That depends. What kind of payment, and for what reason?" Martin returned.

"It's a long story."

"I am willing to listen, if you allow me and my men a seat at your table. We would very much like to warm our food for the first time in a while."

"Please, I would be honored." The man said enthusiastically as he pulled out a chair for Martin to sit.

"James, Jacob. It's safe. Come on in." Martin called behind to the others before walking over and taking a seat.

The others came through the doorway a moment later. James took a seat next to Martin while Jacob took off his backpack and placed it on the floor.

"Do you mind if I use your stove?" Jacob asked.

"Of course. Please, feel free." Aron responded, walking over to turn on the burner.

"So, is it you who is looking to hire us? Or were you just asking rhetorically?" Martin asked.

"It's me. It's probably a long shot, but I need help with something."

"Do tell. I'm all ears."

"Okay, so. Shortly after things went down, this area, Charlottesville, was pretty much completely taken over by a band of marauders led by a man named, Dante Greenskin."

"Hmm. Sounds like a made up name to me." James huffed.

"It doesn't really matter if it is. He is still just as cruel and ruthless regardless of his name." Aron said.

"Don't mind my friend. Please continue." Said Martin.

"Yes, of course. As I was saying. This group led by Greenskin is made up of some of the most barbaric men that I have ever seen. They pillage small towns like they're some kind of Viking clan. They will rape, murder and or abduct anyone they feel like. All this they do with impunity, for no one around here possesses the strength to stand against them."

"Let me guess. You want us to take them out." James stated.

"What about the Chinese?" Martin asked. "Why have they let this go on for so long?"

"They pay the Chinese off. They're in some kind of business agreement with them, last I heard."

"If you can't beat them, join them. I guess the old saying still holds true." Said Jacob, poking his head out from the kitchen."

"Get back in the kitchen, woman!" James yelled, pointing towards the kitchen jokingly.

"Yes sir, daddy." Jacob shot back, causing James to shutter while his face contorted in displeasure at the response.

"What would you have us do? We are only three people after all." Martin said, getting back on track in the focus of the conversation.

"The group, the ones that I've been telling you about... They took my wife and my children. It's probably far too much to ask of you, but I am willing to pay you anything that I have, if you'll only help me get them back."

"Do you know where they are being held?"

"I'm almost certain that they are being kept in the hotel in the middle of Charlottesville. That's their headquarters."

"We cannot guarantee anything." James began. "We cannot be sure what condition they will be in if we can even find them. So I would not get my hopes up too much if I were you."

"I'm not sure how much of the stories about you are actually true, but I'd be willing to bet that you don't give yourselves enough credit. I believe that if they are still alive, then you three will get them out without a hitch."

"We take every bit of the credit that we have earned and all the credit that we deserve, which is none. Because nothing that we have ever done bears us any merit whatsoever." Said Martin.

"Do you really think that?" Aron asked.

"Yes. I do."

"Then why do you bother doing it?"

"First reason is because true charity is doing something for either absolutely nothing in return, or even negative return. Second reason is because I do what I want."

"I think that I understand. So, how much do you want? That is if you even want to help me."

Martin looked at James in the seat beside him, then over at Jacob standing at the end of the table.

"We'll take the job." Martin said at last.

"That's great! I don't have much, but I am willing to give you anything, or everything that I have."

"The fact that you are willing to give us everything you have, is payment enough. We will do whatever we can to save your family. These days good people are hard to come by. Therefore we will not be accepting any payment from you, this time."

# PART: VI

*"Feeling fear is evidence that you care for something. If you care for nothing, then fear becomes irrelevant."*

# CHAPTER: 51

**M**ARTIN walked out onto Aron's front porch early the next morning to the sun hidden by the clouds and a heavy fog moving in like a specter searching for its lonely prey. There was a smell in the air that carried the promise of rain and a rooster crowing from the other side of the barn. The fog was now thick to the point that visibility was nil and it seemed to be blanketing the entire area. Martin and the others then gathered at the dining room table to prepare for the mission that they had accepted the night before. After they agreed to help him, Aron had invited them to stay the night in his home. They were reluctant at first, saying that they could sleep outside like they had been for weeks. But after Aron insisted, they eventually accepted his offer. Not that it mattered though. Because while they did appreciate his hospitality, they all ended up just sleeping on the floor anyway. Apparently after being uncomfortable for so long, sleeping on only sticks, leaves and at best a hardwood floor, James and Jacob had trouble trying to sleep on the beds. Beds that used to be normal but were now just unfamiliar softness that made it hard for them to sleep. Martin of course didn't care either way, being as he sat cross legged to meditate on any flat surface no matter the environment they decided to make camp.

"So, how do you wanna slice this pie?" Jacob asked as he walked into the dining room where the others were sitting at the table going through the contents of their backpacks.

"What pie?" Martin asked, looking up from what he was doing.

"Wait, you have pie." James said with excitement in his voice.

"No no, I meant where about do you think we should start looking for Aron's family?"

"Damn." James said under his breath. "Now I want pie."

"Focus, James. They are most likely being held in the hotel headquarters. Or whatever they call it. I think that we should start there." Said Martin.

"I'll bet they probably have some lame name for it, like the tower of torment or something." Jacob said with a smirk.

"I wouldn't doubt it. People like them are usually morons." Said James.

"Never underestimate a group of organized people." Martin said, as he calmly stood up from the table. "We should get moving before the day gets any brighter."

"Agreed. It's quite foggy outside at the moment and we can use that to our advantage."

"You two use the fog." Martin said, looking at the others. "I will create a diversion while you guys try to get close to the hotel."

"What kind of diversion?"

"The kind that will distract their leader and buy you time."

The fog was beginning to thin as the three of them ran across the rooftops in the direction of the hotel that Aron had pointed out. They still had about a quarter mile left to go when Martin stopped and waved for the others to keep going. Once they were out of view, hidden by the fog Martin went to the edge of the building's roof and looked down. Standing on the sidewalk next to the building he could see the silhouette of a large man wearing what looked to Martin like a bunch of metal and garbage.

"Probably just trying to look intimidating." Martin thought.

He then stood on the very edge of the building directly above the large man. He waited just a few more moments for James and Jacob to cover more ground then he stepped forward and free-fell towards the ground.

Martin landed feet first, kicking into the back of the man's head. The sheer force of the impact drove him to the ground, caving in his skull and snapping his spine before Martin rolled forward to a stop safely in the street. He then stood, turned and walked back over to look at the man in the crumbled, bleeding heap.

"The drop attack is the most powerful move in the game." He humorously said to himself.

Looking over the damage that was the result of someone absorbing the full impact and velocity of his four story fall Martin observed the head wound gushing blood in what seemed like gallons at a time. And with how the man's neck was bent at an unnatural angle Martin knew that he had been dead before his body even hit the ground.

"Hey you! What are you doing?!"

Martin turned towards the source of the yelling voice to find another man about the same size as the one laying before him. He had apparently heard the racket caused by Martin's fall and had come around the corner to find him standing over one of his dead comrades.

There was a moment of confusion on the new guy's face as he observed the body laying on the ground in a pool of blood. Then in a snap like a flip of a switch the large man charged. Martin waited until the last second then he sidestepped causing the charging man to stumble a little, but in the end he was able to retain his balance. Martin calmly removed his bow, dropping it to the ground then he stood up straighter, waiting for the man to turn around and try again. This was the start of a diversion after all, so he figured he might as well have some fun with it. As the large man ran and dove through the air towards Martin he jumped up and kicked off the man's back. Sending the large man face first into the blacktop. Martin landed gracefully as the man slid to a stop by the curb. Then he turned around to observe his work and was suddenly knocked sideways by something wrapping around his entire body. He struggled to get free as he hit the ground hard on his left shoulder. He rolled a time or two before he finally came to a stop laying on his right side about twenty feet from where he had been standing a moment before.

"Well that hurt." Martin said as he wiggled over to lay on his back.

Struggling to get free, he looked around trying to see what it was that surrounded his body. It only took him a second to realize that it was a capture net, and unfortunately, it was a well made one. He struggled some more in an attempt to free himself, but the net was wrapped so tightly around him to the point where he could just barely move. After a few more moments of frustration he was interrupted by the weight of a large foot being placed on his chest.

"Well well well, what good fortune has been brought to us this day?" Said the owner of the foot that was currently standing on him.

"Fortune? One of your boys got his skull caved in, and you got a road rash on your face." Martin said. "An upgrade to your looks if i do say so myself."

"Yes, that would be considered most unfortunate if I cared enough to acknowledge the loss. "Tis but a scratch."

"Well aren't you just a pleasant ray of sunshine on a Sunday afternoon." Martin mocked.

"You aren't exactly in the position to be the one mocking me."

"I'm not mocking you. With a face like that your mother obviously already did enough."

The large, red haired man leaned forward to put more weight on Martin's chest with the intention of causing him greater pain. Martin just cocked his head to the side slightly as if he was confused by what the man was doing.

"Do you really think that you, a pathetic human, can hurt me?" Martin asked.

"I weigh two hundred and ninety pounds, worm. I'll crush your ribs like twigs."

"Sure you will."

Angered by Martin's response, the large man took a step back then raised his foot and aggressively stomped down on Martin's chest. He fully expected to hear the sound of bones breaking as his foot made contact. He had in fact killed many people in this way, and he knew the amount of abuse the average man could take before dying. The sound he heard from Martin however, was not what he expected at all.

"A for effort." Martin said. "I'll at least give you that. Unfortunately for you, you don't weigh enough to bend titanium."

"Titanium?"

"Yes. I'm wearing armor, jackass. Are you gonna stop messing about and take me to your boss now?"

"He's right, Randal." Said someone with a deep voice off to Martin's left. "The boss will probably want to see this one. I think he might be one of those terrorists that the Chinese are looking for."

Martin turned his head to see who was speaking. It was a tall bearded man who was holding something that resembled a very large crossbow.

"Wow, you're pretty intelligent for a moron." Martin mocked.

Randal grunted then removed his foot from Martin and grabbed the net that was still tightly around him.

Martin, being about one hundred pounds lighter than Randal, was easily hoisted onto his large shoulder. Then with Martin secured, they began moving in the direction of the hotel.

"When it comes time. It will be I that gets to kill this one." Said Randal.

"That decision will be left up to the Lord Commander." Said the man holding the net launcher. "You don't get to decide what we do with the prisoners."

"I could just kill him now. It would be your word against mine."

"Do you really think that our master, Lord Greenskin himself, would believe you over me?" The tall bearded man said with a laugh.

"Oh my god. Would you two just shut up already?" Martin said from Randal's shoulder. "You both have enormous ding dongs, now drop it. I'm trying to sleep up here."

"You're right. Maybe you should kill him." Said the tall man, earning a hearty laugh from Randal.

They walked for a while before they arrived at the fence that surrounded the hotel. They continued along it for a few more minutes until they came to the gate that led inside. Martin looked sidelong at the large fence as they passed through the gate, and silently wondered to himself if James and Jacob had made it inside yet. He hoped they had but if not then he would just have to improvise. As they entered through the main door into the lobby Martin observed what he could of his surroundings. He couldn't make out much though, being as he was facing the opposite direction than what he would have preferred.

"You know I have legs, right?" Martin said from Randal's shoulder. "I can walk myself if you untie me."

"Trying to escape already are we? Do you really think we're that stupid?" Randal asked with a laugh.

"Yes. I do think that. Being as you've already made your biggest mistake, I don't see a reason why you shouldn't just untie me."

"What mistake?"

"You brought me here. Right where I want to be. Now, tied up or not, It won't make much of a difference at this point anyway."

Randal dropped him none too gently to the floor where he hit like a sack of potatoes. Then to Martin's surprise he felt his own sword being pulled out of the sheath on his back. A few seconds later Randal began to cut on the net that surrounded him. A moment later, he was free.

"Welcome my friend, to my humble abode!" Said a loud voice. "I am, Dante Greenskin, leader of the Warband."

Martin stood to his feet and turned around to see a man in green armor with a matching cloak standing at the top of the staircase that led to the second floor of the hotel.

"Warband?" Martin asked. "What kind of music does your band play?"

"The Warband is not a music band. We are a band of warriors."

"How nice. You been doing a lot of warring lately?"

"Of course, we've been at war for years now. Only recently did said war go hot though."

Dante descended the stairs and moved towards a chair that was placed in the center of a large red rug off towards the right side of the lobby. He sat down in the chair then motioned for Martin to come closer. Randal grabbed him by the shoulder and ushered him forward to stand on the edge of the large red rug. Now that he was closer and in better lighting, Martin gave Dante a once over to get a better idea of what he was up against.

Dante was without a doubt a man of great stature. He was well over six feet tall, incredibly muscular and he had a beard that could only be described as magnificent. Martin also noticed that he had two different color eyes, his left eye was a shade of hazel, his right eye however was a piercing blue that reminded Martin of his own. Dante also had his hair in dreadlocks, which Martin thought was unusual but didn't think much more of it. Dantes armor appeared to be midieval but well made, however he wore no breastplate and his right arm was also bare. Which revealed a tattoo of a green snake that wrapped around his left arm with the head ending at his bicep.

"What is it that you do?" Martin asked as if he didn't already know.

"I'll be asking the questions if you don't mind. Let's start off with the basics. Who are you?"

"Of course. Where are my manners... My name is, Mr. Blank."

"And what is it that you do, Mr. Blank?"

"I just travel around killing people who piss me off."

"Did you come here to kill me?" Dante asked.

"Most likely." Martin responded.

"So you have failed then?"

"Not yet."

"Persistent even in the face of captivity. I like that. Who else falls into that category of people who piss you off?"

"Humanity."

"All of humanity?"

"Eventually."

"So I take it that you're not too fond of the way things are going then?"

"More or less."

"One last question and then I'll let you ask me some. Why the mask?"

"Sometimes your past is easier to forget when the face of the one responsible for the loss is hidden. It's easy to forget when you don't have a face to remind you of them."

"Ah, so you lost someone too. These things happen to most of us. It's been a while since I've heard a new story, could you do me a solid and tell me yours?" Dante asked.

"No. My story is better off forgotten. What about you?"

"That's fine if you don't wanna talk about it. My story is a lot like everyone else's. I was just a weed smoking, bodybuilding, anti-feminist gym bro who took charge when things went to hell, as strong men do once the cops no longer exist to hold true society back from its full potential. That's about it."

"How have you made it this long without being taken out by the Chinese?" Martin asked.

"Simple, we made a partnership." Said Dante.

"How'd you manage that?"

"We exchange slave labor in return for alliance."

"What happens when you run out of people to give them?"

"There is definitely no shortage of pathetic people who are able to work. When we run low we simply go in any direction and find starving worthless people who will do anything for a piece of bread."

"Sounds reasonable. Does your treason, I mean your alliance with the Chinese, come with any other perks?"

"Treason to what? This feminist hellhole of a country has been dead for years. It was over long before the invasion. Things just finally caught up to it. It was over when men began bowing down to worthless women as though they were godesses when in reality they were no more than dirty, used up whores selling themselves for attention as if it was a currency. It was over when weak men gave emotional women the right to vote to send men to die in war while they stayed here bearing no repercussions for their own actions. The country was dead when men were forced to take responsibility for the failers of women and in turn be the ones shunned and punished for doing so. This country died when women voted for retards to run the country, elected gays to run the schools and allowed pedophiles to teach our children right from wrong. Look how far they have fallen. As soon as the cops, the internet and the government were gone, within a week the gays were all dead, the gender rolls had returned and to survive the whores began doing the only thing they knew how to. If real strong men had been alowed to lead from the beginning and had not been beaten down by bitch ass, simp men who were given guns by the government to make sure we never took power this country would have never been attacked and we would all be at home with our wives and children instead of fighting for our next meal and taking what we want from those who are weaker. The feminists who hated me most are the same people that made me sitting here possible, they destroyed this world with their weakness, and now the age of the strong men has returned. But to answer your question from before I got off topic, of course it comes with perks. You see this satellite phone?" He asked as he pointed to the open briefcase on the table next to his chair.

"I honestly think I must agree with your evaluation of society and why it failed. It actually makes a lot of sense how if the same people who run the country also bear no responsibility for their actions but instead just shift blame to others, failure is inevitable. And yes I see the phone." Martin said with a shrug.

"This is the phone I use in the case of anything I need or want. Air support, reinforcements... call in that I've found the 'terrorist' they have been looking for. You know, normal stuff." He said with a sly smile.

"Yeah, it's obvious that you called the Chinese and that they'll be here within a couple hours, we know. You are predictable, but none of that matters at this time. We will be gone before you can do anything."

"You have a lot of confidence for a dead man."

"You are correct. However you are also mistaken. I am in fact a man who has previously died, but unfortunately for you, I will not be dying again, well at least not today anyway."

"You are my property now. You die when I decide that I want you dead."

"Probably. But we shall see."

"What are you talking about?"

"Patients, you will know soon enough."

"Get him out of here. I've grown tired of this conversation. Take him up to the prison level and put him with the rest of them. The Chinese Commander should be here to fetch them all shortly."

"It was nice meeting you." Martin said as they pushed him out of the lobby.

Randal and the tall bearded man led him through a door and into a hallway. They followed the hallway till they came to the elevator where Randal pushed the up button.

"It always surprises me that people have been able to keep the electricity on for this long." Said Martin.

"People find a way." The tall man said as they stepped onto the elevator.

"So what's your name, tall one?" Martin said, turning towards the man as they stood, waiting for the bell.

"My name is..."

"I don't care." Martin interrupted.

"Hammerlocks." The man finished without expression.

His voice was deep and monotone. Which fit his masculine features and long, thick white hair.

"You're probably pissed about me killing your friend in the street back there. Are you not?"

"I didn't really know him, but from the little that I did know of him, Jeff was a good warrior."

"Ah, well I would say that I'm sorry, but I never apologize for anything, ever. I'm also not actually sorry, so if I apologized then it would be a lie."

"Don't worry about it. He died in a fight. That's a hell of a lot better way to go than starvation or disease. Which is the usual way that people die these days."

The bell dinged and the doors opened to the top floor of the hotel. It made sense that they would make the prison section at the top. It would be very difficult for any normal person to escape. The only way down for most, is either the stairs, the elevator, or of course the quickest way... falling.

"Glad there's no hard feelings." Martin said as they stepped off the elevator. "I wish I could say I cared about any of that stuff, unfortunately I don't. Emotions mean nothing to me, so I refuse to waste any amount of energy on them."

"Fair enough. Ah, well here we are. Welcome to your new home." Hammerlocks said as Randal pushed him into the room and shut the door.

"Thank you." Martin said as the two men began to walk away. "Oh, do me a favor." He called after them. "Tell the front desk I'll be checking out before morning."

Both men laughed at him then continued walking down the hallway back to the elevator. Once they had gone, Martin turned around to examine the room and to figure out what kind of situation he was in. Upon turning he immediately knew that it wasn't the best situation. There were about fifteen people in the room with him and all of them were staring intensely. He examined the faces of the people in captivity both young and old. Some expressions were hopeful, while others discouraged and removed. He then looked to the other end of the room where the glass should have been but had been replaced by nothing but open air. This gave even Martin a sense of freedom while in captivity. He could only imagine the psychological effect that this had on the normal people that had to endure it. To be so close to the outside yet so far from the ground.

He didn't say a word as he moved past the people sitting on the floor. They all continued watching him as he began to walk towards the opening. He then sat down next to the edge and looked out at the forest in the distance. As he sat there with the eyes of those around him still glued to his back, he marveled at the ideas that this prison triggered in his mind. Was this all that life truly was? Just living with the illusion and feeling of freedom while in reality you're trapped with only death as a way out. He struggled to understand why he still even allowed himself to live in such an existence as this. Freedom was as simple as dying for good, and yet he carried on.

"Why." He said to himself.

"What was that?" Asked a woman who was sitting a few feet away from him.

"Why do you stay here when obtaining true freedom is as simple as falling forward?" Martin asked.

"You mean why don't we jump?"

"Yes."

"Well because we would die."

"Is death not the path that leads to absolute freedom?"

"I don't know."

"Is freedom worth dying for?"

"Maybe to some."

"Those who truly desire freedom, do not allow themselves to fall for it."

"Fall... for what?"

"The lies told by those who wish to control you."

"What kind of lies are you referring to?"

"The kind that makes you believe you are free when in fact you are not."

"How do you stop that from happening?"

"You jump. They can not make you believe if you refuse to play their game. They con not make you a slave if you deny them your life."

"Are you okay?" The woman asked with a touch or worry in her voice.

"Yes. I'm only thinking out loud. Do not act upon my questions. I am simply trying to understand."

"I see. By the way, who are you? If you don't mind me asking."

"I am just an empty suit. I am fleeting. Here one moment, gone the next. A single ripple in time, just wishing for a reason why. And wondering who exactly threw the first stone into the water."

"Is that how you want to be remembered?"

"No, it is not."

"How do you want to be remembered?"

"I don't."

# CHAPTER: 52

**T**HE rain began to fall faster with each passing moment as Martin sat alone with his back up against the wall next to the edge of the opening with nothing but air between him and freedom. The woman from before had moved on to the other side of the room to help with something that Martin didn't care enough about to see what it was. He was still deep in thought, staring at his hands which still had the reminisce of blood on them. Most likely from a previous person he had killed but he couldn't remember which one. It seemed like it was never ending, like they all blended together. He couldn't even remember how many it had been.

"How many..." He whispered to himself. "How many lives have died by my hands? Does it even matter?... no, it doesn't. There is no point in worrying about the dead when the living are worrisome enough. Damn, I need to figure out how to get these people out before the Chinese get here."

The clouds got thicker and the rain began to fall even harder. Martin held his arm out of the opening catching some of the drops in his gloved hand. He watched as the blood was washed away, running out of the fabric of his glove in red streaks. When the red stopped he brought his soaked hand back inside to look at it once again. The rain had washed away the dried blood off the surface, but the deep crimson stains could still be seen even in the black fabric.

"The blood on my hands may all wash away, but the stains that remain are too deep not to stay." Martin whispered to himself.

"Yo, Martin." A familiar voice whispered from outside the broken window.

Martin turned his head instantly and to his surprise saw Jacob's face peeking in.

"I found suction cups. Look at me go." Jacob said in an excited whisper.

"Suction cups? Where did you even find those?" Martin asked.

"At the auto body repair shop over there." Jacob pointed off behind himself.

"That's not... that's not how any of this works, Jacob."

"It does though. They are... 'climbing grade'. And look, I brought you a rope."

"I highly doubt that Climbing grade suction cups are an actual thing. Also there isn't really anything to tie the rope off to in this room."

"I assumed that. Don't worry, there's bound to be a railing or something on the roof. James should be up there already. I'm gonna continue up and hopefully find something strong enough to tie off to."

"Okay. I guess It's worth a shot." Said Martin.

Jacob shrugged then quietly moved sideways to the edge of the hole so he could continue up without being in sight of the people in the room. He then climbed up the glass around the corner from where Martin sat and disappeared onto the roof. A few minutes later James came sliding down the rope, stopping right in front of Martin in the middle of the opening.

"There were three guys up top, but they shouldn't give us any trouble now." James said.

"Why's that?" A little girl asked, confused by what James had said.

"Well you see, little one. I have this poky thing that gives people the permasleep. I just tucked them in, kissed them goodnight and that was it."

"Speaking of poky things. I dropped my bow in the street while fighting and they took my sword when they captured me." Said Martin.

"Were they sentimental or important to you?" James asked.

"There are no natural objects in this world that are important to me."

"Alright then. Well here's one of the Glocks. You can use it until we get back to where we stashed our backpacks." He said as he removed the pistol from his holster and handed it to Martin.

"That'll work. Where's Jacob?"

"He's gonna guard the rope at the top. I'm gonna go down to the bottom and start clearing the way."

"Okay. I'll stay here and help people onto the rope."

"Is Aron's family in there?" James asked in a whisper.

"Yes, but I am not going to make it obvious that we are here for them specifically. That would just make it harder to get everyone else out."

James leaned closer towards Martin and in only a little more than a whisper, he said.

"Why don't we grab just Aron's family and leave the rope for everyone else to figure it out?"

"We're already here so we might as well see them all to safety."

"Whatever you say, man. Makes no difference to me."

By that time people had begun to stand up, wondering what was going on.

"Good luck." James said before he disappeared down the rope.

Martin then turned to address the people. Who were now all standing around and looking at him.

"Alright everyone, we're getting out of here. This rope is your ticket out, if you so choose to take it."

"What about the little ones?" A woman asked.

"The men will carry the children." Martin said in answer. "I will show you how to wrap the rope around your body to allow you to repel down safely."

"Why would you have the men carry the children? Do you think that women can't handle it?" Another woman said, putting her hand on her hip.

Martin looked at her for a moment then slowly walked forward and leaned down till his masked face was mere inches from hers.

"No, I simply know that the average man is stronger than the average woman and that there is less of a chance that a man will lose his grip and fall."

"Geez, what's your problem?"

"People like you are my problem. You are everything that is wrong with this world and everything that got us here."

"Oh so you're just a misogynist, and you think this is all women's fault?"

"Incorrect, I in fact appreciate women very much. However, I have only ever met a small handful of real woman in my life, and most of them are dead now."

"Oh, so you think I'm not a real woman?!"

"That is correct, little object. And if you don't shut the hell up and do as I say then I will leave your sorry ass for the Chinese. I have no patience left for weak morons."

"There are women that can do just as much, if not even more

than you can."

"Well why didn't you say so? If that's the case then you should probably stay here and wait for this chick you speak of to come rescue you." Martin said sarcastically before going serious once again. "You are a foolish female. Females throughout all of history have never fought and died for their families, their livelihood or for the defense of others. When times get hard they either cower in wait for men to rescue and protect them, or they spread their legs and accept their captors and their new fate. This is real life, and real life grants no equality to those who are lesser, or to those who are weak."

Without even giving her the chance to respond, Martin simply grabbed the man closest to him and began explaining how to repel down the rope. A moment later the first man carrying a child was at the bottom. And no sooner had his feet touched the ground was Martin sending the next person in line.

James was waiting at the bottom of the rope to meet and point each of them in the direction that they should run in order to get to safety. One by one they repelled down the rope and immediately began running through the hole James had cut in the fence. After about five minutes of this, Martin was the last one in the room. He went to grab the rope to go down himself when Jacob slid by at an alarming rate of speed.

"Hurry up!" He said as he passed by the opening.

Martin looked down after him then grabbed the rope with one hand, wrapped it around one foot and began his descent into the chaos that was undoubtedly awaiting him at the bottom.

# CHAPTER: 53

**Q**UICKLY, you need to take your family and run." Martin said as he ran up to meet Aron, giving him his family. "We will lead the Warband away in the other direction so you can make your getaway. You must go now before it's too late."    "Where should we go?" Aron asked.

"Head for the Appalachian mountains. There's a group there that will help you." Martin said hastily.

"What about you?"

"Don't worry about us. We've been at this for so long that it is normal for us now."

"What are you going to do?"

"We are going to lead them away from here. James and Jacob are causing a diversion as we speak."

"Thank you, Martin. We won't forget this. We'll never forget what you did here today."

"In time, you will forget. And I really hope that you do. Now go."

After leaving Aron and his family, Martin ran to meet back up with James and Jacob.

"Alright, mission complete." Martin said as he slid into the alley next to the others. "Now, let's go retrieve our backpacks so we can get out of here."

They quickly moved out of the alley where they were hiding and began running north, hoping to evade their pursuers. When they made it to the cache where their backpacks were stashed they quickly retrieved their gear. Then they set out running down the block until they exited an alley into a street where they could see the Warband's hotel off to their right. Martin raised his pistol and fired three shots at the building. They were much too far away for the 9mm to do any real harm but he was going more for just getting attention rather than dealing damage. He wasn't quite sure yet if it was a good thing or not but the shots definitely did the trick. They were now being descended upon by an entire army from the looks of it. And when he saw that the Chinese military had arrived he realized that the situation was actually turning into a real mess, and they weren't exactly sure how they were going to get themselves out of it this time.

"Run?" Jacob asked with an unsure shrug.

"Yup, run. Most definitely run." Said James.

They all ran full tilt in the opposite direction of the hotel. They knew they had a lot of ground to cover before they could make it back to the truck and they also knew that the odds of them making it at all were not exactly in their favor at that moment.

After they had been running for about a quarter mile, Martin noticed something wasn't right. He looked around and quickly discovered that he was correct.

"Where's James?!" He shouted to Jacob who was running about ten feet to his left.

They both turned to look back and saw James about thirty feet back, laying on his stomach trying to use his arms to crawl.

"Run!" James screamed at them as he yanked off and threw his dog tags as hard as he could. "Go! My legs don't work anymore! I can't walk! Just leave me!"

Jacob turned and started running back with the intent to save him. Martin chased after him, grabbed him by the arm and tugged him back.

"He's done." Martin said, holding onto Jacob while bending over to pick up James's dog tags. "We can't help him now. We have to go."

"No, James!" Jacob shouted as Martin half pulled, half drug him backwards.

"We can't save him. Just let him go, Jacob."

Martin looked off towards the hotel to see a man standing on top of a truck. He was about a thousand yards away, holding a large rifle perched on his shoulder.

"The weak die, the strong are killed, but the strongest live forever." Martin said to himself, while looking at the man in the distance. "Death is freedom, life is a cage. Therefore, I hope you live forever, Dante Greenskin."

Martin watched as Dante shouldered his rifle and fired, the bullet from his gun whizzed through the air and tore into James's upper back and exited out through his chest leaving a large gruesome wound. The last thing Jacob saw before Martin hurled him over the side of the hill was James dropping his head to the street where the last of his life left him.

Martin and Jacob rolled to stop at the bottom of the hill and Jacob immediately got up and started heading back up. Martin grabbed him again and fought to pull him back down.

"Let go of me! We have to save him!" Jacob shouted.

Martin spun him around and slapped him hard across the face.

"We can't!" He shouted back. "Sometimes people die for good! And believe me, it's better this way!"

"Better for who?!" Jacob yelled.

"Better for, James. Don't you see, he's safe now. Let him go."

"You're delusional, Martin. Stop lying to yourself."

"Your delusional if you think there is anything left of James to save. I only lie in the times when I must. This however is not one of those times. True life does not exist here in this world. You will never experience true life or consciousness until you bear witness to the moment. The moment that is without beginning or end. In the place where there is no shape or measure. The place where there is only knowledge and understanding. After the shade over your eyes is removed by death, you see that which cannot be imagined or retained. James, lived well. Therefore he is now more alive than he was. Let it be so."

Jacob paused for a moment then looked down and patted Martin's arm to let him go. Martin released him and took a step back.

"Alright. I guess it's two down, two to go then." Jacob said somberly.

Martin lowered his head slightly and Jacob walked by him patting him on the shoulder as he went. Martin looked up the hill from where they had come, then turned and followed after Jacob.

After a few hours of stealthy moving around from hiding spot to hiding spot, they finally managed to lose their pursuers once again. They had purposefully moved around in circles, making a flower shape to throw off their scent in case their enemies were using any dogs. Then they waited in a dumpster for about twenty minutes as the enemy passed by on the next street over from them. Once they felt as though the coast was clear they left their hiding place and moved towards the outskirts of the city.

"We really need to get back to the truck." Martin said as they crouched by the corner of a building. "We should be able to use the cover of the trees to circle around the city to the other side."

"Wouldn't it be faster to just go back that way and cut through the city?" Jacob asked pointing to their left.

"Faster? Possibly. Safer? Not likely. With the Chinese now in the area we probably wouldn't make it halfway through before getting found. There are far too many of them for us to evade."

"Fair enough. I guess a little more walking won't hurt."

It took them well into the early hours of the morning, but they finally managed to make it back to the truck. The Warband had gone in a different direction some time before so they figured that they would rest for a little while then head out at the first sign of light.

"Sure did a good job following the plan." Jacob said sarcastically as he threw his bag into the back of the truck and sat down on a log.

"Are you talking about the plan to stay alive?" Martin asked.

"Yeah." Jacob laughed. "Too bad things never go according to plan."

Martin didn't respond. He just sat down next to the truck and began thinking about how everything had gone so wrong in such a short time.

"Do you think that James and Gabriel were heroes?" Jacob asked, breaking the silence.

"I think they died well. But hero is a strong word for someone who was never even the good guy." Said Martin.

"You don't think we're the good guys?"

"There is no good left in this world, Jacob. How could we be?"

"I don't know, I always thought we were fighting for the right reasons."

"In war, it is normally the people who believe themselves to be the good guys that are more likely than not actually the bad guys. There is no right side to be on in war, and there is no person in this world who possesses the merit required to earn the title of hero. There is only the strong and the weak. Those who take and those who are taken from. The weak are killed by the strong and the strong are killed by the stronger. It's just the way it is, and the way it must be."

"I see. Are you afraid of losing what you have left, Martin?"

"No, I am not. For I have nothing left that can be taken. Also fear in general is for fools."

"But why is that?"

"Weak men feel fear to have courage. Strong men do not need courage because they do not feel fear. Fear stems from confusion and from not knowing or understanding pain, suffering and death. They who understand those things, do not fear anything because they know what awaits them. That is what makes someone truly dangerous."

"So wait. Are you saying that you're more dangerous because you're not afraid to die?"

"No, I'm not dangerous only because I'm not afraid to die, I'm dangerous because of the reason I'm not afraid to die."

"What reason is that?"

"Because my death was the best thing that ever happened to me. There is little I have left that is worth living for, but there is so much more that is worth dying for. My only goal left in life is to die for something that is truly worth dying for. So if death is near to me but the reason is not, then I will prevent it until a more suitable time."

"So you're trying to stay alive long enough to die for something that's worth it?"

"More or less. It doesn't really make a difference how you die, but to die well is a good reason to stay alive as long as possible."

"I wish for the same. To live long enough that I may die for something I feel is a worthy cause."

"That is good. You should get some sleep now, Jacob. If we make it through the rest of the night we will probably be on the move again all day tomorrow."

"Are you going to stay up on lookout by yourself all night?" Jacob asked.

"No need, I am going to meditate."

"Shouldn't one of us stay awake on watch?"

"Worry not, Jacob. If it is meant to be, the enemy will wake us."

# CHAPTER: 54

**T**HERE was the sound of thunder as an airplane cut through the sky overhead. Martin's eyes opened slowly and he knew from the sound that it was a jet of some kind. He looked up to try and spot the source of the sound and after searching for only a second or two, he saw it. The cross of death that was the A-10 thunderbolt, or more commonly known as the A-10 warthog. He knew at the first sight of it that there was nowhere to run from a weapon of such awesome power.

"Wake up." Martin said as he threw a small rock at Jacob to rouse him awake.

Jacob jumped up and immediately looked up to scan the sky for the source of the sound.

"This might just be the day our mission comes to its end, my friend." Said Martin, still sitting where he had been meditating with his back against the truck.

"That may be true, but I'll be damned if I don't go out fighting." Jacob said before he ran to the truck they had covered the night before with brush and camouflage.

After climbing into the cargo area, Jacob grabbed the 20mm anti-material, bolt action rifle from the back, inserted an empty magazine then grabbed two 20x102mm armor piercing incendiary rounds from the case.

"I'm probably only gonna get one shot at this if i'm being honest with myself, so you better get going, Martin."

"Let me do it." Martin said as he went to grab the heavy rifle from him.

"No, this is the way it has to be, damn it! I need to do this. Only one of us it gonna make it out of here, Martin. You have to be the one to survive." He paused for a moment to look at the ground then he looked back at Martin. "Survive so you can remember us and how we died, not for the world that didn't deserve our sacrifice but for our friends that did."

Martin was silent.

"Don't take this away from me, man. I can't watch you die too. Please just let me be done. I've found something that's worth dying for. Now please, just let me be free."

Martin slowly removed his hand from the rifle that was firmly clutched in Jacob's and lowered it to his side.

"Thank you, Martin. Now go. Finish what we started."

"Thank you for your friendship, Jacob. You will forever be my brother. And no matter how this goes, I'll see you in only but a moment."

They looked at each other fondly but neither stated aloud how they knew their time was now drawing to a close. Jacob then pulled out the chain which held his dog tags, and after looking at them briefly he tore them off and handed them to Martin.

"A little something to remember me by." Jacob said with a hearty smile.

Martin nodded, and without another word Jacob walked out of the trees, right out into the open and crossed the field. He then took position by an old broken down car in the middle of the road. Taking aim in an upward angle he propped the barrel of the rifle on the roof of the car. As the A-10 came around and faced directly at him he racked the bolt back, threw a single round into the chamber and pushed the bolt back into battery.

"I hope you're not an American. But regardless, whoever you are, I hope you die well."

He flipped the safety off, breathed in deep, exhaled half out and held, took aim, closed both eyes, and squeezed the trigger.

Martin watched the barrage of 30mm rounds from the front mounted minigun of the A-10 rip through the air and onto the ground where his friend had been just seconds before. Martin looked down at the ground in front of where he stood and slowly began removing his mask for the first time since he had put it on. Holding his mask in one hand he looked upwards to the flying death machine and noticed that it wasn't pulling up. A second later it crashed into the ground in a ball of fire.

"Lucky shot." Martin said with a smirk that quickly faded back to a stern expression. "Goodbye, my friend."

He looked down at his hand to the tags he still held. The tags of the last member of his small team apart from himself. The last person in the world that he actually cared about. In that moment a single tear rolled down his cheek. Realizing this, he quickly wiped the tear from his face. Looking at the fingers of his glove, damp with the first and only tear that would ever be shed for his fallen brothers and family, he marveled the fact that it was the first tear he had shed in over 10 years, and the last one he ever would.

And so It was just as he said it would be. He never lied to his team about what they were getting into by following him. They died as he said they would, with honor no one would ever know, and names that history would never repeat. He knew all these things would happen and he accepted them long ago. Unfortunately he was still mostly human and this new reality that he was now completely alone in this world hit a little harder than he had originally anticipated. He would soon die himself for good this time, and having that to look forward to gave him a small feeling of relief. But regardless of that, he would cherish their memory for whatever amount of time he had left, and for as long as he possibly could.

"The only thing in life that is for certain, is death." Said a voice from behind him.

Martin dropped his mask as he turned to the source of the voice and had his pistol drawn before it hit the ground.

"Hello, old friend. It has been a long time."

Martin lowered his gun in surprise while saying only one word.

"Ramiel."

# CHAPTER: 55

**W**HAT are you doing here? Where have you been?" Martin asked as he picked up his mask and put it back on over his face. "I have been building a reputation for you." Ramiel replied.

"Why would I need a reputation? And why are you here now?"

"I have been looking for you. I figured that it was time for you to know the truth."

"The truth? The truth about what?" Martin asked.

"Your purpose in this life." Ramiel replied.

"My purpose? What do you mean?"

"The guilty in this world must be made to suffer, and suffer they shall."

"Explain."

"Life is indeed a gift, but so also is death. Some will say that it is not your place to make the decision of life or death for someone else, but if you have the power to take a life and nothing can stop you then it is absolutely your decision. However, most of those whom you decide no longer deserve life also do not deserve the freedom that comes with death. Some are more deserving of suffering rather than a quick death."

"Are you saying I should have tortured, tormented and made people suffer rather than kill them?"

"People are fully capable of both tormenting and killing themselves. Look at the world today. Everyone who is suffering, is suffering by their own doing. Sometimes however, they must be pushed a little. That is where you come in."

"What would you have me do?" Martin asked.

"What you have been doing. Only more." Said Ramiel.

"Do you want me to kill, or torment more people? Because I have been doing only one of those things, mostly."

"Yes."

"You know, when I was a little kid I always hoped that one day I would have been the good guy, a hero of sorts. Not the bad guy of the story. I know now that heroes don't exist anymore but still, it would have been nice if things had been different."

"This is correct. There is no such thing as a hero. You yourself explained this to Jacob only a few hours ago. You are either a nobody, or the villain. No person alive today has enough merit to be called a hero. So the question is, would you rather be the villain, or be a nobody?"

"I never wanted to be a villain. I always wanted to be good, to be better." Martin said looking at the ground.

"Martin, what is the difference between good and evil?"

"Right and wrong?" Martin asked.

"What's the difference between right and wrong?"

"I don't know. What?"

"Opinion and perspective. The only difference between right, wrong, good and evil, is the opinion and perspective of an individual."

"But there has to be some sort of rule to dictate what's right and wrong."

"Why? What being of authority ever said that had to be a thing? Martin, this world is both more simple and more complicated than you could understand at this time. But I will tell you this. When I offered you power and leadership you turned it down because you did not want it. That is precisely why I gave it to you anyway. If you give power to those who seek it then those will be corrupted and power will be abused. But if you give power to those who do not seek it then those are more likely to remain nutral. Power granted to evil will always be evil and power granted to good may become evil. You cannot be evil for a good reason, and you cannot be good for an evil reason. Evil is inherent, and unfortunatly good no longer exists in this world because there can only be one good and he has forsaken this place. That is why you are not good, Martin. You are simply good at being evil."

"So you are saying I have become evil and there's nothing I can do to change it?"

"Correct." Ramiel said with a nod of his head.

"And what were my powers granted by?"

"Also yes."

"I would like some actual answers." Said Martin.

"Martin, why does the apple fall?"

"Are you talking about Newton's theory of gravity now?"

"Not exactly. The apple falls because it does not understand how gravity or existence works. Why does the human fall?"

"I don't know, why?"

"The same reasons as the apple. The only difference is that humans have the potential to learn how to overcome the clutches of natural physics. They need only to understand."

"Are you trying to tell me that I can use my understanding of existence to defy gravity and physics?"

"Is that such a stretch? I mean can you not already move at the speed of thought?"

"Barely. I can't figure out how to control it."

"It has been so long. How is it that you do not have a full understanding of it yet?" Ramiel asked.

"Probably because I don't know where to start." Said Martin.

"You must figure that out on your own. I can explain why it is, and how it is. But I cannot make you understand something if you yourself cannot decipher it from what I tell you." Said Ramiel.

"Would I be here now if it wasn't for you?" Martin asked after a short pause.

"No, you would not be here if it wasn't for me."

"That's right, isn't it. You trained me. So of course I wouldn't."

"Do not try to shift the blame of your misfortune onto me. I simply gave you direction. You would have ended up somewhere far worse had I not intervened when I did. Also your training was minor. The biggest thing was getting you to wear that mask and swear your service to me."

"What are you talking about?" Martin asked.

"Fulfilling the prophecy." Ramiel said flatly. "That mask is the face of me. It is the face of death. That is why no matter where you have been, or where you go, death and destruction will always be following close behind you."

"You're talking nonsense again. Speak English, bro."

"Since you chose to wear the mask death has always followed in your wake. Had you not chosen to wear it, it would be you that followed death."

"What would my life be had I not chosen what I did?" Martin asked.

"Do you currently have control over your emotions?"

"Mostly, yes."

"If you had chosen otherwise, you would have become the kind of person that you now enjoy killing."

"Was that decision really that important?"

"Did you seek revenge after the death of your family?"

"I gave it a shot, but as of right now am not pursuing it. I actually haven't given it much thought as of late."

"Do you think that you would have had I not given you the information that I did?"

"Vengeance most likely would have been made my final mission."

"Everything happens as it should."

"What?"

"Martin, do you think that your wife, had she still been alive at the time, would have allowed you to take on the burden of my mission?"

"Probably not. I'm sure she would have wanted me to stay for her and our son so that he might not grow up without a father."

"Yes. And also if she had been alive would you yourself have even accepted it?"

"No... what are you getting at."

"Your family had become a problem. So I solved it."

Upon hearing those words, Martin collapsed to his knees in shock, because he knew what they entailed.

"Wait, you encouraged me to talk to her. You were the reason I even knew her!" Martin said, beginning to raise his voice.

"Indeed. I needed you to know what it felt like."

"Know what what felt like?!" Martin shouted.

"Total, absolute loss. I needed you to have everything, in order for you to lose everything. I had to know if you could still press on even after becoming completely broken. And I must say you have exceeded my expectations."

"How did you even do it, how could you have had something to do with it?"

"Years of planning. But the details are not important at this time."

"They didn't have to die." Martin said through clenched teeth.

"Would you have preferred they lived?" Ramiel asked.

"Of course I would have!"

"Why? You should be grateful they were spared. There is no person more innocent than a child, and there is no woman more valuable than one who is virtuous, submissive to her husband and a virgin at marriage. There were no people more deserving of life than your family. That is why they had to die. They were worthy to be spared from the pain, suffering and tribulations of the days soon to come. You should be happy for them. For all of them."

"Why allow me to live then, am I just some sort of experiment or something?"

"Of course. This entire existence is an experiment. And fortunately for you, depending on how you look at it, you are either lucky enough or unlucky enough to be alive to witness the end."

"The end of what exactly?"

Ramiel raised his arms to the sky while looking upwards and said.

"Everything."

"Why now, what is so significant about this time?"

"The dawn of the seventh day is approaching." Said Ramiel. "It will soon be the day that marks 6000 years since the time of our first father. And on the seventh day we rest. For that is the purpose for which it was set aside. It has always been the same, always been the design. And soon time will be no more."

"I still don't understand a word you're saying. What does any of that mean?"

"It means the world is coming to its end, Martin, and it is for the best."

"Why must it though? How is any of this justice?"

"To be both just and merciful, you must give everyone exactly as they deserve. All those not deserving of what shall come to pass were spared, and shown mercy by way of death. Those deserving of torment, and those who shall torment are still here. And even when they pray for death, death will flee from them. For their prayers will be heard no longer."

"Who is responsible for this?"

"My Lord is. You were also a minor part of this. You helped set quite a bit of this into motion. The moment you became relevant was when you accepted my mission, made your promise and received that mask."

"Why is this mask so important?"

"Again, powers granted by evil cannot be used for good but powers granted by good can be used for evil. That mask was both blessed by good and cursed by evil. That is why you have now become as death itself. Blessed by evil for evil and given license by The Great One to do evil and torment the earth. The whole point of your existence now is to bring about torment, destruction and pain to all those you remain on the earth after the Great Cleansing."

"Why are you telling me all of this now?"

"Because you are as a locust; a demon of my swarm. A pest with but a single purpose. A beast bred only to destroy."

"Swarm? Are there others like me?" Martin asked.

"You are one of thousands spred throughout the world. Where do you think everyone has gone, who do you think made them disappear so quickly after the fall and who do you think helped to tear down this great whore of a city that is all of the western world? A few months ago you could not go anywhere without seeing someone else. Now there are few people left to be seen. We set all this in motion. It was I who convinced the Chinese to attack. It was I who made the deal. It was I who made all of this possible."

"Why?" Martin asked in astonishment.

"It was the only way to spare the innocent of what is to come." Said Ramiel.

"What do you mean, spare? How many? How many innocent people have you killed?!"

"Killed? We did not kill anyone. We are not permitted to kill, with our own hands anyway. However, you have not yet taken the vow that most of the rest of us have taken. You kill people all the time. We do not. We simply use whispers to influence others then allow the innocent to be spared by doing nothing. We do Nothing and they pretty much die on their own."

"If you could do something to save them, why wouldn't you?"

"If you could do something to save the ones you killed with your own hands from yourself, would you save them?" Ramiel paused but Martin did not answer. "No, you would not. That is the difference between you and I. You actively seek out death and destruction, I simply allow humans to do what humans do best; kill themselves. The weak are usually the first to go and the first to go are usually among the most innocent, appart from the lucky ones who were guilty but were also just to weak to survive even though they deserved to live and suffer through the darkness that is to come. Because of their weakness they too were spared by indiscriminate death, but soon even the weak will be forced to live. It is quite amusing is it not, how in times of imminent torment even nature favors the weak."

"How is it possible? How did so many innocent people die in such a short time?"

"My friend, you fail to realize just how little innocence was left in this world. there was actually so little left that the only ones who lasted longer than three days was your wife, your son and maybe like three others. The rest died because... well, they were useless savages who were unable to survive without daddy government."

Martin flinched then shuddered at the mention of his family. And when Ramiel finished speaking a moment later Martin looked over at him.

"And what about those who weren't innocent?" He asked.

"When the guilty die they are sparing themselves from the torment that they deserve. And by killing the guilty you are trading in all justice in exchange for mercy, making that same mercy unmerciful. In order for anything to be moral; balance is required. If you trade in part of one for more of another then all becomes corrupted and void. In order to have balance you must be both all just and all merciful. In order to be equally just and merciful you must give everyone exactly as they deserve. You see, Martin, death is not a punishment for the innocent, for they indeed have no fear of torment. And death is not as great a punishment for the guilty as life will be in the days to come. Those left alive after today will suffer greatly. The innocent who live will indeed also suffer, but the guilty will suffer all the more because of the innocence suffering. Soon Martin, soon you will no longer be able to kill the guilty. Soon they will be made to live and refused the ability to be spared from their life of suffering. And yes, even hell itself would be a mercy in comparison to what is coming."

"What is coming?"

"Worry not, my dear Martin, for now just keep doing what you do. It matters not. If you wish to save the mortal lives of the innocent, save them. It makes little difference in the end. Just one small note though: the longer they stay alive the worse their torment becomes. And the more innocent that are left alive the weaker you will be. Only when all the innocent have been spared will you become your best. And when the last of the guilty have been judged, only then may you be allowed to rest."

"When I died I saw many things, including the future. However, I can not remember what the future was. How about you, Ramiel? Have you seen the future? Do you remember what it looked like."

"I have seen only slightly more than you have, Martin. However, my Lord has told me of what will come to pass."

"Who is your Lord, Ramiel?"

"It is not yet the time for you to know that yet. Fret not though, you will know soon and you will serve him as I do."

"If you expect me to serve your Lord as you do, I must say that I will only serve he who is the strongest. He who is without even the slightest amount of fear. He who is subject to no one and he who does not require subjects for him to have strength."

"My lord is all of those things and more. He is stronger than you, stronger than me and soon the whole world will know his name. And they will worship him as they should. For he is the rightful king of all the world, of all beasts and men, both living and dead. He is the giver of both life and of death. The master of both night and of day. He is the stars before the first light of the morning and the rays that shine down to warm the earth."

"If that is true then tell him that I will serve. However, if I find out that he is not all that he claims to be then I will resend my service and he will die as all weak men and liars do. With my blade in his neck."

"Very good. I shall relay your message to my brother. I will come fetch you when the time draws near that everything is near completion."

With those words Ramiel blinked away and was gone.

# CHAPTER: 56

**I**T was almost nightfall as Martin pulled the truck up in front of an old supermarket about an hour north of Charlottesville. He sat for a moment wondering, trying to remember what their plan had even been or why they had even left the group in Appalachia when they could have just stayed there where they would have most likely all stayed alive. Was he running from something, or trying to find something? He thought to himself. He then shook his head to shake away the thoughts, put the truck in park and shut off the ignition. He scanned for any kind of life or movement before exiting the relative safety of the truck. Once he was satisfied there was no immediate threat he popped the door open and jumped to the ground with Jacob's old Steyr AUG in his left hand aimed at the front of the store. He quietly shut the door with his other hand and began to slowly move forward. As he entered through the broken glass of the front door he got the feeling that someone was watching him. He listened intently to the area around him for a moment, then continued into the store. He wasn't quite sure what to make of the feeling he was having, but he wasn't going to take any chances. He moved down the center aisle scanning the area around him as he went. Once at the back of the store he noticed a smell in the air that was different from the rest.

"There's definitely someone in here." He thought to himself.

Just then he heard a scuffle behind him and felt the rush of something approaching quickly. He waited patiently for it to get closer then he spun around and grabbed it. The forearm he now held in his right hand did not come as much of a surprise. It was a teenage girl with brown hair and a snarl Expression. He let his rifle hang on its sling and with his other hand he grabbed the collar of her coat. He then lifted her off the floor with one arm as he quickly took the knife out of her hand with his other.

"Were you going to try to stab me?" Martin asked as he looked at the knife he had taken from her.

"You're one of them." She said as she attempted to kick him.

"One of whom?" He asked as he dodged the kick.

"One of those damn Chinese assassin bastards."

"Do I sound like I've got an Asian accent to you?"

"What's that supposed to mean?"

"I'm an American."

She stopped kicking and looked at his masked face.

"Prove it." She said defiantly.

Martin paused for a second then he simply put her down and presented her with the knife that he had taken. She looked down at the knife in his hand, then looked up at him, then back to the knife.

"You're just gonna give me my knife and let me go?" She asked as she slowly moved to take the knife out of his palm.

"Yes."

"Why?"

"Because you're not my problem or my responsibility. As long as you don't try to attack me again."

With that he turned around and walked away from her, headed in the direction of the manager's office in the back of the store. She stood confused for a second then started after him.

"Hey!" She said as she caught up with him. "Hey. What's your name?"

He ignored her as he opened the office door then walked over to the desk inside, climbing up to sit cross legged on top of it.

"What's your name, mister?" She persisted.

"Don't you have somewhere to be?" Martin asked.

"Yes, I've been trying to get back to DC. That's where all my friends are. Unfortunately I don't know where I even am right now."

"DC? What friends?" Martin asked, looking up at her.

"The DC militia."

"Thomas, Lynn? Were those some of their names?"

"Yes. Wait, you know them?"

"They're in the Appalachian mountains now. You wouldn't happen to have known a man named Brian Parker, would you?"

Her eyes went wide instantly beginning to tear up at the mention of the name and she struggled to speak.

"Yes, I knew him." She said, taking a deep breath. "He died to save me."

"He gave his life to save you, why?"

"He said he made a promise, and that it was just the way it had to be."

"He died so that you could live. That is a steep cost to live up to. You had better make sure that he didn't die in vain. His father would not appreciate the loss of his son in exchange for someone who ended up not appreciating it."

"Who are you? How do you know so much?"

"That's a conversation for another time. You should get some sleep. In the morning I will help you get back to the others."

"Why would you want to help me after I tried to stab you?"

"Because I told Lynn that I would, and I am a man of my word."

"Okay. Well in that case, thanks. Will we be taking the truck you arrived in?"

"It doesn't have a lot of fuel left but we will take it as far as it allows."

"Better than walking the whole way. I'm tired of walking."

Martin looked sidelong at her as she walked over and laid down on the floor in front of the desk.

"What is it exactly that you do?" She asked.

"I do what I want." He answered.

"Why are you dressed like that? Are you actually some kind of assassin or something?"

"Something. Now go to sleep."

After about a half hour of silence and thinking Martin climbed down off the desk and walked out of the room. He made his way outside to the truck and carefully climbed up into the cargo area. Making his way up to the front he knelt down before a large chest. Flipping the latches he opened the lid and began to dig through its contents. A few moments later he withdrew a dark red blanket. After closing the chest and exiting the truck he went back inside. He entered the office once again and tossed the blanket onto a chair off to the side. He then knelt down and felt the floor. It was quite cold. He walked over and felt the desk. It was not quite so cold.

"I just want to be better, and to do what's right." He said quietly to himself.

He then walked over and carefully scooped the girl up into his arms and gently placed her onto the desk. Once she was situated, he grabbed the blanket off the chair, and covered her up. Then he moved to the other side of the room and sat cross legged on the floor.

"Is it not strange how even evil can feel compassion for those who are truly good and innocent?" He asked himself. "Maybe I'm not as evil as I am supposed to be."

# CHAPTER: 57

**M**ARTIN awoke from his meditative state to see the girl sitting on the desk watching him. She had the blanket wrapped tightly around her and she seemed to be thinking about something as she stared at him. She hadn't noticed his eyes had opened on account of the polarized lenses in his mask, and he was curious what she was doing so he refrained from moving for the time being. After about three minutes of not moving and being stared at he finally decided it was time to get going. He slowly raised his head upwards as if he had just opened his eyes. Then he removed his hands from where they were resting on his knees and began to stretch his arms a little. The girl acted as if she hadn't been looking at him by quickly turning her eyes towards the door behind him.

"Are you ready to go?" Martin asked in a level tone.

"Yup. I've just been waiting for you to wake up." She answered. "By the way, how do you sleep like that?"

"I don't sleep at all. I was meditating."

"What? What do you mean you don't sleep?"

"It's a long story and I don't feel like telling you. Let's just get you back to the others so I can be on my way."

"Do you ever take off the mask?"

"Do you ever stop asking questions?"

"I'm young, and a girl. I like to know things."

"I'm sure you do. I also don't care."

"You cared enough to give me this blanket and the desk to sleep on."

"Sometimes you have to do things you disagree with. Simply for moral reasons."

"Did you not want to give me the blanket?" She asked.

"I only do what I want." Said Martin. "That doesn't mean I have to like doing the things I want to do."

"You're a weird guy. You know that, right?"

"That's an understatement. It is accurate, but weird doesn't even begin to explain what I really am."

"And what is that?"

"None of your business. Are you ready to go yet?"

"Yeah, I'm ready when you are."

Martin stood straight up from his cross legged position and walked to the doorway.

"I'm ready." He said looking back at her.

She quickly threw the blanket off herself and got to the floor. She then carefully bundled up the blanket and followed Martin out of the room. They walked through the store heading for the front exit, where Martin walked out first and looked around. Seeing the area was clear he walked to the driver side door and after opening it he climbed up into the seat; putting his rifle on the floor next to it. The girl moved around to the passenger side and opened the door while holding the blanket tightly in one arm.

"What kind of a man are you that you won't even open the door for a lady?" The girl said as she climbed into the seat and closed the door.

"Definitely not that kind of guy. The fact that you're even still alive at all is actually surprising. Being as almost everyone I come in contact with usually dies."

"People really die that often around you?" She asked.

"I'm normally the one that kills them."

"Why?"

"Justice and mercy. See, if I had shown you mercy and just killed you when we met, you would be better off. Rather than having to deal with the remnants of this world. Either way however, I still wouldn't have had to open the door for you."

"Well I'm glad you didn't kill me. My life isn't so bad that I'd wish for death."

"Not yet, but it soon will be. Just let me know if you ever want a quick ticket out."

"Thanks. I'll keep that in mind." She said as she shot him a disapproving look.

"You're welcome. Anytime." He said smugly as he put the truck into reverse and backed out onto the road.

"I'm Scarlet by the way." She said, looking at him from the passenger seat.

"I don't really care."

"So, how did you know Brian?" Scarlet asked after they had been driving for a while in silence.

"His father helped save my life. I was supposed to find him, whether he be dead or alive, and bring the news back to his father."

"Did you find him?"

Martin pulled the dog tags out of his belt pouch and held them up.

"Yes, I found him. I'm going to bring these back to his father before I leave for my final mission."

"What's your final mission?"

"Killing everyone who is responsible for the state of this world."

"Don't you think that's a little extreme? I mean there's probably thousands of people responsible."

"Most likely." ⋅

"How are you going to kill thousands of people?" Scarlet asked.

"You must not understand how fragile humans are. Thousands is not a very large number."

"If they're so fragile, why not just let them die on their own?"

"Because that takes too long. I do it for sport, and I enjoy it."

"Ah, that is actually kinda messed up."

"Depends on your opinion and how you look at it."

"Whatever you say, buddy."

"I'm not your buddy, kid."

"And I'm not your kid, buddy."

Martin slowly turned his head to look at her.

"Stop talking." He said with a touch of annoyance in his voice.

"Or what?"

Martin drew the Glock out of his leg holster and held it on his lap while looking towards her.

"Okay, I'll shut up. No need to act rashly now." She said, raising her hands in surrender.

Martin re-holstered his gun and returned his eyes to the road ahead.

"We only have about an hour's worth of fuel left. You might want to rest while you can. It's gonna be a long walk to the Appalachian mountains once we run out."

Scarlet nodded then snuggled up in the passenger seat with the blanket. A few minutes later she was asleep.

# CHAPTER: 58

**S**CARLET walked next to Martin down the road through the countryside. It was about noon now and the sun was doing its best to peek through the light grey clouds overhead. The truck had indeed run out of fuel and they had left it a few miles back. However, they had been fortunate enough to have run out right next to a dollar store. So they were able to snag a grocery cart to help them haul their valuable supplies. As Martin pushed the cart down the street he looked around, listening intently for any abnormal sounds that might be hostiles.

"You need to loosen up." Scarlet said as they walked.

"What do you mean?" Martin asked.

"You're always looking around everywhere. Like you're either trying to find something, or trying to see everything at once."

"Both of those are more or less correct."

"Well could you just calm down a little? You're making me nervous."

"You should always be aware of everything around you. Surprises are only surprises because you weren't prepared for it when it happened."

"Geez, can't you just be a normal person for 10 minutes?"

"You are annoyed... by me?" Martin asked in surprise.

"Yeah, a little bit."

"Well deal with it. The way that I am is what is going to keep you alive. Or you can just find your own way back to your friends. Either way makes no difference to me."

Scarlet stopped walking but Martin continued on pushing the cart.

"Fine, how about I just follow you from back here instead?" She said as Martin stopped and turned to look at her.

"I don't care." He said before turning back around and continuing down the road.

"Do you care about anything?"

"Nope. Not really." He hollered back to her, then to himself he added. "Not anymore."

She ran back up beside him and matched his pace as he pushed the cart.

"I'm sorry. I'm really just messing with you as a way of coping with all the things that I have lost. It helps me to not think about stuff." Said Scarlet.

"You don't have to apologize. I understand."

"You do?"

"I too have lost something. Would you like to know how I deal with the memories and living nightmares battling out in my head?"

"You try not to think about them?"

"No, just the opposite. I purposefully remember those memories as vividly as I can, then I make them hurt as much as possible. That way it will hurt less and less until one day it becomes just another memory."

"Does it work?"

"Indeed, it does. By the way though. We are being followed."

"What? How do you know?" She asked as she hurriedly looked around.

"I am aware of my surroundings." He said in a whisper as he leaned closer to her.

"How many are there?"

"I'm not sure right now, but I am sure that we will know soon enough. Do you still have that knife you tried to stab me with yesterday?"

"Yeah, it's right here." She said lifting her coat to reveal the knife in her belt.

"Give it to me."

"But what if I need it?"

"Well, if you need it then I'll probably give it back."

"What happened to your pistol?"

"I only have thirteen rounds left, and I'd rather not waste them."

"What about your rifles?"

"Again, low ammo."

"Ah, okay."

They walked a few more steps and stopped when a dark figure walked out of the tall grass and stepped onto the road in front of them. A second later two more did the same. Martin looked over his shoulder to find there were another two stalking up behind them.

"What can I do for you, gentlemen?" Martin called out to the people blocking their way.

"You can start by giving us everything you've got." Said the man in front.

"Yeah. Good luck with that." Martin retorted as he quickly observed the weapons being carried by the bandits while the one in the center started walking towards them.

The rest immediately followed him and began to encircle Martin and Scarlet. The center bandit then slowly drew a sword as he closed in. To Martin's surprise it was in fact none other than his own sword. Martin raised the knife that Scarlet had given him and readied himself for the fight that was about to ensue. The one carrying his sword struck out at him. He parried, deflecting the attack then lunged forward to strike back. The knife's blade found the man's side and Martin wrenched it violently across the flesh, the pain causing the man to drop Martins old sword. He followed through the cut and immediately blocked the blade of a machete that was brought down by one of the other bandits. Martin quickly grabbed his hands and used the machete to block the swing of yet another sword. One of the others then grabbed Scarlet by the arm which caused her to scream. Martin pushed away from the bandits over him and threw the knife into the bicep of the one grabbing Scarlet. She immediately grabbed the handle and twisted the blade as she ripped it out sending the man sprawling in agony. She then slashed at the last bandit that was coming at her from the side.

Martin dived into a roll grabbing for his old sword which was laying on the ground next to the bandit that had been previously wielding it. As the bandit attempted to stand back up, Martin grabbed the sword and completed the roll. Then in one fluid motion he spun around and slashed upwards opening the bandits chest in a shower of blood. He then brought his blade around and prepared for the others who were coming up on either side of the now dead man. One of them swung at him and he deflected the blade of the first right into the leg of the other. Then slashed upwards cutting deep through the first bandit's carotid artery. As the second reached for the machete that was protruding from his leg Martin spun and slashed. The bandit looked stunned for a second, then he collapsed to the ground his head rolling to the side of the road as his body made contact with the pavement. Martin then turned to face the final foe.

"Don't come any closer." The bandit said as he held Scarlet with his arm around her face and the knife against her throat. "I'll do it.

don't even think abou..."

The blade of Martin's sword buried itself to the hilt so that only the handle protruded out from the bandit's face.

"You shouldn't have blinked." Said Martin.

The bandit collapsed to the ground leaving Scarlet standing and obviously shaking.

"How did you do that?" Scarlet asked as she looked down at the man with a sword in his face.

"Do what?" Martin asked dismissingly while looking around at the dead men.

"Throw your sword twenty feet before he could move his knife three inches?"

"I don't know what you're talking about."

Martin walked around the shopping cart and crouched down next to the bandit that had gotten the knife through the bicep.

"Did Dante send you?" Martin asked.

The bandit only stared at him trying his best to hold pressure on his wound.

Martin turned, walked over and ripped his sword out of the face of the one who was laying next to Scarlet. Using the blade he then cut the mans shirt off and tore it into a bandage. Moving back over he tied it around the bandits arm to help stop the minor bleeding.

"Why are you helping me?" The bandit asked.

"Because I want you to tell Dante that Martin says hi, and that he should give up chasing me. Can you do that for me?"

The bandit nodded slowly. Martin stood back up then walked over and began pushing his cart once again.

"You'll never outrun him. He's gonna find you one day!" The bandit yelled from the ground as they began to move down the road.

Martin turned around and looked at him.

"I'm not trying to outrun anyone. I simply want him to stop chasing me."

"He's going to find you and when he does he's going to kill you."

"Then tell him I will meet him on the field of battle where we will settle our differences like men."

# CHAPTER: 59

**L**YNN stood atop the mountain looking out over the side of the rock ledge. There was a breeze in the air and she could smell the scent of food coming from their little camp not too far away. She heard footsteps approaching and she looked back to find Thomas standing at the base of the rock.

"Lunch is ready. I'm here to take over for you." He said.

"Awesome, I'm starving." Lynn said as she slid down to the ground.

"Anything to report?" Thomas asked.

"All has been quiet. If you don't count the birds and the wind." Lynn replied.

"That's good. Go eat now before it gets cold."

Lynn smiled at him then turned and started walking back towards their camp. She hadn't gone far when she suddenly got an uneasy feeling. She stopped walking to listen for any abnormal sounds. As she listened her blood started to run cold for reasons she could not explain. She quickly turned around to look behind her but there was nothing to be seen besides the trees and the leaves on their branches. She let out a sigh then turned to continue walking to the camp. As soon as she had turned a dark figure stood directly in front of her less than a meter away. She gasped and took a step backwards. Then let out a short scream as she tripped and fell flat onto her back. The next thing she saw was the familiar face that was Martin's mask standing over her. He leaned over and offered her his hand to help her back up.

"You shouldn't sneak up on people like that." She said as she got to her feet and brushed herself off.

"Gotta entertain myself somehow, and I thoroughly enjoy watching people flip out as you just did. It amuses me." Said Martin.

"Well I don't like it at all. Are you coming back to camp?"

"Yes, I have... news. Where is Thomas?"

"He's taking his shift on lookout duty. You can tell me over lunch if you want, thats where I'm heading now. I can relay the news back to him once he returns."

"I can tell you now if you would like." Said Martin.

"Let's get food first. I'm far too hungry at the moment to be getting into news and such."

"As you wish. Please, lead the way."

Once back at the camp Lynn got a bowl of stew then led Martin to the bench out in front of her tent.

"So what's the news? and is it good or bad?" She asked as she sat down, offering Martin a seat across from her.

"You have too high of hopes if you are expecting any news to be better than bad."

"So, all bad news then. Well then hit me with it I guess."

"Very well." He paused for a moment and took a deep breath before he continued. "Brian is dead. So is Gabriel, James and Jacob."

"Oh my god." Lynn said in disbelief as she leaned forward in her seat and looked at the ground. "What the hell happened out there?"

"Brian, apparently died in the explosion down in the city that happened the morning we left. Gabriel got shot in the head by a sniper while we were driving. James got shot in the back while we were trying to get away from a Warband in Charlottesville. And Jacob got hit by a barrage from an A-10 warthog."

"My goodness. Are you... are you okay?"

"Yes. I will be fine."

"What about Scarlet and the kids? Did you find them?"

"Scarlet is over there with Tyler and the others." He said as he waved towards the other side of the camp. "She is the only one left."

"So there is at least a small sliver of good news then."

"I suppose it is good to look at things from the bright side."

"I think so too. That's really all we can do anymore. Is there anything else?"

"Yeah, you should probably think about moving everyone out soon. There is a large group that is capturing people to sell as slaves to the Chinese. They're making their way farther and farther out of Charlottesville every day. And It's only a matter of time before they make it here."

"We've actually gotten word of a resistance group to the West on the other side of the mountain. One of our scouts met some travelers a few days ago who said the resistance was preparing for something big. He also said that they were looking for people to come and join them."

"Probably not a bad idea to at least check it out."

"Will you come with us? I know it's a lot to ask, but will you help us again?"

"Yes, I will help you."

Lynn gave a weak pain filled smile then appeared to start thinking about something.

"You probably get this a lot, but just out of curiosity. Why are you doing this? You could go anywhere and do anything. Why come back here of all places?"

He was silent for some time before he spoke.

"I'm just trying to find a reason to live, in a world full of reasons to die."

They talked for another hour about all that had happened in the previous days. He told her how they had saved a group of people from the Warband, and how he found Scarlet. She in turn told him about how they had stumbled onto a former truck driver that still had a semi truck full of non-perishable foods. And how they had built wagons to both haul and store it.

As they talked Thomas came walking into the camp. Upon seeing Lynn he made his way over to her area.

"Did you hear someone scream when you were walking back from the lookout?" Thomas asked.

"Yeah, that was me. I just tripped, that's all."

"Actually, I scared her."

Startled by the voice coming from behind him, Thomas jumped and spun around to see Martin sitting behind him.

"Jeez man. Are you trying to give me a heart attack?"

Martin shrugged.

"Oh yeah, Martin is back. And he found Scarlet."

# CHAPTER: 60

**H**AVE you told the people about the plans to leave yet?" Martin asked as he walked up and stood next to Thomas who was standing at the edge of the camp staring off into the distance.
"Yes, I have. Some of them are against leaving so soon, and some of them are against leaving at all. But I'm sure they'll come around after a little bit of reasoning."

"Have you decided when you want to leave?" Asked Martin.

"No, how long do you think we have?" Thomas returned.

"Not long."

"Do you have any suggestions on how soon we should move out?"

"The sooner the better. But if you need a solid estimation. I would say that we have no longer than three days before we have to be out of here."

"That's what I was afraid of. I'll call a group meeting tomorrow. Hopefully I can get everyone on board before it's too late."

"I think that now would be a better time to have it. Time is, after all, running out."

"You're probably right. Damn, I really don't like public speaking. I get all nervous." Thomas said with a shudder.

"You're gonna have to get over that fear if you want to lead your people well. They will be more likely to respect and follow you if you know what to say and when to say it."

Thomas stood in silence for a moment thinking about the advice he had just received. Then he started walking towards the center of the camp, so Martin followed him.

"Remember, all you can do is tell them the truth." Said Martin. "They will make whatever decision they feel is right for them. Just remember that no matter what they each choose. That decision becomes their own responsibility. And if they choose to stay here, let them. Those people are no longer your problem. There is no need to care for those who refuse to trust or follow you."

"I can't help but care for all my people though." Said Thomas.

"Then you can only hope that they care the same for you."

"Okay. Attention everyone!" Thomas said as he climbed on top of a picnic table. "Please, everyone gather around. I have an announcement." He waited for everyone to gather around then he continued. "You all know by now of our messenger who informed us of the resistance group to the West. You also know that we have been considering trying to join them soon. That aside, it has been brought to our attention that there is a hostile group known as the Warband that is working their way in this direction. Martin here tells me that it is expected that they will be here in less than three days' time. Nobody here is obligated to leave this camp. It is however, strongly advised that you do."

"Why should we trust him?" Said a man standing out front of the crowd.

"You shouldn't." Martin said, addressing the question. "To be honest, I don't care if you do or don't. You can either follow Thomas, or you can stay here and be captured. It makes no difference to me."

"Everyone who is in favor of going be ready to head out by tomorrow night. That is all."

Thomas jumped back to the ground and the people began dispersing back to their duties.

"That was good. Short and sweet." Said Martin.

"Do you think they will all decide to come?"

"The idea was not met with much deference. If there are some that wish to stay, it is a very small number. But I think that even they will follow. If for no other reason, they will come simply to not be left alone out here."

"You make a good point. I think I am gonna go start packing now. Are you good?"

"Yes. I'm just going to walk around and look for anyone in need of assistance."

"Thank you, Martin. I'll see you later."

As Thomas walked away, Lynn came over and stood to Martin's right side. He turned to address her.

"What?" He asked.

She raised an eyebrow at him.

"When I told Thomas that he needed to address the people, he wanted to push the meeting off until tomorrow. How did you get him to do it so quickly?"

"I gave him a boost of confidence. He's a good leader, he just doesn't fully understand it yet."

"We appreciate you Martin. You're a good person."

"I am only a good person to those who are good people. However, I am not actually good. In reality I am far more evil than I am good."

"That can't be true. You are much too sweet." Said Lynn.

"To the ignorant even poison can appear sweet."

"Well then I guess it's better to have poison on our side, rather than on the side of those who wish to hurt us."

"I am only trying to help prolong your lives as long as possible."

"See, that is noble for sure. You shouldn't be so hard on yourself." Lynn gave him a smile then casually moved on through the camp.

"The longer you live, the more you suffer." Martin said to himself. "The more you suffer, the stronger I become."

# CHAPTER: 61

**T**HE next morning the whole camp was bustling with people preparing their things and packing up for the journey ahead. Only three people had argued against going, but just as Martin had predicted, being left alone was scarier to them than leaving their current camp. So by the time noon came around they had eventually given in and agreed to leave with everyone else.

As the day drew into late afternoon everyone was just about packed up and ready to move out when a small group of people were spotted making their way towards the camp. As the group drew nearer, Thomas took a few men including Martin to go meet them to see what they wanted. As they approached the group where Martin could see them a little clearer, to his surprise, he realized who it was.

"Aron?" Martin said in a questioning tone.

"Wait. Do you know these people, Martin?" Thomas asked.

"I do believe that these are the people that my team and I saved from the Warband." Said Martin.

"How did they know to come here?"

"Well, I told them to, of course."

"Ah, that would make sense." Thomas laughed. "If that be the case and you say they're alright, then I'm sure we'll have no issues in admitting them into our group"

As soon as Thomas had finished speaking they arrived before the small group of people.

"Greetings travelers." Said Thomas. "My good friend, Martin, here says that he gave you directions to come here. Is that correct?"

"Yes." Said the man standing out front of the rest. "My name is Aron. Martin and his team saved us all. We seek refuge and have come to humbly request that you let us stay with you."

"We are actually preparing to move out ourselves. We're going to try to join a resistance located West of here. You are welcome to come with us if you wish. However, I regret that you most likely will not be able rest tonight, because we are actually preparing to leave in a very short time."

"We are tired and hungry, but if that is what we must do to survive then so be it." Said Aron.

"Great, just follow us back to our camp and we'll get you sorted out." Said Thomas.

As they walked back towards the camp, Thomas leaned over towards Martin and asked.

"You sure we shouldn't just wait till morning? Do we really wanna travel down the mountainside in the dark with all these tired people?"

"I usually prefer to travel at night. There is less chance you'll be spotted from a distance by undesirable characters." Said Martin.

"But we have children traveling with us. And even more now." Thomas said gesturing towards Arons children.

"What's your point? They need to learn sooner or later, and sooner is better in my opinion."

"Fair enough. I trust you, so we're going to do it your way. We will leave as soon as the rest of the scouts return."

"Scouts?"

"Yeah, I sent four out this morning. One in each direction. I told them to scout out to about five miles or so, just to make sure all was well."

"When are you expecting them back?"

"Two got back about a half hour ago, so I'm expecting the others back any minute now."

Martin and Thomas walked around the camp checking on things when they suddenly heard footsteps approaching. They turned to look in that direction, and as soon as they had, a man burst through the shrubs. He was panting hard as if he had been running for a very long time. He tried to speak through his heavy breathing but struggled at first.

"Oh, hey guys..., so there's like... a literal army that... just made camp... about three miles South East." He said through deep breaths as he pointed back in the direction he had come. "And I'm almost positive... that they are coming this way."

"Vehicles?" Thomas asked.

"Mostly on foot. I think if we leave soon we should be able to stay ahead of them."

Thomas turned around to face the camp, and saw the last scout enter from the Western side. He waved for her to come over then waited as she made her way through the camp.

"Anything to report?" Thomas asked.

"All clear." She replied.

He gave her a nod to dismiss her, then he moved to address the people once again.

"Everyone listen up!" He said in a loud voice. "We are moving out in ten minutes. Be ready, or be left behind. The enemy is closing the gap between us. So we need to do our best to maintain our distance."

Ten minutes later on the dot their group was leaving the camp. Martin walked down the path towards the front of the group, keeping to himself as they picked their way down the mountainside.

"Hey Martin." He heard Scarlet's voice call to him.

He turned to look as she made her way down the path to where he was.

"Who told you my name was, Martin?" He asked as she stopped in front of him.

"Lynn, did. Was she not supposed to? I didn't just get her in trouble, did I?"

"No, it's fine. What do you need?" Martin asked.

"Nothing, I was just wondering how you were doing."

"I'm fine. How are you?"

"I'm good. Also I was also curious how I could become a hero like you?"

"What? Whatever your definition of a hero is, I assure you that I am not it."

"If you're not a hero then why did you save all these people? And all the other people you saved? Everyone talks about you. I've been hearing a lot of stories that sound pretty heroic."

"I doubt that most of them are true." Said Martin.

"Some people seem to think so." Said Scarlet.

"You've been talking to Tyler, haven't you?"

"Yeah so what? He's told me a lot about you."

"A lot of tall tales are all they are. You shouldn't just believe everything that you hear."

"It's not just Tyler that's saying it. Even Mr. Aron who arrived tonight was telling about how you saved him and his family, then refused to let him pay you anything. Actually, according to most of the people here, they all believe that you are some kind of demigod, or something."

"Absolutely not. That is definitely incorrect." Said Martin.

"I don't know. They seem pretty convinced."

"They are letting hope blind them."

"Well if you're not a hero or a demigod. Then what would you say you are?"

"I am nothin, nobody, just an empty suit."

"Nobody's don't save thousands of people. Heroes do that." Scarlet Said proudly.

"That doesn't make you a hero. There are no heroes."

"Someone who stands up for what they truly believe in, even in the face of everyone, and in spite of the entire world is a hero. Or at least is as close to a hero as someone can get."

"What if everything the so-called hero believes in is evil? And everything they have done was for evil reasons? What if they only appear good so that people follow them?"

Upon hearing him say this she was silent. Martin waited for her to answer, but when she didn't he simply nodded and dismissed himself to continue walking with the crowd. Scarlet stood there for a moment deep in thought, wondering what he could have possibly meant by that. She then lowered her eyes to the path before her and began walking once more.

# CHAPTER: 62

**M**ARTIN watched as the people moved down the trail past the rock on which he had spent the night in meditation. They had been traveling tirelessly for three days, and Martin thought it interesting how he felt so near to getting the people to safety and yet he himself still felt so far from it. He knew he didn't belong there with all these people and he planned to leave as soon as he thought it proper. But for now he would be of service. Since the day they had left their camp on the top of the mountains they sent scouts out periodically who consistently came back with word that the enemy was gaining ground on them. With each passing day they grew closer and closer to being overtaken. They just hoped they could make it to the resistance before it was too late.

As they rounded a bend in the road they caught sight of a plume of smoke billowing up over the trees not too far away.

"The resistance is just up ahead!" Shouted one of the scouts. "Hurry up! Just a little farther and we'll be safe!"

With excitement and relief the people all picked up their pace. As the gates of the base came into view more than one of them began to run faster towards it. Expressions of happiness and relief on their faces at the thought of finally being behind the safety of walls. Without warning a shot rang out, and a man towards the rear of the group fell to his knees then slid to a stop on his stomach, blood streaming from a large wound in his back.

"We're under attack!" Lynn shouted.

"Everyone, run for the gates!" Martin shouted. "I'll cover you!"

He then drew his sword and turned in the direction of the gunshots. As soon as it did, another shot rang out. The bullet impacted the tree next to him and his sword was left ringing from when the round had deflected off of it a moment before. He was slightly confused by this because he didn't even remember telling his arm to move the blade in front of his face.

"Well, that's new." He said to himself.

He then heard another shot, and the same thing happened as before. As soon as the bullet hit the ground behind him, off to his left, he realized his blade was once again ringing a high pitched metallic tone.

"Very interesting." He said as he examined his sword curiously.

He then heard movement coming from the trees a little ways up the hill. He sprung into action, racing up towards the sound with surprising speed.

As the last of the people were ushered through the first set of gates, and into the area between the first and second walls, Scarlet turned to see if she could see Martin. That's when she heard the screaming coming from the woods.

"Martin!" She called as she began to run towards the woods. A hand suddenly grabbed her arm and pulled her back.

"That wasn't Martin screaming. That was whoever shot at us." Said Thomas.

"I know. He needs to stop this." Said Scarlet.

"You can't change him." Thomas said. "Just be glad that he's on our side. Some people are better left alone to be who they've become."

Martin suddenly appeared out of the tree line, walking towards the gate with blood splattered across his entire body from head to toe.

The guards stepped aside as he walked through to stand inside.

"How many were out there?" Thomas asked as the guards shut the gate.

"Two." Martin said without emotion. "It's only a matter of time now before they attack this place. We need to start preparing now."

"How much time do you think we have?"

"Little to none."

Just then, two guards in military fatigues came walking over.

"You there." Martin said, pointing towards them. "Take me to whomever is in charge here. I have something to discuss with them."

The two guards looked at each other then returned their eyes to Martin.

"We don't take orders from you." Said the first guard.

"Yeah, and we haven't even decided if you're allowed to stay here yet, or if we're even gonna let you in at all for that matter." Said the second.

"Well, take me to whomever is in charge and I will explain why it is that we are here."

"Alright, wait here. I'll go ask the boss if he will see you."

The guard left through a small door next to the gate, and only a short time later, he returned.

"The boss will see you." He said as he leaned out the door. "But you'll have to turn in your weapons before you can enter."

"That's fine." Martin said as he began walking towards the door.

Thomas and Lynn started to follow as the guards led Martin through. The second guard held his arm out to stop them.

"Just him. You all can wait here." He said before turning to follow Martin and the first guard through the door; shutting it behind him.

Once they were on the inside of the walls they directed him to a table where he turned in all his weapons for safe keeping. He placed them one by one onto the table in a neat and organized fashion. First his sword, then a new set of throwing knives, a karambit knife, and lastly his Glock 19 with only one magazine.

"So, are you the one we've been hearing all the stories about?" The guard asked as they began walking again.

"That depends on what stories you are referring to." Martin returned.

"The one's about a masked man in black that goes around killing the enemy and freeing people from captivity."

"That sounds like something I would do."

"That's what we thought. That's actually why we didn't shoot when you all came running at the gate. Those people are lucky that you were with them and that we recognized you when you came into view."

As they walked down the main road towards a large courthouse-like building, Martin noticed that his presence had begun to draw the attention of the local people.

"Why are they all staring at me?" Martin asked.

"They've heard the stories too. They probably put two and two together. You do fit the description of the man from the stories after all."

"What if I stole the mask and clothes though?"

"If the stories we were told are even somewhat true, then that wouldn't be possible."

"Believe nothing to be true, but anything to be possible." Martin said.

"Are you saying you did steal it?"

"No, my question was hypothetical."

"Oh, well if that was the case we probably wouldn't do anything. There really aren't any laws anymore and even if there was, we probably wouldn't have jurisdiction anyway."

"Fair enough. For the record though, I didn't steal it."

"We figured. Here we are."

They arrived at the front steps of the courthouse and walked up to the doors. Two more guards stood on either side and held the doors open as they approached. They led Martin through the entry way then turned left into a hallway. They followed it down to a door with the name George Issac inscribed on it. The first guard knocked and was immediately answered by a gruff voice.

"Come in. It's unlocked."

# CHAPTER: 63

**P**LEASE remove your mask in the presence of our leader."
Said the guard that now stood inside the office next to
Martin. "Unfortunately my face is classified. So as far as
any of you are concerned, I do not have one." Said Martin.

"Classified by whom?" The man behind the desk asked.

"Classified by me." Martin replied.

"I don't have the time to argue with you about this. Just have a
seat then."

Martin glanced at the soldiers as they moved to either side of the
room. He then sat in one of the chairs that were in front of the desk.

"My name is Admiral George. I see you've already met Sargent
Dave and Private Leon." George said, gesturing to the two soldier's.

"Not formally. But nice to meet you. My name is Mr. Blank."

"I know." Said George. "Word of you and your team made it to
me a few weeks ago through the grapevine. I've also heard about
you from multiple other sources, and so have my men. You're
something of a celebrity to this resistance. It's a wonder that our
paths crossed so unexpectedly."

"Celebrity huh?" Said Martin. "All the more reason to cover my
face then, I suppose."

George paused for a moment as though he was thinking.

"The rest of your team, where are they?"

"They're dead. Everyone is dead now." Martin said as he glanced
down at the pocket on his belt which held all their dog tags.

"I see. Well, for what it's worth and whether you believe it or not,
you and your men did more for the people of this country than you
think. We are in your debt. And If there's anything I can do for you,
just name it."

"You owe me nothing, and any debt you think you owe me I
hereby deem it forgiven. May we get to the actual reasons that I

came here now?"

"Of course. Let's get down to business. What information do you have for me?"

"The first and most pressing matter is that there is a large, hostile group of warriors who call themselves the Warband heading in this direction. And they will be here within a day, maybe two at the most."

"My men are actually preparing as we speak. My turret guards saw what happened when you arrived. Word also spreads very fast around here. We will be ready in any event that we are attacked."

"These men I speak of are not like you're average marauders. Believe me, whatever defenses you have being set up, I advise that you double them."

"They can't really be that bad, can they?" George asked.

"They are."

"Alright then, we will take extra precautionary measures. What's the next bit of news?"

"Not really news, it is more of a proposition for you."

"And what is that?"

"You give me a name and supplies, and in return I will make the bearer of that name no more. After we have taken care of the Warband first, of course."

George leaned back in his chair to ponder this proposal for a minute. Then leaned forward over his desk and wrote down a message on a piece of paper.

"Take this to the supply staff." He said, handing the paper to Sargent Dave.

He then pulled a folder out of his drawer and opened it up on his desk. Martin could see that it was full of pictures and drawings of him and his team.

"So, I take it you were trying to find us?" Martin asked.

"I have a folder on everyone I can get information about." Said George. "But yes I was actually actively looking for you."

George grabbed one of the rubber stamps off his desk and stamped Martin's file page with a stamp that read "lvl4c".

"There, I've given you level 4 clearance. You now have access to everything except for the perks that only come with my level 5 clearance."

"You're going to trust me just like that?" Martin asked.

"These are desperate times, Mr. Blank. And the time to screen and evaluate every single person is a luxury that we no longer have."

"That is understandable. When do you think that you will have my first assignment ready for me?"

"I'll work that out with my command team. We know how good you are at what you do. So we may also want you to help with training in the future, if you're up for it. But when we come up with a job for you, you may do it at your own discretion. We only ask that it's done in a somewhat timely manner."

"What kind of weapons will I be given?"

"Name it. And if we don't have it. We'll get it."

"Excellent. I'll make a list then." Said Martin.

"Blank, I've gotta be completely honest with you though."

"I am a fan of honesty."

"The job you volunteered for just now was the exact job I was going to ask of you."

"I guessed that. That is why I figured I wouldn't waste either of our time."

"And to think I was reluctant to ask you." George said, sitting back with a laugh. "I was worried you might be done with that life by now."

"I'll be done when someone is good enough to provide me the pleasure of a glorious death."

"I like that. You got the right attitude for these times. Is there anything else you wish to discuss?"

"Yes, just one more thing. The group of people I came here with would like to join your resistance. Will you have them?"

"Of course. We've been looking to increase our numbers for a while now. I'll send someone to go fetch them and help get them all settled in."

"Thank you, sir. It's been a pleasure."

"Likewise."

Martin left George's office, walked down the hall and took the exit out of the building. He then moved down the steps, and stood on the sidewalk out front. As he scanned the faces of the people that lined the streets of the base, he noticed some were still observing him. He then saw a little boy staring at him from the other side of the street. Martin cocked his head to one side and waved at the boy who smiled, laughed and buried his face into the stuffed animal that he was holding. The boy kind of reminded Martin of his own son. His son who was only 6 months old when he died. Not wanting to think about that anymore Martin looked at the ground in front of where he stood. But again he wondered how he would have turned out, or the man his son might have become had he lived. When he looked up he saw hundreds of faces, all staring at one thing... him. Not looking for more attention than what already seemed to be on him, he started walking in the direction of the armory. That's where he was pretty sure his weapons were being stored.

The crowd seemed to be getting larger as Martin walked. He could see no hostility in their faces, more like they were in awe at the sight of him and he wasn't sure why. Martin stopped walking and turned around to look at the people crowding around him. Then he heard a voice start singing the words to his song. After the first verse almost all at once, the entire crowd began singing along as if it was planned. The people moved in and encircled him putting their hands on his shoulders, chest and back. Then the people around them put their hands on the shoulders of those around him so on and so forth, creating a web of human connection. Once they finished the song they released him from their gentle touch then stepped back and waited as though they were hoping he would say something. There was silence for a long time until he finally decided to speak.

"I appreciate your kindness, and while I am not sure how you know my team's song, it moved me that you all sang it so well."

"You give us hope!" Yelled a man from the crowd.

"You helped us to believe we could do something!" Said another voice.

"Why?" Martin asked. "I am nobody. I am nothing special. I do not deserve, nor do I wish for your praises."

"You're the reason I'm here! You're the reason most of us are here. When you, with just your small team, saved some of us from that concentration camp back in Pennsylvania. You were hopelessly outnumbered but still managed to make it out alive. I decided right then and there that I would follow you, even if I never met you again and you were just a symbol or idea I could get behind."

"Not all of us made it out." Said Martin. "I am no leader. My men, my team have all been KIA. I am but your humble friend and ally. I'm here to help. Not give orders, but to fight alongside you. Not from the front or the rear, but as equals. All I ask is that to those of you who know my name and face, let it not be recorded or written down in the history books."

"What should we call you then." Asked a man in the front row of people.

"Call me, Mr. Blank, The Empty Suit, for that is what I am."

As soon as he had spoken, the ground began to rumble. It was only slight at first, then the severity of the rumbling increased. Martin looked to the sky expecting to see an armada of planes or something. The skies however, were clear. That's when the ground began to shake violently.

"An earthquake? In Appalachia, of all places?" Martin said to himself.

The magnitude of the earthquake increased until it caused even the vehicles to slide around on the asphalt where they had been parked. The earthquake grew so severe that it began to knock the people themselves off their feet.

"What is this?" Martin thought. "What could be causing the world to shake so violently?"

Then there was a loud crack that sounded as though the world was split in two. And then as soon as it had come, the earthquake ceased, and the ground became stable once again.

"What the hell was that?" A man asked as he arose from the ground where he had fallen.

"I do not know." Martin replied.

"How did you remain standing?"

"I'm not exactly sure."

Martin then turned and saw Dave and Leon hurriedly coming in his direction.

"What the hell was that?!" Dave yelled as he approached.

"If I had to guess. I would say that it has begun." Said Martin.

"What has begun?" Asked Leon.

"Just like everything else in this existence, all things that have a beginning must also have an end."

"What are you talking about?"

"The final stage my friend. I believe that we have entered the final stage."

"The final stage of what?" Leon asked.

Martin paused for only a moment, then he said just one word.

"Everything."

# CHAPTER: 64

**M**ARTIN looked around at the broken buildings as he walked through the base. Almost everyone was hard at work cleaning up the debris and repairing the damage that was caused by the earthquake the day before.

"Hey Mr. Blank." Called a voice from behind him.

He looked over his shoulder to see George approaching. So he stopped walking, then turned to greet him.

"Good morning." Said Martin.

"Yeah yeah, morning. It's actually not very good though." Said George.

"Is that so? Might I ask why?"

"Have you not seen this place? That damn earthquake messed up a lot of stuff around here. It's gonna take weeks to recover from this."

"Is that what you came over to talk to me about, or is there something else?"

"No, it's something else. I wanted to talk to you about the people who chased you all here."

"Ah yes, the ones that will be here soon."

"That's what I'm worried about. That earthquake set us back. I wanted to ask you again how much time you think we have before they arrive?"

"Not long." Said Martin. "I would be surprised if they weren't here by tonight or tomorrow morning."

"Damn it. That's so soon. I really wish you guys wouldn't have led them here."

"They would have come here regardless. It's what they do. They need people and resources, so they take them from anywhere and everywhere that they can find them."

"Don't take that the wrong way. I don't blame you, I just wish that we had more time."

"Don't we all. Unfortunately, time is something you can never get more of by simply wishing for it." Said Martin.

"I know. And yes, that is quite unfortunate." Said George.

"Was there anything else you'd like to discuss?"

"Yes, do you have any experience in tactics and strategy?"

"A little. Why do you ask?"

"I'd like a second opinion on our current battle plan. if you'd be interested in helping me out that is."

"I'd be delighted."

"Great. Right this way."

Martin followed George into the courthouse which surprisingly enough was still mostly intact. They then moved into a large room where three men were standing around a table. There were chairs on either side of it so Martin took a seat and waited for George to begin explaining his plans.

"Mr. Blank, these are my generals, Mathew Barns, Stephen Night and Joseph Redney." George said, pointing to each of them as they were introduced.

"Pleasure to meet you all." Martin said with a nod to the generals.

"The pleasure is ours. We have heard much about you." Said Joseph.

"All bad things I hope." Said Martin.

Not knowing how to respond to that they all looked at each other and began to chuckle nervously.

"Just a joke. Don't worry about it." Said Martin. "Let's get down to the meat and potatoes. Explain this plan of yours to me."

"So, if you'll look over here at this map." George began. "This is where we are going to set up our defenses. A row will wait just inside the wall, with another row lining the top."

"So, similar to a battle formation that would have been used in a castle from the medieval times?" Martin asked.

"More or less. If you think about it though, we kind of are back in the medieval times."

"What kind of weapons do you actually have?" Martin asked.

"We currently have about five hundred guns of all different kinds, swords, bows and arrows, and some explosives. Speaking of which, have you figured out what kind of weapons you want?"

"I haven't had the chance to think about it yet."

"No problem. Just let me know."

"So, why don't we just attack them first and hit them hard when they don't expect it?" Martin said without so much as a hint that he wasn't completely serious.

Some of their facial expressions turned to complete shock for a moment at the proposition.

"You can't be serious." Said Mathew, who appeared to be the oldest of the three generals.

"What I have found throughout my days of hunting humans is that the element of surprise is always more useful when it is on your side." Said Martin.

"That may be true, but we can't just go marching out there into a hostile environment and expect that we'll make it back in one piece."

"Why not? I do it all the time."

"Well no offense but most of us are still normal people." Said Mathew.

"What makes you think I'm not normal?" Asked Martin.

"Normal people don't do the crazy things that you do."

"Fair enough. But I think we should give it a shot. We can charge their camp and with any luck, catch them unaware."

"You aren't even a real soldier. What makes you think you are even fit to fight with us?" Stephen asked.

"You're probably right. I never signed up to be a soldier in the military. However, I have both seen more combat than you have, and killed more of the enemies than you could imagine. So next time you speak you should probably think it through first."

"Enough." George said sternly. "Now, I don't know what the right decision is right now. All I know is that your plan sounds extremely risky, Mr. Blank."

"It's a high risk, high reward situation. As are most operations."

"I just think that the risk is not worth the potential reward. How many lives will it cost, how many will it save and how many is it worth?"

"The answer to that varies based on who you ask." Said Martin.

"I'm asking you."

"Me? That's probably not the best idea."

"Why's that?"

"Because I do not value life in general, let alone human life. I am willing to help you, but it really doesn't make much of a difference to me whether or not everyone on earth dies. I'm just here to enjoy the ride."

"How can I trust you with the safety of my people when you have an attitude like that?" Asked George.

"I would advise that you don't. However, I am pretty much your only hope of survival. So you just have to ask yourself. Do you want to win and live a little longer, or do you want to lose and die today?"

George thought about the question for a moment, then turned and walked over to his generals. They had a private word for a few minutes while Martin waited patiently for their answer.

"We've come to a decision." George said, walking back over to Martin. "What do you require to get the job done?"

"Give me a third of your men and I will see to it that your enemies never reach your gates."

"Very well. I will send Joseph and his squadron to follow you. Don't make me regret it."

"Every decision you make gets you one step closer to where you're going." Martin said as he got up and started for the door.

"Oh and Mr. Blank." George called to him. "Try to protect them and get them all back in one piece."

"I will do my best, but I never make promises that I cannot keep." Martin then turned to Joseph, and said. "Prepare your men, we leave in one hour."

# CHAPTER: 65

**M**ARTIN walked at the front of the line of soldiers that Admiral George had given him charge over earlier that day. Their plan was to go and try to attack while the rest of the army would stay to defend the people in the event that Martin was defeated.

As they moved quietly in the direction of their foe's camp, Martin began to sense that something was about to go wrong. They arrived at the edge of a large field and Martin began to cross through the knee high grass. Once he had gone about ten paces he spotted a dark figure step out on the far side of the field. He stopped for a second then continued moving forward with caution. The figure began moving towards him as well. After a few more paces, Martin raised his hand and waved for the soldiers to advance. The figure copied his motion and the two small armies moved into the field. Martin understood what was happening almost immediately. But there was no need to project that to those outside his own mind.

"Dante, is that you?" Martin called out to the figure.

"Indeed it is." Said Dante. "Are you the masked man who's name I have forgotten?"

"That sounds about right. Where are you headed?"

"I could ask you the same question."

"Me? I'm just out for a stroll."

"With an army?" Dante chuckled.

"These are dangerous times. Can't be too careful."

"Yeah. For sure. So how are we going to do this?"

"You could turn around and leave. We could avoid conflict." Martin suggested.

"Not gonna happen. You pissed me off, so first I'm going to kill all of you, then I'm gonna go and take all of your women and children."

"Well, good luck with that. Where are all your Chinese friends at?"

"Hunting people is my sport. And I take it seriously, so I told the Chinese to stay behind."

"How nice of you."

"Mr. Blank, why are you wasting your time trying to talk down an evil brute?" Joseph asked.

"Even If we were battling against angels sent down from heaven itself we would still find a way to make them appear as devils in our own minds. We do this to justify our violence as though we are the righteous ones, when in fact there are no good guys in an unjustifiable war. We choose to lie in order to make both ourselves and our men hate the enemy and make them appear as if they are not just normal people like the rest of us. Their views, opinions and intentions may be different, but they as a people are no different from you or I."

Dante raised his sword to the orange sky and let out a battle cry that cut through the afternoon air.

"Warband, assemble! Charge!"

Both sides then yelled out and began sprinting towards each other and also to their likely deaths. Martin ran out front of the rest of the army. Heading directly for Dante who appeared to have the same idea. As they ran at each other, Dante took out a handgun and fired. The shot was expertly made and would have been a direct headshot, had Martin's blade not been in the way. Dante fired again as he ran, but with each shot he took, Martin effortlessly blocked it as if he wasn't even trying. Deflecting the bullets downward so as to not allow them to hit the soldiers running behind him.

As Martin charged forward preparing to strike, he changed course abruptly to jump and kick off of a rock. This sent him flying through the air just a little higher than he had expected. Dante smiled then he slowed his charge to wait for Martin to bring his blade down on him. Dante raised his own sword to block the attack, and to his surprise, the unexpected force of the impact drove him to one knee. Then all at once both sides collided and the thundering clatter of battle ensued. Dante pushed back hard against Martin's blade, his muscular arms easily overpowering Martin's slightly smaller stature, causing him to slide backwards.

"This sort of fighting is definitely not my strong suit." Martin said as he slid to a stop. "This was supposed to happen differently."

"Let's not be picky. Just take what you can get and adapt." Dante said as he advanced.

"I guess that some advice is better than no advice at all."

Martin blocked over his head as Dante brought his sword down on him. Dante pulled back and quickly cut sideways towards Martin's side. Martin quickly flipped his sword around into an underhanded grasp just in time to block Dante's blade from taking a chunk out of his side. Martin then flipped his sword around and stabbed foreword. Dante jumped back, evading the potentially lethal blow. He then rushed Martin and slashed sidelong at his head. Martin ducked then in return slashed down at Dante's head. Dante reared back just fast enough to avoid the downward blow to his face. However, not fast enough to avoid getting a small cut on his chest.

Dante grunted in frustration at the sight of his own blood. He then looked back up at Martin who was preparing to attack once again. He slashed at Dante's leg, but Dante parried and returned, cutting upwards towards Martin's arm. He was rewarded by a small spray of blood that jetted from Martin's forearm. Martin spun away from the source of the pain and blocked the attack from a man who had come up behind him. He quickly dispatched him, driving his sword through the man's throat. He then turned to face Dante once again, and reflexively blocked a downward slash from Dante's blade. Martin pushed up then immediately stabbed forward into Dante's leg. The blade tore deep into the muscle causing Dante to shout out in pain. Then to Martin's surprise Dante grabbed the hand that he was holding his sword in. He then moved his grasp to Martin's wrist and squeezed his grip from the handle.

Martin struggled to free himself, but with powerful speed Dante grabbed him by the throat and slowly lifted him off the ground. As his feet lost purchase, Martin looked first into Dante's green eye then into his blue one. He thought it quite strange how the beauty of the blue and radiant color of it brought back so many fond memories. Memories of Ellis. Memories far to beautiful for the now hideous world that he helped to make. And then as quickly as the hand of a clock suddenly stopping its ticking, he decided that it was finally time to go. He stopped struggling, then closed his own eyes to let his mind flow deep into the depths of his consciousness. He drifted through the darkness and the light for what seemed like an eternity, through the parallel planes of existence and into that which is the single moment, and that which is all of time. The one and only true moment where everything is now. Where there are no emotions, feelings, beginnings or ends. Where there is no life or death. Where there is no shape or unit of measurement. The place where everything simply, is.

Martin then suddenly felt a slight pressure travel through his chest and touch his heart. This confused him because you're not supposed to be able to feel anything while in the fourth dimension.

He then felt his feet hit solid ground and he opened his physical eyes once again. Looking up he saw Dante smiling wide with satisfaction. Martin slowly looked down to find the hilt of a sword sticking out of his chest. He then fell down to one knee while putting a finger to the hilt of the sword to check if it was really there.

"We have won!" Dante shouted as he turned and raised his arms in triumph. "Your hero is dead!"

Throughout their fight, the soldiers of both sides had slowly stopped fighting each other to watch as their leaders fought. All of the soldiers looked on now, not quite sure what they were supposed to do. Then as Dante looked at the faces of both his enemies and his own men, their expressions all suddenly turned to shock and horror.

"Why do people keep mistaking me for a hero?" Said a dark, hollow voice from behind him.

Dante slowly turned around, and what he saw was the last thing that he expected. Not only was Martin not dead, but he was now floating about three feet off the ground, holding Dante's sword in his right hand. There also didn't appear to be any blood whatsoever on Martin or the blade that had pierced him.

"How?" Dante asked, his eyes wide in surprise.

"You cannot kill that which is death. For I am. And my power comes forth from death. Evenso, as I have seen, so also shall you see. For I have been sent forth to make you believe."

As Martin spoke a darkness began to overshadow the earth. Everyone around began to look up, and they saw as it were, the sun turned to black. It wasn't alike, or even similar to that of an eclipse, but more so that the sun simply changed color so that it was now emitting a strange shade of completely black light. There was no reason for this that anyone, including Martin, could explain. However, for the sake of instilling fear, Martin played it off as though he was the cause for it.

"Dante, I do not wish to kill you." Martin said. "I respect your drive and determination. You may have won this battle but you cannot win this war. Killing me only makes me stronger. leave now and take your men with you. Or I will send you all into the place where I gain my power."

"What the hell is this?! Who the Fuck are you?!" Dante shouted.

"Well." Martin said softly. "That escalated quickly. I am but a man, Dante. However, I am also more. Take what is yours and go. Or I will blot thee out of this life."

Martin then descended about a foot and presented Dante's sword back to him. Dante reluctantly accepted it then sheathed it whilst glaring at Martin.

"I will also take back that which is mine." Martin said as he waved his hand towards the sword in Dante's leg.

Still glaring at Martin, Dante reached down and quickly pulled the sword out and handed it up towards him. A man then came running up and bandaged Dante's leg.

"I don't know what sorcery this is, but I'm going to figure it out. And when I do, I will be back here to finish what I came here to do." Said Dante.

"That is reasonable. I hope that you do figure it out. I'm counting on it actually." Martin said in a now much friendlier tone.

With one last cold stare Dante turned and walked away, waving for his men to follow. Martin gently floated to the ground as his most formidable adversary disappeared into the forest.

"I really hoped that was the way I died for good." Martin mumbled to himself. "I just want to be free. What did I ever do to deserve the curse of everlasting life?"

Shortly after the battle the sun had gone back to normal. It was now bright and warm as Martin and what remained of the army walked up to the gate of their home base. The gate opened and after they moved through it into the courtyard, it shut behind them. Closing off the path they had walked, but unfortunately it couldn't shut out the memories of all those they had lost that day.

# PART: VII

"If you know my face you'll know my works. If you know my works you'll know my charity. If you know my charity then my works and my face will become my pride. And my pride will then in turn become the cause of my destruction."

# CHAPTER: 66

**M**R. Blank, we have a job for you." George said from behind the table in the large war room. "Alright, what might it entail?" Martin asked as he walked across the room and sat down in one of the chairs.

"We have acquired the location of a Chinese Commander."

"I do believe that there are many. What one might you be referring to?"

"Commander Wong. The one you attempted to kill back in DC. You fired ten shots from over a mile away, and all of them would have hit him were it not for the bulletproof glass."

"It was 1,400 yards actually, and it was one of my many failed missions." Said Martin.

"Failed or not, It was still a true testament to your skill. And the impact you made that day showed the Chinese that there are some who can, and will go the distance."

"What would you like me to do?"

"Finish what you started." Said George. "Complete the mission. Show them that we won't just bow down and give up."

"Where will I find him?"

George set a map down on the table then drew a circle around a town about twenty miles from where they were.

"You'll find him here." He said pointing to the circle he had drawn. "We received intel on good authority that he's made a base in an abandoned warehouse towards the center of this town. I'm sure you know what to do."

Martin stood up from the chair, paused for a moment then nodded and walked out the door.

As he stepped down onto the sidewalk he noticed Joseph walking over to meet him.

"Hey Blank." Joseph said as Martin stopped to greet him. "I just wanted to say thank you for your help saving our town."

"Don't mention it." Said Martin.

"I have to. You got stabbed through the chest for us. I'm not really sure what to think about that, but still, we owe you a debt of gratitude."

"You owe me nothing. I do what I want. And that was what I wanted to do at that time. So there is no need to thank me, my friend."

"Okay then, I won't say anything after this. I just wanted to let you know that we are all grateful." Joseph then paused for a moment before he continued. "One last thing though. Do you mind if I ask you something?"

"Not at all. Go ahead."

"Okay. Blank, I know this world is messed up and all. I do understand that. But honestly I saw what you did out there. So I'm just wondering how is it that you can do the things that you did? How exactly did you not die? And for goodness sake how does one just levitate?"

"The human mind cannot imagine that which is not real or possible. Everything you can imagine can be done, you need simply to figure it out, then understand how to apply it."

"So anyone can learn to do what you do?" Asked Joseph.

"Yes. A long time ago I was just a normal man. Then I learned far too much about our existence. Far more than anyone ever should. But I did, and it changed me completely. I also died and went to the supernatural on two separate occasions, yesterday being one of them. But that is a long conversation best saved for another time."

"Sounds pretty awesome. You're probably the most powerful person alive to be honest." Joseph laughed.

"I hope not. I would not wish that upon anyone." Said Martin.

"Do you not like being powerful?"

"I do not. I would have preferred that I wasn't."

"Do you really mean that? I mean come on, man. Everyone wants to be a superhero."

"I don't." Said Martin.

"Why?" Asked Joseph.

"Because anyone with as much power as me can never be a superhero."

"Why not?"

"Because life is not a comic book. Understand that when someone is faced with obtaining true power, they will inevitably be corrupted by it. Power In the hands of man is either evil now, or it will be soon. humans do not possess the ability to control true power."

"But you weren't corrupted. You used your power for good."

"I have killed more people than you have even met in your entire life. The bad things I've done far outweigh the good."

"I don't know, man. I think you're alright, but I guess that I probably just don't understand such things yet."

"Do you want me to give you some advice?" Asked Martin.

"Well, yeah." Joseph said sounding interested.

"Just make sure that you become who you want to be, Joseph. Remember, there is no man more peaceful than one who has the capabilities to do terrible things and chooses not to. There is no man more destructive than one who seeks out power for personal gain. And there is no man more dangerous than one who fears nothing but will still fight till his last breath for a cause."

"Wow, I guess this is like a 'choose wisely' type of situation?"

"It's whatever you want it to be. All I know is that I made a choice once. Someday I hope that I become more peaceful than I am destructive. Unfortunately, this is not that day because I still have much to do. And as much as I wish that it wasn't, violence is still very necessary."

# CHAPTER: 67

**M**ARTIN looked out over the rooftops to the warehouse that sat just a few blocks away. He was currently staked out towards the top of a large tree; waiting for nightfall. He had been sitting on a limb for about an hour now, just watching the comings and goings of the Chinese soldiers. Before now the twenty mile trip to the warehouse he was currently looking at would have taken him hours to walk. But with his new skill he was able to make it there in only a few minutes.

As the afternoon pressed into evening and evening into dark, Martin decided that it was time to start preparing his attack. He calmly allowed himself to slide off the branch and gently drift towards the ground. Once he was back down on the street he drew out his sword then disappeared, reappearing on top of the warehouse with his blade plunged through the neck of a very surprised Chinese soldier. He then disappeared again allowing the soldier to fall to the ground clutching at the hole left by Martin's blade. As the man lay dying another soldier walked around the corner. After he snapped out of his sudden state of shock he ran over to try to help his comrad. As soon as he knelt down to help stop the bleeding there was a sudden swoosh sound. The man wasn't sure what it was, but he was sure that he could no longer move. At first the man thought that it might have just been fear but when his head hit the floor before his body began to fall. He knew it was over.

Martin looked down at the bodies of the soldiers laying before him and wondered if this was fair to them in the slightest. He was certainly incredibly outnumbered, but what use are numbers when they don't even stand a chance of fighting back? He thought about it for a few more seconds then decided he didn't have time to play with them. He would kill them all quickly then go back to the base to relax. He disappeared again, moving through the warehouse like a phantom he began killing one soldier after another, without a care. As he was pulling his sword from his most recent victim an alarm began to sound.

"Well then." Martin said to himself. "Maybe now it will be a challenge."

"Sir, we are under attack!" Said the Chinese soldier as he burst into Commander Wong's office. "We found bodies throughout the building so we sounded the alarm."

"I can see that." Said the Commander as he looked at the flashing red light. "Who is attacking?"

"No idea, sir. The men are getting into defensive formation as we speak."

"Why aren't you down there helping them?"

"Sir, the Captain gave me orders to get you to safety."

"Very well." The Commander said before closing the book that he had been reading, then placed it off to the side of his desk and stood up. "Alright soldier, lead the way."

"Yes sir."

The Commander followed the soldier down the steps from his office. He could hear gunshots coming from the other side of the building, and then there came a scream that almost curdled his blood.

"What the hell is going on?" The Commander asked.

"I don't know sir, but I think we should run." Said the soldier.

"Agreed."

There was another scream and then all gunfire stopped. The soldier stopped running then turned to look towards where the gunshots had been coming from.

"Why'd they stop firing?" He asked in bewilderment.

"It's possible they might have got them." The Commander said, turning to look in the same direction. "What do you think?"

When there was no answer to his question, the Commander turned to find the soldier was gone. Confused, he looked around in an attempt to figure out where he went or if he had simply abandoned him. Just when he was about to write him off a severed human leg hit the ground in front of him. He stared at it for a moment, eyes wide in surprise. With adrenaline coursing through him, he slowly started to look up. His eyes then fell upon the masked face of a monster clinging to the ceiling above him. Crippled by fear he stood motionless in the face of death. Then all at once the remaining pieces of the soldier who had been leading him to safety, hit the ground. The sudden noise and jolt of excitement caused him to snap his eyes shut for just a second.

"Run." A voice suddenly whispered in his ear.

Knocked out of the trance by the word, he immediately started running. He sprinted through a doorway and down a hall when his foot suddenly caught on something causing him hit the ground hard on his shoulder. He frantically looked around, scanning the shadows for a sign of his pursuer. He started to get back up and quickly looked ahead into the darkness. The  Commander blinked and then there in front of him was the face of the monster in all black looking directly into his eyes.

"Who are you, what do you want?!" The Commander cried, as he fell backwards onto his hind end and scurried backwards.

Martin stood up straight, walked over to the commander then bent over him whilst raising his blood soaked sword to strike.

"I am the voice among the four." Said Martin. "I am the the last one left alive and one day I will be the last voice to ever speak. You saved my family from the life that will soon come to pass and for that I thank you. However, for that same reason I choose to also spare you by way of death. I wish for it to be so and so it will be as I wish."

"You will never win this war! You have already lost! All shall hail The Order!" The Commander yelled.

Martin then smiled and brought his sword down, ending the life of the man who started him on the dark, heartless path that he currently walked. And even though he had gotten his vengeance, it did not change anything. He was still the same as he was before. Emotionless, cold and empty.

The moon rose red as blood in the East as Martin stepped outside the warehouse carrying a duffle bag he had filled with all the weapons, ammo and canned food that would fit inside it. He watched the moon for a little while as the red rays of light cast shadows over the parking lot before him. He then turned away and with his eyes to the ground he began walking back in the direction of the resistance base.

"How much longer must I wander this earth without purpose." He said to himself. "Is this all there is left for me? Is this the only thing that I will do for the rest of my time? Or am I meant to just wait for my purpose to become obvious? No, if the end is drawing near then I will be what I wish, and I will do what I want. To hell with prophecy and destiny."

He paused for a moment to consider what was going through his mind then continued talking to himself.

"I am a fool. What point is there to life if not to serve the reason that I am here now? Maybe I just need a break from everything."

Martin walked through the forest with his blood soaked sword still in hand and slightly dragging on the ground. He had been walking throughout the night in silence. As he rounded a bend in the path he was walking he saw a rock ledge that looked to be a good place to stop for a moment to rest and meditate. He set his duffle bag down as he stepped up and sat cross legged upon the rock with his sword across his lap. He took out a rag he had tucked in a pocket on his belt and began cleaning the blood off his blade. It had been so long since he was able to just sit and think, and it felt good. He wasn't hunting anyone, he was probably being hunted by someone but he didn't care about that now. He looked out at the scenery and it reminded him of the days back when he would sit on the bench in his favorite spot back home. The place where he met his best friend Ramiel not so long ago.

He looked to his left wishing his old friend would be there next to him to tell him something, anything like he used to back in the beginning. Back when everything was so simple. He looked down at his sword remembering all the faces of the lives it had taken while in his hands. So many lives. Yet he felt nothing. No remorse, no regret, no hatred, simply nothing.

"I have no sympathy for the foolish." He said aloud to himself. "I am all out of empathy for the weak and I no longer possess the ability to give a damn about the worthless."

He felt nothing for the lives he had taken, for he knew that what they had now was what he himself wanted. Death.

For death was the goal, the end result and the only thing that had the power to answer the questions that nothing in life could answer. What is this existence, why must it be and who are we to experience it.

This life was strange to him and he had come to realize the more he knew about the reason for life, the more he wished to see the final result after complete death. He did not actually wish for death. But whenever it might come he would embrace it with open arms. He only hoped that it would be glorious and that once all the innocent were dead and all the guilty judged then maybe he would be worthy enough to see the truth and finally go forth into true and complete existence.

# CHAPTER: 68

IT was closing in on noon as Martin walked down the main street towards a small town. He wasn't quite sure where he was or where he was going. But he had a lot on his mind so he decided to take a detour before going back to the resistance base. He also wasn't sure what it was exactly that he was thinking about, but he knew that it was a lot. He also knew that once he figured it all out in his head he would be better off. He was sure about one thing though. The Commander was finally dead so his wife and son could now Rest In Peace knowing that he had avenged them. Even if it was not his place to do such a thing, vengeance wasn't the only reason he did it. So he figured that it would be alright.

As he walked into the town he of course caught the attention of almost everyone who was out on the street. Most of them only looked for a minute or two then went back to what they were doing. Some of them however, watched him intently until he was well past. He made his way down the street then he stopped short and looked up at the handmade sign that was above the door to his right. It was a blacksmith shop. He reached down and drew his sword part way out of the scabbard to inspect the blade. It was clearly getting dull now so he decided that he might try to have it sharpened.

As he stepped through the door he heard the sounds of a hammer hitting an anvil coming from the back of the shop. He moved to go around a table and was met by a little old lady.

"Hello dear. Can I help you?" The old lady asked pleasantly.

"Yes, I would like to have my sword sharpened. Can you help me with that?"

"Yes, of course. Wait here, I'll go get my husband."

The old lady walked through the back door, and a few minutes later she returned, followed by an elderly man in a blacksmith apron covered in soot.

"Good day, sir." The old man said. "What can I do for you?"

"I was hoping to get my sword sharpened." Said Martin.

"That shouldn't be a problem. May I see the blade?"

Martin drew his sword and placed it onto the counter between them. The old man then picked it up and began examining it.

"How much do you want for your time?" Martin asked.

"There really isn't a currency anymore, my young friend. Do you have anything to trade?"

"I have guns and ammo."

"Do you have .45acp?"

Martin set the bag on the floor then knelt down and opened it. Inside were a few AK47's, a TEC9 and two 1911's with boxes of ammo for all of them. He had gotten most of the guns off dead bodies back at the warehouse. One of the AK's and the boxes of ammo however, he had found in a cabinet inside one of the offices. He pulled out a fifty round box of ammo and handed it to the old man.

"That is far too much." The old man said, holding the box out for Martin to take it back. "Ten rounds is more than enough for this small job."

"Take it. I don't need it. I got them for free anyway."

"Oh, well in that case, thank you. I'll get started on this right away." Said the old man.

"No rush. Take your time."

The man bowed in thanks then turned and disappeared back into his workshop behind the store.

"Feel free to look around." The old lady said. "Just let me know if you're interested in anything."

Martin nodded to her then turned and began walking around the small store. It was mostly junk cluttering the shelves, but he had nothing better to do so he looked through it anyway. He walked around the backside of one of the shelves and looked up at what was hanging on the wall. Almost immediately his eyes fell upon a black compound bow. It was similar to the one that Parker had given him, the same one that he had lost back in Charlottesville. As he looked at the bow hanging on the wall, he contemplated whether or not he should get it. Before he had a chance to decide, the old man came back in from the workshop carrying Martin's freshly sharpened sword.

"It's done, good as new now." The old man said as he walked over to Martin and handed him the blade. "Did you find anything you like?"

"Yeah, what would you take for that compound bow up there?" Martin asked.

"Hmm, I don't know. Make me an offer."

"If you supply at least twenty arrows and a quiver to go with it, I'll give you an AK47 and four loaded thirty round magazines."

"Why would you trade so much for so little?"

"These guns here mean nothing to me. I have left both more valuable and more sentimental things on the side of the road. Do you want to trade or not?"

"You drive a hard bargain, but okay you've got a deal."

"Excellent. Where do you keep the arrows and quiver?"

"They're in the back. Wait here, I'll go fetch them."

He returned a few moments later, carrying a quiver full of arrows.

"Here, this is all I've got." The old man said as handed Martin the quiver.

"There are thirty two arrows here. We agreed on twenty." Martin said sternly.

"Take them. That was my only bow. I have no use for twelve arrows by themselves."

"Thank you. That's very kind."

Martin then reached into his duffle bag and withdrew the rifle and the ammo. He handed it to the old man then turned and grabbed the bow off the wall. As he was heading for the door he slung the quiver onto his back, he then pushed the door open to continue on his journey.

"Wait." The old man called from behind him.

Martin stopped and turned slightly to look back.

"Yes?" He asked.

"I'm Greg. What's your name?"

Martin stood there for a few moments before answering.

"Nobody, I'm just a wanderer who was never here."

Without another word Martin slipped out the door and made his way down the road towards the edge of town.

# CHAPTER: 69

**M**ARTIN made his way up the path he ended up on while walking aimlessly and he wasn't even sure where it was leading him just yet. It was almost noon the day after he had left the town where he had acquired his new bow. He had gotten an early start that morning and after a few hours of walking and looking at the ground, he finally decided to look up at the path ahead of him. As soon as his eyes were raised he saw a small group of people standing in a circle up ahead gathered a little ways off the path. He quickly decided that he would take precautionary measures to see who they were before they spotted him. Crouching down he silently faded into the tall grass and moved towards the group. He had been observing them for some time when he noticed someone else coming up the path from the direction that he himself had come shortly before. From what he could tell from his current location the body shape of the traveler suggested that it was most likely a young female. Turning away from the approaching girl Martin crept forward a little bit more to get a better look at who the group was. And to his displeasure they appeared to be some kind of marauders. Looking similar to Dante's men, only less well kept and rougher looking.

They were still on the other side of the path from Martin, just standing around as the hooded female traveler walked down the path between them simply oblivious to anything going on around her. Martin lowered his head and shook it in disappointment. Once she was passing Martin's hiding spot the group seemed to take notice of her and also take a fancy to her.

Martin watched from his spot in the tall grass as the group of marauders began following the girl. He counted six as they passed by him. There were four men and two women, and he had a feeling that they probably didn't want to just talk to her. So he decided to follow them himself. After a few seconds the girl finally noticed that she was being followed and so she started to jog. The marauders started after her so she broke into a run. The marauders gave chase, so Martin flew up the hillside to get a better angle on them. As they closed the distance between themselves and the girl he watched her stumble and fall on her face.

"Stupid girl." Martin said to himself as he knocked an arrow to his compound bow and took aim at the man bringing up the rear of the pack.

The group had slowed to a predatory walk after the girl fell, licking their lips as they got closer and closer to her. Martin loosed his arrow and it found its mark in the rearmost man's spine at the base of his neck. Martin reloaded the bow in a flash and picked off the next in the line, working his way towards the leader. After the fourth one was down there was only one woman and one man left. Martin thought about his remaining targets for a moment trying to decide which one would be dying first.

"It doesn't really matter which one I hit first. So just for fun let's see who's more fit to survive." Martin said to himself in a low voice.

He let his arrow fly and it hit the leader directly behind his right ear and pierced out through his left eye. The female marauder screamed in horror and confusion as a little bit of blood splattered across her face. She then looked around her and realized she was now all alone.

"What did you do!" She screamed as she turned to the girl they had been chasing, who was still laying on the ground where she had tripped.

"I, I didn't." Stuttered the terrified girl.

"I'll kill you!"

Just then an arrow stuck into the ground right next to the girl's hand. She looked at it, then looked at the woman charging her.

"Let the fittest survive." Martin said as he sat back against a tree to watch the impending fight.

The girl snatched the arrow about four inches up from the broadhead, and got into a defensive crouch as the woman dived for her. She evaded to the side and stabbed out at the same time, slicing the woman's shoulder with one of the razor blades in the broadhead. The woman landed into a roll. Then standing back to her feet she spun to face the girl once again. As she stared menacingly at the girl, she drew a small knife from a sheath on her belt and charged again. She swung the blade at the girl's throat but the girl leaned back just in time, then countered with a stab of her arrow. The woman blocked it with her knife twisting her wrists causing the blade to flip to the other side of the shaft. She then pulled upwards, slicing the backside of the girl's hand. She pulled back with a cry of pain as blood began to flow from her newly acquired wound. The woman smiled with glee at her success in drawing blood.

The girl switched the arrow to her other hand and without warning charged forward. Using her already cut hand she blocked the incoming knife while simultaneously flicking past the woman's blocking hand and stabbed her in the neck with the arrow. Both of the woman's hands shot to her neck to try and stop the bleeding, but it was no use. The arrow had found its mark perfectly into her carotid artery and was now hemorrhaging blood. She collapsed to the ground gasping for air as she slowly began to choke and suffocate on her own blood. After a few more seconds of anguish the woman finally twitched and then went limp. The girl looked down at her hand to find the woman's knife had gone clean through, right between the two bones in the center of her palm. She gasped and tears began to roll down her cheeks as she knelt to the ground holding her wrist.

"You'll be fine." Said a voice from behind her.

Startled, she spun around to see a man dressed all in black. He was wearing a long coat with a hood covering his face, and he was holding a bow in his left hand.

"Oh god! Please don't hurt me!" She cried as she spun around and fell onto her back and tried to crawl away on her elbows.

"I'm not going to hurt you." He said as he silently made his way around her to look at the now dead woman. "You did well. Here let me help you with your hand."

"Wait a second." She said as she looked past the hood to see his mask. "Martin? you asshole! Why didn't you just save me?" She said with a touch of frustration and anger.

"I did. I simply made the odds even so you could prove that you were worth helping at all."

"Six lives for one. Why not just let them kill me?"

Martin took her hand with the blade still protruding out of it and said.

"True strength is being able to defend yourself against those who wish to harm you." He then ripped the knife out of her hand and quickly applied a bandage to the wound. He did it so fast that she didn't even have time to cry out until after he was done.

"It is a show of weakness when a pack of people band together to give the illusion of strength in order to pray on the weak." He said.

"Is that why you helped me at all?" She asked through teary, pain filled eyes.

"Yes. But I only help those who can help themselves. If someone can't even hold their own in a fair fight and stay alive, then they don't deserve to. If you die, it's because you were too weak to live. When the weak die that is just nature's way of making more room for the strong."

"So you wouldn't have even cared if I had lost that fight and died, instead of her?"

"It makes no difference to me. I barely even know who you are. And even if I did, I still wouldn't care. Probably."

"I'm Scarlet. Don't you remember? You helped me get back to Lynn and the others."

"I remember, I just don't care."

Martin then stood, turned and started walking away from her.

"Hey, wait up." Scarlet said as she got to her feet and started after him.

"Why are you here, Scarlet?" Martin asked.

"I found out where you were going so I tracked you. Are you mad?" She asked once she had caught up and started walking next to him.

"No, I am not someone who is quick to anger. I am however, impressed that you were actually able to find me though."

"Okay cool. Yeah I try my best. So where are you headed?"

"Not that it's any of your business, but I'm heading to see an old friend." Martin said, deciding on the destination only a moment before.

"Where does he live?"

"Why do you assume that it's a he?"

"I just figured that it was. Is your friend not a he?"

"He is indeed a he. I am just messing with you."

"Damn, man. Why do you gotta be like that?"

"Because if you're going to be following me around then I am going to find amusement at your expense."

"I just figured that we could team up. We're both probably better off if we stick together rather than go it alone."

"You're better off keeping me around to protect you. I have nothing to gain from you. I require nothing and no one to survive. I have survived even death; you being here is of no benefit to me. My presence is only a benefit to you."

"Wow, tell me how you really feel, why don't ya."

"I just did."

"If you want me to leave you alone, I will."

"You should have just stayed with the resistance, Scarlet. But do what you want. You are not my responsibility. Therefore I won't stop you either way. As I said, my presence is a benefit to you. Keeping close to me is your best chance at surviving for the longest amount of time."

"So you don't mind if I stick around for a while?"

"It's all the same to me. But if you do stick around then at least make yourself useful and carry this bag."

Martin held his duffle bag straight out with one arm and Scarlet instinctively moved to take it from him. Not yet realizing what was in the bag, she took hold of it without a second thought. As soon as he let go of the handles the unanticipated weight of the bag caused Scarlet to almost face plant into the ground. Puzzled, she looked at it for a moment then looked up at Martin.

"What the hell do you keep in this thing? Bricks?" She asked, hefting the bag up and pulling the strap over her shoulder.

"Just the normal everyday things." He said.

"Like what?"

"Guns and ammo."

"I see why you are always alone now. Your jokes are unbelievable."

"You are either alone now, or you will be someday. I have always been alone, even when I wasn't."

"What's that supposed to mean?"

"No matter how much things change, everything always remains the same. Even if you're in a crowd of people, it is meaningless, if they don't understand the language that you speak."

# CHAPTER: 70

**S**O, you've been wearing that mask a long time." Scarlet said as she walked down the path not too far behind Martin. "As far as you're concerned, I've been wearing it since the day I was born." Said Martin.

"That seems a little extreme. Why can't you just take it off?"

"I am a man of only three rules. Never show my face, never break a promise and never feel emotion."

"Isn't that a pretty dull way to live?"

"It is the only way to live."

"How can you live at all if you don't feel?"

"Once you understand why you exist, it is no longer possible to feel emotion." Said Martin.

"Why is that?" Scarlet asked.

"Because feeling emotion is human. And humans are not permitted to understand why they exist. So once one does they are no longer allowed to be human."

"What would you become if you were no longer human?"

"Simply, more."

"Can you teach me?"

"Why would I do that?"

"I don't know. Because I'm curious and I want to know things."

"What does that have to do with me?"

"Well if you are the way you say you are. Wouldn't you know enough to spread your knowledge and teach others?"

"Others, meaning whom?"

"Me, for instance?"

"What makes you think that you would be the person that I would teach?"

"I'm here, and I'm interested. So can you teach me?"

"The question is not; can I teach you. The real question is; Can you learn?"

"Of course I can."

"Hmm. We'll see."

"I can learn. I'm not stupid." Said Scarlet.

"I will be the judge of that." Martin said flatly.

"Okay then, let me ask you this then. How do you understand existence?"

"It cannot be explained with sound or word. It can only be understood through revelation of the mind."

"How does that happen though?"

"You choose it."

"You really don't make much sense. You know that right?"

"Yes, that is by design. If you can not understand on your own then you will never understand at all."

Scarlet was silent with her frustration obvious on her face.

"Allow me to explain then." He continued. "Everything you do is an answer to a simple yes or no question. And you are always required by the laws of existence to make a choice. If you take that to the absolute extreme then you can choose to know things without learning them."

"Bullshit, that's definitely not possible. You're just screwing with me again."

"You're right. Life is never anything more or less than what you believe it to be. Whether you believe it or not, you are always correct."

"That sounds a little narcissistic."

"Not exactly. It's more like, you can only believe that which you choose to believe is possible. You cannot make a difference if you do not believe that a difference needs to be made. My advice is that you believe nothing to be true but anything to be possible."

"Okay, I'll have to remember that. Not to change the subject or anything, but the sun is beginning to set. Should we find somewhere to make camp for the night?"

Martin looked to the west at the red sky, then turned back to Scarlet and nodded.

"Let's move a little ways off the path. Just in case someone comes by." He said.

"Okay."

Martin led the way into the trees about twenty paces and stopped.

"This looks like a good enough spot. Are you hungry?" Martin asked.

"I'm starving." Said Scarlet.

"Okay. I always carry a little bit of food just in case of a situation like this."

"What? I thought you didn't care. And you don't carry food for yourself?"

"No, I don't eat human food anymore."

"You've got to be kidding me." She said as she dropped the duffle bag.

Martin walked over and knelt to the ground next to it. He then reached in and pulled out a can of stew, opened it then handed it to her. She took it without further question and immediately began eating. Martin closed his bag then he dropped down to sit with his legs crossed in front of him as he usually did.

"So, what have you been up to these last few days?" She asked with her mouth full.

Martin looked up, and after a short pause he sighed.

"Just wandering around and killing bad people."

"What?"

"Exactly what I just said."

"I can't tell if you're being serious right now, or if you're messing with me yet again."

"I only speak two languages, girl. English and sarcasm, and both are fairly easy to differentiate between."

"Geez, I'm sorry. No need to snap."

Martin sighed again.

"I didn't snap at you. If I ever snap it's almost a certainty that someone is either going to die or already has."

"Why are you doing it though? Why don't you just leave this part of the world? Why put yourself through it when you could just go somewhere else and settle down or something?"

"I do it because I want to. Because it makes me feel alive." Said Martin.

"Killing makes you feel alive?" Scarlet asked with one eyebrow raised.

"Taking life is what sustains mine. The energy I absorb from the dead is what gives me my power."

"Why must you always speak in riddles? What do you actually mean by that? I've heard many people call you a superhero. But I'm starting to think that you're actually some kind of sociopath, or a serial killer."

"Sociopath, probably. Not so much a serial killer. Serial killers prey on the weak and the helpless. I prey on the strong and the powerful. I kill those who are at the top, and those who are the hardest to kill."

"Why? What's the point though. This world is gone. Why go after those people? Why not just let them kill each other off?"

"I could do that. But as long as I am killing, I cannot die. Not from starvation, not from being shot. As long as people die then I cannot. Once everyone is dead then I will also die. I do it because once everyone else is dead, I myself may finally rest."

"None of what you say is real or based in science... it's not even based on religion."

"Do you believe in science or religion?" Asked Martin.

"Of course. Don't you?"

"I use my mind to defy all known laws of physics and reality. I believe in everything, because I have experienced what true consciousness truly is. What you have been taught, and what you think you know, is a child's play thing in comparison to the truth."

"So you're telling me that all the scientists were wrong?"

"There has never been anything proven incorrect more often than science. Nor used to disprove itself. Science is only a means to understand nature in its most simple form. But it does not possess the means to prove anything to be true, because there is very little that can be proven true at all."

"So how do we answer all the questions that we have if we can't trust the way we research them?" Scarlet asked.

"Sometimes the answers you get for the questions that were asked were correct. But the questions that were asked were the incorrect questions for the answers that you require. Science and religion are never the answer because they were never questions to begin with. Both science and religion are simply formulas and ideas based on faith that allow one to believe. However, both do have truth to them, neither are absolute. Science and religion are like two plus two. Put both together and it equals something. Each by themselves is an incomplete equation that possesses no real answers for anything. Knowledge is vast, intelligence to decipher it is rare. You can easily prove to yourself that you exist, but can you prove to me that I exist?"

"Why are you the way you are?"

"The human mind is a powerful thing, more powerful than you would believe. If you wish to know something you need only think. The knowledge is already there because we are all connected as everything is. So if you think for long enough, you can understand anything."

"How is that possible?"

"Our existence is a solid mass with each and every thing in it completely and totally connected with absolutely no empty space between. This is how energy can be transmitted from one end of the universe to the other by mere thought."

"No space between? What about actual space?"

"What about it? If it exists in our universe then it is a part of the solid mass."

"What do you mean by solid mass?"

"Solid meaning without spaces between. However, understand that when I say solid, it is in comparison to the supernatural which is not the same."

"How so?"

"The comparison is similar to comparing oxygen to concrete. Our universe would be concrete, but both these are natural things so the comparison is still incorrect."

"If what you're saying is true then how are we moving?"

"You are looking at it far too literally and intently. The answer is in your mind. You need only choose to know it, then pursue the knowledge deep into your own head."

"That doesn't work. I'm not buying it."

"You are correct."

"What?"

"Whether you believe something to be true or false. You are correct. It is impossible to make a difference if you do not believe that a difference needs to be made."

# CHAPTER: 71

**T**HE light from the morning sun had just begun to peak over the horizon when Martin came out of his meditative state. He looked over to find that Scarlet was still sleeping soundly, about five feet from where he was sitting. He thought about waking her so they could get going, but then thought better of it. He was in no real hurry to get where he was going, as long as he got there eventually. He decided that he would give it another hour before he would wake her so that they could head out.

He watched the sun rise as the hour passed by slowly. Every so often holding his hand out sideways against the horizon to check the time. After a long while he checked it for the final time. The sun was now four fingers above the trees in the distance, marking one hour after sunrise.

"Hey Scarlet. It's time to wake up." He said before standing up.

Scarlet lifted her head up from her arm where it had been resting, revealing the imprint her sleeve left on the side of her face.

"What time is it?" She asked through a yawn as she stretched.

"Morning." Martin said in answer.

"You don't have to be so specific, you know?"

"Get your stuff. We're heading out in five minutes."

Martin and Scarlet followed the small, overgrown path through the woods. As they walked, the trees suddenly began to thin until they finally opened up to a field of tall grass. They continued across the field until they came to a paved road stretching from north to south. Martin looked south then north, and after a brief pause he began walking north. Scarlet looked around for a moment then turned and followed after him. Once she caught up she began walking next to him.

"I've been thinking." She began.

"That explains the smell of burnt rubber." Martin interrupted.

Scarlet glared at him for a moment before continuing her previous thought.

"As I was about to say, I'm starting to wonder if the Chinese had the right idea. Like what if their plan for America was the right one and we in our stubbornness did all this to ourselves?"

"That's always a possibility. But you must not have met the same Chinese that I have. I watched them execute hundreds of people for no reason. They were going to kill us regardless if we fought back or not."

"Yeah, probably. But still, do you think that their ideas of society can work if properly implemented?"

"No, I do not. No sane person does. Communism and freedom cannot coexist. You are always free to be bound, but you cannot be free by allowing yourself to be bound. The only way to achieve freedom through bondage is with violence. And they only wished to bind us."

"Do you think communism could ever actually work though?"

"The day that food grows on shelves instead of plants is the day communism will work the way the fool wants it to. The truth however is that communism has been 100% successful every time it has been tried, because those who implement it, gained power. That is what communism really is, a few powerful people on top with everyone else completely equal and equally starving."

"Oh, I see. So in your opinion, what would be the best form of society?"

"The only society that works long term is one that is based on individual responsibility and accountability for personal action. A society where if you can't make it on your own then you don't deserve to. One where only the strongest of people survive, and procreate. This is the only way to attain the closest thing to a strong, civilized, polite and perfect society. To allow the weak and the worthless to die of their own weakness is the only way the truly strong can keep all that which they have rightfully earned. True freedom is being allowed to die because of your own failure."

"I guess that kinda makes sense. It's something to think about at least. But do you think we should try to find a car or something in the next town we come to? I'm getting pretty tired."

"We could do that. Or we can just fly." Said Martin.

Scarlet laughed at what she thought was an obvious joke.

"What do you mean fly? What are you talking about?"

"Oh yeah, did you not hear that I can fly now?"

"Ah, I get it. You're actually insane. It all makes sense now."

"I'm surprised you didn't hear about it from someone who was at the battle the other day."

"Are you just mocking me because of the fact that I called you a superhero once."

"No I'm not. You are reading too deeply into it."

"Ah, so you're not just trying to get some amusement at my expense?"

Martin stopped walking and Scarlet stopped a step later.

"What? Did I offend you or something?" She asked.

"Nope. I don't get offended. Here, let me just show you what I'm talking about."

Martin then floated up about five feet off the ground and began to hover. Scarlet's mouth dropped open, and after a second or two her eyes rolled back in her head and she began to fall backwards. Martin darted forward, catching her just in time to keep her head from hitting the pavement.

"Scarlet, wake up." He said as he lightly smacked her cheek.

She came back around a moment later and her eyes suddenly snapped open.

"You can fly!" She said in a surprised gasp.

"Indeed. That's what I was saying. Are you gonna be alright?"

"Yeah, it's just that I didn't expect that. I mean you flying was definitely not something I had on my doomsday bingo card."

"I felt the same way when I discovered that I could too."

"Wait a second." She quickly stood up and pointed at him. "You mean to tell me that we've been walking the past ten miles when you could fly this whole time?"

"Yes. I felt like walking. What's the problem?"

"Oh, there's no problem. I'm just tired as shit on account of having to walk pretty much everywhere without a break."

"Are you finished?"

"Yes. Can we just go? I'm tired of being out here on this road."

"Yeah. Pick up my bag and climb on my back."

Scarlet picked up the duffle as he ordered. Then she grabbed onto his shoulders and jumped up onto his back.

"Hold on tight." He said as he crouched down in preparation to take off.

She wrapped her arms and legs around him tightly, then Martin jumped into the sky. He didn't fly very far up, only high enough to stay above the trees, but not so high that Scarlet might freak out completely.

"Are you good?" He asked as she squeezed him tighter.

"Yeah. I'm just really afraid of heights." She returned.

"You should probably keep your eyes closed for the time being then."

"Okay. Just let me know when we're back on the ground."

Martin flew smoothly for a while in silence, then he turned his head to look over his shoulder.

"So, do you have any family?" He asked.

"Are you asking if I have any family left?"

"Yes."

"I don't know. My parents both died on the day of the invasion, but some of my cousins who lived out West might still be alive. I'm not sure though. How about you?"

"My family lived over in Illinois. Haven't heard from any of them since the before days. I used to have a wife and son, but they were killed by the Chinese."

"What! Holy shit, really?" She said as she opened her eyes and then immediately shut them again tightly.

"Yes, but it was a long time ago now."

"Is that why you do the things you do? And also why you're kind of a dick?" She laughed. "Sorry, not a time for jokes."

"It's alright. But no, I did what I do now even when they were still alive. The only difference is that now when I take them with me I travel lighter, because I'm only carrying their memory."

"How did they die? If you don't mind me asking."

"Execution, I was forced to watch."

"My god. I can understand now why you hate them so much. Did you ever catch the bastard who did it?"

"I got the one the pulled the trigger, but the one responsible is still out there somewhere. The only problem is that he is more powerful than I am."

"Wait, you mean there's someone else out there who can fly?"

"He can do far more than that. He's the one that taught me everything that I know today."

"What are you going to do?"

"Haven't really thought about it yet." He said tilting his head slightly. "That's kinda why I'm going to my friend's place. He's old and wise and he might be able to help me. I also just want a place to think."

"Sounds good. How much longer till we get there?"

"We're already there. Open your eyes."

Scarlet opened her eyes and saw that they were now standing on the ground. She dropped down off his back and felt the grass beneath her shoes. It was tall and green and she quickly sat down then with a smile on her face she fell onto her back. She laid there for a moment until Martin leaned over her.

"Are you done? I would like to get going."

She groaned then sat up.

"God you're such a drag. Can't you just enjoy life a little?"

"Nope. Let's go."

Scarlet stood up and after looking around for a moment she followed Martin into the trees. They had only been walking a short time when a small cabin came into view. Martin stopped walking and Scarlet did the same.

"What is it?" She asked.

"A lot has changed since I was here last." He said.

"Do you think that he's expecting you?"

"I couldn't tell you. But I guess we'll find out soon enough."

# EPILOGUE:

**E**LIJAH Parker sat on his front porch cleaning his shotgun in preparation to go duck hunting. It had been a long time since he had helped and housed Martin and Mr. Blank, and as he sat there in thought he wondered what ever came of them.

"I'm actually surprised they haven't found your old ass yet." A voice came from the chair on the other side of his little table.

Parker jumped in his seat and aimed the shotgun at the source of the voice. He held the gun to Martin's masked face for a few moments, then they both began laughing.

"There's not even any ammo in it, you old bastard." Martin said through his light laughter.

"You scared the hell out of me, you little shit!" Parker returned.

"My apologies. By the way, Parker. This is, Scarlet. You wouldn't by chance have some extra food for the girl, would you?"

"I do, but she will have to cook it herself. I'm actually very busy at the moment." He said with a friendly smile.

"That's fine. I wouldn't have it any other way." Scarlet said.

"Make enough to go around, if you don't mind." Said Parker. "It's not every day that someone else cooks a meal for me."

"It would be my pleasure." Said Scarlet.

"You'll find everything you need through there in the pantry." Parker said pointing towards the doorway into the cabin.

"Thank you. I will come fetch you when it's ready."

Once she had disappeared through the front door, Martin moved over to the chair next to Parker. They sat and talked for a long time where Martin told him all that had happened. When he got to the part where he found the dog tags he drew them out of his dog tag pouch, sorted them until he came across Brian's pair and presented them to the old man. Parker took them into his hands and examined them closely with tears welling up in his eyes.

"I figured you would have wanted them, as a remembrance." Said Martin. "I keep the ones that belong to my men. You should have the ones that belong to your son."

"You were right. I would have rather had my son, but if this is the best the good Lord can allow me then I will accept it. Thank you, Martin. Your debt is repaid as per our agreement. You owe me nothing now."

"A friend doesn't need a reason in order to help a friend. I would have brought them to you even if I had previously owed you nothing."

"You really are a good man, Martin. It's too bad about the state of the world and that it dictated that you've become what you have."

"It's hard to be charitable after you watch your family's cold blooded execution and all your friends die right in front of you."

"What happened to your friends? Were you not able to rescue them?"

"I was. They were killed off afterward, one at a time. It is what it is."

"Did you finish it?"

"Finished what?"

"The fight. Get the enemy back for what they did."

"I kill enough people already. There is no need for me to add to the number by seeking out personal vengeance."

"Revenge is mine. So says the lord. But the lord has been known to work through people. And I've gotta say, you're probably as close to the angel of death as a person could be."

Martin then told him the rest of the story about the events that transpired since the time he had stayed there while his wounds healed.

"How many days has it been, Martin? Since the day you left here?"

"For you? Not many. For me? All of them."

"Food is ready." Scarlet said sticking her head out the door.

The two men then made their way to the dinner table where Scarlet supplied them each with a can of stew she had warmed up on the stove top. She placed one can in front of Martin then one in front of Parker and sat down herself.

Martin did not touch the can. He instead just waited for the others to eat.

"Aren't you hungry?" Scarlet asked.

"I don't eat food, Scarlet. Remember?"

"Now is not exactly the kind of time that you can be picky about food."

"It's more complicated than that." Said Martin. "I might tell you someday. Might."

"Suit yourself." She said before she finished off her food then stood up. "Are you sure you don't want it?" She asked pointing at the can in front of him.

"Yes, I'm sure. Thank you."

"If you're interested in staying the night." Parker said. "There is a spare room next to the kitchen. Blankets are in the closet down the hall."

"That would be very much appreciated. It's been a long time since I've slept in a bed." Scarlet said as she took the can that was in front of Martin and started off towards the kitchen.

Once she was gone Parker turned to face Martin.

"Are you allowed to take your mask off in my presence, or are you still forbidden?" Parker asked.

Martin thought about this. Ramiel, the man who had given the mask to him was gone along with everyone who knew his face, save for Parker, was dead now. He was silent for probably a little too long when Parker continued.

"I am dying, Martin. It is very possible that you will be the last man that I ever talk to. I promise to carry your secret to my grave. I would just like to have one last actual face to face talk with you before I go."

"The promise I made to wear this mask forever, never permitting more than one living person see my face, has become irrelevant and the promise I made has become void by the one whom I had promised. It however, was a promise nonetheless. And I shall keep said promise until the end. Ramiel is not of the living, therefore you may see my face once more."

He then removed his glove and put his finger to the print reader in the side of his helmet. There was a click and a seam cracked open between the mask and the rest of the helmet. Martin then reached up with both hands and pulled the helmet off his head. After placing the helmet on the table he reached back up and removed the mask off his face revealing his blue eyes, pale white skin and now shaved head.

Parker hadn't realized how loud he had been talking. Or that his voice had carried to Scarlet who was now in the bedroom. When she heard him ask Martin to take his mask off, she was driven by a strong sense of curiosity. She slowly and carefully crept out of the room and down the dark hallway. Martin came into her view just as he was taking off his mask.

"You know, before Blank left here. I overheard him say to you that he had too much evil in his heart. What did he mean?" Asked Parker.

"His name is Ramiel Asmodeus actually, and he is evil." Martin replied. "It is not only his heart. He has attained a level of knowledge, and understanding of existence that by default he has lost all traces of his humanity. He is evil, and is without remorse or consideration for any human life. He is as I am now becoming. Pure evil, and content with life to the point of disregard."

"Do you really believe that, or are you just forcing yourself to believe that it is true?"

"Sometimes lying to yourself is the only way you can cope with something. However, I am not lying at this time. What I am saying now, is the truth of how it is."

"The truth may hurt, but sometimes it's better to live the truth to let it hurt and overcome it rather than live a lie and revel in your misery." Said Parker.

"I healed myself on my own. Alone. Nobody helped me get through any of my sorrows. I delt with them on my own, and I overcame them all."

"Was it worth it, going through everything by yourself?"

"Yes. The most dangerous thing to you, is yourself. If you can't protect yourself from yourself, and heal on your own, then you deserve to fall victim to your own weakness."

"So your saying that healing on your own made you stronger?" Asked Parker.

"Yes. To overcome the worst things in life by your own power. This is true strength." Said Martin.

"That sounds like something he would say. And he'd be completely correct as you are."

They sat in silence for a while until Martin spoke up once more.

"Ramiel is evil. But he is also my brother. I am also evil, but I do not wish to remain this way. What can I do?"

"When the time comes, you must do what is necessary. And you must not hesitate or falter."

"I will try to save him. I must also try to save myself."

"As you should. But do not allow yourself to become too hopeful. Only bad things will come of you believing in false hope."

"Hope is for fools and children. I know what is coming. I know the tribulations we must soon overcome."

"It isn't over yet is it? We've got a long time yet to go, don't we?"

"It is over, when He says... it is done."

As soon as Martin finished speaking, Scarlet slowly and quietly moved back into the bedroom.

"Damn. He looks so much younger than I thought he would." She thought in reference to Martin as she carefully shut the door.

She had heard all of what he said, and she had no idea what most of it meant. Maybe one day she would ask him about it. But until that day, she would keep the fact that she saw his face a secret. Because even though she now understood a little bit more about the man in black that had come out of nowhere to change the entire way she looked at life. He was still a mystery to her. And now she only wanted to know and understand more, and one day hopefully become more like him.

"Where have Martin and Scarlet been?" Thomas asked as he walked up behind Lynn, who was sitting in a chair, holding a backpack in her hands.

"I think they went on a mission or something." Lynn said looking up at Thomas.

"Do you think they will ever come back?"

"Martin, seems to do what he feels like. But I'm pretty sure he'll come back. I mean, he didn't seem like he disliked being here."

"What if they die like Brian and so many others have?" Asked Thomas.

"Martin once said; if you die it's because you were too weak to live. But you wanna know something? I saw Martin die during that battle against the Warband, and yet he lives. Don't worry, Thomas. He'll be back one way or another. He always seems to return eventually."

"What's with the backpack?" Thomas asked.

"It's Martin's. He gave it to me for safekeeping while he went on the mission."

"What's in it?"

"Just a book and a metal rose. He said that they are the only possessions that he places any amount of value upon." Lynn said as she opened the backpack and withdrew only the book.

"Existence? Never heard of it." Thomas said reading the cover as she pulled it out. "Who wrote it?"

"Someone named, Ben David."

"Interesting. Do you think Martin would mind if we read a few pages? It's been a while since I've read anything."

"He didn't say I could read it, but he also didn't tell me I couldn't."

"Let's just read the first page or so. What could be the harm in that?"

# TO BE CONTINUED

TO BE CONTINUED

# ABOUT THE AUTHOR

## Charles Lite

 Charles Lite is a Fiction/Philosophy author who grew up in a in a small town so remote that it is not worth even mentioning. Charles did not receive an education as a child. Not for lack of his parents trying, he just simply wasn't interested. So he dropped out of school before even completing fourth grade and began building engines in his fathers garage. One month after he turned 18 he left home and moved across the country to begin working towards a career in engineering and tech development. He got a job shortly after moving where at the same time that he was working 16 hours a day he also wrote his first book 'From Linen to Sackcloth: Vol 1. A Voice Among the Four'.

By age 28 Charles had eared enough money to retire from his career to persue his dream of writing full time with the hopes of finishing his trilogy within the next few years.

Something he said once was, "A persons mind will only retain the knowledge which it is interested in learning. If a mind is not interested in the subject being taught then it is a disservice to that mind to force it. All unwanted knowledge is only clutter that the mind will eventually throw away. Therefore, it would have be better that you learned nothing rather than now have to exchange forced knowledge with desired knowledge. All knowledge that is forced will become knowledge that is lost."

# BOOKS IN THIS SERIES

*From Linen to Sackcloth*

# THANKS FOR READING

If you have any questions, compliments, disagreements, criticisms or insults for the author, feel free to contact Charles at:

CharlesLite7@gmail.com

Please be nice though... I'm very fragile.

Also don't forget to leave a 5 star reveiw.